WYNNE FROST AND THE SOUL OF REMORSE

Wynne Frost AND THE SOUL OF REMORSE

Paula Apynys

PIRBRIGHT PUBLISHING
AKRON

WYNNE FROST AND THE SOUL OF REMORSE.

This is a work of fiction. All of the characters, organizations, and events portrayed in this novel are either products of the author's imagination or are used fictitiously.

Copyright ©2016 by Paula Apynys.
All rights reserved.
Printed in the United States of America.
For more information,
address Pirbright Publishing, 822 Orlando Avenue, Akron, Ohio 44230.

www.soulofremorse.com

The text of this book is set in Warnock Pro & Humanist.
Book layout and cover design by Ted Lamarsson.

Library of Congress Cataloging-in-Publication Data
LCCN Control Number: 2016945197

ISBN: 978-0-9977186-0-7 (hardcover)
ISBN: 978-0-9977186-1-4 (softcover)
ISBN: 978-0-9977186-2-1 (ebook)

First Edition: July 2016

To my husband, Ted, who has always been the music to my words.

The Spirit World

In this story the Spirit World is the dimension where souls are born, develop, and reside between lifetimes.

The Immortals in *Wynne Frost and the Soul of Remorse*

Veliastan is Wynne Frost's Spirit Guide.

Lersaliaz is Dash Fordhyme's, Reve Tierney's and Barbara Tishkin's Spirit Guide.

Xe is a soul who has not yet incarnated physically but has lived several mental lives.

Akmaritee is Olivia Chipley's Spirit Guide.

Neriante is Wynne Frost's immortal soul name.

Ukutmanu is Dash Fordyme's immortal soul name.

Fadraya is Reve Tierney's immortal soul name.

Metemnia is Barbara Tishkin's immortal soul name.

Heciyanth is Olivia Chipley's immortal soul name.

Chapter One

Between Earth and the Spirit World:

Dennis "Dash" Fordhyme had never been so despondent. Although he had shed his physical body and was freed from the constraints of gravity, he felt as though his astral arms and legs weighed a thousand pounds each.

With a growing sense of revulsion, he replayed the last minutes of his life:

"Let's go to our next caller, Mark, in Portland, Oregon. Mark, what's on your mind?"

He'd punched the "on air" button and gleefully awaited the caller's comments — he'd told Bruce "Bucky" McIntyre, his long time call-screening assistant, to pass through a live, unscripted caller. From its inception, the Dash Fordhyme *Voice of Reason* radio show had been built on the *illusion of spontaneity*; unbeknownst to his loyal listeners, some of the calls originated from the same building housing his studio. These callers were actors reading from scripts provided by the show's major underwriter (and GOP think tank): The Institute of Priority Research (IPR). Meanwhile, genuine fans got on the air only after careful pre-screening. But sometimes Dash enjoyed the challenge of mixing it up with one of the self-identified liberal Democrats who were forever calling and being screened out.

The exchange had commenced:

"Dash, on yesterday's show you said the President and other Democrats hated our troops and were actively working to undermine our national security. While I know that's boilerplate republican rhetoric . . . "

"Wait just a minute, Mark . . . "

They'd gone back and forth for a few rounds as he'd worked himself up to the rant that would conclude the call.

". . . your listeners should know," Mark was saying, "that over the past six years, the Republicans have either blocked or voted against *every single* proposed piece of legislation written to help our veterans and their families. Just last week, the Republicans in the Senate filibustered S.B. 1974 which would have provided counseling and related services to veterans suffering from PTSD . . . "

He'd hit the "mute" button then. So while Mark (unknowingly) continued talking, Mark's voice was no longer being heard.

Leaning into the microphone he'd bellowed in his deep, full-bodied baritone: "Mark, you misguided ignorant liberals are all the same! You take time out from collecting your welfare to call in and read your talking points — which you've undoubtedly pulled off of some far-left, radical, America-hating website — and you think you're making a valid argument. Patriotic citizens are tired of your worn-out lies! We won last fall's elections in a landslide! We control both houses of Congress! You lost! You stinking liberals and Democrats have nearly destroyed th . . . urg . . . "

Then he'd slumped backwards and onto the floor.

He was still shouting when he'd realized he was outside of his body — he was floating near the ceiling and looking down at his prone figure, red face fading to pale, sightless eyes bulging. His producer was frantically calling 911; the door burst open and Delilah, the radio station's receptionist, had crouched down and tried, clumsily, to find a pulse.

Then he'd heard a roaring sound followed by absolute stillness as awareness overwhelmed him — he was dead!

After a timeless interval of paralysis, shock had been replaced by a wave of relieved recognition — he was just dead. He'd been dead many times he now remembered. Nothing to worry about; he'd soon feel a pulling sensation that would rocket him upward, then he'd see light and his spirit guide would come to meet him. His guide Lersaliaz. Good old Lersaliaz. Good . . . Lersaliaz.

Lersaliaz was good. He resonated with the purest energy — the energy of the Source. Lersaliaz would arrive on a tide of total acceptance and love. But Dash had just completed a life of, oh dear . . .

Reviewing his life rapidly, considering the manner of his death, Dash admitted to himself *resonance* was conspicuously absent.

Yet he'd meant well.

He wanted to think he meant well. He'd simply tried to guide people to right thinking, for their own good. And he'd made some jokes. Nothing wrong with jokes. Where was the harm?

Then he remembered there were no excuses here. Rationalizations evaporated and everything he had done and thought was stripped of all pretense.

His life, encapsulated before his inner eye, revealed to him all the rage he'd generated and spread. All those, quite clever he had thought at the time, insults. His brilliant invective. His penchant for selecting people who couldn't fight back and eviscerating them publicly. Ruined lives, damaged careers, left in his wake. All that pride. The self-regard. The self-centeredness. So much money and so little charity. He'd scorned people who needed money; convinced that their poverty and struggle were deserved, just as his wealth and power was deserved. He had been sure being rich meant he must be worthy.

Dash's form began to writhe as his energy transformed itself into sound — screeching discord erupted — a blurt of notes that thrashed in distorted counterpoint to the music of the spheres.

After a stupendous exertion of concentration, Dash reassumed his previous form.

More memories came, of previous lives now, a string of misspent lives in which he'd failed to restrain his worst impulses; he'd given in to pride and hubris repeatedly. He'd engaged in a wide range of cruelties — at least in this life he'd confined himself to verbal cruelties! That was progress, right? Still, he had entered this life possessed of a tremendous gift for communication and he had used his abilities — he had used his abilities to —

Lersaliaz would blanket him in forgiveness but he would never be able to forgive himself.

Meanwhile, in the Spirit World:

"Welcome, Xe. My name is Veliastan. I am in training as a Soul Guide, at present charged with the care of three souls who have been incarnating on the planet Earth. As I advance I will care for more souls. I am told all of your incarnations have been on Immion, a purely mental world, and you now wish to commence a cycle of physical lives. Your Guide believes you are ready and requested my help in introducing you to the earth plane of existence. There are many complexities to consider. The imprints of your mental lives will impact your earth experience in the beginning. The adjustment can be extremely challenging."

"So I understand. But it is said if I succeed in the transition my soul energy will gain considerable strength, elasticity and resiliency."

"Correct. Therefore, the effort is worthwhile. After much thought I have decided to begin your acquaintance with Earth by having you follow the activities of a selected group of individuals now incarnating. Initially, we will focus on one of my charges. Once you are oriented we will expand your awareness to additional souls whose lives are soon to intersect with my charge. Through their thoughts and activities you will gain exposure to several aspects of modern earth life."

"I am ready!"

"Then let us begin. My charge is named Wynne Frost. Her earth age is 34 and she is in the 3rd decade of her current physical incarnation. Wynne is entering a critical phase of her development requiring close attention on my part. I very much desire she succeed in meeting her life goals and assignments."

"Of course."

"Failure is always possible, however, and is neither unusual nor shameful. Soul evolution is a slow, mostly incremental process and Earth offers a particularly challenging existence mode. We all require — pardon me Xe, Lersaliaz is communicating with me, he has been confronted with a situation."

"What is happening?"

"I will share with you . . . Oh . . . well . . . Lersaliaz has a soul in his care who is refusing to come home. This soul has much to account for and, upon his death, recognized the enormity of his errors and does not want to face his soul mates, Lersaliaz, or his Advisory Council."

"Is this a common occurrence?"

"No. Souls who incarnate on Earth usually feel a great sense of release after each death, especially the sick or aged who have suffered physical deterioration. They also enjoy an overwhelming feeling of relief. Some will remain for short periods to try to comfort those who mourn their loss, but then they look forward to coming home."

"Relief?"

"Because they recognize their immortality. When you were incarnating on Immion did you fear death, Xe?"

"No. We determined there was meaning to our existence and were taught upon cessation our questions would be answered. We anticipated our endings with interest, though we regretted losing contact with our companions. This differs, I surmise, from what Earthlings experience?"

"Correct. Earth experience is so rich with sensation and emotion — great pleasures, great pains — it is difficult for humans to imagine existence outside the physical realm. Consequently most humans exist in a state of fear regarding their deaths."

"What do they envision?"

"Many things — you will learn. Some fear oblivion. Some fear cruel and punitive punishment. Some believe they will be reunited with God, as they have variously imagined God, but they also harbor doubts. Altogether there is much disagreement among humans about the afterlife, and much confusion. This can complicate matters when a human dies."

"Ah. So this soul — "

"This soul — his immortal name is Ukutmanu — was called Dennis Fordhyme in this incarnation. Lersaliaz tells me Dennis was revered by humans consumed with fear and hate; loathed by humans concerned with justice and kindness, and isolated from true intimacy. He used his gift for communication to instill and amplify both fear and hatred among humans and took no responsibility for harm he wrought. This he now knows and his regret has paralyzed him. Lersaliaz will have to fetch him."

"What will happen to Ukutmanu?"

"Lersaliaz and his Council will confer. They may recommend a period of isolation — Ukutmanu may request a period of isolation. There will be much work in his soul group when he rejoins them — if he rejoins them. They will work to help him understand where he went awry and why."

"May we observe Lersaliaz as he contacts Ukutmanu?"

"I will offer to assist Lersaliaz. Neither of us have previously dealt with a reluctant soul; we will both learn. I will inquire . . . Lersaliaz is conferring with Ukutmanu's Life Planners. We will proceed meanwhile until I hear further.

My charge, Wynne, is the current human incarnation of a soul named Neriante. When souls incarnate on Earth a portion of them joins a physical body while the rest of their soul energy remains here. Neriante has agreed to allow you to merge with her reserve energy for intervals, enabling you to follow Wynne's thoughts and emotions as they happen. Wynne will have no conscious knowledge of this."

"When can I visit Earth?"

"Soon."

"Will I feel anything?"

"Not in the way a human feels as you won't be corporeal. But you will gain a sense of the energy there and will be able to visually engage with the plane. Your Advisory Council will inform us when a fetus that will not survive to term is available. You will be introduced to physicality then and we will see how you do."

"How can I prepare?"

"By observing and questioning. But you must never interfere or intervene. Unless I or another guide gives you permission."

"May we begin?"

"First you will consult Wynne's Life Archives and review her life up to now. Her birth, childhood and so on."

"And then?"

"Then I will open a portal when Wynne is sleeping — "

"What is sleeping?"

"A kind of resting. Powering physical beings demands substantial energy. They must continually rejuvenate. While she rests we can contact her. She will experience the communication as a dream and will recount her current life situation as she sees it. Then you can follow her in her waking life and witness developments. Finally I will enlarge your window of observation to include other lives — you will behold how a web develops connecting people whose destinies will intersect."

"May I consult Ukutmanu's Life Archive as well?"

"With his permission. Ukutmanu here must await resolution of the situation with the portion of his soul energy still bound up with Dennis Fordhyme. However — just a moment — Lersaliaz informs me the Life Planners see a probable connection developing between Dennis Fordhyme and Wynne Frost. Their main lines of probability did not cross while Dennis lived; now new lines are forming."

"Do humans commonly alter their main line of probable destiny?"

"Certainly or there could be no free will. There are often many paths leading to the same destination; alternatively humans may take paths leading away from their destinations. Ukutmanu veered off his intended path many years ago."

Wynne Frost's Dream Communication with Xe:

My name is Wynne Frost. I am known as a Career Counselor, although I don't have any special credentials which would officially justify the designation. It's the term people use to describe me so I adopted it.

I prefer to think of myself as a strategist, albeit in the realm of careers. Careers are so challenging nowadays. There's so many ways they can go wrong; there's so many obstacles to getting started. And here in the Greater Washington D.C. area, people face nonstop moral dilemmas. The realities of political life here — the egos, the money, the power and power-seeking — transform career setbacks into *catastrophes.* (Or at least make them feel like catastrophes.)

That's where I come in.

My mentor, Congresswoman Klara Tesarik, got me started. (I worked on the campaign that elevated her from a city council member to a U.S. congresswoman from the great state of Ohio.) Having graduated with a Political Science degree from Kent State University I found it hard to obtain satisfying employment. The local job market was conspicuously lacking in well-paying, interesting, meaningful and steady jobs for liberal arts types with fuzzy goals, no money, and vaguely romantic notions about contributing to society. (Or even low-paying jobs of that description.)

So, I waitressed while sending out resumes, eventually responding to an ad seeking Activists to perform GOTV (Get Out The Vote) projects in Northeast Ohio. I got (in company with about 20 others) the job.

One might think "duh! why hadn't I previously considered political activism?" I plead ignorance. I didn't know any activists personally and such jobs weren't quite real to me. To me, *real* meant medicine, insurance, law, construction and service, service, service — fields in which the people around me worked. I'd pursued a political science degree because I was interested in politics and current events, but I hadn't formulated any concrete career plans. My background was working class; I was a first generation college graduate living in the Rust Belt, with, as I would later recognize, very limited exposure to the world.

But my GOTV grunt work prepared me for greater things: I worked on several local campaigns and was introduced to Klara Tesarik. She faced a well-funded Republican opponent, a local newspaper that reflexively endorsed Republicans, and a very divided electorate consisting of dispirited Democrats, smug Republicans, pugnacious Libertarians, and a pool of disaffected, unexcited, apolitical voters who outnumbered Democrats, Republicans and Libertarians combined.

But, as I was to learn, many elections are won and lost by narrow margins — half the electorate routinely sits out all elections and the real battle is getting just enough of the right people to the polls to eke out a win.

Technically, I was one of the crew of folks in charge of groups of volunteers who toiled making house-by-house contacts, but my real work was keeping Klara's spirits and confidence in the upper half of the continuum. She knew the odds were against her, and so did I. But I knew something else, something that I was sure of deep in my soul: Klara would be an exemplary congressperson; honest, dedicated and maybe even great. And she needed to persevere because if she did so, she would win. I just knew it. It was her destiny.

When she won she took me to Washington with her.

I had a mixture of duties in Klara's office "on the Hill", but over time I gravitated more and more to communicating via the internet. I submitted posts to influential Progressive and Democratic blogs as well as to a handful of Ohio-based blogs and I managed the congresswoman's Facebook page and website.

During my minimal free time I acted as an unpaid strategist for people trying to develop their careers. Most people's situations were (so it seemed to me) simple enough. But some people were like Congresswoman Tesarik — they had a particular destiny and I could discern what it was and help them bridge the space between where they were and where they needed to go.

I don't know where this ability comes from. I can't predict it, but it manifested often enough that Klara noticed it, began to follow it, and one day opined that treating my intuition as an interesting oddity might be a miscalculation.

"You have a gift," she said.

"I don't know if it's a *gift.*"

"It's a gift."

Long story short, I set up an office in my apartment and began seeing clients.

An advantage of working in the D.C. area is the ready availability of well-educated people with discretionary income — more than enough to furnish me with a good living. People are also very networked; initial clients yielded a generous chain of referrals to get me started.

D.C. also has a plentiful supply of roving idealism: unhappy well-educated idealists. That, in a nutshell, described my early client base.

I reveled in the work. D.C. is such a stark contrast to the employment environment back home. The Washington Post classified section routinely lists more interesting job openings on a slow weekday than I saw in my local newspapers, well, ever. My clients are rarely constrained by lack of opportunity. Instead, they are hampered by what I call *mental grooves.* For various reasons, people develop narrow views of their situation; just as water always travels downhill, their thoughts and ideas flow inexorably into the same narrow channel offering no satisfactory exit.

In the Spirit World Xe has a question for Veliastan:

"Why do people develop narrow views of their situation?"

"Because it's built into the human brain, Xe — part of the design."

"Elaborate please."

"When you are human you exist in a stimulus-rich environment. To negotiate through each succeeding moment you must simultaneously absorb *and* ignore a vast amount of data distributed among your senses. To be effective, you must be able to select relevant data from irrelevant data and you must do this quickly and while remaining physically active. You cannot be required to stop all motion while you ponder choices as every waking second is filled with choices. So your brain functions, among other things, as a filter and habit generator. You — yes?"

"How do humans distinguish the relevant from the irrelevant?"

"Their brains filter incoming information based upon their past experiences, their knowledge and exposure, their interests and preoccupations, as well as previously developed habits. This means they do *not* consciously process most incoming data in any given instant, but they always have the option to change their focus. Indeed, learning *on what to focus* is one of the most fundamental lessons undertaken by souls when on Earth."

"Their focus is subject to their will?"

"That is a simple question with a complicated answer. Humans have the inherent ability to evolve throughout their lives; they can learn, they can adapt, they can improve, they can advance. All this requires examination of new information. However, many aspects of the earthly experience hinder receptivity to new information — habit being one."

"How does habit affect focus?"

"Habits are thoughts or actions that occur without conscious involvement. Habit frees human minds from needing to consciously process information previously selected and accepted. Once something has become *habitual* it is no longer scrutinized. An individual in the habit of filtering out a particular data packet will not be stimulated to notice it even when the data is highly relevant. Unless they deliberately seek awareness and purposefully examine their habitual thought patterns, they will routinely miss information they could use or would benefit them."

"Awareness."

"Yes."

"It sounds simple enough."

"Yes, it sounds simple enough. But, when human, you will learn that simple is not always easy."

Back to Wynne:

A typical client would be someone like Piper Ferrar. When we met she was in a negative groove — she didn't know what she wanted, only what she didn't want.

Piper was a tall woman, thin, angular and simmering. She had dark eyes that telegraphed a barely restrained rage, longing for an outlet. She was a good example of an idealist-gone-cynical: so completely awash in disillusionment she could no longer envision a fulfilling professional existence. Everywhere she looked she saw compromises, sell-outs, and, worst of all from her point of view, *lobbyists.*

"How can I help you?" I asked.

"When I got my job with Senator Thompson (Democrat, Indiana) I was thrilled. I was going to be working on legislation; I was going to make a difference. What I didn't know was that Senator Thompson has zero intellectual curiosity and almost zero knowledge about economic issues, education issues, environmental issues — -just about any issues really. He avoids anything the least bit controversial. He's a poster boy for bad conventional wisdom. I think he's angling for a very cushy job in a lobby shop for fossil fuels after he finishes his term. I don't think he's going to run again, and he shouldn't — at least he realizes that. But he's playing coy; if he'd be clear about his intentions, there's at least two serious contenders back home who would start putting together campaigns."

"Have you been in touch with either of them?"

"I've got feelers out to both. If Thompson doesn't run again, I'm out of a job and I want to land somewhere. But I don't want to make the same mistake."

"Have you been exploring alternatives?"

"I'd like to, but I don't really know where to start. I sure as hell don't know who to trust." She looked at me.

"You don't trust me." I said. Not a question.

"I want to."

"Good. That's a start. Your trust muscle may have taken a beating, but its not healthy to distrust everyone on principle, even in D.C."

"I should have listened to his office manager back home. She told me Thompson was an empty suit, but I thought she was just bitter. She'd worked for him for ten years and, well, I thought she was angry that he hadn't brought her to D.C. My mistake."

My main question about Piper was whether she could be constructive. I've known people who've gotten trapped in a bitterness loop; they've lost their faith in life and view all possibilities as inevitable future disappointments. I can't work with them. Careers, ultimately, are leaps of faith. Jobs are things people do for money, security, and sometimes external validation. *Careers* invest a larger meaning to a series of jobs. The jobs are steps that offer lessons, contacts, credentials and, to the person, are worth pursuing and sometimes enduring.

Disillusionment divests jobs of meaning and erodes people's faith in their lives. Disillusionment is a spiritual wound that must heal or it will disable the soul — and where did that come from? I get these thoughts from the ether, I swear to God. I don't know where they come from — souls being disabled, what does that mean?

In the Spirit World Xe asks Veliastan about Wynne's reincarnational background:

"Wynne has spent several recent lives as a male soldier and she developed many strengths. But there are no further lessons for her to absorb on that path and she needs to reacquaint herself with the female experience. In this life her work is to reach out to other humans and provide spiritual and emotional strength, rather than physical strength. The warlike components of political intrigue provide a bridge from her lives focused on survival, defense and conquest. She was given a body equipped with a psychically sensitive, intuitive character, one with a strong open channel to us."

"Was the alignment between her soul and body successfully achieved?"

"For the most part. All incarnating souls carry the essence of their previous lives into their new lives. You have amassed strong mental powers which will inform your human lives. Humans bring to their lives hard won strengths, the weaknesses they battle, scars from major emotional wounds and traumatic events, and certainties from significant successes. Each life builds upon the last. Each life presents both new lessons and old lessons yet to be conquered. Life situations provide both a learning environment and avenues to resolve karmic debt. Souls will often live a group of consecutive lives with a particular emphasis, such as Wynne's soldiering lives. Some souls will live the occasional vacation life — one with easy circumstances and few challenges. Some impatient souls continuously choose formidable situations. But all periodically change directions and such shifts cause discordant moments. Wynne, for example, must meld the soul imprints of a warrior with the body and personality of a female sensitive. There are times when she senses a disconnect."

"How does the disconnect manifest?"

"She experiences unsettling qualms when she cannot identify the source of her perceptions. She has genuine insights, but she questions them. However, she acts on them, which is what we desire. Her survival instinct is unerring; her helping instinct is weak in comparison. Her previous lives have been life and death oriented. Her challenges as Wynne are less primal, but more complicated. Modern humans face very different trials than they once did. They live in mental spheres on a physical plane. They must find meaning in activities that engage them beyond sheer survival. They must think in longer terms and make more nuanced choices."

Back to Wynne:

Fortunately Piper was resilient. But helping Piper land another staff job with a politician didn't strike me as a good idea.

"How would you feel about lobbying . . . "

"Are you insane? I told you how I feel about lobbyists."

" . . . for an environmental group? I heard the Center for Sustainable Manufacturing is working on promoting legislation offering incentives to companies willing to adopt cradle-to-grave manufacturing processes. They could use an advocate who's been on the inside."

Piper chewed this over for several minutes. Then she said: "I know a guy who knows someone who consults with them. I could probably get a meeting and find out what they're like over there."

"They look legitimate. You can check out their website and see their donors. You know the drill."

Piper did. People inside the beltway now realize (mostly) they must do serious due diligence before they accept the validity of any group. Over the last 30-plus years shady political groups have multiplied like fleas. D.C. is home to scores of front organizations for egomaniacal billionaires with idealogical or financial axes to grind (usually both) and/or grift operations by sociopathic political operatives. The front groups have legitimate-sounding names and claim a variety of hard-to-argue-with-but-vaguely-described-goals and they raise a lot of money which gets spent on lobbying, underhanded skullduggery, the buying-off of media figures and Academics, and assorted misinformation campaigns. The grifters stuff most of the donations they receive into their pants and purses while doling out small percentages to help "the cause." The Center for Sustainable Manufacturing could be working to transform manufacturing through sustainability principles, or they could be working to suppress sustainability principles, or could be simply pretending to work while diverting donations to their personal bank accounts.

But, in actual fact I'd heard positive things from some good people, so I was confident they were on the level.

In the end, Senator Thompson landed at a law firm serving the oil industry and Piper went to work for the Center for Sustainable Manufacturing. Obstacles abound: politicians still disappoint; big monied interests claim the lion's share of attention by the media, and political classes and the doors continue to revolve between public service positions and lobby shops. But now, at least, Piper is surrounded by intelligent and dedicated people who are on a mission. She is, as they say, fighting the good fight; she can sleep at night and get up each day feeling her work has merit.

I enjoy my practice. My work puts me in constant touch with "players" in the big game of politics, but I am now on the sidelines. When I worked for Congresswoman Tesarik I was, at least, *involved*. I assisted a (relatively) powerful woman in doing important things. (Power in Washington is subject to many different measurements, dependent on many different contexts.) Over time I found myself wanting an avenue to influence events and the zeitgeist. I had been an avid follower of a progressive blog called *In the Works* and commented there frequently (under a pseudonym). Several months after leaving the Congresswoman's team I contacted Aidan Lorimar, the blog's owner.

Aidan is a reporter and blogger who writes extensively about employment issues and their place, or lack thereof, in the current Democratic Party's platform. Plugging along with minor success for a decade, he's become "hot" as a result of the Occupy Wall Street protests and the attention they brought to the "One Percent". People began talking about inequality and the persistence of unemployment and underemployment. (People in D.C. that is. Back home my friends and family had been talking about the dreary employment climate for years. But inside the beltway interesting jobs are plentiful and well-paying. Here, unemployment is an abstraction, not a living, burning problem. Here, people tend to benefit from the policies that favor the One Percent — this is where a good deal of money trickles *to*.)

I floated the idea of being a "front pager" for Aidan. He was receptive. Now writing under the handle *Winvision,* I post blog entries three times a week.

Aidan recently referred a new client to me, a young woman he believes has considerable potential who is trying to decide on a career direction. She cleans his apartment once a week. He wondered if I'd be willing to work with her, perhaps in exchange for cleaning services?

I've always intended to work with some deserving people who can't afford my services. Plus, my apartment could only benefit from a good cleaning. Not that I'm a bad housekeeper — I don't even mind cleaning occasionally, but I can't say I love house chores and I'm willing to make the sacrifice of letting someone else do the work.

Olivia Chipley was a born-and-raised local from D.C. where there's a large and largely poor black community living a few miles from our nation's capital. *The District* (officially The District of Columbia") is a unique territory originally created to house the national government. It falls under the authority of Congress, while not itself having a representative in that body. Statehood is an ongoing aspiration of many residents.

Olivia was the fourth of six kids. Her mother had died of breast cancer when Olivia was eleven and her father died of complications from diabetes right after she graduated high school. Two younger brothers, ages 14 and 16 at that point, were still in school. Olivia's oldest brother was in the Army, her oldest sister was married and living in Michigan. So, it fell to her next sister Diana to assume the role of official guardian to the boys with Olivia as her second-in-command. Diana had completed a degree in Nursing, which provided their primary income, but there were loans to pay and two teenagers to support. And so, Olivia postponed her own plans for college, started doing housecleaning jobs and helped fund the household. By the time we met, Olivia's brothers (James and Lawrence) had both completed high-school; James had entered the Army and Lawrence had gotten a scholarship to Virginia State University.

Now it was Olivia's turn; she was 25, had managed to save $4,000, but was looking at a high tab for college and was very concerned about needing to take out student loans. Olivia felt it was critically important she make judicious choices regarding her education.

Olivia was tall and shapely with a gorgeous headful of long braids which she confined to a ponytail when working. Dressed differently, you could imagine her as a credible Cleopatra: she had large eyes, a classic nose, high cheekbones and plump lips. In her sweatpants and athletic shoes she looked less exotic, but the impression of strength remained.

I showed her around my apartment and Olivia assessed the spaces, sizing up the labor required to keep the rooms dust-free, cobweb-free, cat-hair free(ish), and neat. Then, we went to my office and, after removing my cats (Penelope and Winston) from the cushioned chairs, sat, and talked about my piles of books (okay to dust them but otherwise leave them where they were), my piles of papers surrounding my laptop (okay to lift them, dust under them, and put them back) and the cat litter box (I'd keep it clean — it had to be scooped daily as I was already in the habit of doing). Interestingly, she would use only non-toxic cleaners. Some cost a bit more; baking soda and vinegar were cheap.

"You have to live with the product residue, I have to work with the products. It's healthier for both of us," she said.

She would clean my apartment once a week until she'd worked off what she'd owe me for our sessions and then we could decide whether I'd start to pay her, or let her go.

Offering her a glass of iced tea, which she accepted, we began.

"What are your thoughts about what you want to do?"

"That's the problem, I don't know. I don't want to be a nurse, doctor, dentist, or anything medical; I don't want to be a teacher or an accountant. I was good in math and science, but not really interested. I mean, I don't want to be a chemist or something. I did like biology. I thought about being a lawyer, but I've been reading there's a glut of lawyers and jobs are few and very competitive. Law school is also expensive. But I really don't know what all is out there, you know? You see stuff on TV and in movies and you get ideas, but I know jobs in real life are different. Like lawyering. I've read that you do more paperwork than anything."

I agreed.

"I don't want to be a house cleaner all my life. I don't mind doing it, but it's not really meaningful or well-paying. I'd always planned to go to college, but had I gone right out of high-school I don't know what I would have majored in. So its probably just as well I didn't go then. But I'm kinda mad at myself because I feel like I should have figured it out by now. I'm twenty-five!"

"Choosing a career direction can be really hard. Some lucky people are born knowing what they want to do and there are people who don't much care — they'll do whatever's available if it's reasonable and they can make a living. But if you don't fall into one of those two categories, it can be tough."

As I was talking my mind was on another track: Olivia, Olivia, what am I getting from you? Strong, physical, practical, looking for meaning . . .

"How were your math and science grades?"

"Oh I got A's," she said offhandedly. You'd almost think it wasn't important, but there was a tiny flash of smile as she said it.

"Did you do any activities in school? Sports? Band? Debate team?"

Again there was that quick smile, "I played volleyball and was Captain my senior year when we were state champs."

"I think . . . hmm."

"Yes?"

"What do you do for fun? When you have free time?"

"I garden," she said promptly. Then she seemed to have to think: "I do the normal stuff I guess. Watch TV, read . . . I follow politics but it makes me crazy."

"Why is that?"

"Nothing ever seems to get done. Or worse. Something good, like Obamacare, happens and then people try to repeal it. Half the states in the country refused funds for Medicaid — are they crazy? We elected our first Black president and some folks got more racist instead of less racist. They've been disrespectful, threatening . . . it works my last nerve."

I nodded. I had attended President Obama's first inauguration. It had been a frigid day starting with an early rise at 5:00 a.m. I was part of a gigantic crowd on the National Mall watching the ceremonies on one of the many Jumbotrons provided for those of us far from the action in front of the Capitol building. Squashed in close with a million-plus strangers, it was notable how everyone was happy, polite, jubilant, orderly. Of course, reality set in. Like all good progressives, I have various bones to pick with this President, but any disappointments I've felt regarding specific policies have been eclipsed by my utter loathing of the Republican Party's behavior since his election.

But I didn't want to get into all of that with Olivia; we had work to do.

I shifted back to business. "I hear you and I agree with you. But if I get started talking about politics we'll be here all night. I need to think about you, about how I'd recommend you approach this process."

"Okay. Sure. We'll talk next week?"

"We will."

After Olivia left I went into my living room with my iced tea, sat down on my very comfortable recliner, reclined slightly, and began to review my impressions.

In the Spirit World Xe consults an archive record of Veliastan having a conference with Olivia's Spirit Guide:

"Greetings Akmaritee! My charge, Neriante (Wynne in her earth incarnation) wishes to assist your charge Heciyanth (Olivia in her earth incarnation)."

"You have an open channel to Wynne?"

"I do."

"Please inform her Heciyanth is working here to preserve the earth's health; she is showing great promise as a potential builder, most likely of planet features. At present, she is one of Earth's Watchers."

"Are the Watchers working on the planet directly, or attempting to communicate to humanity the necessity for stewardship?"

"Their hopes are that humans will clean up their own messes without our intervention, so they are filling the thought stream with awareness. They are feeling some guarded optimism."

"How was Heciyanth's adjustment to this incarnation?"

"As Olivia she is well-balanced. She merged with her human body well — they are very compatible in temperament. She is capable of excellent work in this incarnation, although she will face obstacles as a brown-skinned female. Her sister and two younger brothers are from the same soul group; they intended to support one-another through their youths as their mother's life was to be short. They have done well."

"Xe, do you have a question about this conference?"

"What are the obstacles to being brown-skinned? I had not realized this was a distinction in humans. They have all looked very similar to me."

"That is because they are so unfamiliar to you. Humans have many physical distinctions in skin color and the shape of their features, limbs and so on. Specific skin color can be an advantage in one part of the earth and a disadvantage in another. It depends on the dominant color in a region."

"Is brown skin not dominant where Wynne and Olivia exist?"

"Light skinned people dominate the region, although in the immediate environs all the races are present. But brown skinned humans have a tumultuous history in that part of the earth. Less then two centuries ago many of them were enslaved."

"Enslaved?"

"Treated as property, as objects. Purchased and sold. Separated from their offspring and companions and brought to the area by force. Beaten, starved, imprisoned and murdered."

"Humans do that to one another?"

"Oh yes. They have found many ways to enact cruelties upon one another. Slavery is but one example."

"I cannot conceive of it!"

"We will talk further."

Back to Wynne:

What did I think of Olivia? My surface impressions were straightforward but I was groping for the seed, the center from which her life could blossom, more fully formed and lush.

When I am considering a person, I deliberately relax and empty my mind (as much as possible) and wait. Eventually a thought will slink in, subtly. Usually it will seem meaningless, but I have learned to grab it as my starting point, and follow where it leads me.

After a few minutes of contemplating my living room, I began to think about the seed I was seeking . . . the seed . . . why a seed? Why am I using that word? What has "seed" got to do with Olivia? Because she likes gardening? Because that was the first thing she mentioned when I asked what she likes to do? Gardening . . . something with gardening . . . but I don't think that's the crux, though it's on the path somehow.

I waited some more. I started thinking about how she uses only non-toxic cleansers. I liked that. I cleared my mind again.

And then it bloomed. Point her in the direction of environmentalism, have her explore that world. What did people study? What could people do? I would start there. At this thought, I was suffused with a gratifying sense of completion which reassured me I had uncovered a valid direction.

Our next meeting went well.

Olivia was intrigued by the idea of environmentalism as a career direction to be explored. I asked if the idea of environmental work in any form had ever occurred to her.

"No, not really. And, now that I think about it, why is that?"

"Do you know anyone who works in the field professionally?"

"No."

"That's probably why. When we first met you said you've seen lawyers and doctors on TV, so they're on your radar. Environmentalists don't come up much, and when they do they're usually portrayed as fanatics, or shown in faraway places like the Amazonian rainforest or something."

"I see what you mean. Gardeners, I know. Dentists, I know. Environmentalists, I don't know."

"And it's a big area. People work for all kinds of non-profits and agencies. There's a lot of traditional fields that can have an environmental angle, too. For instance, you can design regular office buildings, or you can design *green* office buildings with rooftop gardens. Or, living roofs and all sorts of other features to help reduce energy consumption. People work with solar and wind energy in different ways. People work to clean up lakes and rivers and brownfields. And that's just off the top of my head."

Olivia's braids flew as she nodded. She started smiling in just the way I like to see: a smile of dawning excitement about an idea.

"There's a lot of exploration you need to do," I said. "You'll be looking for an niche that would especially interest you, and — this is very important — would be able to make use of your innate aptitudes."

"What do you mean by aptitudes, exactly?" she asked.

"I mean things that you are naturally good at, including things you're so naturally good at you take them for granted or discount them as unimportant because they come so easily to you."

"Oh! Okay, but where do I start?"

"First I want you to begin researching schools in the country that offer programs related to environmentalism. There will be several variations I should think. Some will be entire programs; some will be more like majors within traditional areas like biology, geology, agriculture, or architecture or even public planning."

"Oh my."

"So first, let's get an idea of what's out there educationally. Then, we'll start finding working professionals and arrange information interviews. They'll be the people who are realistic and who can tell you both what's wonderful, and what's not wonderful about what they do. Every job and profession has it's down sides. You want those to be negatives you can handle which are more than compensated for by the positives."

"You'll show me how to talk to people?"

"Oh yes. You'll get the hang of it and you'll enjoy it. I have a couple of people in mind already."

Olivia appeared to think about that for a minute, then she asked: "Do you really think I can do this?"

"Of course I do. Why not?"

"Well, I mean, it all sounds really great but, well, its like it's alien, you know?"

"The unfamiliar can be intimidating but that passes," I said firmly. "You are intelligent, responsible, disciplined and dedicated. Those are powerful qualities. And I think you're brave. You've been through a lot with your family and you've been strong for them. Now you need to use that courage for yourself, and let yourself aim for something wonderful for you."

"For me, yeah," she said, nodding.

"For you," I repeated. "We'll just take it one step at a time."

"OK. Sounds great!" she said, just a bit uncertainly.

We talked for some time about targeting and researching schools and Olivia left me carrying a stack of notes and wearing a very purposeful expression.

I was pleased. All Olivia needed to do was start: one thing would lead to another and along the way her confidence would grow. With that in mind, I scribbled a list of people to contact who could hook me up with information interview prospects. Once she started talking to people she'd be launched.

As weeks passed my instincts proved sound. Olivia was digging up information about all sorts of programs at different schools around the country. She was also reading about environmental topics, arming herself for the meetings we were contemplating.

Starting with people I knew myself and, through them, making additional connections, I had amassed list of eight people for Olivia to meet with. Some of these meetings would inevitably yield more contacts. I wanted Olivia to get comfortable asking for referrals and following up on them. But first things first.

As we sat together reviewing the list we decided to arrange her first interview with a Barbara Tishkin, a good friend of a friend (Sonya Helvender) of a friend (Natalie Vilano) of mine. This Barbara had a small organic sheep farm in Maryland. She harvested the wool to make yarn for knitters and weavers and her entire operation was eco-friendly. I thought she would be a nice, unintimidating first interview for Olivia, who was game, but a bit nervous. My friend Natalie had already approached Barbara through their mutual friend Sonya, and Barbara was open to the idea. I had Olivia call her and they scheduled a meeting.

That done, I wanted dinner. It was Friday, I felt good about Olivia's progress and wanted to celebrate. I called Natalie and invited her to meet me at Madeline's, a restaurant we like in Dupont Circle.

Natalie is an activist who works on nuclear energy issues. Her group, *No Nukes,* has most recently been following efforts to mitigate leaking nuclear waste at several sites. They've been following efforts to find new places to store new nuclear waste and, of course, they're keeping an eye on the Fukushima disaster. *No Nukes*' position was simple: if we can't safely store nuclear waste, then it's insane to continue using nuclear fuels to generate energy. Nuclear waste remains potent and potentially fatal on contact for tens of thousands of years — we're not talking a generation or two. Operating on the assumption that people in the future will figure out solutions we haven't is gambling with *their* lives — something worse than shortsighted and stunningly irresponsible. I was with her all the way and greatly admired her dedication.

We met outside the restaurant entrance. Before us was a fenced patio area with outdoor seating, but today's temperature was high enough to drive us into the air-conditioned interior. Natalie is a slightly plump but athletic woman with thick, wavy, dark hair, brown eyes with naturally long dark lashes and an unexpected scattering of freckles. She has one of those perfect complexions that doesn't require makeup which (in combination with her lashes) inspires my undying envy. Temperamentally she's optimistic and good-humored, buttressed by a gritty determination. She is dating a fellow *No Nukes* activist whom I also liked and admired. His frequent travels makes managing their separations their greatest challenge.

"So where's Brady this week?" I asked her as we sat down.

"Portland — Hanford's had an event."

"Serious?"

"Not clear yet. DOE (Department of Energy) says no. But that's what they always say."

We both opened our menus, musing on the DOE and their perpetually optimistic reports about nuclear incidents.

The segue from that to whether I wanted a steak sandwich or a crabmeat sandwich was immediate. Unlike Natalie, I had long since given up any sense of empowerment regarding nuclear energy. If something blows up, melts down (like Fukushima) or leaks we'll just have to live with the results. There are potential nuclear accidents lurking all over the country and throughout the world and our survival will depend on where we are at the time the event(s) occurs. Even the more subtle damage done by lower levels of contamination is unavoidable. I felt completely fatalistic about it.

Crabmeat it is.

Natalie chose a steak sandwich and we split a giant order of fries. I had a glass of Riesling, she a dark microbrew ale. Eat, drink and be merry, I thought, for tomorrow . . .

"Did you hear about Reve Tierney's latest op-ed?" Natalie asked.

"Oh God, what did he write now?"

Reve Tierney is a conservative pundit and occasional campaign consultant. As a *Fellow* at The Institute of Priority Research (a totally-undeserving-of-the-honor "prestigious" rightwing think tank), his primary job is to take reactionary and incoherent conservative ideas provided by the tank's funders and present them as serious, thoughtful views. IPR regularly cranks out spurious studies and polls all crafted in advance to come to the preferred conclusion. These are then fed into the maws of the rightwing propaganda media machine to be spit out on radio, television and the internet.

Tierney has the priceless gift of being likable even as he spouts dreck. He does television well and is the go-to guy for news shows needing a conservative guest who doesn't foam at the mouth.

"He did a New York Times editorial explaining how that looney guy from Florida . . . what's his name?

"Uhhh . . . Henry Phillpott — Congressman Phillpott," I supplied.

"How Phillpott's speech about outlawing birth control pills was really an expression of respect for women who honor the sanctity of sex for procreation. And Phillpott's calling pill users sluts was . . . "

"Let me guess: taken out of context?"

" . . . exactly! Cuz you know how many contexts there are where calling women sluts for using birth control is totally appropriate."

"Oh sure. Did Tierney specify any?"

"Of course not! I guess Phillpott was so sexist in his speech even Tierney couldn't spin it. He just phoned the column in — that's what people were saying."

"Seems like Tierney's been doing that a lot lately. Of course Phillpott is pretty hard to spin."

"Where would you rate Tierney in comparison to, say, Dash Fordhyme?"

"Oh man, I don't know . . . Fordhyme is a class by himself. If there's a hell they'll be preparing a special place for him."

"There is a hell, but he's so loathsome they kicked him out. That's why he's here."

"Maybe," I said, grinning. There had to be some explanation for the continued existence of Dash Fordhyme. Someone that repellent should surely have spontaneously combusted by now, but then humanity is never that lucky.

Our food arrived and we dived in. The crabmeat salad was delicious, the fries crispy and tangy with vinegar.

"Fordhyme's taken a big hit in the ratings since the Smash Dash group started contacting advertisers and sending them quotes from his show," said Natalie a few minutes later. "Apparently ad buyers purchase time in bulk and don't select whose shows their commercials run on."

"Yeah, I read about that. I think his numbers have been padded forever. I don't think he was ever as popular as was claimed. But nobody challenged the numbers for years so he got a lot more attention than he merited."

"He does have a devoted fan base, though. But at least he doesn't appear on cable news anymore."

"No, they prefer guests like Tierney. Tierney doesn't say unforgivable things, just makes excuses for people who do."

Our waitress materialized with dessert menus.

"I'm up for dessert tonight," I announced, "It's been a good day."

Natalie raised an interrogative eyebrow.

"Olivia set up her first interview with Barbara Tishkin," I explained.

"Oh Good! Sonya thinks a lot of Barbara; she'll be good for Olivia to meet. Dessert sounds good for me too. Should we split something? The chocolate thing?"

"Which chocolate thing? The double-fudge layer cake or the hot-fudge brownie?"

"Either."

We got the layer cake. It was rich, it was dark, it was moist. Yum.

Natalie's cellphone made a restrained little sound (Natalie doesn't do musical ringtones; she thinks they're unprofessional). While she greeted Brady, I licked the last molecules of fudge frosting off my fork.

Natalie made a sudden wave at me, "Oh my God! Really?" she said into the phone.

"What?" I asked.

"Hold on Brady." She looked at me, eyes wide. "Dash Fordhyme dropped dead today — massive heart attack apparently."

"Wow! Really? Wow!"

Natalie went back to talking to Brady while I got out my phone and googled Fordhyme. Sure enough, the word was out. Dead at the age of 56. One of those big ol' heart attacks, popped off in the middle of an exchange with a caller during his radio show.

I wondered who he'd been yelling at. I wondered if whoever it was knew Dash had died in mid-conversation. I hoped he or she didn't feel bad.

I waved to our waitress and asked for another drink for each of us. I wanted to savor the moment.

Chapter Two

Xe begins to follow Wynne in Real Time:

Dash Fordhyme's death dominated the news cycle for the next three days. The internet went berserk over the weekend with tweets and posts; cable news was all over the story and rightwing propaganda machine operators went into the deepest mourning.

I spent the first two days of the post-death feeding frenzy virtually glued to my office chair tirelessly scanning the web for commentary, online discussions, and tweetfests. Having thoroughly detested the man, I happily surfed on the waves of schadenfreude that erupted at news of his passing. It's unbecoming to rejoice when someone dies, but I didn't care — Fordhyme was so acutely preferable dead.

Nature abhors a vacuum. Hence, speculation soon began percolating about potential replacements for talk radio's "Jaws of Pestilence." But that was a side note proffered with lukewarm enthusiasm. Fordhyme's hate-spewing-how-ugly-can-I-get routine had been growing stale. He had single-mouthedly coarsened political discussion and public dialogue, ultimately reaching a point of diminishing returns. Well, he didn't do that all by himself, but he lead the way and created a huge market for professional haters. Maybe, some of us thought (and wrote and tweeted), just maybe, hysterical and malicious invective was becoming passé.

Meanwhile, Democratic luminaries preserved a (wholly appropriate in my opinion) decorous silence. A few years ago many of them would have felt compelled to make respectful noises, however insincere. No longer. That, I felt, was true progress.

This wholesale disinclination to offer praise inspired spittle-flecked denunciations by rightwing fanatics, threats of various boycotts and marches on Washington as well as online petitions calling for Democratic office-holders to step down. These reactions, in turn, provoked spirited, indeed inspired, mockery on the part of the Left's most gifted humorists — basically, a good time was had by all.

At about 7:00 p.m. on the Monday after Fordhyme's death an airplane from the Philippines went down somewhere in the Pacific Ocean — CNN was on it! — with other cable outlets putting their own spins on the material. The Fordhyme fever was broken. Only FOX News persevered, presenting breathless segments about Fordhyme's life interspersed with fulminations about liberal disrespect, Democratic disrespect, late-night-news-host disrespect, and Comedy Central's disrespect — asserting all this disrespect was the result of the knee-knocking fear Fordhyme had inspired in his detractors. In other words, the usual.

I had clients scheduled and was working on my next blog post for Aidan when my phone chimed. It was Connie Milleray with whom I used to work in Congresswoman Tesarik's office. (She'd been an intern and became my replacement.) She wanted to make a referral.

"Great!" I said. "Who?

"Well, it's a bit delicate."

"Because?"

"It's like this. You know Congressman Wayland?"

"Ick. I know of him of course. I've never met him and wouldn't want to. Why?"

"He has an assistant named Peter Gilen. From Missouri. I've, uh, I've been seeing him for awhile. Secretly."

There was a strained silence.

"He's really darling; he's passionate, and he's become very disillusioned with the Republican Party," she offered.

"Connie, I know God made Republicans too, but really? You're seeing a guy who works for *Wayland?*"

"I know. And Peter wants out. But he wants to land on his feet so he needs to strategize his way into another job."

"Does he have political ambitions for himself?"

"He's not in any position to run for office. He doesn't come from money and he has sizable student loans to pay off. So his immediate goal is to stay employed. But he really, really wants to detach himself from reactionary Republicans."

"Let me ask you this: does he want to become a Democrat or just stop being a Republican?"

"Fair question. I don't think he knows. Most definitely he wants to stop being a reactionary. But he was raised in, and has worked in, an environment that despises Democrats. So crossing the aisle isn't something he'll do lightly, and it isn't an easy decision."

"So he's going to call himself an Independent?"

"I — well — maybe. At first."

There was another silence. My first instinct was a pretty solid "screw him then" but I have learned to step back from knee-jerk reactions and wait. Often I feel quite differently after few minutes or hours. Sometimes I don't. In this case, the first question was whether I wanted to oblige Connie — I did. I liked her; I'd enjoyed working with her, and she'd been unattached for awhile. If this relationship had merit I was prepared to help out. If Peter Gilen was unworthy, however . . .

"Is he worth it Connie?" I asked.

"I think so."

"He works for Wayland — is he a Born Again?"

Her hesitant silence screamed a big "yes" to me.

"Oh Connie. Those folks are practically unreachable. Plus they think being psychic is evil. Have you told him?"

"I have and actually that's what sold him. Here's the thing, Peter's paternal side is all Baptist but his maternal Grandmother was an Irish-Catholic who married a Baptist. And Peter says she was psychic. He remembers her being able to foretell events and read people. His father even made use of her abilities in his business a few times. Maybe that's why Peter was open to me; there was always that little crack in the wall."

"Huh," I said, thinking. Not necessarily hopeless. Resistance was probably futile, but I gave it one last shot.

"How is he with cats?"

"Love's them. And dogs. And horses, in principle."

If a person however different from me is an animal lover, then we have a starting point. I gave in.

"Okay then," I said, "I'll talk to him. No promises — "

"Of course not!"

"And if we don't hit it off or I feel I can't help him, I'll tell him so. Politely."

"Of course." I could hear her smiling now. Worst was over, big relief, etc.

Connie would let Peter know, he'd send me an email, could we meet tomorrow?

Sigh.

In the Spirit World:

"Xe! We are to accompany Lersaliaz. He will assess Dash's state of mind and approach him. We are not to interfere but we may observe."

Between Earth and the Spirit World:

Dash felt a sensation of pulling. He resisted. He would not go home yet. He saw a glowing ball of yellow light with green and blue sparks and a white halo.

Had he completed a successful life, that ball would form itself into a shimmering, welcoming human-like figure and they would meet as long separated, much-loved friends. He would be looking forward to his energy cleansing and rejuvenation — and the subsequent reunion with his soul group — and the part of his soul energy that had never left the spirit world: Ukutmanu.

But he turned his back.

No further exchange was needed. Lersaliaz had arrived, as was customary for a soul at Dash's level of development, and Dash was declining his escort.

After a pause, Lersaliaz sent a telepathic message: there was nothing for Dash to do on Earth; his energy would be cleansed and his soul healed at home, and then they would consider how best to address his future.

In reply, Dash expressed his unwillingness to proceed. He would remain where he was for the present. That was all.

Lersaliaz receded.

Veliastan and Lersaliaz confer.

"How much deformity to his energy?"

"Many dark layers; grey sections; tears and holes."

"Salvageable?"

"Borderline. It is up to him, of course. He did not commit physical cruelties. The great error in this life was his reach; he gained significant influence and used it to spread darkness. He now has a large karmic debt to contend with — he cannot face it."

"And now?"

"I have consulted with my Guide. She advises me to visit him periodically, offering support, until he realizes the futility of exile. She believes he will resist for a time and will not be hurried."

"I have heard that some souls, reluctant to return home after a great failure, will construct spaces for themselves to inhabit. Angry souls may reproduce places where they were happy on Earth; remorseful souls such as his may create dark rooms, holes, prisons. Yes Xe?"

"Why does he refuse forgiveness?"

"Lersaliaz?"

"Dash's energy is greatly contaminated — this impedes clear thought. He can no longer recall how differently he will feel after his energy has been cleansed and reunited with his reserves. His soul has the capacity for great power; right now that power is working in reverse, filling him with overmastering regret. I will give him time to reflect. With no other forces working on him he may begin to repair his energy himself. Let us observe."

Back to Dash:

Dash's spirit hovered in a space between Earth and his spiritual home. From his location he could (with some effort) travel to his studio, his house, or anywhere else he chose. But he was tired. He had relied on rage and righteousness to fuel him for so many years and now the rage was gone.

For an interval that could have lasted five minutes or years he remained stationary. Then he made an attempt to regenerate some anger, hoping for a spark of energy to overcome his massive inertia. Like a failing alternator in a car, he felt a sputter of power that immediately dissipated. There was no reason to go anywhere, he thought. There was nothing for him to do on Earth — the window of opportunity was gone. He couldn't change what he'd done or not done as Dash Fordhyme.

He'd become a radio talk show legend by relentlessly attacking people who disagreed with his (and his financial backers') political ideology. He'd been especially savage towards women, minorities, and people of color. Outright expletives were forbidden under FCC guidelines; his genius had been his ability to craft impressively vile yet technically compliant slurs which he flung with abandon at his opponents. Following the repeal of the Fairness Doctrine in 1988, an entire genre of radio talk show — dubbed "hate radio" by its detractors — had sprung up in his wake with imitators and admirers filling the airwaves. He'd been a trailblazer, proud of his legacy.

And there was nothing he could do about it now.

Sadly, if he was still alive on Earth, every thought, word and deed would continue be counted, so if he'd turned himself towards the Source, if he'd atoned for harm while alive, he could have changed the outcome he now faced. Improved it. Reduced his karmic debt. Not disappointed his guide, his soul mates, his council, or himself.

His soul mates. His soul mates . . . souls from his group, with whom he worked and learned between lives, and who incarnated with and around him on Earth. Some had already died, but some were still living. The discarnates might be trying to reach him, but he couldn't face them yet. But of the living, could he reach one of the living? Could he help any of them?

Who had he been in contact with? Who might he be able to reach?

Ovirem? No, their lives had barely touched in recent years; there was no closeness. Kopojil had died three years ago. His sister Barbara (*Metemnia* in the spirit world) was estranged. He was estranged, in fact, from all of his soul mates currently living, except for Fadraya.

Fadraya . . . Fadraya was . . . was . . .

Reve Tierney.

Reve, yes, Reve. Could he contact Reve?

Dash experienced a moment of lightness thinking about Reve/Fadraya. Fadraya was a steady soul. Fadraya needed to develop more spiritual courage and conviction while Ukutmanu needed to develop more spiritual strength and compassion. Fadraya was gaining strength, but he hadn't risen to any major challenge. Instead, he attached himself to powerful institutions and dutifully carried water. As Reve, he'd refrained from the sort of aggressive hate-mongering Dash specialized in, but he *had* compromised his higher values for money and prestige.

In the spirit world, Fadraya worked hard — much harder than Ukutmanu. Ukutmanu had secretly admired Fadraya's seriousness of purpose. They both had a long way to go, but Fadraya was advancing more rapidly. Still, Fadraya would have to account for his work in support of people whose actions resulted in harm — for his willingness to sacrifice the well-being of people who were weaker, poorer, less gifted, less influential.

Dash pondered. If he could get through to Reve, perhaps he could convince Reve to better use his remaining time. Then Reve's homecoming would be happier and Dash could feel better about himself as well. Maybe he would then be able to face Lersaliaz.

But could he make contact?

Veliastan and Lersaliaz confer.

"So Dash will attempt to contact Reve Tierney."

"That is his intention. His skills are limited, however, and he does not have enough energy to materialize for long or to make himself heard. He will need to cleanse some of his energy and build up his concentration. The effort will be beneficial to him."

"Yes. But there will be repercussions."

"Yes."

"We cannot violate Dash's free will. But nor should he violate Reve's."

"No."

"Xe, would you like to follow the forks Dash will generate?"

"Yes!"

"If Dash succeeds the chain of events he will instigate may prove disruptive. And it is hard to anticipate what you will make of it all, Xe."

"Yes. But I would like to study how the events unfold."

Back to Dash:

Dash had never tried to contact a human from the discarnate state. He knew souls occasionally reached the living by haunting a place, but he wasn't (he told himself) commencing a haunting. Hauntings happened when souls were in shock, overcome by grief or rage, with compromised energy — usually due to years of despair or in response to an especially traumatic death (or pre-death) experience. Such souls were either unaware of their effect on the living, or were haphazardly acting out, impacting any random person(s) who happened along. Other souls haunted in an effort to complete a deeply desired objective and, since time for discarnates is divorced from "living time," a seemingly centuries-long haunting on earth could represent days in the spirit world.

But such hauntings were unanticipated.

Dash knew some souls *planned* post-death contacts: between earth lives they made a point of developing the expertise (it was one of the panoply of competencies souls may choose to master). It was all about concentration and matching wave forms.

As he understood it, direct contact was difficult because recently departed souls are usually trying to provide comfort to grieving loved ones, but grief clogs the channels of communication. Nevertheless, the departed soul could seize an instant when a channel cleared, and connect. The living human might then see the the soul, hear it, smell some associated scent, or simply be enveloped by a feeling of love, reassurance or peace. Mission accomplished, the discarnate would then proceed to the spirit world.

All souls learn how to match wave forms in order to travel dimensionally in the spirit world, but in the spirit world souls have access to all of their energy and the energy is pristine. Dash knew his available energy was degraded; he didn't think he could manage direct contact.

What about dream contact? Between lives and among other pursuits, Dash had dabbled in dreamweaving. It was a skill-set with broader uses than comforting the bereaved, but discarnates did occasionally harness it to that end. Dream contacts induced mixed results though, as the receivers tended to dismiss dreams (however well-remembered or comforting) as *just dreams* — night-time, unconscious wishful thinking.

Still, Dash thought it was worth a try.

First he needed to find Reve.

He concentrated, visualizing Reve's condominium in Cathedral Heights. Summoning all of his tattered essence, Dash condensed and then transported himself. He arrived, providentially, in Reve's bedroom, where he spent an unquantifiable interval recovering. Eventually, he was able to survey the room and see Reve's body curled up in his queen-sized bed. Then the room disintegrated around him and Dash was floating in a sea of particles. He couldn't sustain physical sight for more than a few blinks. But now he could direct a ray of energy towards Reve and, if he found an opening, slide into a dream.

After several misfires he succeeded in infiltrating a succession of Reve's dreams spanning three nights, but getting Reve to register the correct interpretation of his message ultimately proved unachievable. Reve awoke daily to the sound of a clock radio which normally blasted his dream impressions into fragments that quickly vaporized. Reve put little stock in dreams anyway, so he was not motivated to try to remember them. But he was growing conscious of an *offness.* In fact, he had correctly sensed an intrusive presence in his nightly unconscious milieu, but lacking any context in which to process this recognition, his conscious mind converted this knowledge into a disturbing feeling of disquiet with Dash Fordhyme overtones.

After several attempts to convey the message Reve was on the wrong path, Dash gave up. In his efforts to tell Reve he should do good and not harm or his homecoming would be painfully disappointing, Reve had only picked up *Dash, pain* and *wrong.* Reve was spooked and was blocking further contact.

Frustrated, Dash concluded he would have to materialize.

On Earth:

Meanwhile, Reve Tierney was having trouble sleeping. He didn't know why; there was nothing wrong with his immediate environment to account for the sleeplessness. He had plenty of money and had lavished a good deal of it on his surroundings. His bed was large, his mattress the perfect combination of softness and support. His sheets were of Egyptian cotton with a thread count of 1200. The room temperature was 70 degrees. His pillows supported his neck (he was a back sleeper). Although he'd been sleeping alone since his divorce (not his ideal), he normally enjoyed satisfying slumber.

But since Dash Fordhyme's death, he'd done nothing but churn around on his bed and, while he'd swear he hadn't slept at all, he kept remembering snatches of bad dreams with Dash playing a prominent role. So, he must have fallen asleep. Or had he been daydreaming? He wasn't sure. Dash's death had been all over the news for days — everyone had been talking about it everywhere he went. It was all a blur.

Reve stretched, adjusted his light cotton blanket, stared at ceiling for a few minutes then resolutely shut his eyes.

Naturally, he thought, there was shock to deal with — he and Dash had been friends — of sorts. Dash didn't conduct relationships like normal people, but they were members of the same country club and often saw one-another at events where rich people and Republicans gathered. Dash was the undisputed emperor of the radio wing of the conservative propaganda machine while Reve was one of the lesser aristocrats in the think tank wing. Thus, while they were both working for the dominance of the Republican Party, they labored in different areas and were never in direct competition.

Examining his feelings, Reve discovered more relief than sadness. Dash's death could *almost* be seen as a blessing, he thought. Dash's radio show had been declining in popularity and advertiser support was being steadily eroded. (Activists had discovered the efficacy of informing individual advertisers what precisely was said on Dash's show and sharing those communications on social media. The resulting feedback loop exerted increasing pressure on advertisers to disavow Dash, and they did.) Dash's show was being dropped from radio stations around the country and Reve considered the trend irreversible. Dash had gone out, not quite on top, he thought, but definitely higher than he would have been five or ten years hence. He'd been spared that humiliation.

Dash's death also spared Reve from having to publicly distance himself from Dash, something — to his own surprise — he'd begun to consider doing.

Until recently he'd considered himself fortunate and fully appreciated every luxury, every mark of prestige, and every dime he'd earned during his career as a conservative pundit and consultant. For years, the world had seemingly conspired to keep him in this happy state. He had interesting work to do; he got to appear on television, senior politicians asked his advice and their aides took his calls. High-ranking politicians, operatives and media figures attended intimate soireés at his condo — life was good!

But lately he was sensing subterranean shifts in the world that left him increasingly ill at ease.

There was a lot of talk about income inequality; he didn't know what to make of it. The Party's position was income-inequality agitators were motivated by envy and their complaints should be suppressed. It was verboten to even *suggest* there might structural reasons for the phenomenon and heresy to think anything should be done about it.

There were schisms in the Republican Party that needed to be resolved; they'd let the Tea Party get too powerful. A lot of quiet work was being done to defang the rabid dog element, though, so far, with mixed results. It was worrisome. Tea Party politicians were embarrassing — they expressed themselves with an unbecoming crudity, opening up all Republicans to accusations of racism, sexism and every other "ism" by extension. These people were supposed to be the reliable and obedient foot soldiers for the party, not the generals. And, really, their ideas ranged from startlingly harsh to outright lunacy.

Between the Tea Party and the NRA things were getting out of hand. People waving guns everywhere, militias throwing their weight around, various municipalities voting for secession — that was going too far.

Dash had been right in the thick of it all, Reve thought, ratcheting up his invective and coming perilously close to inciting violence and, even, depending on your viewpoint, treason.

More tossing and fussing with his pillows. Then, Reve started visualizing himself being chased by an Occupy protestor only to be shot by a Tea Party/militia man.

He shook off the image. Resigned to a bout of insomnia, he reluctantly opened his eyes again.

The ambient light of the city shone through his window, lighting up a portion of the bedroom. For two seconds he could have sworn he saw Dash Fordhyme standing there, looking supremely unhappy. A jolt shook Reve's entire body; his heart rate skyrocketed and his mouth went dry.

He closed his eyes, opened them again and forced himself to inspect the corner of the room. There was nothing there — naturally there wasn't!

Of course there wasn't!

Maybe he was coming down with something. Although, if he was, it was probably a bad idea to do what he was about to do, which was to get up, go into his dining room, pour a glass of brandy and drain it in three gulps. If he kept the brandy down, it would (he hoped) quiet the chatter in his head, shut down his overheated visual engine, and help him fall asleep.

Chapter Three

I wasn't really looking forward to meeting Peter Gilen as I was extremely ambivalent and had never attempted to counsel someone about whom I felt less than good. I wasn't sure I wanted to help him.

Gilen's boss, Congressman Herbert Wayland (Missouri), has a number of noisome, but mostly failed, legislative efforts to his credit. He is a union-busting misogynistic corporate toady overlaid with a thick layer of evangelical self-righteousness. He has a classically downtrodden yes-sir wife who depresses me profoundly when I see her on television. Gilen working for Wayland is hard for me to overlook.

His wanting to move on from Wayland is laudable, of course, and Connie thinking well of him is more meaningful still. I shook my head impatiently. My reservations were irrelevant now; I'd agreed to meet him and, if I didn't like him, I could refuse service.

I had thirty minutes to kill. I poured myself a cup of coffee, settled at my desk, and surfed the web. I owed Aidan a blog post, but was unable to concentrate on the career-related topics I usually write about, wanting, instead, to compose a screed about Dash Fordhyme. It had been four days since his death; the media hysteria had peaked and was dissipating, but there were still things to be said.

Oh hell, I thought, I'm going to write my piece, maybe send it to Aidan, maybe not send it, but at least I'll get it out of my system.

On The Passing Of Dash Fordhyme

I cherish my anonymity as a blogger and therefore will not share what I, specifically, do for a living. But between that, and my posts here, I touch the lives of many people. Those of us who are privileged to live and work in our nation's capital all, directly and indirectly, touch the lives of many people, in some cases quite profoundly. So, I always feel it behooves us to be exceedingly aware of our responsibilities.

I am, as a human being, imperfect. I don't know, have never met, and don't think there exists, a perfect human being. While I believe we should all attempt to hold ourselves to high standards of behavior and thought, I'm well aware that I, and everyone around me, will repeatedly fall short. So, while we need to strive, we also need to forgive.

Sometimes we need to strive *to* forgive and sometimes our inability to forgive becomes another failure. That is the case with me as I find I cannot forgive Dash Fordhyme.

Dash Fordhyme came into this world a blessed being. He was bright, he was quick-witted, he was persuasive, he was entertaining. There are many ways he could have used his abilities to make the world a better place: lighter, funnier, smarter, happier. But he chose to use his gifts to make the world darker, more suspicious, more fearful, more prejudiced, more hateful.

Dash Fordhyme made it socially acceptable, among some people at least, to be publicly and proudly hateful. He sowed, nurtured, and celebrated scorn and intolerance. He turned his wit into a weapon and used it against people who were often in no position to fight back. And like virtually all professional haters, he took no responsibility for his influence on his followers. Many mentally disturbed people who committed beatings, shootings, bombings and murders, listened to him and others like him. Where the line of responsibility begins and ends is murky; perhaps such disturbed people are on some inescapable path to violence. On the other hand, perhaps those same people, if they couldn't marinate in a daily brew of calculated, manufactured vitriol served up by media personalities who strive to make the despicable acceptable, maybe those people would be less angry, less miserable, and ultimately, less violent.

On a larger scale, Dash Fordhyme and those like him provide cover for politicians who use intolerance as a political wedge.

Dash didn't do it all himself — he has plenty of company. But he was a pioneer of sorts; a towering figure of infectious toxicity who showed others the way to profit from serving the powerful by hurting the powerless. There have always been people like him and probably always will be. He wasn't the first and won't be the last. But he was what he was. His death doesn't nullify the damage he wreaked on the body politic, public discourse and the bitter seeds he planted will not, unfortunately, die with him.

Well, I thought, that says it anyway. A catharsis. Maybe I can get some work done now!

With that in mind, I started looking forward to Peter Gilen's arrival.

The first impression I got from Peter Gilen in the flesh was, and this was untypical, visual. I saw an image of a shining light. It passed promptly and was replaced by a feeling of solidity and great sweetness.

I was so occupied with receiving and evaluating these impressions it was a few minutes before I inspected Peter in a normal way. He was looking at me with visible apprehension which surprised and slightly amused me.

I don't usually frighten people. I describe myself as "medium" (medium-height, medium brown mid-length wavy hair neither curly nor straight), eyes that are green sometimes and blue sometimes with unremarkable but not unattractive features. I'm one of those people who can be dressed up to look striking or dressed down to look unnoticeable. I have a good, serviceable figure, but it wouldn't win me awards. With me it's all about mood — I can effervesce, glow, hum or fade. I've been told my directness can be intimidating on occasion, and I was about to be very direct with Mr. Gilen.

But first I took a good look at him. He, in contrast to me, was indisputably attractive. Indeed, he was one of those people who literally cannot be unattractive. He was tall, muscular without being overbuilt, and blessed with thick, blonde hair, a square chin, large hazel eyes with dark, long lashes, arched eyebrows and a nose that was exactly the right size. What was odd was that his obvious external beauty kept receding in my attention, reduced to insignificance by the strength of his internal signal. He was the first person I'd ever met whose spirit struck me first.

Interesting.

I was beginning to understand Connie's attraction. Still, I needed to discover what his character was made of. And pursuant to his character, were his reasons for ever working for a man like Wayland and his reasons for wanting to stop.

"You must know," I began, "I can't stand your boss and have a hard time understanding how anyone with a brain, a heart and a conscience could ever work for him. So what's the deal?"

First he winced, then he swallowed, then he rallied.

"Brain, heart, conscience — that's pretty intense."

"Yep. Sorry. But whether I say it nicely or bluntly, that's what I think. I can't do anything for you if I can't be honest with you and I won't do anything for you if I don't buy your story. So let's have it."

There was a pause while Peter stared at his hands (which were clasped on his lap) apparently organizing his thoughts. He looked up at me, narrowed his eyes, then lowered his gaze to his hands again.

I waited.

"You have to understand where I come from," he began, looking me firmly in the eye now.

I nodded and raised my eyebrows encouragingly.

"I grew up in a strict evangelical family. My father is a deacon in our church. He is a good man — he was never violent or mean and I know there were other dads who were. He isn't a total chauvinist either — my mother is a strong woman, not some kind of doormat — "

"Like Wayland's wife?"

"Right. Like Muriel Wayland. My mom isn't like that at all. But she and my dad are Biblical fundamentalists and, as you can imagine, that colored every aspect of my upbringing. We are taught obedience and respect for authority. We are not encouraged to question anything — quite the opposite. Kids in my church were systematically kept from exposure to alternative points of view, shall we say. Television and internet access were closely monitored. My dad likes sports, which was the only reason we had cable TV. And, of course, he watched FOX News. Not all day long (like some people I knew), but he watched it. I think you can figure out where this is going."

I nodded again.

"I got interested in politics as a teenager, because, well, I don't know why really. Why is it that some of us find politics so fascinating when most people we know couldn't care less?"

I nodded a third time, and I could feel myself softening.

"Yeah," I said, "I know what you mean. Are we born with a politics gene or what?"

"Exactly. For whatever reason I got interested in politics in high-school, and, after college — "

"Which was where?" I interrupted him.

"Bob Jones University. I did a degree in Journalism and Mass Communications at BJU."

I nodded a fourth time, feeling some rigidity creeping back in.

"You know how, during the Bush years, there was a lot of active recruiting at Christian schools for government jobs?"

"I do."

"I was, I'll say fortunate to have been interviewed by someone who knew someone who worked for Congressman Wayland. Where I come from, Wayland is very popular. My parents were thrilled when I got hired and I felt very lucky. I started out in his Missouri office, but about four years later moved here. And that's when everything started to change."

"What happened?"

"D.C. happened. I'd grown up in a very closed, sheltered environment and college was the same. Coming here, suddenly I was seeing and mixing with all kinds of people who are really, really different from people I grew up with and met at college."

I nodded yet again. In D.C. you can meet someone from *anywhere.*

"Back home, things are very simple. Or seem simple. Things are black and white; you're with us or against us. Here, there's so many layers and so many people with different agendas." He paused. "Everyone is smart and people who believe things completely contrary to what I was raised to believe can make their cases persuasively," he went on. "At home and at Bob Jones we never heard the other side to anything. We heard our side, period. I mean, we were told what other people believed about things, but we didn't hear it from the people themselves. We never debated people who were passionate about their ideas. We were taught to argue straw-men and we were taught what to say. But we were never taught to think for ourselves."

"So you . . ." I began.

"When I first arrived I was a true believer. I was quite confident about my beliefs and thought Wayland was a principled warrior for good."

I swallowed the "ugh" I wanted to utter.

"But little by little my feelings started to change. I was seeing how things work from the inside — seeing the dealmaking, seeing the actual legislation being proposed by others and seeing how it might get changed, rejected, stalled, and lied about. Especially lied about. And the media is all over the place: sometimes accurate, sometimes way wrong and sometimes misleading; right about some technicality but wrong about the larger picture. Or, right about the larger picture and completely wrong about specifics."

"Maddening, isn't it?"

"Yes ma'am! But it doesn't bother Wayland at all. He told me confusion is a good thing."

"He did, did he?"

"He said everything he stood for was for people's own good, but if they actually knew what the party was trying to do they'd never elect another Republican. He said they weren't smart enough to know what was good for them; they needed people like him to make their decisions."

"He really said that?" Not that I was surprised, but, apparently, Peter had been.

"He really said that. To be honest, at first that didn't really bother me. I mean, from our point of view, most people are wrong about Jesus and being saved. Extending that into politics is easy. Except that with respect to Jesus we are taught to go out into the world and spread the good word. We're expected to try to convince others of our rightness. In politics apparently we're just supposed to believe everyone is stupid, including people that vote for us. That they won't understand what's good for them. It's okay to fool them rather than convince them."

He shook his head and looked at this hands again.

"I kept thinking about it," he continued. "I started watching different news shows and compared them to FOX. I noticed FOX is very big on opinion and does very little with factual information. Some other shows presented real information and explained what it all meant. FOX does a lot of innuendo and assertion and there's a lot of inconsistency. When you have nothing to compare it to it seems fine. When you start comparing it it's just embarrassing."

"I certainly agree with that!"

He looked sheepish for a few seconds, then said "It's not easy, or pleasant, to feel the foundations of your life wobble, you know."

"No, I suppose it isn't."

"Then I met Connie. She believes the opposite of practically everything I do, well, politically. Or did believe. But it didn't matter. I really liked her, right away, and I started listening, for the first time, to opposition. I hadn't realized how completely I blocked out alternatives; how I had never worked with an opposing idea — chewed on it — thought through implications. I considered what she had to say because I liked her — was attracted to her. I guess that supplied the motivation."

"It usually does." At least for awhile, I thought. I wondered if his new open-mindedness would remain if his attraction to Connie wore off. How deep did it go?

"For awhile I wavered, going back and forth. I wanted to be able to salvage what I could from my upbringing. I haven't lost my Christianity, but I've been shucking some of the attached baggage. I haven't shared any of this with my parents; I have no idea how they'll react."

"You have my sympathy," I said, feeling inadequate. I was starting to comprehend the enormity of what he faced.

"Thanks. Is that what you wanted to know?"

"Pretty much. I appreciate your honesty. So tell me what assistance you'd like from me."

"According to Connie," he began, with a glint of humor now appearing in his eyes, "you have some kind of gift for helping people in and around politics to find the most direct route to career satisfaction."

"Ah," I said, smiling.

"And that's what I want."

I rested my chin in my palm and my elbow on my desk and looked at him consideringly.

"The thing about politics," I said, after a moment, "is what you *should* do depends on which part of you is the driver."

He clapped his hands together and leaned forward.

"Are you driven by idealism? By ego? By competitiveness? By ideology? Are you more intellectual or emotional? What itch do you want to satisfy? A desire for power? Prestige? A desire to serve people? To help people? A desire to fix things? A desire to change things? A desire to prove yourself?"

Peter looked thoughtful. "I really have to think about it," he said. "I have to separate my religious motivations from the rest. If I had been raised in an entirely different environment; if *saving people* wasn't part of my universe — what would draw me to politics?"

"You're saying that you were drawn to politics, at least in part, because of your religion? How do you mean?"

"Well politics offers positions of influence and avenues to spread the good word. Political leaders also have the power to make things happen or stop things from happening. My problem is, oh, there's so many strands. Where does offering salvation cross the line into enforcing it? What's the right balance of politics and religion? How can we separate church and state without sacrificing religious beliefs? Does the end justify the means? Always? Sometimes? Never?"

"Good questions," I said.

"But separately, I just find the political realm interesting. I think I would no matter how I was raised."

"Probably. The question becomes: what drives you to work in politics rather than merely follow politics?"

"Right. I don't think it's ego or power. I don't think I'd ever want to run for office, though never say never. But right now, no."

"Okay then. I'd like you to explore that question between now and when we meet again. "

And with that I knew I as going to work with Peter.

Chapter Four

In the Spirit World:

"Xe! Metemnia has given you permission to view her Archive entries for her current incarnation as Barbara Tishkin. The Life Planners expect her to intersect with both Dash and Wynne soon."

On Earth:

Barbara Tishkin (née Fordhyme) was in the uncomfortable position of having inherited the estate of her estranged brother Dash (or Dennis, as she had stubbornly continued to call him although he'd never liked the name and preferred his nickname). While he often referred to his disapproving sister as a sanctimonious witch (with a "b"), he also trusted her and retained enough brotherly affection to make her the primary beneficiary in his will. (He certainly wasn't going to leave anything to his squad of ex-wives.) Whatever her qualities, Barbara was his only close relative. And now she was extremely wealthy.

Although Barbara had occasionally wondered whether she'd be remembered in her brother's will, she had done her level best to live with no expectations. They had barely spoken in five years and the previous ten had been marked by escalating rancor on both sides. This had pained her considerably as, at one time, she had adored him. Seven years separated them; through her childhood he was her heroic older brother — funny, bold and charismatic. As an adult, her assessment of his virtues began a gradual metamorphosis. Dash's charisma started to grate as he commandeered center-stage at all gatherings; his wit became barbed and sarcastic and his growing success was accompanied by corresponding increases in arrogance and insensitivity. Barbara's husband came to find Dash so insufferable he wouldn't attend events if Dash was invited. That development several times landed Barbara in the middle between her husband and her parents — the senior Fordhymes were disappointed and disapproving of this perceived disloyalty. But the senior Fordhymes were also retired, living in Florida, and too busy (so they said) to listen to Dash's show.

Barbara wasn't too busy to listen to Dash's show, she was too horrified. She couldn't believe many of his statements were allowed to be said on the air. (She would later discover the nullification of the Fairness Doctrine created the opening for hate-radio). When she questioned him he dismissed her concerns; he was just a "shock jock" he insisted. And if his "jokes" were aimed exclusively at women and minorities, that was simply where the humor took him.

Initially, she did her best to ignore Dash's professional activities. She was not much interested in politics; she voted Republican because her parents and husband did and she was too busy building a career in marketing to invest significant time in following current events (outside of business). But Dash's growing prominence ultimately made him inescapable; first friends, then co-workers, then business contacts, and finally strangers, started confronting her about "something-Dash-said." And while she agreed with his detractors, she didn't like having to publicly criticize him, but neither could she defend him. Praise was even worse; anyone who supported Dash instantly alienated her but she found it personally difficult and often professionally risky to make her feelings plain. Her husband, a lawyer, was similarly impacted, though to a lesser extent. A fair man, he didn't *blame* Barbara for the professional difficulties her brother occasionally caused him, but he couldn't help feeling sporadic surges of resentment. But there was nothing she could do. Dash was enjoying a dizzying ascent in popularity and influence; he was unstoppable.

Inevitably Barbara and Dash's relationship frayed. Most of their conversations degenerated into heated arguments. Politically, Dash grew ever more rightwing and Barbara found herself driven to the left. Dash's proclivity for making confident assertions that sounded, to Barbara, like spurious nonsense, became unbearable and she began researching his stated positions and, when they next met, refuting them. As Dash's mode of argument relied heavily on his ability to yell louder than most people as well as his gift for creative invective, enormous sound and fury resulted. But after shouting himself hoarse, Dash would find Barbara, still standing, neither intimidated nor remotely convinced. Her bleak eyes, telegraphing unyielding rejection, made him defensive and abusive by turns. Her common response was to tax him with his inability to conduct a substantive debate using reason and facts, a thrust that usually precipitated another round of vituperation. Depending on their location and the presence or absence of other people, these encounters might be concluded by a loud departure of one or the other; the throwing of small objects, or the intervention of a bystander (and on one memorable occasion, the police).

During these years Barbara mastered the facts about a number of controversial political issues, something she found both empowering and enraging. Disgusted by the Republican Party's unflaggingly rightward migration, she felt forced out. But while she gradually became sold on the Democratic Party's purported platform she was continually dismayed by party leaders' seeming inability to actually lead, remain firm, sell an idea, or — and this was damning — condemn the kinds of rhetoric Dash and his many imitators spewed, unchecked. She couldn't understand why no one in power pushed back. To her, it seemed Democrats held worthy beliefs but didn't defend them, while Republicans were increasingly adopting unworthy beliefs and defending them to the last ditch.

And Dash lead the charge. The extreme views he offered up (as comedy, so he originally claimed) slowly penetrated his brain; he stopped saying things because they were "funny" and started saying them because he believed them. The money poured in, becoming, in his mind, evidence of God's approval. To Barbara the money was simply evidence that he was doing work for people even richer than himself.

Quite possibly they would have argued in circles indefinitely, but life intervened. In the space of six devastating months, Barbara's husband was diagnosed, treated for and killed by an aggressive form of cancer. Six months later both senior Fordhymes were also dead. Throughout that exceedingly painful year Barbara coped, mourned and handled the physical and legal hassles engendered by each death. Dash was not able to provide much in the way of emotional support. Work pressures kept him from making more than brief appearances at the three funerals and they already had difficulty communicating under far less demanding conditions.

During her husband's ordeal Barbara used up her available vacation and sick days. A life insurance payout enabled her to contemplate quitting her marketing job, but she hesitated, unsure about her next move. When her father fell ill, Dash sent her check for $250,000. Barbara accepted the money with mixed feelings. Pride told her to send it back; exhaustion convinced her to keep it as she saw more trials looming ahead and doubted she could fulfill the requirements of her demanding and competitive corporate position. She resigned and spent the next several months in Florida, dealing with her parents' final illnesses, then sorting through their accumulated possessions.

Between the life insurance, Dash's gift and her parents' estate, Barbara felt financially secure. She also felt lonely, depressed and rudderless. Most of her friends, she realized belatedly, were work-related (either her work or her husband's) and their relationships didn't survive her absence both from the corporate world and the state of Maryland. But she remained close with a couple of people and it was one old friend, Sonya Helvender, who pointed her in a constructive direction.

Sonya and Barbara had met in college (University of Maryland), but while Barbara had studied business, Sonya had studied biology and had gone to work in the then fledgling field of ecology. She'd later completed a graduate degree and now made her living doing urban planning with an emphasis on energy efficiency. Before embarking on her graduate studies, she had taken a sabbatical and traveled around the country exploring various green projects and meeting with several practitioners of assorted new age arts. She'd been introduced to yoga and meditation, both of which she recommended highly. At her suggestion, Barbara sought out teachers; spent several months visiting tranquil and inspiring locations, and emerged from this odyssey with a plan for her future.

Purchasing a small farm in rural Maryland, she now raised merino sheep and converted their wool into artisanal hand-dyed yarns for knitters and weavers. Her work was physically demanding and creatively satisfying. In her limited leisure time she practiced yoga, meditated, knitted and was learning how to spin and weave. She kept an eye on political events. but from a distance — entering into political conversations rarely and only with likeminded individuals. She remained close to Sonya and a few others but otherwise avoided people from her previous life — preferring to socialize (when she had time) with new acquaintances she met through her business. These relationships were, if somewhat superficial, blessedly removed from Dash's orbit of influence as she never divulged their connection.

Her goal was to live a Dash-free life. She and Dash exchanged Christmas cards and spoke on the phone occasionally and always awkwardly. Barbara was determined to abstain from the sort of violent arguments they invariably fell into, having concluded the exchanges led nowhere and accomplished nothing. But even brief conversations required hours of decompression time as Dash couldn't resist trying to arouse her ire, always making inflammatory statements and reacting petulantly when she didn't take the bait. She wondered if he'd lost the ability to interact with people any other way — did he do nothing but pick fights? That might explain, she thought, why wife numbers three and four bailed.

Fortunately for her peace of mind her fledgling business was absorbing; dominating her time and attention. She acquired a well-trained herding dog for company and, if she was sometimes lonely, she was otherwise content.

The 2008 crash had interrupted what had been a very satisfactory business trajectory, but Barbara was making a reasonable profit and adding to her nest egg. She didn't need Dash's money; rarely thought about it and hence, was as much perturbed as delighted when informed by Dash's lawyer that she'd inherited several million dollars.

In addition to this windfall there was a list of sombody-has-to-do-these jobs to be fulfilled, starting with funeral arrangements and ending with the distribution or discarding of Dash's personal possessions.

Although Barbara was still in shock, she had dealt directly with three deaths in a year's time and well-remembered the flurry of decisions that had to be made. While Dash's sudden decease flooded her with contradictory and chaotic emotions, on one point she was absolutely clear: there would be no public calling hours, funeral service or burial. Dash would be cremated and she would figure out what to do with his ashes when she could think more clearly. In the meantime, she chose to delegate the making of the relevant arrangements. Fortunately, Dash's personal attorney was able to offer the services of his assistant, who took charge with flawless competence, eventually appearing at Barbara's door with a stack of paperwork and prepared checks.

"If you can sign these," said this paragon, "we'll be all set. The cremation can take place and other than collecting his ashes, there is nothing else you need to do."

After a quick review of invoices and agreements, Barbara did as directed, noting without comment the spectacular fee she had approved for attorney services. Worth it, she thought, all things considered.

"Now," continued the assistant, "regarding Mr. Fordhyme's personal effects, you can consider them to be your property as of today, although his estate will take time to work through probate. His estate is more than ample to discharge his obligations and no one has any legal claims to anything he owned so all (after taxes) will transfer to you. Do you have keys to his condo? No? Here you go."

After promising to be in touch as needed while Dash's estate wound it's way through probate, the assistant conveyed the law firm's condolences and appreciation for Dash's business and departed.

"Well!" thought Barbara, both relieved and a bit appalled at the efficient neatness with which her brother was legally ushered out of existence. While she lacked any desire to have to wrestle with emotional choices, there was something depressing about not having to do so.

Is that what will happen when I die? she wondered. I don't even have a me to leave things to — at least Dennis had me.

My sheep would miss me, she thought after awhile. And my dog.

I may have hit rock bottom, she thought after that.

Then her phone buzzed.

Oh God, she thought tiredly, "the attorney again? Or his assistant? Or a reporter (she'd been dreading the moment one would track her down.) Teetering on the edge of letting the call go to message, something made her answer.

"Is this Barbara Tishkin?" said an unfamiliar male voice.

"It is."

"This is Reve Tierney."

Chapter Five

Reve Tierney had seen the end of his rope dangling over his head, laughing maniacally. First, there'd been more glimpses of Dash Fordhyme in the corner of his bedroom. Then, his recent dreams began swimming to the surface of his consciousness demanding acknowledgement. While the details were sketchy, their overall trend seemed to point to one conclusion: a dead Dash was experiencing something dreadful and was appealing to him for aid, the nature of which was unfathomable.

Reve felt both unnerved and helpless. Nothing in his education, experience or upbringing prepared him to deal with supernatural problem-solving. His circle of friends, family and acquaintances offered no potential succor; upper level conservative pundits who work for right-wing think tanks do not mix with people who have a working knowledge of the occult. He knew plenty of Christians who felt themselves equipped to speak for God, but instinct told him they were unlikely to be constructive allies in this circumstance. Anyway, he couldn't imagine trying to tell anyone he knew about what he was experiencing.

Yet the need to talk to someone was becoming imperative, but who, who, who? Then he thought of Barbara. Dash had talked to Reve about Barbara over the years, expressing the opinion that his sister was a liberal who possessed every stereotypical flaw of that execrable class of people. He had railed about her judgmentalness, her naiveté, her "bleeding-heart" tendencies, her desire to spend everyone else's money on the undeserving, her intolerance for his intolerance and her openminded acceptance of differences (other than his). But his grudging coda had always been that Barbara was decent, honest and trustworthy.

Had Barbara been actively political, Reve would have ruled her out as she belonged on the other side of the aisle and one couldn't be too careful these days. But she wasn't. Thus her open-mindedness could be seen as a positive — she wouldn't dismiss his story automatically. And, given that she'd never gone public with her views about her brother, she might also be trusted to maintain confidentiality.

So he called her.

Barbara had seen Reve Tierney on television. She thought he was well-spoken and seemingly intelligent which made the content of his comments all the more reprehensible. He took the crudely unforgivable slurs served up by Dash and his imitators and repackaged them into semi-palatable material, assuming one didn't scrutinize too closely. Under normal circumstances she would have politely declined a request by him for a personal meeting.

But he was one of the few people who had contacted her with condolences and her self-imposed isolation meant he'd had to do some digging to find her. And whereas her friends struggled with their and her ambivalence, until Tierney had called, she hadn't realized how welcome an unequivocally sincere expression of sympathy would feel.

They met at The Cosmos Club, just outside of Dupont Circle, near downtown D.C. Tierney was a member and the club was quiet and offered privacy. He greeted her outside the main entrance and ushered her to a secluded table in the dining room.

Tierney was an elegant man in his mid fifties. Formally dressed, he was trim; was just under six feet tall, and had the posture and carriage of a dancer. His hair was still brown and barely receding; he had expressive eyebrows and a smile that had, by itself, increased his income by twenty percent over the years. His eyes were large, brown and shadowed at the moment by lack of sleep.

Barbara's figure was youthful for a woman approaching her fiftieth year. Her small farm and it's requirements provided ample opportunities for vigorous exercise and she'd developed a pleasingly energetic demeanor. As a corporate professional she'd displayed the necessary sophistication in wardrobe and appearance. Now she dressed for comfort, though she chose clothing made from high quality materials, classically styled. Her hair was a dark reddish-brown; shoulder-length, thick and straight. Her resemblance to Dash rested primarily in her lips and jaw, which both shared with their mother. Her hazel eyes had also come from their mother, while Dash's brown eyes and dark, wavy hair had been their father's.

Barbara, anticipating an awkward meeting, found herself somewhat disarmed. Tierney was polite, friendly, and observably exhausted. Was he really this distraught at the passing of her brother? Or was he bedeviled by some other problem?

A waiter was on hand immediately so a few minutes were occupied with selecting drinks (brandy for Reve, white wine for Barbara) and listening to the evening's specials. Choices made, they were left to contemplate one another: he somewhat blearily; she, puzzled.

After a period of silence that seemed fraught with some unstated significance, Barbara ventured a remark: "You seem to be troubled, Mr. Tierney, in some kind of strange way that I don't think is grief for my brother. Yet, since you asked to meet with me I have to assume your distress has something to do with Dennis's death. Is there something you need to tell me?"

A series of expressions passed swiftly over Reve's face: first surprise, then indecision, then gratitude and lastly, relief. But he remained mute, methodically taking minute sips of his brandy in what appeared to be an effort to prolong the supply in his glass while maintaining a steady level of slight inebriation.

Finally, he spoke: "Do you believe in life after death?"

This was unexpected and, for lack of any better reaction, Barbara deflected the question.

"Um, isn't that a bit personal, considering we've just met?"

Reve shook his head impatiently, "It is, yes, but could you please, please just indulge me?"

For a moment confusion battled with pity while alarm stood aside, thinking about entering the fray, and then Barbara decided to be honest and see where the conversation went.

"I was raised as a Lutheran, which is a faith predicated on life after death, of the traditional Christian flavor. Yet I wouldn't be prepared to go to the stake to defend Lutheranism. In recent years I've also learned a bit about Buddhism. Buddhists see the world quite differently from Christians. So, I suppose you could say I hold a mixture of beliefs, but am never entirely sure what is ultimately true. Overall I *think* there's life after death; I don't believe in hell, and if there's a heaven it's probably very different than the Christian conception."

Reve absorbed this and sipped his brandy. Then he asked: "Do you believe in ghosts?"

Barbara blinked.

"Mr. Tierney, are you alright?"

Again, the impatient shake of the head. "I am not alright. I am very, very tired and slightly drunk. But I am also completely serious. Please call me Reve, by the way." Then he waited.

Correctly interpreting this as a request that she answer his question, Barbara shrugged and spoke: "I don't know. Like most people, part of me believes in things like ghosts, but probably not in a deep way. I've never personally experienced anything ghostly, or supernatural, so it's all academic to me. Obviously there are many highly respected, well-educated people who reject the notion of the supernatural but I've never been convinced by skeptics."

"Why not?"

At this point salads and bread arrived. After the application of dressings, salt and ground pepper; butter on warm bread and a couple of bites, conversation resumed.

"Why haven't you been convinced by skeptics?" Reve prompted.

"Well," said Barbara, munching, "for one thing, I meditate and that can get very . . . *otherworldly*. And I suppose some part of me just likes the idea of the supernatural. Plus, if you believe in life after death, who's to say there can't be ghosts? But there never seems to be irrefutable proof."

He nodded. Barbara, who'd realized she was famished, noticed that Reve was pushing his salad around but wasn't really eating.

"Eat," she said, firmly.

He smiled faintly and obediently levered a forkful of salad into his mouth. This was followed by a bite of quite tasty bread — he seemed to consciously notice the taste and began to eat with more energy.

For a few minutes they ate companionably.

Barbara considered this. She wanted to retain her dislike for him, indeed, she wanted to express it. Tierney was part of the same apparatus that supported people like Dash; both had blood on their hands, metaphorically speaking. The problem was she could see his spirits improving — due to her company — which made it hard to deliver the verbal beating she felt he had coming.

Oh well, she thought, some other time. At the moment her hostility was trumped by her fundamental kind-heartedness — and curiosity.

"What about you?" she asked. "Do you believe in life after death?"

Reve laid his fork down (he'd been eating a expertly prepared piece of tilapia), wiped his lips with the starched cloth napkin and appeared to gather himself.

"You're probably wondering why I asked you that," he said.

"Well, yes."

Looking like a man who is debating whether the parachute will really open if he's mad enough to leap out of the airplane, he spoke: "I think I'm being haunted. I think I'm being haunted by your brother. I don't know why and I don't know what to do about it and — don't look at me like that — I'm really not crazy."

"I didn't say anything!"

"I could see it on your face. You were thinking it. Please don't."

Barbara blinked a few times, tilted her head back and took a deep breath through her nose. She rubbed her eyes, lowered her chin, and realizing she had no other response to offer, spread her hands in a gesture of acceptance and said: "why don't you tell me about it?"

Reve described his sleepless nights, confused and disturbing dream fragments and Dash's brief ghostly appearances, followed by a diplomatically edited recitation of her virtues as seen through Dash's eyes, which had convinced him she was the one person in the world he should call.

"So you," she said, "just to be clear, called me because Dennis described me as open-minded?"

"Among other things, yes."

"Well if he thought that," she said, diverted, "it would have been nice if he'd shared it with me! The last time we spoke he called me an idiotic granola-crunching tree-hugger and that was the nicest thing he said."

"You know how it is," said Reve, "people often say nice things *about* people, but not *to* people."

Barbara looked skeptical at this. "If Dennis told you I was open-minded he didn't mean it as a compliment."

"Perhaps he didn't," Reve conceded, "but I do."

"And why would you trust me to keep my mouth shut?" she asked.

Looking at her steadily, he said: "I decided to take the risk. You know what this town is like. You could cause me a lot of trouble, but you never did for Dash and I know you disapproved of him — "

"Very much so!" she interrupted

"Indeed. But you've never behaved vindictively. At the same time, I'm talking about *Dash*. We were friends for years and you are his sister. If I'm not crazy; if what I'm experiencing is real, then he's in some kind of trouble and I have no idea how to help him."

Her brow furrowed, then she said, "Nor do I. I don't know a thing about hauntings or ghosts or the occult. I'm just a Lutheran-cum-Buddhist, not a Wiccan."

"Yes, but you're probably the only other person in the world who might be bothered to find out."

"Oh. True. That's really sad, isn't it?" she said.

"It is sad," he replied, weary again.

They sat sipping their respective drinks, both near the bottom of their glasses. When their waiter asked if they'd like refills, both declined.

"I'm very tired," Reve announced, after the waiter left "and I don't know where this is going. But I don't want to drink any more, and for that I thank you. It's been a relief to be able to talk to someone."

"Did you drive?" Barbara asked. He might be feeling better but he was in no condition to drive.

"I took a cab. And I've booked a room here for tonight — its silly, really — I'm thinking that, maybe if I don't sleep at home I won't have bad dreams."

"Because Dennis won't be able to find you?"

"Right. Although I suppose ghosts have ways of finding people. Or do they? Don't they haunt places?"

"Beats me," said Barbara. "I'm sorry, I still have to come to terms with this. The only ghosts I've ever heard about are fictional, which isn't much help. And with all due respect, you *could* be crazy."

"That's true. But I'm really not."

"You don't *seem* crazy," she conceded, "but I don't know you so . . . "

"I understand."

"And frankly, a lot of the stuff you write about seems very nearly insane to me, so — "

"Well — "

"Well it does! But," she waved him down as he prepared to speak, "lets not get into that now. We're neither of us at our best and I'm not in the mood for a debate."

Reve opened and closed his mouth, then said: "Agreed."

"Let me sleep on this and I'll call you tomorrow. Will you be reachable?"

"I'm taking some vacation days so I'll be available, yes."

They exchanged phone numbers, then Barbara got his room number, and rose. Reve came around the table and took her right hand. He clasped it in both of his and said: "I can't thank you enough."

Touched, Barbara patted his arm with her left hand and said: "You're welcome. We'll get this figured out."

He nodded and they walked to the main entrance, where he stopped and said goodnight.

"Goodnight Reve. Sleep well."

Heavens, she thought, descending the club's front steps, that was not the evening I expected.

In the Spirit World, Veliastan, Xe and Lersaliaz confer:

"Xe! Have you been following Dash? What has he been doing?"

"He has made several attempts to get a message to Reve Tierney."

"And his message?"

"He's tried to exhort Reve to make good use of his remaining time."

"Hmm. That, at least, is constructive. Although the specifics of his message are important. Reve should not be frightened into change — he should decide for himself what is best."

"Why should he decide for himself? Can he not be told?"

"Each soul, within it's capacity and level of maturity, must choose what to believe and on what to act. It is the only path to growth. Humans *are* told by other humans what is good and what is bad. But they are given many conflicting directives and must decide for themselves. It is a fundamental earth lesson and is routinely failed. But Fadraya has advanced enough on the continuum to meet it — we would not want his opportunity for growth to be compromised. Changes made in response to external forces are weakening, not strengthening. Lersaliaz?"

"Yes. This effort is beneficial for Dash; it is pulling him out of his blank despair. I am encouraged; I think he will work himself through his turmoil and come home. But you are right — he must not violate Fadraya's free will or nullify his opportunity for growth. I will have to monitor them closely. His attempts at contact have borne one good result: Fadraya has sought out Metemnia."

"Indeed?"

"They were intended to meet some time ago. But Metemnia was so angry at Ukutmanu's way of life she had no interest in meeting his friends. Ukutmanu does not yet remember that one of his life assignments was to bring Metemnia and Fadraya together."

"So he is completing an assignment — that is good. Yes Xe?"

"What is the nature of their relationship to one-another?"

"Fadraya and Metemni are soul mates. They often partner in Earth lives although in this life as Reve and Barbara they were to partner with others first. Now they may be together."

"Why not earlier?"

"Each had challenges to surmount without reliance on the other for assistance. Now they may help one another."

On Earth:

Barbara drove home in a trance. Her mind was such a chaotic swirl of impressions, opinions and questions, she nearly passed her own driveway and had to brake abruptly and back up to turn in. Approaching her house, a yellow, three-story clapboard sided structure with a generous wrap-around porch and gingerbread details, she parked her Subaru Outback along the side, and, exiting the car, decided to stroll over to the fenced meadow to visit her sheep.

Her sheep soothed her. They were simple; their needs were straightforward. And they weren't spooky. Her dog Sabrina, an Australian Kelpie herding dog, came out of the house through a dog-door in the kitchen. Sabrina was a working dog, happy to be on duty and loaded with energy. She herded sheep, and when not so occupied, made it her business to keep an eye on Barbara, the house, the barn and the environs. Sabrina was also steadfastly un-spooky.

There's nothing scary here at all, Barbara told herself firmly. In any case, if Dennis is haunting someone, it isn't me and if he did haunt me I wouldn't be scared. I don't know what I believe about God or life after death, but I don't believe in demons or devils. If Dennis is an unhappy spirit he's unhappy, not evil.

So thinking, she lifted her chin and proceeded to the barn. This was a classic red-painted building with multiple sliding doors on both stories. She used part of it as a garage. Now empty (the sheep were all outside), it echoed when she spoke to Sabrina and Barbara found herself fighting a slight jumpiness.

Stop it! she ordered herself. With Sabrina at her side she'd often walked around her property at night and had never before been the least bit nervous.

The key, she thought, is to figure out how . . . to figure out if . . . how do I know Reve Tierney isn't simply delusional? Granted he didn't *seem* delusional but is that a guarantee of anything? I mean, really. Dennis died and I reacted ambivalently, which is perfectly natural given our history, but that was it. I didn't have the slightest inkling anything unusual was happening. Why Reve Tierney? Why would Dennis haunt him and not me? What am I saying? As if I want him to haunt me!

As she moved through the barn her mind continued to churn furiously.

Lets say Tierney isn't crazy and Dennis is really trying to ask for some kind of help, she thought, what should we do? Pull out a Ouija board?

Barbara remembered fooling around with a Ouija board when she was a teenager. She and a couple of girlfriends set up the board during a sleepover. They'd deliberately staged the scene for fright; sitting by candlelight at a table in a basement family room. They'd put their hands on the planchette and asked if anyone had a message for them. After a moment they experienced that uncanny feeling of the object moving on it's own with their hands as passengers instead of drivers. All three swore they weren't pushing or exerting any force at all yet the object was flying around the board spelling words.

The words themselves were innocuous — she couldn't remember them now. But eventually a sustained message seemed to manifest: someone calling himself a strange name she couldn't recall, told them to *beware of* . . . at which point Barbara's friend Jane had screamed and pulled her hands away, refusing to continue.

"It could be an evil spirit!" Jane croaked.

"Who?" Barbara had asked.

"Whoever was talking to us. I didn't really expect anyone to make contact. It's creepy."

Barbara had been scared, but just enough for it to be enjoyable and she would have gone on but Jane was genuinely rattled and wanted to stop. So they turned on the lights and trooped upstairs to make popcorn.

Barbara had thought about trying again but never got around to it. That episode, a visit to a fortune teller who used Tarot Cards, and the occasional reading and dismissing of a horoscope represented the sum total of her experience with the occult.

Was now the time to try again? Or should they find another Tarot reader? Did card readers talk to ghosts? Or just tell fortunes? Anyway, could you believe anything they'd say? At least with a Ouija board it was you and whoever came through, without intermediaries. (Unless the messages were purely subconscious productions as skeptics asserted.)

She visualized herself and Reve Tierney sitting at a Ouija board trying to contact Dennis and suddenly giggled.

After Barbara left Reve had gone to his room and commenced his nightly bedtime ritual, feeling curiously lighthearted. Rightly or wrongly he felt as though he'd left Dash at home — Dash didn't know where he was and therefore couldn't bother him tonight. He knew there were flaws in his logic and holes in his knowledge but chose not to examine either too closely. A placebo effect was just fine, he thought. He couldn't think clearly anyway but if he could just sleep normally, just sleep, everything would be better in the morning.

And if Barbara could help him — Barbara — he'd liked her. He'd felt at ease with her which was unusual. That she was attractive to him was normal; he reacted (privately and considerately) to all attractive women. But with Barbara he'd felt relaxed and unguarded, an untypical response to a new acquaintance. Of course, he'd also been both tipsy and tired — his defenses accordingly weakened. But that had been nice too. His normal state was one of alert wariness; his motto: "you can't be too careful." He couldn't remember the last time he'd been able to interact with a person without simultaneously scanning them for secondary motives, subtle traps, and hidden agendas. Political punditry was a world rife with competition, temptation and scores to be settled, at least on his side of the aisle. The need or compulsion for self-protection had become so much a part of him that its absence was striking.

Tomorrow, he thought as he drifted off. Things would be better tomorrow.

Chapter Six

Reve awoke with a moderate headache, a sour mouth and a large appetite. On balance he decided that was good; he could have felt a lot worse. He felt, not completely rested, but reasonably rested. His sleep had been blessedly undisturbed.

He toyed with the idea that his notion of a haunting had been a passing mistake, compounded by insomnia. But only briefly. He had not been mistaken, or rather, if he had been mistaken, then he was also flirting with delusional behavior, something he would not accept. No, something weird had definitely been occurring and might well occur again. Probably as soon as he went home. Could he not go home? For awhile, but not indefinitely. No, he would have to deal with Dash.

Maybe he could get Barbara to go with him. Having someone there would help (he pretended he hadn't thought having *her* there would help) and maybe she'd see something too.

He wondered what she'd thought of his claim. Doubt, probably. Understandably. But she'd been incredibly decent about it and he felt sure she'd do her best to help. In whatever way one helps another person deal with a haunting, he added to himself. He mused for awhile on his sudden plunge into the unexpected. Since the first night after Dash's death he'd been unmoored. He wasn't on solid ground yet, but Barbara had thrown him a rope and he'd caught it. It was a start.

After breakfast he would call her.

When Barbara's phone buzzed she was sitting at her kitchen table, coffee in hand, an unread newspaper spread out in front of her, thinking.

Dennis haunting Reve Tierney — it had to be nonsense, didn't it? Ghosts didn't happen in real life, did they? Whereas drunken delusions, psychosis, or the side-effects of sleep deprivation were perfectly possible, plausible, explainable and documented.

It was far more likely that Reve Tierney was disturbed, wasn't it? That would explain a lot, she thought. She had never liked him when she saw him on television, but she'd been rather drawn to him in person. How that squared with him being disturbed wasn't clear, really, but it made a sort of mangled sense.

When she saw who was calling she froze for a moment in indecision. Talk to him or have him go to message and talk to him later? Or not call him? But she'd promised she'd help him, more or less. What exactly had she said?

Oh drat! she thought, stuff it. Answer the phone and get it over with!

"Hello?" she said.

"Good morning Barbara! This is Reve. Did you sleep well?"

"Pretty well. You?"

"Better than I have in days, thanks to you. I feel, not great, but pretty decent, which is an improvement."

"That's good."

There was an empty space as each considered where to go next. As discomfort started to build Reve said: "Have you . . . "

Just as Barbara said: "Should we . . . " and they simultaneously burst into a babble of speech that ended with them laughing.

"This idea of Dennis haunting you — I don't know what to think of it," Barbara went on frankly.

"I don't know what to think of it either," said Reve. "I'm afraid to go home and was wondering if you'd go with me? Maybe you'll see him or hear him or feel something and you'll know I'm not crazy."

"Or that I am," she replied.

"Now don't be silly. Craziness isn't contagious, after all."

"Well . . . "

"It's not . . . how about this? If we both go and nothing happens, that proves, well, nothing. But if we both go there and *something* happens to both of us, that proves I'm not crazy. If we both go there and only *I* experience something, I'll go to the doctor."

"That seems reasonable."

"Good!"

They decided to meet in the lobby of his condominium complex at 2:00 p.m. and tackle his unit together. Each rang off with a pleasant sense of anticipation. Ghost hunting was out of the ordinary and could be looked at, in the clear light of a bright and sunshiny day, as a bit of an adventure.

In the Spirit World Lersaliaz and Veliastan confer:

"Lersaliaz! Has Dash made any progress?"

"At present I am keeping him under observation. He is on a quest now and must succeed or conclusively fail."

"I think you are right."

"Although, if he makes a mess I will have to clean it up."

"Yes."

"Still, Xe is enthralled."

"He is. He is now following many event lines. It is my hope this exercise will help prepare him to address dilemmas in his first incarnation. Although there's no avoiding a period of sheer culture shock."

"Familiarity may help soften the impact."

"So I hope."

On Earth:

Entering the beautifully restored historic building that Reve Tierney called home, Barbara whistled to herself.

Nice, she thought. Very nice and very expensive. Barely discernible security cameras endlessly monitored the tastefully landscaped entrance, marbled foyer and silver elevator doors that opened and closed with the inaudible breath of meticulously maintained machinery.

To the right of the elevator doors was a small, furnished waiting area. Reve Tierney, seated in a plushly upholstered chair and reading a copy of the Washington Post, rose gracefully and, moving towards her, offered Barbara his hand.

Barbara, shifting her purse (capacious enough to hold standard items *and* portable knitting projects) to her shoulder, grasped his hand and shook it firmly. Firmness, she felt, was of the essence. There was something disconcerting about Reve Tierney that kept her off-balance even as she warmed to him. Or maybe it was just the strangeness of the situation compounded by the tangle of disjointed emotions she'd felt about Dennis's death. She *was* off balance. Maybe he was simply in her orbit during a confusing time . . . Reve was talking.

"Thank you so much for coming! I really couldn't face this alone."

He looks much better than last night, she thought. Casually but nattily dressed, he appeared tired but not haggard and was completely free of the suggestion of panic, distress or overindulgence. His smile struck her, almost physically.

He's much more charming in person, she thought.

Meanwhile Reve thought Barbara looked absolutely sparkling and delicious. Hearing those words in his head he double-checked himself — did I really just think that? *Sparkling and delicious* — where did that come from? She wore a sleeveless blouse, a linen skirt and her bare, toned legs ended in sandals. She brought the outside in with her; he could smell a faint suggestion of grass and fresh air in her hair and for one instant, quickly repressed, felt the urge to bury his face in it. But she was talking . . .

" . . . is what I think. So let's go up and see what we see. Are you ready?"

"As ready as I'll ever be. Shall we?"

They entered the elevator, each hoping something definitively occult would happen, confirming Reve's sanity, and simultaneously that nothing at all would happen, relieving them of a problem they both felt ill-equipped to solve.

They walked towards the door at the end of the hallway slowing as they neared it. The door was of dark mahogany, heavy and paneled. Reve pulled out his key, extended his arm, hesitated and looked at Barbara who was staring rather wide-eyed at the number 12 in gleaming brass on the door. She met his eyes, took a breath and said, quietly, "Let's get this over with."

He nodded, manipulated the key and opened the door. They peered in through the doorway, surveying the dimly lit vista and seeing nothing unusual.

Slowly they advanced. Barbara intently scanned spaces while simultaneously taking in the expensive but tastefully restrained furnishings, thick oriental rugs and gleaming wood floors. The living room, with its large flat screen television mounted over an elaborately carved wooden fireplace surround, multi-paned windows, deep cushioned couch and two easy chairs covered in a dark green tweed and dark floral pattern respectively, exhibited no signs of supernatural activity.

The only thing this room needs, Barbara thought reflexively, is a hand-knitted afghan draped over the back of that floral chair. What color would I use?

Moving towards the east, bright sunlight filtered through real wood blinds, casting a grid of light over the formal dining table. The remains of Reve's last bad night filled one end of the table: an empty brandy snifter, an empty bottle, a crumpled cloth napkin, a coffee mug with a tiny pool of liquid in the bottom, a spoon, a jumbled newspaper. Nothing notable, though a bit sad, Barbara thought. Reve, correctly interpreting her expression, looked down. She didn't notice.

"Kitchen?" she asked, pointing to her left.

He nodded. Together they moved toward the doorway, Reve reaching around her to push open the door.

The kitchen was silent. There were a few dishes in the sink and a small trail of coffee grounds on the counter. Otherwise the room was clean, elegant and unremarkable.

"Well," said Reve, "so far so good I guess."

Barbara nodded. They turned together and, exiting the kitchen, headed toward the west end of the unit, which included a study/guest bedroom, a full bathroom, and Reve's bedroom with it's own full bath.

The bathroom, a gleaming, cream-toned space, looked spotless and empty. The study, dressed up to resemble the educated American's notion of an English country estate master's retreat, looked more lived-in than the rest of the unit, and inspired an appreciative nod from Barbara.

Reve looked pleased. People always liked his study.

On the wall behind his large antique wooden desk hung an arrangement of framed photographs. Barbara looked closely at one sporting a scribbled message — she couldn't quite make out the handwriting. With a half-smile on her face she looked at Reve inquiringly.

He cleared his throat and said: "That's from Congressman Wayland of Missouri. It's a *Thank You* for helping him win his last election. He gave it to me the last time he was here for a dinner-party. He lives near here."

"Oh," Barbara said, keeping her tone neutral. She didn't care for Congressman Wayland.

But there was no indication of anything untoward.

Re-entering the hallway they looked toward the door at the end, which, slightly opened, and seemingly innocent, caused them to pause warily. Both thought "this is it!" after which their thoughts descended into incoherence. But each felt a weight of significance; crossing into that room was going to change their lives.

For a full minute they stood, heart beats speeding up, hesitating, then Reve grunted and pushed the door open.

They entered.

It was a good-sized room filled with expensive, solid-wood furniture with overtones of Art Nouveau. In particular Barbara liked the oval floor mirror that stood in one corner. Reve accepted her enthusiastic comments somewhat wryly, explaining his ex-wife had picked it out some years ago.

It took a moment for them to process the image that was joining their forms in the mirror's reflection. Then, as one, they turned and saw a tall, shadowy shape in the opposite corner of the room which was coalescing into a recognizable figure. It was a bit blurred around the edges but, Barbara acknowledged, *it was him.*

The voice in her head said: he certainly looks unhappy, then, more fully absorbing what she was seeing, blacked out.

Dash looked *frayed.* She couldn't make out what he was wearing and his form wasn't complete.

Barbara's mouth went dry and her body stiffened. Her fight or flight instinct fought for expression (flight won), but her body rebelled, rejecting the order to move and substituting a thunderous rendition of her heartbeat while immobilizing her lungs.

Having been through this before, Reve was able to think and his thoughts were: Oh damn, there he is. Oh good, there he is — she sees him! Oh damn, there he is!

After an eternity lasting some eight seconds, Dash faded.

Barbara, feeling the strength ebb out of her legs, began sinking toward the floor. Reve, frozen to his spot, reacted when she slid against him, clutching her right arm and holding her steady, until she signaled to him that she was recovering. He guided her to the door, then to the living room, where he steered her to the couch.

"Lie down," he said, then, with shaking hands he placed a pillow with a soft covering of earth-toned stripes carefully beneath her head.

Barbara was taking deep breaths; Reve could practically see her heart beat slowing.

He felt almost giddy with relief — he *wasn't* losing his mind.

"Can I get you anything?" he asked, forcing his voice to be steady.

"If I were a different type of person I'd say whiskey," Barbara replied. Then she chuckled briefly, "but I am very thirsty. Do you have anything cold to drink? Water is fine."

"I do have whiskey."

"I know. That is, I expect you do — not that I mean . . . "

"I understand. I am not, contrary to the impression I may have made, a heavy drinker. But I usually have the basics on-hand for myself and visitors."

"I've just never had an experience before that seemed to call for a slug of something strong. But I don't actually want any alcohol right now."

"Hold on," he said, disappearing and returning a minute later with a glass of Perrier.

She drank from it gratefully and sat up.

"Well!" she said.

"I know."

"Do you think he'd be there if we went back in?"

"He comes and goes. I don't think he can be visible for long. But I expect he'll be back."

Barbara waved her hands helplessly.

"I am gobsmacked," she said. "I have no idea what to do with this."

"Tell me about it!"

She examined him. He was the picture of the well-dressed man gazing at her earnestly and she was overcome by a sense of unreality.

"This is freaky, you know."

"Tell me about it!"

That made her smile.

"Alright," she said, turning her body ninety degrees and putting her feet on the floor. She patted the cushion next to her.

"Sit down. Let's figure this out."

Some hours later they were no closer to a plan of action, although they had ruled out several possible paths to follow. They agreed consulting anyone professional was unacceptably risky, at least at this point. Reve had his public reputation to guard (Barbara accepted this assertion without comment.) and Barbara shuddered at the vision of the media circus that would develop if word got out that *Dash Fordhyme's sister sees ghost of dead brother.* Psychic consultants might be bound by discretionary ethics, but could one count on that? When the topic was this juicy?

Similar considerations ruled out consulting friends, family or co-workers, assuming any might have something useful to suggest, which seemed highly doubtful.

"I can think of people who would thoroughly enjoy getting involved in this," said Barbara, "but whether they'd be of any help is a different question entirely. And could they keep quiet about it? I don't think so, and I wouldn't blame them. Not that they'd blab all over town, but not tell a single person?"

"And all you need is one," said Reve.

They discussed consulting a priest. Reve was a Catholic, nominally, he suddenly realized. He'd not actually been to church for years and he didn't know any priests personally. He'd encountered a few priests at various political gatherings, but his encounters were limited to introductions and brief, polite conversations, quickly forgotten.

Still, it made sense in theory.

Barbara objected on the grounds that the involvement of a Catholic priest automatically imposed a point of view she disagreed with.

"I don't believe in evil spirits or demons or possession or Satan," she said firmly.

"Well I can't be sure, but I don't think a priest has to automatically assume an unhappy spirit is a demon. Though, to be honest, I have trouble imagining a priest taking me seriously anyway."

"If he saw Dennis like we just did he'd take it seriously! But would he be able to do anything?"

"I really don't know. Maybe."

"I suppose we could research that a bit. Maybe priests get some kind of training in dealing with spirits. Probably not a lot. Still, some of them do perform exorcisms . . . " Barbara's voice trailed off and she frowned.

Reve looked at her inquiringly. They'd gotten quite relaxed on the couch together and were talking as though they'd known one another for a long time. Every so often he was struck with how odd that was.

"I just don't like the idea," Barbara went on after a moment. "It implies there's some magic formula or incantation to be used — as though a ghost is, is not an individual. I mean, whatever's going on with Dennis has got to be unique to him, don't you think?"

"I suppose so," said Reve. "But maybe it doesn't matter why he's a ghost, just that he *is* one."

"True." she conceded. "Do you know a priest?"

"No. But we could find one easily enough I should think. There's definitely been clergy at some of the events we both attended — I could check my member lists in . . . "

"Any minister or priest that participated in the kinds of events Dennis favored are off limits as far as I'm concerned!"

"Well — "

"No!" Barbara straightened her spine, throwing back her shoulders and faced him, suddenly angry. "It's probably not the right time or place to say this, but you know I thoroughly disapproved of Dennis's politics, and to the extent you agree with him, I disapprove of yours. Dennis talked a lot about religion in ways that I think defiled the basic messages of Christianity and I couldn't stand it. And any clergy person who agreed with Dennis's politics has no moral authority for me."

"Aren't you being a little harsh?" Reve asked, but he could tell it was a weak rejoinder.

"Look, people aren't perfect and I don't expect perfection from priests or ministers or nuns or whatever. But it seems to me their whole point is to try harder than the rest of us to emulate the teachings of their faith, and provide guidance and examples. If they don't do that, they're just bad at their jobs. Any priest or clergyman who associated with Dennis has to have questionable standards."

"What if they were trying to get him to — "

"To what? Repent?"

"Well, it's possible."

Barbara laughed derisively.

"Are you saying you know of such a person?"

"No," he admitted.

"So?"

"I just don't like you thinking everyone who knew Dash is some kind of horrible person. Or that I am."

She inspected him then, dispassionately but with a discomforting intensity.

"Are you a horrible person?" she asked after a moment, tilting her head and raising her eyebrows.

"Of course I'm not!" he said with an attempt at a laugh. It was short-lived. "How can you ask that?" he then said, with an attempt at indignation.

"You spend your professional life asserting a kind of racial and class superiority over other people and you support and defend people who are openly prejudiced in practically every way — many of whom use violent and demeaning language to describe others. You have been an apologist for the Iraq War, one of the greatest debacles in American history. You've written in support of Paul Ryan's pretend-budget, privatizing Social Security, repealing the ACA, and Antonin Scalia, and I could go on. All of which argues either stupidity — and I don't think you're stupid — or intellectual dishonesty."

Barbara stopped as Reve, who had turned pink, struggled to speak. She waited.

"I can defend every opinion I have ever spoken or published!" he produced, his voice vibrating slightly.

"Can you now? Really? You want to defend, let's see . . . repealing the ACA?"

She jumped up from the couch and started pacing.

"You've supported that, haven't you? After years of escalating prices and people losing access to healthcare, something finally gets passed that helps people and those sanctimonious, entitled, windbags in Congress vote over and over to repeal it. Granted, the ACA isn't a perfect law, but it's a huge step forward. But you guys don't give a damn about how many people you would hurt do you?"

Reve, who was still pink, said: "The question of the best way to deal with healthcare is — "

Barbara shook her head impatiently and interrupted: "Do you have medical coverage?"

"Yes," he said, "but — "

"Ever been without it? Has it ever cost more than you could afford?"

"No, but — "

"Does the individual American citizen have any control over medical costs?" Barbara asked, her volume rising a notch.

"Well, that's a complicated question. People have some choice over procedures and — "

"Do they have any control over what procedures *cost?*"

"Well, the market always has a say — "

"Do individuals?"

"Individuals don't have direct control, no. But the market will work if given a chance."

"The market *was* given a chance. The market had decades of chances and all that happened was that more and more people were priced out of it. And we're talking about living and dying here. Illness and pain. Grinding financial stress. Not someone being unable to afford a luxury car. Can't you grasp the difference? Don't you understand how utterly, utterly fortunate people like us are?"

"The ACA was the largest entitlement program since — "

"So what? It's better than letting people suffer and die who don't need to; it's better than ruining people financially; it's better than spending that money on hideously stupid and expensive wars and it's better than the alternative Republicans offered *which was nothing.*"

Reve, holding tight to his temper, stood and tried again: "If you will calm down and listen I can explain our rationale."

"No you can't," she replied, just calmly enough to be aggravating to a sensitive listener.

"Yes I damn well can!"

Barbara walked up to Reve and tapped him on the arm three times as she said: "No. You. Can't. You can make arguments that *sound* plausible, but in the end, what you're saying is that serving your ideology is more important than sparing and saving people's lives."

"That's not true!"

"It is true. When you talk about the market you are talking about a collection of rules, laws, taxes and tax-exemptions which, in combination, create outcomes. The market failed to deliver a solution to people being priced out of affordable healthcare. For years. So a new set of rules were imposed that ensure most people now *have* access to healthcare. Those rules offend your idealogical sensibilities so you would sacrifice them in one stroke even though people would once again suffer and die. It doesn't matter how you dress it up, that would be the result and what's more, I think you know it."

"I do not! That is — "

"Well then you should!"

Their eyes locked for several seconds. Then the silence between them assumed a liquid quality and began to drip: plip . . . plip . . . plip.

Reve collapsed into the dark green recliner.

"Wow . . . so on top of everything else you think I'm just heartless." he said.

Barbara looked at him detachedly, then felt an unwelcome but irresistible tinge of sympathy. He was *hurt*. Which he bloody well deserved to be! Still . . . sigh.

"I don't think you're *heartless*," she said quietly. "I think you block yourself from recognizing consequences and by doing that you can rationalize your work."

"Oh," he said sardonically, "that's so much better!"

This made her smile and despite himself, he smiled slightly in response. They hesitated, each in the grip of a disconcerting mix of hostility and amusement, not sure to which to surrender.

"You know," said Reve, "I don't think I've ever been so comprehensively insulted. I don't know why I'm not asking you to leave."

"Maybe because you have a ghost in your bedroom and you don't want to be alone with it?" Barbara's smile was firming up.

"Well there is that. Still, I don't know that I can just leave my character on the floor in shreds like that without making some effort to defend myself."

"I *could* leave," she offered, "if that will make you feel any better. Do you want me to leave?"

"No. But I ought to."

"Well how about this? We'll return to the topic at hand — Dennis's haunting — and you can defend your honor some other day when you feel more up to it."

"But if that's what you think of me, why are you here?" he couldn't help asking.

"Because it's Dennis, my brother, we're dealing with. We were close at one time. And, I suppose, because for some reason I like you."

"You do?"

"I do. Strange, isn't it?"

"Strange seems to be where I live now," said Reve.

He reflected for a moment even as part of him struggled with competing feelings of outrage and gratification. The sense of being unmoored, from which he'd been suffering since Dash's death, returned with a vengeance. He was about to attempt an elucidation of his emotions when Barbara looked over her shoulder, in the direction of his bedroom.

"What?" he said.

"Did you hear something?" she whispered.

Very quietly Reve replied "No. What did you hear?"

"I'm not sure. I don't know. But I think he's back. I feel . . . that he's back."

"Should we go see him?"

"Um . . . I guess. It can't hurt can it?"

Reve's expression said that it probably could hurt, but he knew that was an instinctive fear reaction and he couldn't bring himself to say it. Time to show some guts, he thought. So, while his face vehemently disagreed, his mouth said: "No, it can't hurt, per se. How can it hurt?"

"I guess we've already been shocked and scared. The worst we can expect is more of the same, right?"

"Right," said Reve. "Right!" he added, more forcefully. He stood, put out his hand and secured hers and began walking towards the bedroom.

Walk confidently, he told himself and hoped he was. He couldn't be sure because he was nervous and a buzzing in his ears was jamming the other signals his system was trying to send him. All he knew was that Barbara was gripping his hand tightly, following his lead.

When they reached the door Reve opened it straightaway and they entered the room quickly, which made, when they saw Dash's fluctuating figure, their dead stop the more jarring.

Transfixed, they stared as Dash seemed to grow more solid. But not solid enough. There was something wrong — his outline disintegrated into broken lines. He seemed to be wearing the clothes he'd died in: a cotton polo shirt and tan pants, but they kept fading into a melange of grey and black criss-crossing edges with holes and tears and wisps that re-solidified into a facsimile of a cotton polo shirt and tan pants.

His mouth opened. No sound emerged, but the fact that he was clearly attempting to speak was peculiarly paralyzing. Neither Reve nor Barbara took a breath while Dash issued a stream of soundless remarks.

Then his mouth closed and he looked at them. Expectantly?

He *saw* them.

They gaped.

Exercising a considerable effort of will, Barbara summoned her ability to speak. She was still in mid-gargle when, with an expression of sheer frustration on his face, Dash faded.

With her hand still tightly clasped, Barbara felt herself being pulled backwards. She allowed herself to be propelled out of the room, although she could have stayed. Shaken, but not panicked, she was sure now Dash was specifically trying to communicate and therefore their first priority must be to receive the message. Instead of leaving the room, they should probably camp there.

"We should what?" demanded Reve, after they'd reached the living room. His adrenaline was still surging.

"We should probably stay in the room and be there when he appears. He's trying to tell us something. Or you, I guess. He did choose you after all. He wants to tell you something."

"Stay in there?"

"Well we want to figure out what he's trying to tell you, don't we?"

"Do we? Do we?"

"Reve, calm down!"

On the verge of shouting "calm down!" Reve checked himself and, waving his hand to silence her, pulled himself together.

"You're right, of course. It's just — he was trying to talk! It's bad enough to see him, but I don't know what I'll do if I *hear* him! Holy hell! What on earth could he have to tell me? Why me? We weren't *that* close!"

"I don't think Dennis was really close to anyone in these last years," said Barbara.

"Right!"

"Which means, even if you weren't really close, you probably were still closer to him than anyone else."

"Ohhh hell. Yes, probably. Probably that's true. That could be true."

With a bend of the knees, Reve crumpled onto the couch and covered his face with his hands. After an interval, Barbara sat and, pulling her legs up beside her, waited quietly.

Finally Reve straightened up and, resignation contouring his features, said: "I suppose we could do that. I mean, not try to find a priest or anyone else. Just go in there and see if he can do whatever he's trying to do. Tell me whatever he wants to tell me."

"He seems to be progressing doesn't he?" said Barbara, wrinkling her forehead. "It started with you dreaming about him and then just glimpsing him and working up to us definitely seeing him and him even trying to speak. Can he be learning how to appear?"

"God knows. Is that how it works? Whatever he wants to tell me can't be good I don't think. Does he want me to do something for him? What could he want?"

"How often did you used to see him? I mean, when he was alive?"

"Oh, not that often. Maybe every few months. We had dinner a few months ago at the Cosmos. I would see him at different events; we'd have a drink at the bar type of thing. We didn't talk about anything deeply personal. Well, we commiserated with each other about our divorces but — "

"Your divorces?"

"His four and my one."

"Oh . . . do you mind my asking what happened with you? Why you got divorced I mean?"

Reve's expression was grim. "Kind of," he said.

"Sorry."

"It's alright. Its natural to wonder. We just . . . lost each other I guess. Over time. It was all very civil. She had her own money and we didn't wrangle over anything. She said she felt empty. Her life, our life together, was empty. Had become empty. And it had. I agreed with her. We didn't do things together, we had different friends. No children. She was a lobbyist and was burned out. She's in Italy now. She sent me a postcard."

Barbara was trying to compose a comment that wouldn't be trite or overly familiar when Reve added: "It's been two years. I'm fine with it."

"That's good," she said, not believing him but grateful for the out.

"Although, between my wife leaving and this haunting, I'm starting to think I ought to move!" he added.

"I can imagine!" Barbara said.

"But not just yet, I guess."

"Not quite."

"Alright. Well, what time is it anyway?" Reve looked at his watch and, registering surprise, said "It's already after seven! Did you think it was that late?"

"No! My goodness. I need to feed my dog! Not to mention that I'm hungry."

"We can't spend all evening here — we need to eat. You have stuff to do. What shall I do? I don't think I want to sleep here tonight. I can go back to the Cosmos. Isn't Dash's funeral tomorrow? I would go, but I read that it's for family only. Do you suppose he'll show up there?"

"I don't think so. He hasn't even come out of your bedroom. That's probably where he's focused or anchored or whatever you'd call it. Anyway, there isn't going to be a funeral. I couldn't stand the idea of open calling hours. I have nothing to say to most of the people who would have come. I had him cremated and his lawyers released a statement about a private family ceremony, which boils down to me going to the funeral home and picking up his ashes."

"I see. I wondered. I know you don't have any close immediate family so I thought maybe you were having some friends or cousins . . . If this was a . . . a normal death, I'd be concerned about you not feeling, you know, closure."

Barbara acknowledged the comment with a small shrug. Closure was not currently on the table.

"Would you like me to come with you to get his ashes?"

After a pause she said: "Sure, why not. It makes sense, really. And it would be nice not to go there alone. Thanks."

"Don't thank me. It's the least I can do. Let me pack some stuff. I wonder if he's in there now. Would you come with me?"

As they entered the bedroom they immediately sensed it was empty. Moving quickly, Reve collected a sport coat, pants, shirt, tie, socks and some underwear. Quickly zipping them into a garment bag, Reve then looked a bit distractedly around the room as if searching for something. Then his brow cleared.

"My bathrobe and pajamas are still in my other bag," he said. "I took them to the Cosmos Club yesterday."

"Maybe you should pack some informal clothes too, just in case," Barbara suggested. She was thinking . . .

"Um, well, that might be a good idea. Let me see."

He opened a drawer and grabbed, seemingly randomly, a yellow short-sleeved polo shirt and from a closet shelf, a pair of olive-green cotton pants. Back to his dresser for some cotton socks, a handkerchief and, from his closet, some athletic shoes and a pair of sandals. He stuffed them all into the suit carrier and said "let's get out of here!"

Back in the living room, Barbara came to a decision and asked Reve whether he'd like to join her at the farm for the evening.

"Really?"

"Sure. I have a guest room if you want to spend the night."

"I'd love to," he said, visibly relieved, "but is that really okay with you? We've only just met."

"I think we can consider the formalities to have passed, don't you?"

With a smile Reve said: "Pretty much. Still, I don't want you to feel obligated. I would be fine at the Cosmos."

"It's okay, really."

"Well good then. I've never been to a sheep farm. Are you going to cook dinner? Can I help? I make a good salad!"

"I don't know what I have in the refrigerator. It's been such a crazy week. We'll have to look. Do you want to drive with me or follow me? If you drive with me we can go to the funeral home tomorrow and then come here, and check in, so to speak. But for tonight" she added mischievously, "you can help me tip a sheep and trim its hooves!"

Reve, an urbanite by upbringing and habit, squared his shoulders manfully and said, "No problem!"

In the Spirit World, Veliastan, Lersaliaz and Xe confer:

"Lersaliaz, how is Dash?"

"I am encouraged. In his effort to make contact with Reve he is becoming frustrated and aggravated."

"Excellent. Yes Xe?"

"Why is that excellent?"

"Previously he felt despair."

"Frustration energy is active, Xe, while despair energy is incapacitating. You will find that frustration is unpleasant but despair is far worse. There are experiences on earth to which despair is the only reasonable response, but they should be few and brief. Prolonged despair is extremely damaging. If Dash languished in despair for long I would intervene but fortunately he is helping himself."

"He is still very unhappy, isn't he?"

"Oh indeed. But unhappiness has many modes and levels. Dash will have to deal with the ultimate cause of his unhappiness — his poor life performance and steep karmic obligation — but he will be better able to deal with it if he starts to repair his energy. Should he succeed in his current effort, he will feel better still, and that will open the channel to positive energy. An infusion of positive energy will assist his thinking and, in due course, lead him home. Do you concur Veliastan?"

"I do. However, he must be resolved to succeed in his effort. He is attempting a complex communication and he lacks the necessary skills. Yet, he may find a way. For now it is a pretty puzzle for him and, as you say, creates the conditions for improved energy. Will you endeavor to aid him?"

"I may drop an idea or two if he becomes more receptive. My Guide believes this struggle will make a lasting impression on him. His soul must be seared with the reckoning so strongly that it affects his actions for many lives to come."

Chapter Seven

I was looking forward to my session with Olivia. We were going to prepare her for her first information interview. She was nearly finished cleaning my condo and I was enjoying the delightful feeling of having everything dusted and neat without myself having lifted a finger. Everything smelled fresh; she'd used assorted essential oils in various preparations which gave me an agreeable feeling of virtue. While I waited for her I mused about Peter Gilen and the challenge he presented to me as a counselor.

I thought about my last conversation with Connie, who had called to relay the intelligence that Peter had been encouraged by our meeting, though he'd found my bluntness intimidating at first. But that had passed.

"He said he's used to people being aggressive and intrusive, but always in an effort to impose their beliefs. He's not used to someone delving into him because what he thinks and feels matters, you know?"

I didn't know, actually, having trouble imagining the kind of environment Peter came from. But I got the gist and made concurring noises to Connie.

"He's really hopeful you'll help him work out a strategy for going forward," Connie went on, "and soon, because he's starting to have trouble going to work."

"What kind of trouble?"

"It's getting harder for him to go along with things. He wants to make objections and disagree with people."

"It would be hard," I said. "He's acting now, playing a part. And not for much longer," I hastened to add. "We're going to meet again tomorrow."

"That's great! Can you share anything with me?"

I thought about saying: "I have no idea what I'm going to advise him to do," but I didn't think that would inspire confidence.

I told Connie that Peter needed to be the first to know and she agreed. We would be meeting again after he left work on Friday.

"Pretty much anything you come up with is going to cause an earthquake in his life," she said.

"Yeah, there's no escaping that. But in the end, the important people are his family who I hope will be able to forgive him and accept him. Exile and excommunication, even if just figurative, would suck."

Olivia's appearance in front of me brought me back to the present. Her situation was uncomplicated. Peter Gilen, on the other hand, had something to end. And then what?

Peter Gilen was relieved Friday had arrived. First, he had another session with Wynne. Second, although his job was virtually all-consuming, it was summer, nothing especially hot was on the burner and he could, barring some unforeseen event, actually anticipate a free weekend.

Congressman Herbert Wayland, who had intended to make an appearance at Dash Fordhyme's funeral, was surprised when informed by his chief of staff there was to be no public mourning for Fordhyme: no calling hours, no graveside ceremony (No photo-ops, Peter, who was passing the two men on his way to his desk, thought with uncharacteristic cynicism.) and, apparently, no grave.

"Are you kidding me?" Wayland demanded. An imposing figure, his weight had been skyrocketing recently necessitating a new supply of suits. He attributed this weight gain to the increase in stress he'd been enduring since the second he'd learned he was going to be primaried by a Tea Partier. But he carried himself well, and was aging attractively. His hair, while gray, was thick; he kept his eyebrows groomed, his teeth had been touched up and he had always been photogenic.

"No sir, " said Melvin Thornery, "the word came out yesterday — I meant to tell you this morning. There will be a family-only ceremony and the body will be cremated. I guess there's a sister who calls the shots now and those were her wishes."

"Hm, yes," Wayland said, "I seem to remember hearing Fordhyme's sister wasn't a fan. It was decent of her to keep a low profile — she's some kind of crazy eco-femmy liberal, but she has no stomach for public life. I wonder what will happen to Fordhyme's money?"

"I would imagine she'll get most of it," hazarded Thornery. "I suppose it's possible he'd leave it to someone else, or maybe a group or institution, but seems unlikely. Though you never know."

"Shame," said the Wayland, "that money's gonna change sides now. Too bad. Wonder what she'll do with it if she gets it?"

Thornery had no information to offer so he shrugged his shoulders. A thin, angular man with a sharp chin, small eyes and a prominent nose, he managed to create the impression of good looks. A beautifully-fitted, expensive wardrobe contributed to this impression, as did his overall air of assurance. Thornery knew himself to be smarter than most people, even inside the beltway where IQ's were high, and he was notably competent.

He said he knew a man who knew a woman who might be able to find out something. Would the Congressman like him to look into it?

Peter had never liked Dash Fordhyme, even before his change of heart. He hoped Fordhyme's sister did something outrageously liberal with her windfall and, thinking this, he smiled.

"What's funny?" Wayland asked.

"Oh nothing, sir, some thought. Forgot it already."

"You haven't been yourself lately — I've noticed. Something on your mind?" He looked at Peter intently. Thornery, scenting *something,* also fixed his gaze on the young man.

This surprised, then alarmed Peter. The Congressman was usually too busy to notice the moods, or, many times, even the existence, of junior members of his staff.

Or so he thought. In point of fact, Wayland was acutely conscious of the currents that surrounded him; they were part of an internal radar system that had helped him survive politically for many years. He didn't necessarily *care* how people around him felt, still less what they thought, but he registered both. Now he was getting faint but unmistakable signals that something was up with Peter.

Meanwhile, Thornery, who was very good at reading his boss, was picking up Wayland's unease which was increasing in response to Peter's undeniably guilty grimace and evasive response.

"I, uh, haven't been sleeping well," Peter tried. "I'm looking forward to the weekend. You know how it is."

"Sure son, I know how it is. The job can take a lot out of ya," Wayland said, looking avuncular. Thornery, following Wayland's lead, murmured something about all work and no play.

Peter smiled gratefully and retreated to his desk where he began "getting-ready-to-go" activities while the hammering in his heart subsided. Turn computer off, he said to himself. Put files away. Put pens in drawer. Find laptop bag. Looking up, he saw Wayland and Thornery in close conversation and wondered if they were talking about him.

No matter, he told himself. I'll be out of here soon. I'm a small cog in this wheel. I'm dispensable. Something will come up to distract them.

Affecting nonchalance, Peter walked past Thornery and Wayland and wished them both a nice weekend. Both smiled at him and reciprocated. After he was gone, Thornery turned to Wayland.

"Think we have a problem?"

"Not sure. Maybe. He's a good kid, but you know what happens. He's in the big city now, rubbing up against all kinds of people he's not used to. There's always some who fall off the straight and narrow if the opportunity arises. Depends which way he falls."

"Right."

The Congressman, remembering his own forays into forbidden territories when he first came to Washington, thought Peter was probably undergoing a fairly routine rite of passage. He put this to Thornery.

"Very likely," Thornery agreed. "And usually I wouldn't worry too much. But lately, what with your poll numbers dropping, we don't need any scandals."

Wayland sighed heavily. He was beginning to wonder if it was time to retire. The political landscape was becoming ever more difficult to navigate, even for an old hand like himself. The Tea Party faction, initially so useful, was forcing choices on him he preferred not to make. Sooner or later, he feared, he was going to have to bow to them, or defy them. There didn't seem to be any middle ground any more. The question was whether he needed to make that choice soon, or could he eke out one more election. He'd won 12 elections, mostly handily, especially recently. The Democrats had fielded one weak candidate after another. Now he was being primaried *from the right.* After all these years, he thought bitterly. How was that justice?

Thornery, who had a pretty good idea what his boss was thinking, also brooded about the prevailing state of affairs. Over the years he had assiduously nursed a collection of connections throughout beltway and had been confident he could secure a plumb position minutes after the Congressman retired. But loyalty, so richly rewarded for so long, was beginning to look less like a sure thing. It all depended on which faction of the Republican Party regained control. At the moment, no one was really in charge — the party had devolved into fiefdoms with no clear leader. Politicians like Wayland were usually, if nothing else, superb survivalists, but it seemed like the rules were changing and no one knew where it would all end

His sigh made the Congressman look up and narrow his eyes.

"Just thinking," Thornery said quickly.

"About what?"

"Whether we should, uh, you know . . . keep an eye on Peter. I can have Wilksie tail him for a few days and see if he's up to anything we should know about."

Wilksie was a retired FBI Agent who performed low grade surveillance assignments for D.C. functionaries. If you paid him, he kept his mouth shut and, as such, was an extremely useful person to know. Knowing him was one of Thornery's many achievements in the realm of contact development.

"What could he be doing?"

"I don't know. But better safe than sorry."

"I suppose. Fine. Let me know if he discovers anything."

The minute Peter walked into my apartment I sensed a change in him. He had solidified since we'd last met — his doubts were allayed and his purpose was now firm.

His first words were: "I have to get out of there as soon as possible — I can hardly stand going to work anymore."

"And hello to you!"

"I'm sorry," he said contritely. "That wasn't polite."

"No problem; I'm just kidding. I understand and I agree. Certain jobs — once they go bad — you have to leave."

"Yeah. Every minute I feel like a liar and a fraud. Plus I'm starting to dislike my coworkers, which really isn't fair. I just . . . I just feel judgmental all the time."

While speaking, Peter had followed me to my office, moved his chair, removed his suit jacket and generally arranged himself. He now sat directly across from me and looked expectant.

"Do you have any vacation time you could use?" I asked.

"Unfortunately, no."

"Ok then — lets get busy. " I marshaled my thoughts, then continued, "Basically you have two ways of handling this. You can leave your job without making a political statement, or you can *make* the leaving of your job a political statement."

Peter looked slightly puzzled.

"In other words, you can simply resign, citing apolitical reasons — we could come up with something. You don't have to share your, I'll say, conversion, with anyone. Or not yet, at any rate. Or, you could make your reasons very public. The first approach buys you more time and leaves old doors open. The second approach sets you up to pursue jobs on the other side of the aisle, immediately. By being public you will impress Democrats with your sincerity — the fact that you are willing to burn bridges. All partisans enjoy a conversion story."

"Okaaay," he said slowly.

"If you play it low key, you can pursue jobs that aren't political. For example, you could look at jobs in various federal agencies — administrative positions that exist regardless of who's in power."

"I see."

"You can pursue jobs in lobby shops or any number of issue oriented organizations. You would be likely to have to explain yourself in interviews, but that's okay — it will come up. The point is you don't have to explain to the world at large, just to your potential employers."

Peter nodded.

"Or you can go the other way and pursue something that represents a clear and public repudiation of your past. As I said, there would be payoffs to that approach, but also prices to pay you can avoid if you go stealth."

"Hmm. Well, its not like I'm famous or anything. Who's gonna care what I do?" he asked.

"Depends. You could make yourself a *little* famous. All it would take is a guest column on one or two of the prominent progressive blogs and you could create a mini-sensation. Go public with your reasons for being disenchanted with the Republican Party and you will get noticed. That could be parleyed into a job if you handle it well. You're a staffer for a Congressman whom Democrats love to hate and there are those who could make use of you: Wayland's opponent in the next mid-terms, for instance. If you created some stir and went to work for that person, he — or she — could use you for outreach to Republican voters who might be feeling like you do."

"I don't know about that. I had to come to D.C. and be exposed to a lot before I saw the light. Folks back home are cocooned — if anything they'll just hate me and consider me a traitor."

"All of them? There are no dissatisfied Republicans in your district? They all love Wayland?"

"Weeell, it's hard to say."

"How many voters does a Democrat need to peel off in your district to flip it?"

"Wayland used to win by wide margins, but things have been tightening up," Peter conceded.

"And you could appeal to other Evangelicals. A lot of them are getting disenchanted with their political involvement, feeling the Republican Party makes a lot of promises it doesn't keep."

"True, but Democrats don't speak to born-agains at all. They are usually dismissive and mocking,"

"I'll bet if you went to work with Wayland's opponent you could help that person better appeal to your folks, couldn't you?"

"I don't know — maybe."

"Maybe. But maybe means its possible, right? My point is you could position yourself as a significant asset to someone. We could do some digging in your home district and find out if any promising Democrat is considering a run. I could put out some feelers and so could Connie."

"Wayland has had things locked up for years. The Democrats haven't fielded anyone with a prayer for decades."

"Right, but things are pretty volatile right now and upsets happen. Yes it's a long shot, but its not impossible. And it would be a natural transition *if* you want to continue to work directly for an elected official. A Democrat in a bluer district doesn't need you."

"That's true."

"And it would be a way of paying your dues, so to speak. You help flip a district and Democrats will "forgive" your past allegiance."

"I can see that," Peter agreed, "and yet . . . "

"Or here's an idea," I said, interrupting him. Suddenly my thoughts were coalescing around a central idea, the idea I'd been groping for since I'd meet him. "I mentioned that you could be helpful to a Democrat running in your district because you could provide outreach to your community of believers. But what if that became your primary purpose?"

"What do you mean?"

"What if you began to work, specifically, on building a bridge between evangelical Christians and the Democratic Party?"

"You mean as a consultant?"

"Or something. I'm not sure. I just have this idea . . . can you be an evangelical Christian and a Democrat? Or are they mutually exclusive?"

Peter's forehead puckered as he considered the question. He started to speak and stopped twice, then said: "My first instinct is to say yes, they are mutually exclusive, but I don't think it should be true."

"You mean, evangelicals should be able to be Democrats, but not many of them are?"

"Right. And I can cite chapter and verse for various issues, particularly about abortion and homosexuality, that seem to fall in line with Republican positions. But there are other chapters and verses that fall in line with Democratic positions too. Somehow they never seem to have the same impact."

"I've noticed that," I said.

Peter smiled wanly.

"I know," he said. "Connie has been pummeling me about that for awhile now."

Good for her, I thought.

"Some evangelicals don't believe religion and politics go together at all, but they're in the minority. The Republican Party has done an outstanding job of courting conservative Christians for years so it isn't surprising we skew Republican," he went on.

"That's true," I said. "the Democratic Party is the big tent, as they say, and a majority of Democrats define themselves as Christian — but very few as fundamentalist or evangelical. A growing percentage of Democrats describe themselves as spiritual, but not religious. And many Democrats are atheist. Then there's Jews, Muslims, Buddhists, Hindus — America's non-Christians lean Democrat because the Republican Party denounces them."

"I can't deny that and I think it's bad, but you have to admit that Democrats denounce fundamentalists too!"

"Touché," I said, "and that's wrong too — in principle. But there's really a couple of different disagreements going on that muddy the waters and preclude constructive communication."

"Do tell!" Peter said, smiling.

"Well first, we have our own internal squabbles about religion, primarily between militant atheists and everyone else. Most atheists are perfectly tolerant but some are incredibly arrogant and are convinced any form of faith is stupid, period. As a group they tend to be well-educated, which increases their confidence. They are not shy about sharing their views or their scorn, which does not endear them to others."

Peter nodded in agreement.

"Many of the most vocal atheists are scientists and, broadly speaking, Democrats hold scientists, as a class, in high esteem. Within the scientific community there are plenty of believers of all stripes — by no means are all scientists atheists. But many scientists *are* and they put believers on the defensive. And since faith, by it's very nature, is not susceptible to proof, there's no logical way to argue for it. The result is a kind of uneven stalemate, because believers on our side of the aisle are comfortable co-existing while disagreeing with atheists, but many atheists have trouble responding in kind. They want you to agree with them, not simply accept their right to believe what they believe."

"I know a little about that point of view," Peter said, grinning.

I grinned back.

"Right," I said. "in point of fact the Democratic Party is bursting with Christians. They still outnumber all other groups put together, but you don't hear about their religious views. Still less do you hear about Americans who practice Islam, Buddhism, or Hinduism — the big societal debates seem to happen between fundamentalists and atheists as though no other ways of believing exists. One of the problems we confront is: where do the lines get drawn between people's beliefs and our laws? I certainly don't want fundamentalist Christians to be able to impose their worldview on me. I don't want our laws to be based on so-called biblical law; I don't want an *official American religion* and I don't want non-Christians to be subjected to discrimination, pressure, threats or violence on the basis of their non-Christianity."

"True Christians aren't violent; they don't hurt or threaten others," Peter objected.

"Yeah, well, a lot of Christians apparently didn't get the memo. They use violent rhetoric, scorn tolerance and seem to delight in the idea of other people suffering."

Peter looked down, frowning. After a moment, he said: "They do give us a bad name."

"Yep. But worse, they are actively undermining democracy in this country and that is intolerable."

"Can I ask what you believe? said Peter.

I had to pause to organize my thoughts.

"I accept," I said slowly, "the basic tenets of *all* the great religions: love, honesty, charity, kindness, tolerance. But I don't consider any strain of faith to be the ultimate truth. I don't believe we can know the ultimate truth for certain. However much we believe any particular thing, we are all simply making our best guesses. We can dress them up with whatever ancient texts or religious or cultural traditions we choose, but in the end they are still guesses."

"So you're a nonbeliever."

"Not at all. I believe in a lot of things. I believe we live with purposes; I believe our lives matter; I believe in reincarnation — that's the only life after death scenario that makes any sense to me. I reject the notion our existence is purely an accident of chemistry, but equally I reject the concept of original sin. I don't believe there is a hell, but I do believe in something like angels, oddly enough. And God. I just think what we call God, is a being, or even a collection of beings, that we can't really conceptualize."

"Well!"

"You did ask."

"I did. So you reject the Bible?"

"I think the Bible, the Koran, the Tao Te Ching and other texts are rich sources of human thought and history, but they are all human creations and should be treated as such. They can be mined for their wisdom, but should not be treated as infallible and certainly not literally."

"So you reject faith."

"I think any and all spiritual connection to God — whatever God is — is holy . . . is good. I think people make that connection in numerous ways and many of them have nothing to do with religion as such. To believe in the rightness and value of that connection is what I call having faith. It can't be proven other than anecdotally, so it's pointless to argue about. People either have or gain some form of faith, or they don't. You can't talk them into it and any form of coercion invalidates it. All the rest is detail."

"The devil's in the details as they say," Peter said, smiling.

"Yeah they do!" I replied. "Anyway, I'm fine with people having their own details. I'm not fine with them having any ability whatsoever to force their details on me and I'm not fine with any use of force to advance any religion. This is America and one of the beauties of the American idea is that people are free to practice their religions unimpeded by the government or other people. We're not doing so well with that principle right now, but it is a very worthy aspiration."

"Do you believe in karma, like Hindus or Buddhists?"

"In the general concept, yes. But I don't think people reincarnate as bugs, for instance, nor do I believe people who may be poor, or sick, or victims of violence are being karmically punished. Likewise, I don't believe that because someone is rich or good looking or healthy or smart, they are being karmically rewarded. Instead, I *think* we intentionally reincarnate in all kinds of settings and situations to undergo a range of experiences, including challenging experiences. If all our lifetimes were easy what would we learn? How would we stretch ourselves or find out what we're capable of? That's my theory anyway."

"Then how does karma fit in?"

"I would define karma as the law of fair accountability — its repercussions are proportional to the intentions and the acts. Over the course of multiple lifetimes karma ensures *we will get what we have given* and what we encounter offers, among other things, opportunities to make needed restitution — if restitution is needed. Karma does not dictate the totality of our life conditions; it plays a role in some of them. And once we're here we have free will to respond to all people, conditions and events however we choose."

"Isn't that kind of a fairy tale?" Peter asked.

"Isn't having a white-bearded old man on a gold throne floating in clouds surrounded by people engaged in eternal worship kind of a fairytale?"

"Well, when you put it like that — "

"As opposed to?"

"I, well, you know what I mean!"

"I do. But all we're doing is exchanging our best guesses. Your best guess has the gloss of widespread acceptance here in the West, but it is ultimately as much a fairytale as the notion of reincarnation. You are more comfortable with your fairytale because it's what you were raised to believe — but that doesn't prove anything. I'm more comfortable with my fairytale because I find it persuasive — but that doesn't prove its validity either. There is no proof for either of us. There's only and ultimately, faith."

"But how can you know right from wrong without sin and religious laws?"

"I think we know — I think it's part of human packaging. We aren't taught to listen to our deepest selves, we are taught to listen to external authorities. Think about your tradition: isn't being saved an exercise in finding and listening to an inner voice that connects you with goodness?"

Peter frowned at this. "No, to be saved is to accept Jesus as your personal savior. Consequently, you are freed from God's wrath for your sins."

"Saved from God's wrath for sin. Which means what, that you can sin all day long so long as you believe you're saved? A spiritual get-out-of-jail-free card?"

"No, of course not! In accepting Jesus, you are acknowledging God's sovereignty and the primacy of the Holy Spirit in your life. At least, that's how my church sees it. There's a lot of dispute and debate on the topic. Some believe you are saved by grace alone, meaning God's grace, when accepted, is all it takes. You don't need to do good works; you can sin and will still go to heaven. The idea is God's grace has no strings attached."

"That's what I mean by get-out-of-jail-free. It seems to remove any requirement to act morally, doesn't it? It's like buying a ticket."

"Well, but true acceptance of Jesus in your life *makes* you want to do right and be moral."

"But if, in practice, you find yourself breaking commandments or whatever you're still covered, right? Seems like an awfully convenient way to have your cake and eat it too."

"That's why there's disputes. There's a lot of disagreement among evangelicals as a matter of fact, about scriptural interpretation and the meaning of salvation."

"But in the end you believe those who aren't saved won't go to heaven? Even if they lead good, moral lives?"

"People who are saved go straight to heaven when they die, no questions asked. There's a whole range of views about what happens to everyone else. The strictest believe everyone else will go to hell. Others believe people are given a chance to accept Jesus right after death. Others believe good people are held somewhere to be evaluated on Judgement Day. There's a bunch of variations. Personally, I believe God welcomes everyone who tries to live a good life. But maybe not right away."

"And you believe in hell?"

He looked uncomfortable, but answered readily: "Yes, I believe in hell. But I'm not sure what it's like. Myself, I don't like the idea of people being tortured for eternity. Hell was the place the fallen angels went. But Jesus talks about hell too. He was pretty descriptive. That's one of the reasons we evangelize — we want to spare people."

"I see. Well, I don't believe in hell, but it's nice of you to care. And I don't want you to evangelize me because I've got my own faith worked out."

"I'm trying to imagine you having this conversation with my parents and am wondering what would disturb them the most! So many choices!"

"Well, fortunately that's not my problem. It's not your problem either. Your problem is what to tell them about what *you* believe. Which brings us back to business; let's talk about your career!"

Chapter Eight

For Reve, the evening spent with Barbara at her farm was wholly pleasant. The rural environment relaxed him. The escape from his troublesome houseguest relieved him. And the feeling of being half of a duo kindled a welcome sense of familiarity for Reve was intended by nature to be a partner. Single life didn't suit him.

Not, as he told himself, that any assumptions should be made. He and Barbara had just met and they inhabited different worlds. She was a solid embodiment of the type of person he spent his professional life discrediting. Politically and philosophically their priorities *diverged.* They were on the opposite side of practically every issue, and she'd already demonstrated she would not be shy about voicing her vehement disagreement. And there was the little matter of her complete condemnation of his work and, by extension, his character. He'd made a few attempts to line up defensive arguments on that front, but couldn't seem to sustain the effort. He fully intended to crush her assertions with a set of masterly responses.

Later.

For the time being it was far more enjoyable to tramp around a meadow with Barbara as she visited with selected members of her herd. Mercifully, he thought, they did no hoof-trimming. He needed to work up to that.

As they walked they were accompanied by Sabrina, a well-trained animal with whom Reve was rapidly falling in love. Watching as she expertly herded a group of outlying sheep, Reve was captivated. At Barbara's command Sabrina sat and offered her paw; he took it gravely, wishing he had a treat in his pocket although Barbara told him no such reinforcement was needed — for Sabrina the work was its own reward.

Reve helped pour grain in a trough (supplemental feed said Barbara) and watched with unexpected satisfaction as the sheep gathered to eat.

After their walk, Barbara gave Reve a tour of her inviting, informal and colorful home. She showed him the guest bedroom and he noted the size of the bed and the inviting plumpness of the pillows and mattress. Draped over the end of the bed was an intricately patterned throw knitted (she told him) using several colors of a cotton-and-wool-blended yarn. It looked amazing and difficult to him and he said as much. She smiled and said it was easier to knit than it looked.

There was a bookcase with a selection of old classics and 1930's murder mysteries; he wondered vaguely if he'd ever read a 1930's murder mystery. Barbara seemed to think a lot of them.

In the living room, Reve saw a relatively new flat screen television next to a stack composed of a CD player, a DVD player and an old VHS player. There was a pile of remotes — he counted seven of them, which seemed like a lot relative to the available equipment. Barbara mentioned something about never getting the hang of remotes and needing to resolve some problem between the DVD and CD player. She watched very little TV she explained, and, in a pinch, used the portable in her kitchen.

Together they brainstormed a dinner menu out of the odds and ends in her refrigerator. They made mixed-cheese, vegetable and leftover mashed potato omelets with toast on the side. (Neither had ever included mashed potatoes in an omelet before and they were delighted with the outcome.) Rejecting a browning and wilted head of lettuce, they settled for thinly sliced cucumbers with onions and sour cream in lieu of a salad.

They moved around the kitchen quite chummily; within minutes Reve felt at home.

After eating, they migrated to Barbara's office/studio. The room was dominated by a French solid-oak antique armoire (cedar-lined to discourage moths) stuffed to the exploding point with skeins, hanks, balls and twists of yarns in a wide range of colors, patterns and weights. About half were her own products, she explained. The rest had been collected from other artisans and shops from around the country. There was a drawer full of needles in various lengths and widths, made of plastic, metal, bamboo, wood and other exotic materials. She had very few of the straight metal knitting needles Reve remembered his mother using. Barbara's looked like needle-ends connected by lengths of flexible plastic. *Circulars,* she called them, and explained they could hold more stitches and could be held closer to one's lap, which was less fatiguing on the arms. Reve mentally filed that tidbit away as mildly interesting.

She also had a small loom with a striped item partially woven — one of a set of placemats, it turned out.

While Barbara had a laptop in her kitchen, the office was home to a desktop computer and widescreen monitor equipped with specialized software she used to design and produce knitting patterns for her yarns. Settling into a couple of rolling office chairs, they spent a few hours online looking up stories about purported hauntings. After scanning a series of vignettes in which sudden, violent, gruesome or wretched deaths were central (lightened by a few tales of spirits who seemed to have hung around simply because they liked a place), Reve had had enough.

"What have we learned?" he asked, pushing himself backwards in his rolling chair.

"Hmm. Well," said Barbara, "ghosts mostly seem to *appear* but not talk, or people don't see them but hear cries, whispers, individual words or other sounds like footsteps, music playing, horses galloping, knocking or banging. Sometimes there's cold spots, and with poltergeists all sorts of weird stuff happens."

"But aside from poltergeists, ghosts appear in the same sets of places over and over and usually repeat the same actions don't they? A few seemed to interact with people, but very minimally. They aren't like . . . like Jacob Marley in *The Christmas Carol*. They don't make speeches."

"No. And nothing they do lasts for long; things happen for seconds, not minutes."

"So how typical is Dash?" Reve asked.

"Not sure. Most of the accounts are about hauntings that have gone on for years or even centuries. Did any of them start out with the ghost trying to talk to a particular person?"

"Good question."

But they found no answer.

When they parted for the night, Reve kissed Barbara's cheek, almost absently, as he might kiss someone he'd known for many years. It didn't seem especially momentous at the time, although Reve would awaken in the middle of the night in some confusion over its significance. Likewise, Barbara accepted the gesture composedly, and patting him on the shoulder, wished him a good night. That the imprint of his lips lingered in her consciousness for awhile was something she did not, in fact, register. But she did sleep quite well.

The next morning, she and Reve were at the kitchen table companionably sipping coffee and formulating plans for the day when the doorbell rang.

"I wonder who that could be?" said Barbara. Still clad in a pair of light green summer pajamas and a green plaid cotton robe, she didn't want to answer the door, but, in response to an internal nudging, found herself facing a young black woman who was looking at her with an expression of slight nervous anticipation. Her nervousness visibly increased as she took in the blank non-recognition on Barbara's face. Meanwhile, Barbara, groping, had the feeling . . . "Can I help you?" she asked tentatively.

"Um, this looks like a bad time," said the young woman. "I'm Olivia Chipley.

We spoke on the phone. I was referred to you by Sonya Helvender? We were going to do an information interview."

For a moment Barbara remained blank. Then it came back to her. Sonya . . . oh, yes. Oh yes.

"Oh my gosh, yes. I am sooo sorry. Please forgive me. I had completely forgotten. Not your fault!" she added, anticipating Olivia, who looked like she was about to apologize. "My brother died suddenly and, what with one thing and another my whole life has been out of kilter for the last several days."

"I am so sorry for your loss," said Olivia, taken aback. "I should have called ahead and double-checked." She pulled out her smartphone and started tapping into it. She looked up at Barbara and said: "Note to self: always confirm information interviews the day before. This is my first one," she explained.

"I feel terrible," said Barbara. "You came a long way — you live on the other side of the beltway don't you?"

Olivia nodded in affirmative. The drive had taken almost an hour.

"Well, please come in at least. I'm really not in any condition to be helpful today. I have a guest here now and have to get to the funeral home in a few hours. But please, have some coffee and we'll arrange another date." As she spoke, Barbara was herding Olivia through the door and then walked ahead of her to the kitchen where Reve, also still in pajamas and a robe, looked up in surprise. He stood.

"Reve, this is Olivia Chipley. We had an information interview scheduled for today and I completely forgot it. There's still some coffee isn't there?"

Turning, Reve was able to confirm there was coffee in the pot. He then put his hand out and introduced himself.

Olivia, politely shaking his hand, exhibited no signs of recognition, not that Reve expected her to. He had given it a fifty-fifty chance. In the world of political junkies he was well known, outside of politics, not so much which was fine with him. Celebrity had plenty of drawbacks.

"Well!" he said, "this will get us moving at any rate! We've both had a long week and were having trouble getting motivated. I'll go shower and get dressed, okay Barbara?"

"Of course," she said, "although you haven't eaten."

"Um, is there anything to eat? We finished off the eggs last night and you're out of milk."

"Oh dear," said Barbara, deflated. She looked helplessly at Olivia, who, sensing an occasion to be risen to, rose.

"Do you like bagels?" Olivia asked.

Barbara looked at her questioningly.

"I had stopped and bought a dozen bagels this morning before heading out.

And cream cheese. You two go ahead and get dressed. If you don't mind, I'd love to take a look at your gardens and then we can have some bagels and set up another meeting. Okay?"

"You're a lifesaver!" said Barbara. "Please, take a look outside and visit the sheep. Give us twenty minutes and then we can talk for a bit at least. Keep you from wasting your trip."

She looked at Reve who expressed delight with the plan and, waving, exited the kitchen and was then heard climbing the stairs.

"Thanks again for being so understanding" said Barbara.

"Not a problem. Not a problem. I know deaths in the family. Don't worry about a thing — we'll work it out. Shoo, go get dressed. I'm going outside."

Barbara, opening the back kitchen door, thanked her again and fled to her bathroom.

Olivia, feeling she'd handled an awkward situation with aplomb, began a slow tour of the farm. She'd been told Barbara was a very nice person and felt her reputation had been vindicated. Which made it more surprising, she thought, that there was an empty refrigerator. In Olivia's world a death in the family was followed by mammoth amounts of prepared foods and frozen casseroles. And lots of people. But maybe the people had come and gone. Or were coming later. None of her business anyway.

Retired FBI agent Lloyd Wilksie was on the case. It was Saturday and Peter Gilen had the day off. If he was sowing wild oats, Saturday was oat-sowing day. For Gilen's sake, Wilksie hoped some bar-hopping would be the extent of his activities. It might not be acceptable behavior for a *good Christian* but by regular people standards it was harmless enough. Unless the kid was developing a drinking problem. But drinking problems were solvable.

Of course, Gilen could be into something worse. Drugs, for instance. Or maybe he was going to strip bars. Or discovering he was gay, or bi or gender-confused.

He could be sleeping with someone he shouldn't. That happened a lot. With surprising people too. Gilen was a good-looking kid if the photos he'd seen were accurate. And, in this town he could be involved with *anyone*: an underaged illegal, a female judge old enough to be his grandma, a male reporter swinging in from a war zone — D.C. was filled with fascinating people and lots of high-stakes maneuvering. People had to takes risks, or had to risk not-taking risks. And once you've done risk-taking in one area, it got easier to take risks in another.

And that looked like Gilen (yes . . . bullseye!) coming out of his apartment building and heading for the bus stop. Probably going to the Metro. Sigh. Gonna be one of those days. Bus-riding, on and off the Metro, probably walking around downtown. Well, I've got my back-pack and comfortable shoes. Anyone looking at me will see a harmless sightseer enjoying the nation's capitol. The great thing is I can take pictures and even film people without raising a single eyebrow. Not everywhere, of course, and not all the time. But on a summer Saturday? I'll blend right in.

Of course I might do a lot of unnecessary walking and it's early. The good stuff usually happens later in the day. But not always.

Peter was looking forward to seeing Connie. In the interests of discretion they usually met at her place, at least during the day. At night they sometimes went to dinner or a movie in Baltimore or somewhere in Virginia where they felt reasonably sure they wouldn't be seen by anyone they knew. Both were looking forward to the day when they could officially go public, but until then, a clandestine relationship had a certain appeal.

Still, it's getting tiring, Peter thought. Probably because I have to work so hard to fake my way through work. And Wayland suspects me. And Thornery suspects me. And I'm a bad liar.

Getting on the bus, Peter found an empty seat and, gazing out the window, went into a trance. He'd been thinking hard about Wynne's idea. Consulting with Democrats about outreach to Evangelicals — it was intriguing but terrifying. But, at the core, it was brilliant because it enabled him to keep faith with his deepest beliefs while letting him continue to work in politics. It didn't negate the confrontations he'd have to endure, but it gave him an angle that just might work with his family and friends back home. He could tell them he'd been in the belly of the beast and it had changed his outlook. He could make the case that there were good people outside the Republican Party who were committed to good works and he wanted to build a bridge to them. He could ask them to trust him and he thought they might. He could use them as test cases, learn what spoke to them and what opened them up. He might even convince some of them! But even if he didn't, he wouldn't necessarily have to be cut off.

Connie loved the idea. Even better, she had found some consultants who were doing that kind of work already.

Today Connie would be sharing the information she'd gathered and maybe he could start putting together a plan of action.

Arriving at his stop, still preoccupied, he didn't notice the tall, fit-looking older man with a backpack getting off the bus behind him.

In the Spirit World, Lersaliaz and Velistan confer.

"Has Xe been following the forks?"

"He has. The Life Planners see a large array of probabilities developing. He is following several lines radiating from Wynne Frost. He is closely following developments between Dash, Barbara and Reve, as well. There is now some crossing of connection lines."

"Is he learning?"

"He is fascinated by human thought processes, but he is baffled by human emotions, especially self-deception and indecision."

"Ah."

"He is being introduced to internal-conflict as experienced by humans. At this point he can only observe it, he cannot understand it."

On Earth:

Barbara, Reve and Olivia ate bagels and, on the surface, shared a very agreeable half hour.

Olivia, unaware of subterranean currents, was thoroughly enjoying herself. It was her first public airing of her potential new identity as an environmentalist and it felt good. She'd had many interactions with educated professionals in her housekeeping role — this was different. She was being evaluated for her ideas and her intelligence instead of her ability to dust or scrub floors. Not that she was ashamed of her housekeeping job, but it wasn't something people sat up and noticed.

She directed most of her attention to Barbara, who had briefly shared how she'd gotten started and why environmental concerns affected her. Apologizing again, Barbara provisionally scheduled a second meeting for the following Friday, during which she promised to provide more in-depth information and a personalized tour of her operation.

Mr. Tierney, as Olivia called him, said very little while she and Barbara talked. Olivia was grateful for this. He looked well-off and well educated and could have been very intimidating had he interjected anything negative (not that he gave any indication of wanting to do so). For Olivia, the new persona was still fragile and needed to be protected from doubt.

But Reve was more bemused than anything. He'd written many words questioning the validity of global warming and composed many a dig aimed at environmentalism and environmentalists. In all cases he was simply completing assignments and he'd rarely troubled to assess the accuracy of the positions he stated and defended. He served a certain sector; that sector had a list of arguments and his job was to state and restate those arguments, not to challenge them.

To be breakfasting with two people who accepted global warming as fact and who discussed environmental issues, albeit briefly, as though they were critically important, was a bit unsettling. They sounded so reasonable. And informed. Also intelligent. And this Olivia — so excited, made him feel . . . he wasn't sure. Something uncomfortable.

Meanwhile Barbara was nursing a quiet amusement. Olivia, in all innocence, was making remarks that Barbara knew Reve, in his professional role, would oppose. In this same situation Dennis would have — she didn't even want to imagine. Pounced. Chewed up. Spit out. Not that he'd have had anything valid to say, but he'd have been aggressive and rude anyway. Validity was irrelevant. He had enjoyed dominating arguments through sheer lung power and bellicosity.

It pleased her Reve was polite and friendly. Had he said anything to dampen Olivia's enthusiasm, she'd have intervened without compunction, but was glad to have been spared the necessity.

Not wanting to outstay her welcome, Olivia drew her visit to a close. She said she knew how crazy things could get with funerals and she didn't want to keep them. Were they going to calling hours or straight to a cemetery?

"We're going to the funeral home," Barbara said. "Fortunately I didn't have to make a lot of arrangements; my brother's law firm handled everything."

"That's good," said Olivia, politely. There was something not-quite-right with this funeral thing, she could tell. In a rush to change the subject she found herself saying "If there's anything I can do, please let me know. I clean houses you know. If you need help with your brother's stuff, or anything, give me a call. I'm very efficient."

"Oh dear," said Barbara, "I will have to handle all his stuff. I'm not looking forward to it. I might need some help. Thanks."

"Sure," Olivia replied. "My rates are reasonable," she added firmly.

Barbara smiled at this.

Reve's phone vibrated just then. He looked at it, then, with a gesture he started for the hallway.

"I'll take this call . . . nice to have met you Olivia. Good luck with your interviews."

"Nice meeting you too," Olivia replied. "He's nice," she added as she found her purse and notebook.

Barbara agreed.

Reve returned to the kitchen just after Olivia left.

"That was my boss," he said. "He sends his condolences. For what it's worth."

They stared at each other for a long moment, both thinking a lot, neither speaking.

Finally Barbara said: "Thanks."

There was more silence.

"And thank you for being nice to Olivia."

"Of course!"

"Not that I'd think you'd be rude! Just that . . . " she trailed off.

He wanted to say: it's just my job. He couldn't. He wasn't sure that was true. He wasn't sure what it meant about him if it *was* true. He settled for giving her a look which combined sincerity with an appeal for understanding.

It worked. Barbara cleared her throat and said: "Anyway . . . I had forgotten about Dennis's condo and all of his things. I had to go through all of my parents' stuff after they died."

"My father's gone, but my mother's alive so that ordeal is still ahead for me. Although my mother moved into a retirement community after Dad died so we did a lot of purging then. Still — "

"She's still the keeper of the family history?"

"Yes. Old photo albums; my Dad's war medals and books; stuff from both sets of grandparents. I don't know what I'll do with it all when the time comes."

"Well, at any rate I don't think there will be much of Dennis's stuff I'll want to keep. I'll have to hire one of those companies that do estate sales I guess. Dennis has a lot of expensive furniture I never liked. I could just give it to the Goodwill or something, I suppose. It's not like I'll need the money."

"You could do an estate sale and donate the proceeds to, whoever — ?"

"That's a thought!"

"This is a delicate question and, you don't have to answer it, but, did you, um, that is, are you — "

"Do I get the money?"

"Yeah."

"I do. Several million."

Reve looked like he was trying to frame a response. *Congratulations!* didn't seem right, but what was?

Recognizing his dilemma, Barbara said:

"It's hard to know what to say, isn't it?" To his affirmative she added: "I don't even know what I think about it."

"You must be pleased on some level, aren't you? I mean, all things considered?"

"I suppose. It's just, its a huge responsibility. And, well, it's like the money is tainted, you know. Like he made it from drug running or something."

Again Reve found himself unsure what to reply only this time Barbara didn't help out. She looked at him challengingly but he didn't bite.

"Whatever you think about how he made it has nothing to do with you having it," Reve said firmly. "And you can do good things with it, you know."

"Like what?"

"Whatever you want! Donate to charities or causes. Create endowments. Build a library somewhere. Start a liberal think tank!" And why did I say that? he asked himself, ruefully.

She laughed.

"A liberal think tank. That's a great idea!"

"I lean towards the library or endowments myself, but it's your money," he said, with a smile.

And suddenly they were comfortable again.

Hmm, thought Wilksie, as Peter entered a tall apartment building, there's probably a hundred units in there.

He strolled nonchalantly towards the entrance. A few people were passing one another going in and out at the same time. Peter was out of sight.

He went back outside and looked around. What he wanted was a cafe with outdoor seating facing the apartment building. What he had was crowded sidewalks on both sides of the street, more apartment buildings, a shoe repair shop with a closed sign — How do you like that? he thought. Do people still get their shoes repaired? — and a lot of parked cars.

After due consideration, Wilksie decided to take the bus back to his car (which was parked down the street from Peter's apartment) and drive back. He might be able to get a parking spot and, if not, well, he'd have to see. There were always near misses and wasted time on these kinds of gigs. You needed time to learn a person's habits.

Peter, meanwhile, was engaged in greeting Connie by means of ardent kisses and rapturous pronouncements. They were often unable to see each other for days at a time partly because they both worked demanding hours, and partly because they couldn't meet in public places or when they were with other people.

The feast and famine dynamic of their relationship was straining Peter's commitment to honor a pledge of abstinence he'd made in high school. Sex, he'd been taught, went with marriage. Inside a marriage sex was a gift from God; outside of marriage, it was *beastly.* At Bob Jones University his male friends had acted as a support group; they'd discussed their struggles with temptation openly and encouraged one another to be strong. It had worked and he'd arrived in D.C. still in technical possession of his virginity. (Out of sheer self-preservation he and his friends had decided that masturbation, if not excessive, was acceptable. Jesus had been mum on the topic and some evangelical leaders had weighed in with cautious acceptance.)

He didn't have that support near to hand anymore and Connie wasn't making his abstinence any easier.

As a matter of respect, she stopped short of attempting to seduce him into the ultimate state of sin (as he thought it), but she disagreed with his premise and told him so. Frequently.

In a perverse way Peter found her openness comforting and, gradually, liberating. *She talked to him about sex.* He'd never been able to talk about sex to females he'd dated in high school or college. There was so much baggage bound up in it. But Connie was unselfconscious and she set the tone, allowing him to express his feelings honestly. Although being able to talk about sex was sexy, and it wasn't like they needed additional stimulation.

Connie thought Peter's views were regrettable. She was on the pill; she was serious about Peter and she was an adult. She thought adults should have sex lives since they had sex drives. Although she had no unusual tastes, she believed people had the right to do whatever they liked so long as their partners consented, were of age, and were in their right minds.

From their first kiss she'd concluded they'd ultimately be good together in bed and everything they did up-to-but-not-including intercourse cemented her impression.

Neither was sure how much longer they'd hold out and Connie's information about consulting was not forthcoming until after the conclusion of more immediately pressing activity.

"We're going to have to get married," Peter said, a bit thickly, after everything had settled down.

This made Connie laugh. "Maybe," she said, "but only if you actually want to and not just for the sex."

Many protestations later they were provisionally engaged. Connie cautioned that they needed to see how they felt after they were able to go public.

"We've been in our own little world," she added. "We haven't been around each other's people. After we are, we'll know for sure."

A few hours later Barbara and Reve were walking towards her Subaru, Reve carrying the sturdy cardboard box containing Dash Fordhyme's ashes.

Although it had been her choice to forego a public ceremony to recognize Dennis's death, Barbara now found herself feeling unexpectedly deflated.

Notwithstanding the fact that she'd actually seen Dennis yesterday and might be seeing him for some time to come, it seemed wrong to simply collect a box of ashes and go home.

I suppose that's what Reve meant when he mentioned closure, she thought. Although, would calling hours have done me any good? I don't think so, she concluded.

But, she realized, frowning, it's clear I'm going to have to do something. Something symbolic and ceremonial.

"Are you okay?" Reve asked.

"I don't know," she replied. "I mean, dealing with his ashes is really the least of our problems, but I don't feel like I can just stick them in a fancy urn and be done with it. I feel like I need to do something to commemorate his death. Which is really silly, when you think about it, since he doesn't seem to be quite dead."

"Well, whatever the status of his spirit, we have the remains of his body. I think it's just human to want to do something ceremonial with them. But maybe not today. Maybe you just need some time to decide what to do."

"Yeah."

They got into her car, putting the ashes in the back seat. In the time it took her to get arranged and seat-belted, Barbara was picturing herself lighting candles, and . . . should they go to the seashore? Somewhere in nature? Not that Dennis had had much interest in nature. He hadn't been one to hike or stroll or cycle or in any other way enjoy the outdoors. For him the outdoors had been spaces between buildings.

No, lighting candles by the seashore might be ceremonial, but not particularly appropriate. Although, maybe that didn't matter. She didn't think Dennis would care what she did with his ashes. She was the one who needed closure. She should do whatever would make her feel the best.

Whatever that might be.

Lost in thought, Barbara started the car automatically, then realized they hadn't decided what next to do. Did they go straight to Reve's condo and wait for Dennis to show himself? Or did they go somewhere to eat first? It was only 3:00 — late for lunch but early for dinner. Still, the morning's bagels were a distant memory and Reve's larder was even barer than Barbara's.

A few minutes discussion settled the matter: food first.

Reve, who ate out regularly, recommended a nearby restaurant, and Barbara, who ate out infrequently, readily assented.

Fifteen minutes later they were seated, waiting for drinks to arrive. Reve, who was a frequent patron, was greeted by name by the waiter and had been waved at by people seated at two different tables.

"You come here a lot," Barbara remarked.

"I like the menu. I order takeout often as well. I like to cook, but not just for me. What about you?"

"Do I like to cook for myself?"

"Yes."

"I don't mind. But it is nicer to share meals, certainly."

A middle-aged, portly man was approaching.

"Reve! How are you?" he said, heartily, coming to rest next to their table.

"Hello Gerald. I'm doing well. You?" Reve's answer was polite but Barbara got the impression that he was not pleased.

"Fine! Fine! And this is?" said Gerald, looking at Barbara with a smile on his lips that was not reflected in his eyes.

"This is Barbara Tishkin. Barbara, Gerald Kaboulis."

"How do you do?" said Barbara. She noted the absence of any qualifying information about both her and Gerald and was prepared to follow Reve's lead but Gerald had other ideas.

"And how do you know Reve?" he asked, still in his hearty voice, but with an intent expression on his face.

"Oh we're old friends," Barbara replied, smiling. "And you?"

"I work for Kineal and Brybson, a law firm that works with conservative interest groups. Reve's used me as a source for some of his work on trade policy."

"Ah," said Barbara, "how nice."

She made herself beam but made no further remarks. Since Reve was also speechless, Gerald, after a few seconds, took the hint.

"Well enjoy your lunch!" he said. "I'll see you soon Reve."

"See you," said Reve, watching him move away.

When he was out of earshot Reve said: "You wouldn't like Gerald. He does a lot of work for the NRA."

"Ugh. You're right. Although what does the NRA have to do with trade policy?"

"Gun manufacturers make a lot of money selling arms around the world."

"Because they just aren't moving enough product domestically?" she asked dryly.

Reve frowned.

"I don't like Gerald myself." he said, "Nor do I approve of his work or gun proliferation in general. But he and my boss were fraternity brothers and I had to use him for a piece I wrote recently which was not well received, by anyone. He and my boss didn't think I was supportive enough and liberal critics, well, you know . . ."

Barbara looked at him searchingly. She didn't know what to think or say. A few days ago, when she didn't know him at all, she'd have asked him why he was willing to sell his soul for money, but now she couldn't. Yet, she didn't know him well enough to discern whether he wanted sympathy, a slap upside the head or absolution. He seemed a fundamentally decent man. So how did he live with himself? She'd moved from wanting to ask the question rhetorically (as an insult) to really wanting to know. Though, she thought, it was probably just a matter of simple compartmentalization. Americans were good at that. Go to church Sunday, screw the environment, or pension holders, or your employees, or customers, or the general public, on Monday. It was just business. Still . . .

"I — how can I put this — if you want to talk about your work and how you feel about it, I can listen. I mean, you know what I think — "

"That what I do is basically evil?" Reve cut in, one eyebrow raised.

"Well, more or less. Evil is a harsh word, clearly."

"Ya think?"

"But!" she replied spiritedly, "I stand by it in principle. I'm not saying you're solely responsible, but I do say that there is an underlying dishonesty driving conservatism today and you, through your work, participate in that dishonesty. If you like, I'll retract *evil* and replace it with *bad.* But!" she interjected, forestalling him as he looked about to speak, "You can certainly tell me to jump in the next lake! Who the hell am I after all? Someone you barely know."

He looked her over, his eyebrows lowering and his expression one of bafflement. How she managed it he couldn't explain, but she kept insulting him while simultaneously reaching out to him and being surprisingly irresistible. His ego demanded he wither her, but he couldn't summon anything. Not even much genuine chagrin. He wanted to change her opinion of him, but not by trying to argue that she was wrong. Which meant, what? That she was right?

At that point his brain tripped into a groove and started repeating was she right? Was she right? Was she right?

He shook his head to clear it.

"Are you mad at me?" she asked.

"What? Oh, no. Sorry."

Just then their food arrived, and after the waiter had finished his ministrations and removed himself, they chose to move to less charged topics.

"So I can put you in touch with at least two people who are doing consulting work right now, with a focus on religious and evangelical outreach by the Democratic Party," said Connie, triumphantly.

"Really?"

"Wynne is big on information interviewing, you know. This is what she'll tell you to do: find people working in the field you're considering and talk to them. Don't ask them for a job, just explore what they do, what they like, what they don't like, how they got started and all that."

Peter felt a tingle of excitement. The idea was coming to life — taking form. It was becoming something he could act on. Although . . .

"You know," he said, hesitantly, "I haven't committed to going Democrat yet."

"You haven't, huh?"

"It's a really big step. A big shift. A total slap in the face of a lot of people in my life."

Connie's face was understanding, but her voice was firm.

"Realistically, what else is there? To call yourself an Independent is pretty meaningless. Who would you be working for? It's not like there's an Independence Party right now — a functioning party. There's the Green Party. Do you have any interest in them? I mean, if you do, fine, let's check them out. But do you?"

Peter grunted. "Not really. I don't know much about them. I know they surface occasionally with some good ideas, but that's all."

"For better or worse we're in a two-party system. If you want to do something third party then your goal should be to help make a third party become a contender. But I don't think that's where your heart truly lies."

"No, you're right."

They were seated at Connie's tiny kitchen table in her small and cheery kitchen. Connie had bookmarked the consulting firms she'd located and had shown Peter the websites on her laptop.

The air conditioner was keeping the room moderately cool and the table was littered with the remains of cold drinks and sandwiches and small piles of Connie's notes.

Peter got up from the table and began clearing glasses and plates. Connie watched. He was going to have to make the decision. She would try to help him, but she wasn't going to push him. This had to be his choice and, ideally it would be wholehearted.

"It's just — " he stopped. Then he put dishes in the sink and returned to the table with a damp dishrag.

"I know honey. But let me ask you this, what is more important to your folks: their religion or their political party?"

"Their religion, of course!"

"Well then. Which would you be choosing?"

"That's true. But man, they don't like Democrats!"

"Do you think they dislike Democrats more than they love you?"

"Ooh that's a loaded question." But he smiled, then started wiping crumbs into his hand with the cloth.

"You know what might help?"

"What?"

"Why don't we find a liberal evangelical minister for you to talk to?"

Peter's face lit up.

"That's a thought!" He returned to the sink with a new spring in his tread.

Connie could see him thinking about it. He stood by the sink, washing, rinsing and stacking and she marveled at how divinely sexy he was for her.

It had been a long hot afternoon for Wilksie.

He'd driven back to the apartment building into which Peter had disappeared and, after a few trips around the block, managed to get a parking space not far from the building's entrance. The time elapsed since his departure was just under an hour.

Of course, the question was whether Peter was still in the building. Wilksie was prepared to bet that he was. It was just a feeling he had, but, over the years he had learned to trust such feelings.

He had some snacks and drinks, although he limited his liquid intake to postpone the need for a bathroom break. He had his smartphone and an iPod to play tunes. He was often tempted to web surf but knew how easy it was to get distracted.

People were continually coming and going; walking past his car, getting into their own. He had to appear like someone just arriving, or just about to leave, or innocently waiting for someone. Fortunately few people noticed him — they were busy about their own affairs. And those who did note his presence quickly forgot it. He looked harmless. It was none of their business.

But he knew that if he was still in the car when people who were leaving began returning, attention would ratchet up. There had been occasions when he'd simply flashed an old FBI ID at people, who, moved to curiosity, approached him. That was usually enough to scare people off. This was D.C. after all. All kinds of stuff went down every day. The average person preferred to avoid the attention of the FBI and so would quickly move on.

But to his relief, that would not prove necessary. Right around dinner time Peter emerged from the building's parking deck, in a bright red Volkswagen Beetle driven by an attractive brunette. Wilksie quickly snapped pictures of the woman, her image slightly distorted by the sun striking her closed window. He saw bangs, straight hair held up with a clip and a wide smile. More importantly, he got her license plate number.

Hah, thought Wilksie. Peter's got a girlfriend. Wayland and Thornery were under the impression Peter was not dating anyone in particular.

Wilksie started his car and, with practiced ease, slid into traffic and began following the little red car.

Chapter Nine

Between Earth and the Spirit World:

Dash had been pondering. He had seen both Reve and Barbara. He was torn about Barbara. The part of him that was Dash still resented her disapproval, but the part of him that was Ukutmanu was beginning to recall his history with Metemnia. She was a member of his soul group and had been part of most of his lives in one guise or another. She would be disappointed in him, but forgiving. Barbara might not be able to forgive Dash, but Metemnia would forgive Ukutmanu (although she would probably lecture him). He felt gladdened at that thought, and then sad. He could not surrender himself yet. And if he did, he would likely not see her or the others for some time.

Meanwhile, he was battling with the difficulty of making a meaningful contact with Reve. He had tried speech and failed. If he couldn't speak how could he transmit his message?

He attempted to construct a spiritual blackboard to write on, but could not keep it conjured for long enough to display words. This was partly because his energy was low and malfunctioning and partly because he couldn't decide what words to use. He kept changing his mind. It would be easier if he could speak. He would just present his thoughts as he used to when alive. He had been one of those people who figured out what they were thinking while talking. Oftentimes he himself didn't know what he was saying until he'd said it. One of the things he'd liked about Reve was Reve's ability to listen. Reve would offer an opinion if asked, but did not feel the need to have an opinion on everything.

He decided to make another attempt at vocalization. He had to create sound. Or the illusion of sound. It might be that he could look like he was speaking while actually sending his thoughts telepathically. Reve might not block him then.

But that would only work if he could keep his communication clear and simple.

On Earth:

Having finished their late lunch, Barbara and Reve deliberated their next move. They considered grocery shopping as Reve was out of various foodstuffs and they were in for a long evening. Sated for the moment, they were quite likely to be hungry again before the day ended.

Both operated on the assumption they would spend the rest of the day together. It didn't need to be said, it was assumed.

"I usually order groceries online and have them delivered," Reve said, in answer to Barbara's inquiry about where he normally shopped.

"Do you? I can't do that where I live. That must be convenient."

"My ex-wife used to like to shop for groceries, but I'm usually too busy." He didn't add that he sometimes felt conspicuous and had been approached a few times by people who didn't like his political views. The confrontations had been disquieting and embarrassing.

Barbara, who favored seasonal farmers markets, food coops and stores featuring organic foods, had no preference regarding the chain grocery stores in the area. Driving down a main thoroughfare, she decided to stop at the first grocery store on her side of the road.

This turned out to be a Safeway, a popular regional chain. It was busy and crowded, but there was something comforting about doing such a mundane activity. The problem was simple: supplies are low. The solution was simple: get more supplies. It was nice to focus on an eminently solvable problem.

There was also just the barest hint of a "new relationship discovery" vibe happening; that tinge of specialness in connection with learning little details about someone new.

Barbara learned that Reve loved full-strength organic coffee cream and hated flavored coffee creams.

Reve found himself enjoying the spectacle of Barbara testing and selecting peaches and avocados. She seemed to have a sure hand with them and hummed in satisfaction when she found one she liked.

They joked as they tossed out ideas for snacks and sandwiches for later and became quite serious as they considered whether they should shop just for Reve or for Barbara also. She could only buy items that wouldn't spoil in the car — maybe she should just get a few things? Left unspoken was whether she would stay at Reve's that night or he return to her house. Much depended on the nature of their interactions with Dash's ghost, if any.

Both felt confident Dash would appear. Barbara wondered if his next appearance would be definitive in some way. Conclusive? Maybe their possession of his ashes would mark some kind of turning point. Maybe spirits hung around until their bodies were buried or cremated. She put this to Reve as they were loading bags of groceries into the car.

He shrugged and made a "who knows?" face.

"It would be nice," he said. "I hope there is a specific message. It would be terrible it he's just generally haunting me and won't ever leave."

"Ick. That *would* be terrible."

"Do you think he could be hanging around because his death was so sudden? Maybe it makes some kind of difference if you're sick for a long time."

Barbara shrugged.

"Lots of people die suddenly, but you don't hear about ghosts very often. I mean, for real."

"Thats true."

Groceries stowed, Barbara was pushing the cart to the closest cart holder when she noticed a young man with a hostile expression walking towards Reve. Quickly releasing the cart, she rapidly walked back to the car just in time to hear:

"You're Reve Tierney, aren't you?" The voice indicated its owner would not greet an affirmative reply cordially.

"People ask him that all the time!" Barbara said loudly, infusing cheeriness into her voice. "He looks like Reve Tierney doesn't he? It's something of a trial since some people really don't like Reve Tierney!"

"Yes, happens all the time," Reve echoed. "I'm going to have to get surgery!"

He then got nimbly into the car and shut the door while Barbara waved a friendly hand at the not-quite-convinced young man and got in her side, shutting the door quickly and starting the car with slightly trembling fingers.

The young man stared at them suspiciously for a moment and then turned and entered the store.

"What was that?" Barbara asked as a wave of relief swept over her.

"Someone who doesn't like me I guess," said Reve, evenly. "Thanks for jumping in. What made you do that?"

"I didn't like his expression and I wasn't in the mood for a scene. Does stuff like that happen often?"

"Only recently. It never used to be like this. And before you comment, let me just say the adage about chickens coming home to roost has already occurred to me."

Although that was precisely what she was thinking, Barbara had not intended to say so, but she couldn't think of anything else. On impulse, she reached over and threading her fingers through his hair, smoothed it into bangs on his forehead.

"Maybe you need to change your hairstyle when you go out in public," she said, smiling. And instantly the air was *charged.*

Reve smiled crookedly and said "Good idea."

For a few seconds the space between them sizzled, then Barbara faced forward resolutely and said: "well, we'd better go" in a bright, bracing tone and, checking her mirrors, began backing out of the parking space. Thus occupied, she didn't see Reve's hand, which had started moving towards her, slowly fall.

They said nothing on the drive, and, after securing a space in the visitor's section of Reve's building's parking deck, were careful not to touch each other as they gathered bags of groceries from Barbara's car. Dash's ashes, forgotten, remained in the back seat.

By the time they reached Reve's door they'd entered a state of mutual hyper-awareness; feeling as though an aura of energy surrounded each of them and the auras were touching although their bodies were not.

But Barbara felt Dash's presence almost immediately after crossing the threshold and when she informed Reve of her awareness, the tension was effectively broken.

"Um, should we put the groceries away first?" Reve asked. He felt his mood beginning to plummet from a place which he wouldn't have been able to adequately describe, but which he knew was in a "good" zone to somewhere less good and equally indescribable.

Barbara thought for a moment.

"Yes," she said decisively. No point in letting the coffee cream spoil.

They hauled bags into the kitchen and for a few minutes almost forgot about Dash as Reve explained which things belonged in what cupboard. But Dash's presence affected them; they bumped into each other and brushed fingers in passing as they handed each other items, all without noticing the contact.

Suddenly, Barbara remembered Dennis's ashes left unceremoniously in the car. First she felt bad about this, then she asked herself what exactly she should have done? Brought them in to show to Dennis?

Frowning to herself, Barbara tried once again to think of an appropriate thing to do with the ashes, but absolutely nothing came to mind.

Reve was starting a pot of coffee. Glancing at Barbara and noticing her expression, he asked if she was alright.

"I'm fine. Was just thinking about Dennis's ashes again. Wondering what on earth I'm going to do with them."

Reve, having no suggestion to make, nodded sympathetically and asked "Are you ready?"

Barbara took a deep breath and held out her hand. He took it and, holding firmly, gestured towards the bedroom with his head. She dipped her chin in reply and they started walking.

As the door loomed their pace slowed. Arriving, Reve pushed the door and they entered the bedroom.

It was empty.

They both halted and looked at one another, nonplussed.

"I was sure he was here," Barbara said, uncertainly.

"I thought so too," Reve replied, brows lowering in puzzlement. "Maybe because we delayed coming back here?"

"Probably. Something like that anyway. I'd bet he was here. Should we wait here do you think?"

The realization that the bed offered the only surface on which to sit struck them both simultaneously. It was followed by a wave of mutual awareness verging on awkwardness. Fortunately, before the awkwardness became acute, the light flickered in the corner of the room as Dash's form began to appear.

For the first time Barbara focused on Dash's transparency. She could see the edge of the window-frame through him. She started looking at him intently, noting details. Doing this helped her feel more in control.

As before, his body seemed to fluctuate between near-solidity and looking like a kind of smudgy, shredded blotch. His face was always his face, though.

Really, she thought to herself, it's quite interesting. I am having a paranormal experience.

"Reve," she whispered, "you can see the buttons on his shirt and then they're gone."

"Yes," he replied.

Dash now seemed to notice their presence.

His eyes traveled from Reve to Barbara and back. He flickered a bit and then, slowly, opened his mouth. They watched as he seemed to form words, but they heard nothing.

"Are you — I can't hear you," Reve said, with the tiniest of tremors in his voice.

Dash didn't respond, continuing to say whatever he was saying. After several more seconds of this silent monologue, Barbara gave tongue:

"Dennis! Can you hear me?"

This seemed to penetrate. Dash's mouth stopped moving and his gaze moved back to Barbara. His mouth moved again and she said:

"We still can't hear you. Can you . . . nod? Nod 'yes' if you can hear me?"

There was a suspenseful wait and then, very slowly, Dash nodded.

"Oh my God!" Reve whispered hoarsely. His grip on Barbara's hand convulsively tightened.

Dash's mouth opened again, and with a discernible expression of chagrin on his face, he began to fade.

"Dennis! We'll stay here all evening! Try to come back!"

When he was completely gone, they remained immobile for over a minute.

Unstiffening, Reve said: "He heard you. He's conscious — reacting. He's really there."

"Did you think he wasn't?"

"I knew he was there, but thought he might be some kind of projection or something. I don't know. Or maybe we were both hallucinating."

"You believed it, but didn't *really* believe it."

"I guess."

He looked down at his hand, still clasping hers, and gently disentangled their fingers.

"Let's go," he said.

"Where?"

"Just to the kitchen. He's gone for now."

They went to the kitchen and Reve checked the coffee-maker.

"It's like he got weak all of a sudden," said Barbara.

"I could see he was frustrated when he started fading away. Did you see that?"

"Definitely. Does — I guess it's some kind of energy thing, don't you think? He needs energy to be able to appear. He can't appear for long. He can't keep his form intact. He must need to get more energy to appear again. I wonder how that works?"

Reve was thinking he didn't really care how it worked, he just wished it would stop.

"Why aren't you more . . . scared?" he asked, curiously.

"I don't know," she replied, looking thoughtful. "I was quite shocked at first, but it *is* kind of interesting, don't you think?"

"I haven't made it to interesting yet. I'm still stuck at shock."

"You're worried about what his message will be?"

"I can't think it will be anything good, can you?"

"Well, whatever it is, maybe we can do something to help," she said. "Or, maybe you can since he *is* reaching out to you. And if there's something we can do for him, isn't that good? Maybe it means whatever trouble he's in isn't hopeless."

"What if it's not? Reve replied. "What if he's here to tell me he's damned to hell for all eternity? Or that he's going to haunt me until I die?"

"Do you really, I mean *really,* believe in eternal damnation?" Barbara asked.

"Until all this I never seriously thought about it. I mean, they talked about hell in Catholic School and all that. But, you know, you tell yourself you believe it, but you don't believe the way you believe that if you fall off a fifty-story building you'll die. But then, I didn't believe in ghosts either. Right now I don't know what I believe, other than the fact I'm being haunted."

"Raises a lot of questions, doesn't it?"

"What, being haunted?"

He came to the table with two mugs of bracingly fragrant coffee. Barbara took hers, and sipping it, issued a little "mmm" of appreciation.

"Yes, being haunted," she answered, after another sip. "At minimum, it does seem to prove there's life after death."

"I suppose so. But, oh my God, what if there *is* a hell?"

"I've always thought the concept of hell was really primitive," said Barbara decidedly. "I just can't fathom the idea that a Supreme Being who is capable of creating all the miracles of existence would be an unforgiving sadist who tortures people for eternity."

"I don't think religious scholars are literal about hell. They see hell as having to exist separate from God. Maybe that's what happened to Dash. Maybe he isn't allowed into heaven."

"Whatever heaven is."

"Well, whatever it is, what if he can't get in?"

Barbara thought about this. Reve looked at her with the air of someone needing a reassuring answer.

"Let's not get ahead of ourselves," she said. "Everything is hypothetical at this point. Anyway, if Dash is barred from heaven, whatever heaven is, I have no idea what can be done, if anything. He's the one on the other side; it may be that he knows and wants to tell you."

Reve took this in and said: "Okay. You're right."

"I'm curious about one thing, Reve," Barbara said after another moment's thought. "If you are afraid Dash is damned, so to speak, what do you think he did to deserve it?"

Reve's mouth opened immediately and then he stopped, closed it, and looked at her, first blankly, then with consternation.

"You appreciate the irony, right?" Barbara said, with hints of both humor and sympathy in her voice.

He got up, turned his back to her and went to look out his kitchen window.

Before either could speak again, Barbara's phone buzzed.

Reve, staring out his kitchen window, heard her greeting, then exclamation of concern.

"Of course, I understand. No, it's fine. I'll get someone else. You take care of Terry. I'll talk to you tomorrow."

Hanging up, she explained to Reve that the woman she arranged to feed the sheep their grain and Sabrina her dinner was in the emergency room with a son who had broken his arm in a skateboarding accident.

"I'm going to have to find someone else or I'll have to go home. My other helper is on vacation. Should I go home and come back?"

Reve turned and, with a sense of relief, applied himself to the immediate problem.

"You could do that. Or . . . why don't you call Olivia? She seemed interested in what you do and, if you pay her well, would probably appreciate the money."

"Hmm. Maybe. Can I trust her? I hardly know her and she's inexperienced."

"Well, she was a referral from someone you do trust, wasn't she?" said Reve.

"That's true."

"And if I can feed a sheep, I should think anyone could."

Barbara laughed. She retrieved Olivia's business card from her purse and placed the call. Fortunately, Olivia could make herself available (after rearranging some not-very-important plans) for a few hours. Barbara, explaining what needed to be done, was thankful to receive the right kinds of questions and the right kinds of answers. She told Olivia how to handle Sabrina who was trained to be obedient when given certain commands.

"I'm not exactly sure where I'll be tomorrow. I'll call you at noon and we can figure out where to meet so I can pay you. Okay?"

"That was a great idea," said Barbara after hanging up.

"Thanks."

Reve returned to the table and sipped his coffee. He stared resolutely at his coffee mug and tension started to build.

"Do you want to talk about it?" asked Barbara quietly.

"You know," he replied, "before I met you, before Dash died, I was satisfied with my life. I'm not saying it was perfect, but I felt no need to question what I was doing or why. But since then I feel like . . . I feel . . . "

"Doubt?" she prompted.

Looking goaded, he said: "Yes, doubt! Alright?"

"No need to be defensive."

"I'm not being defensive!"

She raised her eyebrows.

"Fine, I'm being defensive!"

"Look at it this way," said Barbara, "doubt is the first step towards change. Maybe you need a change. Maybe you've been needing a change."

"That's very new age-y of you."

"That's very dismissive of you!"

"I'm sorry," he made himself say, "I didn't mean to be dismissive."

Her look said she knew damn well he meant to be dismissive, but would let it go.

It would help, he thought, if she'd just be unreasonable, but instead she was being understanding and holding her fire. It was *maddening*. While Dash's haunting was violently upsetting him, it wasn't rocking her at all. She was taking the experience in stride, notwithstanding some natural shock. For her it was becoming *interesting*. How could she be so certain in herself? Or was she just more comfortable with uncertainty?

The people around him, he realized, were all about certainty. They insisted on it. They asserted it. They proclaimed it loudly and belittled the irresolute. How would his boss react, he wondered, if he was haunted by Dash Fordhyme? Would he experience fear and doubt? Or would he find some way to rationalize the situation and carry on, unaffected and undisturbed?

No, Reve realized, his boss might carry on, but he'd be affected, disturbed, and probably very loud. He would reject, he would deny, he'd probably panic for awhile, and all at the top of his voice. He'd then subdue any acknowledgement the world might be more mysterious than he'd thought and to compensate, would grow more rigid.

He'd observed the same pattern with a colleague who was gay and had no intention of ever admitting it.

Meanwhile, Barbara, seeing that he was lost in thought, got out her phone and googled "what to do with cremated ashes?"

She read until, looking up and catching his eye, she said: "I was looking up on Google what to do with cremated ashes."

This was sufficiently diverting and Reve asked if she'd gotten any ideas.

"Well," she said, consulting one of the articles, "they can be buried in a cemetery plot of their own, or added to an existing plot, or put in a crypt thing that cemeteries have for people's ashes. They can be buried on my property. I don't want to do any of those things because I don't want people doing pilgrimages to his grave."

She paused, then continued: "I can scatter them outdoors, in woods or the ocean or something, but Dennis wasn't an outdoorsman at all. I can keep them in an urn. I can — oh, this is interesting — I can have them blended with fireworks and shot off in a fireworks display."

"That seems kind of appropriate for Dash," Reve said thoughtfully.

"Possibly . . . I can have them added to a coral reef, or, my goodness, I could have them crushed into a diamond. Imagine that!"

"Really? Let me see."

Barbara handed him her phone and he read the description of the process.

"Intriguing," he said, handing her back the phone. He got up and began to wander restlessly around the kitchen.

Barbara, watching him, thought "here it comes" and waited.

Having crisscrossed the room a few times, he began.

"Dash said things about people that were — "

"Terrible? Nasty? Prejudiced? Hateful?"

"Well — "

"All of the above?"

Reve gave her an exasperated look and said: "Do you mind?"

"Sorry. It's a sore subject."

"Granted." He paused to see if she wanted to add anything, but she waved at him to indicate he had the floor, so he continued: "Originally I saw him as a fighter — as someone who said things that needed to be said and wasn't afraid to say them. You know how it is with politicians, they won't just come out and say things. They hedge. They don't want to offend anyone and end up exasperating everyone. Plain speaking was so refreshing."

He looked at her.

"Go on," she said evenly.

"Somewhere, at some point, he stopped being about ideas and started being about winning. Beating Democrats. Anything to win."

"Yes."

"He didn't used to believe half the stuff he said, you know. He thought he was a comedian pushing the envelope, saying things because they were shocking, seeing how far he could go."

"So he told me."

"But there were people who lapped it up. And he could get those people out to vote. And it was as simple as that, really. He could deliver a certain segment of voters to the party, so the party supported him."

"So — "

"So I supported him. Personally, we just got along. I don't know why, really. Professionally, I thought he was good at a dirty job."

"That's an interesting way to put it," said Barbara, "what do you mean exactly?"

He looked at her speculatively, and replied: "I always thought one of the characteristics of being a conservative was realism. Liberals are idealistic, conservatives are realistic. I — "

"It's funny," Barbara cut in, "because, while I agree liberals tend towards idealism, I disagree conservatives are realists. They use realism as an excuse for every other ism: racism, sexism, corporatism. And greed. And lack of accountability. And — "

Reve made a sound like "grtttt" and Barbara stopped. She watched with interest as he teetered on the edge of losing his temper.

Speaking through lightly clenched teeth, Reve said: "Can we have that debate another day?"

"You made a blanket statement about liberals and conservatives; I'm replying in kind."

"Fine. Touché. Do you want to hear what I mean by a dirty job or not?"

"Yes. But I also want to discuss what it means to be *realistic*. But I guess that can wait. Go on."

"What I meant was getting people out to vote is a constant challenge. People are often more motivated to vote against someone than for someone. Dash was very good at generating opposition to Democratic candidates and officeholders. The way he did it wasn't pretty, but it worked."

"The end justifies the means."

"Yes."

"Doesn't matter if it's immoral as long as it's legal, right?"

"Which is what I mean by realism. Morality is a concept that is subject to debate."

"And yet, you have been fearing that what he did was, in fact, immoral — so immoral he could be barred from heaven as a result."

Reve was silent.

"Haven't you? And you went there because in your heart of hearts you *knew* what he did was bad. Unless you think he did something else? Something I don't know about? Do you know something I don't know?"

"No!"

"So — "

"Fine, yes, I've been thinking what he did was bad. Maybe unforgivably bad. Are you happy now?"

Barbara pushed herself away from the table, leaned back and emitted a mirthless laugh.

"No. Not happy. A teeny bit satisfied, maybe. It would have been nice if Dennis had come to the same realization. I told him often enough and we had some vicious fights. I probably made him worse."

"How do you mean?"

"He was very defiant. He wasn't going to be told how to act by me. That kind of thing."

Reve nodded, "Yeah." That was Dash, he thought.

"I am curious about one thing," she went on.

"What's that?"

"What about his behavior do *you* think was so bad? I know what I think, but what do you think?"

He didn't answer.

"I guess I'm just wondering why it didn't bother you before. Why now but not then? You didn't think there were consequences before? Now you do?"

"I told you I thought it was a dirty job."

"But you thought it was okay to do it if it worked?"

He stared at her for a few seconds, then looked away.

"It was the realism thing, right?"

"You could say that," he replied. "Anyway, I didn't listen to his show — I tried a few times, but I didn't . . . enjoy it."

"It was horrible. It made me ill to listen to him."

"It was . . . pretty awful," he conceded.

"He was poisonous." she said, her tone sharpening. "He filled the airwaves with dishonest, demeaning diatribes. His fans were plague carriers. He made scapegoats out of powerless people. Scapegoating, especially when times are hard and people are stressed, is *wicked.* It creates the conditions for violence."

"Barbara — "

"And all sorts of powerful people encouraged him! Even honored him. They didn't denounce him; they didn't censure him. They gave him cover. They legitimized him. You legitimized him!"

Reve's face had become blank.

"I know," he said.

"Why? Why did people like you do that?"

"I've told you why."

"How can you live with yourself?"

"By knowing people could turn him off! No one was forced to listen to Dash; he gave people what they wanted! It's a free country!" Reve shouted, jumping up and backing away from the table.

"Oh I see, not your responsibility, right?" Barbara almost whispered.

"It's not my responsibility!"

"You could reap the benefits he brought you, but wash your hands of the damage he caused," she went on, still quietly.

"Collateral damage," Reve said, now calm.

"Collateral damage," Barbara repeated. "Exactly. That's how you all see it. It's war. We aren't fellow citizens with different ideas, we're *enemies.*"

"Metaphorically! Not literally."

"Not literally. You say. So maybe Dennis stirred up the occasional nutcase who turned around and shot someone, or beat someone up or put a burning cross on a lawn — "

"Look crazy people are crazy — "

"And guns don't kill people, people kill people right? But God forbid we try to keep crazy people from getting guns!"

"I told you I don't agree with gun proliferation!"

"Oh that's right. At lunch. That lawyer . . . "

"Gerald Kaboulis."

"But you wrote about it."

"Badly. I got hammered from all sides."

"Do you think," she said, pronouncing each word distinctly, "that absolves you of responsibility?" When he didn't answer she went on, "I am asking you in all seriousness."

He pushed a breath out and said: "I don't know."

Then he stared at the floor, feeling her eyes searching his face. He felt as if his mind, containing hosts of explanations and justifications, had seized up. He could produce nothing. Dimly he recognized that if he started down that path he'd wind up somewhere he didn't want to go. Things were connected to other things and underneath it all, the support structure was feeling rickety. Just how rickety — no. Not tonight. Not tonight.

Barbara was thinking "On a different day, with a different person, I would go in for the kill right now."

But she refrained.

Is it a liberal thing, or a womanly thing, or an idiot thing, she wondered sourly. Worrying about the feelings of people who . . . oh hell. He's not a "people" anymore; he's a "him". He's here. He's conflicted and unhappy . . . what is wrong with me?

After a moment of indecision, she stood and asked ungraciously "Would you like a drink? Of alcohol?" she added.

Reve raised his head. "Yes," he said. "I would. Sit down. I'll get it."

He went to his refrigerator.

"Beer? Wine?" he asked, his hand on the door.

"What are you having?"

"Brandy."

"I'll try some of that."

He smiled faintly.

"Are you sure?"

She gave him a look and he said, "If you're not used to it you might find it a bit strong."

"I'll risk it."

He went into the dining room, collected two snifters and poured a small amount into each. Returning to the kitchen, he sat at the table and handed Barbara her glass. She watched as he swirled the liquid in his glass and then sipped.

"Swirl it," he said.

She did.

"You can sniff it — breath it in, before sipping it. It enhances the taste. But I always feel self-conscious doing it around other people. It does make a difference, but it looks really pretentious."

Barbara chuckled, reluctantly, but it broke the tension.

"It does," she agreed, "but I'll try it."

She brought the snifter to her nostrils and breathed in, eyes closed. She thought she could discern both fruity and woody odors and others she couldn't identify. Then she took a tiny sip. At first it was strong, too strong, but she attempted to find flavors beneath the general sensation of alcohol on her tongue and thought of nuts and oils. And warmth.

Reve, watching her, made himself look away.

"What do you think?" he asked.

"It's growing on me."

"Take it slow, it's insidious."

"I can tell."

She did a few more small sips and felt the pleasant sensation of pending light inebriation. She decided to surrender all of her tangled emotions to the universe; philosophical and political battles could be rejoined at any time, but for now she wanted clarity and peace.

"Do you meditate, Reve?" she asked.

"Not successfully. I've tried a few times — not recently — and didn't seem to get anywhere."

"You tried by yourself?"

"Yes."

"Leave your drink for now," she said, then stood and gestured for him to follow her to the living room.

She sat on the far end of the couch and waved him to the other end.

"Sit and get comfortable. Lean back; stretch your legs, whatever is relaxing."

She waited while he, wearing a slightly skeptical expression, ensconced himself into his end of the couch.

"Now, close your eyes and imagine all your worries, fears, angers — anything painful or disturbing — are being held in your lungs."

Obediently he closed his eyes and after a moment, Barbara, opening one eye, looked at him and asked "Are you with me?"

"All my worries and fears are held in my lungs — I'm imagining that."

"Okay. Now, imagine that every time you breathe out, you are expelling clouds of dark smoke and the smoke is made up of all your worries, fears and the rest. As you exhale, the smoke is leaving you and starting to move away . . . far away from you . . . to the end of the universe." She spoke slowly. "Breathe in and out, deep breaths."

Reve told himself he was just humoring her, but he *was* relaxing. He began to breathe in and out deeply, and managed a decent visualization of smoke exiting his nostrils."

After a few minutes Barbara began again.

"Now, imagine that your lungs are clear, there's no smoke left."

"Okay," he said, nodding. My lungs are clear, my lungs are clear, no smoke left, he said to himself.

"Now, imagine that when you breathe in, each breath pulls energy into you that is pure, clear and blessed."

"That's nice," he said. "Are you doing it too?"

"I'm going to now. Give me a few minutes of quiet and we'll be done. Our heads should be clearer and what remains will be good."

He continued to breathe in and out slowly, thinking it couldn't hurt and was probably good for him. While part of his mind continued to chatter and dissect his actions, another part acknowledged the results — he was feeling more . . . tranquil.

Barbara, who had used this technique many times, felt serene and clear. With the clarity came a definite, not entirely surprising decision.

Opening her eyes, she looked at Reve closely, observing the softening of his jaw as he relaxed. His hands were loose, unclenched; his body, for the moment, unguarded.

She was feeling a connection to him she couldn't explain. She was pretty sure he felt the same.

The only question that remained was the nature of the connection: were they to be friends or lovers?

That will come down to chemistry, she thought. We'll have it or we won't. Might as well find out.

Reve, opening his eyes and meeting her gaze, read something of her intention and consequently felt his heart begin to pound and his active inner dialogue abruptly cease.

Wordless, she began moving towards him, crawling on her hands and knees across the couch. Without conscious intention he reached out, and then she was there, with her mouth on his and his eyes closed again.

Barbara, tasting brandy, experienced an infusion of warmth similar to the sensation her earlier sips had induced, but more far-reaching. It seemed to enfold all of her and the surrounding space and him in a private sensuous bubble.

Reve, enjoying the simple bliss of feeling without thinking, did what he had wanted to do since their first meeting — he wrapped his arms around her and buried his face in her hair.

"Was it . . . are you . . . " he asked, his voice muffled.

"I think so. You?"

His answer was to find her mouth again.

"Well!" said Barbara, some minutes later. Their clothing was askew, his hair was disordered and her cheeks were flushed.

Reve started trying to untangle his shirtsleeve which had gotten twisted behind his back and said: "I'm beginning to wonder if I went through the looking-glass without realizing it."

"So you think this is bizarre, do you?" Barbara said, eyes crinkling in amusement.

"Not bizarre, just surprising. Unexpected things keep happening. Mysterious and now magical things. You must admit this is unlikely. A few days ago all I knew about you was what Dash didn't like and you certainly had a low opinion of me. And yet here we are."

"Here we are."

"We are awake, right? This isn't a dream, is it?"

She pinched him.

"Did you feel that?"

"Yes."

"Then you're awake. And this is real."

"No," he replied. "I still think it's a dream. The only way I'll believe it is if you kiss me again."

"If we start again we may not stop."

"I'll risk it."

She laughed and moved towards him, feeling weightless, as though a cushion of air lay between her and the couch. There was a lightness in her head and tingles streamed from her center through her extremities and out into infinity.

Reve's response was rather more earthy — he was aroused, he was inflamed, but he was also conscious of feeling simple thankfulness. He had always considered himself lucky. He was feeling very lucky now.

It took several seconds for Barbara's buzzing phone to secure their attention, but once it did Barbara said "It might be Olivia with a problem!" and, detaching herself, moved swiftly to the kitchen to retrieve her phone.

It was Olivia. And by the time she and Barbara were through talking, Reve had straightened his clothing once again, flattened his hair, and joined her at the kitchen table. He took another sip of brandy, now with a slightly celebratory air.

"I arranged for Olivia to stop here tomorrow morning — is that okay?" Barbara asked.

"Absolutely. Does that mean you're spending the night?" he asked, eyes gleaming.

"I was leaning that way."

"Do you want to . . . ?"

"I want to, but I don't think we should just yet. What if Dennis appeared?"

"Oh. Right."

"He would put a damper on things don't you think?"

"In a big way. But, er, where do you think we, or you or I, should sleep tonight?"

"We could sleep together . . . you know, just sleep."

"Yes."

"In your guest bed maybe?"

"It's a pullout couch in my study; I've been told it's very comfortable."

"Let's have a look. And then we should check to see if Dennis is back. Although, I don't think he is. I'm not feeling him. Are you?"

"No," said Reve, "but I've been a bit distracted."

Chapter Ten

Wilksie, two cars back from the red Beetle, wondered where Peter and the young lady were bound. He hoped they were going somewhere to eat so that he could get some dinner and use the bathroom.

But instead of stopping at one of the many eateries in the vicinity, the Beetle got on the beltway heading for Virginia.

Okay, he thought philosophically, there's some great places to eat in Virginia.

Forty-five minutes later he was feeling less philosophical; his bladder had been issuing increasingly urgent status reports for the last 30 minutes.

Where the hell were they going? If they didn't stop soon he was going to have to pull off somewhere and lose them which he hated to do. He'd already invested most of the day and besides he was curious. The route was taking them down single lane roads, making it harder to remain unnoticed. He wasn't too concerned; he doubted Peter was in any way on his guard — why should he be? Still, if things got too rural he or the girl might begin to pay attention to the vehicles immediately behind them.

When they pulled into the parking lot of a white clapboard building identified by it's sign as the Baptist Fellowship Church he sighed. He drove on past and continued for a quarter of a mile where he came to an intersection and could see a gas station-convenience store in the foreground.

Ten minutes later, feeling much relieved, he reentered his car and considered his next move.

Church. Wayland wasn't going to care if the kid was spending Saturday evening at church, was he? Wasn't church the big thing with them? Of course, church people could be very touchy about *which* church was being frequented and the Southern Baptist Convention had been splintering in recent years hadn't it? He'd read something about Jimmy Carter . . .

Checking his cell for a signal he was relieved to find he could google the Baptist Fellowship Church on Sperry River Road. After a few minutes he whistled. He didn't think Wayland would be too pleased about *that.*

Reverend Fenimore was short, muscular and electrically intense. He had a two-inch-high thatch of thick brown hair that stuck straight up and out, dark eyebrows and blue grey eyes, surrounded, most noticeably, by deep laugh lines.

Connie liked him immediately; Peter, who was suffering from an acute attack of irresolution, regarded him warily.

The Reverend, whose intelligence was only exceeded by a bone-deep kindness, noticed Peter's withdrawal and responded by dialing down his energy. Peter, he divined, was poised between past and future, certainty and examination. A crisis of faith, particularly in a fundamentalist, needed gentle handling.

He lead them down the stairs into the large room used for meetings, luncheons, Christmas pageants and Bible classes. Currently there were several folding tables set up with chairs, he explained, for a training session after the next day's service. The air held the (relative) coolness of a basement mixed with the odor of humid dampness. There was a oscillating fan on a table cyclically rustling a distant stack of papers; the Reverend patted the papers absently as he passed.

"I only use the air conditioner when a lot of people are here," he explained. Then he waved at the tables and papers and said: "We're preparing to conduct a poverty simulation."

"I've heard about those," Connie said, interested, "how do they work?"

"They're very powerful," Fenimore replied. "I went through one and it really opened my eyes."

He lead them to the table at the furthest end of the room and seated himself across from them.

"The basic idea," he went on, "is you have a collection of identities and situations that you assign to your participants. For instance, you might be a twenty-five year old single mother of two working at a McDonald's, Peter might be a thirty-two-year-old man just out of prison living with his mother, and so on. The scenarios are based on real life people in real situations. You're assigned their income and the simulation begins. You go through four intervals, representing the four weeks in a month, and see how you manage your bills, job, transportation, etc., on your income. Volunteers play the parts of people working in the kinds of places poor people deal with: low-paying employers, check-cashing companies, pawn shops, homeless shelter. As you go through the weeks, you get wild cards like car breakdowns, foreclosures, late fees, and utility shut-offs."

"My! So what happens?" Connie asked.

"What happens is participants get tense and tired. They learn how much juggling has to go on in poor people's lives; how many obstacles they face — obstacles you never run into if you have sufficient funds. They see how problems spiral into bigger problems and holes get deeper and every day presents a chain of survival decisions. It opens your eyes to the powerlessness and stress poor people suffer. You get a taste of being emotionally drained and you wonder how these people get up in the morning at all."

Peter, getting interested in spite of himself, asked: "How does it end?"

"You wind up by asking people if they finished out the month better-off, worse-off or the same. Almost everyone will be worse-off. Many will also have committed crimes or considered committing a crime."

"You're kidding!" said Connie.

"Oh no. That's part of what makes it so powerful. You find out what happens to your head when you're confronted with continuous crises, always about not-enough-money. You see, while we have a terrible poverty problem in America, we have a good portion of the population making enough or more than enough money, and they — "

"Most Americans don't seem to think they make enough money," Connie interjected.

"Lots of people would like to make *more* than they do, but they are above the survival line. For now, anyway. They may not be able to get everything they'd like or want, but they don't go hungry and they can pay their bills. And when you have *enough* money you get in the habit of paying your way out of difficulties. And, depending on whether you were ever poor or were never poor, you may have literally no conception of what life is like when you can't just write a check to solve a problem. That's one of the reasons I'm so happy to be talking to two people who work for congresspeople. Most folks in Congress have no idea what many of their constituents face every day. Zero. Which translates into their pitiful lack of urgency for doing things that would help poor Americans."

"Congresswoman Tesarik is very concerned about constituent poverty," said Connie.

"I believe you. But, with all due respect, and I speak as a new convert on the topic, concern isn't enough. Concern, sympathy, empathy — these are all worthy emotions and reflect well on those who feel them, but they haven't lead to *action.*"

"You think this is because people don't really know what it's like to be poor?" asked Peter.

"To be poor in America — correct. That is to say, people don't know *viscerally.* They may have, as I did, knowledge of the facts — of the statistics. But they don't know what the stress is like; they don't really appreciate what it means to have nothing but bad decisions to make every day — if I do this I can't do that — or what it means to have all sorts of powerful institutions seeking to exploit or penalize you. For example, many police departments around the country make up for budget shortages by targeting low income people and charging them with all sorts of petty crimes in order to extract fines. People who can afford lawyers would never tolerate it."

Peter and Connie digested this.

"And that's just one example," Fenimore added. "But the key, again, is the simulation causes people to *feel* desperation, frustration and fatalism. Even if just for a short time. Indeed, part of the power is that participants feel desperate very quickly. They usually start out thinking they're above it all and they'll be able to manage their situation successfully; they're humbled and disturbed to discover how remorselessly they get pushed to the edge. The simple fact is you have to have money in America. It's not like you can go live in a tent in a park if you can't afford housing. Being homeless is essentially a crime in most places. Everything costs money and many of America's poor work full-time and still can't afford to live where they live. They have to constantly go without. I didn't fully understand this before."

"Well, from a legislator's perspective, what can be done?" Connie asked.

"About a hundred things. Would you like a list?"

I had an ecstatic phone call from Connie. She and Peter were visiting a liberal Baptist minister in Virginia and he and Peter were deeply engaged in a debate about scriptural interpretation when Connie ducked outside to call me.

"At first I could tell that Peter was holding back," Connie was saying, "so Reverend Fenimore started telling us about a poverty simulation project he's doing — that's really interesting by the way, I'll have to tell you about it — and Peter got loosened up. And then they started getting biblical and I left them to it."

"Does it bother Peter that you're not as biblical as he is?" I asked.

"Well . . . it's not easy. We're attempting a mutual respect approach. But over time it could be a problem — I don't know. I think it will depend on whether he can use his work for an outlet. Back home, he used to go to church every Sunday and every Wednesday night. Since he's been in D.C. he's hardly had time for any services, but he felt that he was expressing his religion through his work. If he can continue to do that going forward, we may be okay. He asked me to marry him, by the way."

"Oh Connie! So soon? I mean, congratulations!"

She laughed.

"I know. I told him we can be provisionally engaged. We have to give this relationship a public airing and see how it goes before we make it official."

Connie went on to tell me about the poverty simulation. She was going to see if she could get Congresswoman Tesarik to participate in a simulation with her and suggested I consider doing so too.

"You could write about it on the blog — if it's as powerful as Reverend Fenimore claims. I think Peter's hooked, although I don't know if he'd be able to get away from work."

"It does sound intriguing," I said. (I'm always looking for new angles for blog posts.)

"I really like Reverend Fenimore," Connie went on. "I think he can help Peter."

I was happy to hear it.

When I finished talking to Connie, I saw a message from Olivia. I returned Olivia's call and she described her meeting with Barbara Tishkin. It sounded to me like Olivia had handled a difficult situation quite well.

"We didn't get to talk that much, but she liked me enough to hire me to take care of an emergency at her farm."

"Really? What kind of an emergency?"

"She needed someone to see to her sheep for tonight. She'd had a funeral today and can't get home and her usual person's kid landed in the emergency room."

Olivia told me more about Barbara and the farm, only mentioning in passing that she'd be going to Cathedral Heights tomorrow to pick up a check at the house of a friend of Barbara's, a man named Tierney.

"Tierney," I said, "I wonder if he's related to Reve Tierney," I added.

"His name *is* Reve Tierney."

"What!"

"Yeah, that's his name. Why, do you know him?"

"What does he look like?" I demanded.

She described him vaguely — he hadn't made a strong impression on her, other than being "nice" and "polite". Still, the description fit.

Okay, I thought. Well, well, well. Small world.

"No, I don't know him," I replied. "I know *of* him. He works for a conservative think tank and appears on news shows."

"He does! Well I never."

I didn't share my views about him; I thought it would be more interesting to get her untainted impressions. But it struck me as odd that Sonya would refer Olivia to someone who hung out with Reve Tierney.

After we disconnected, I googled Barbara Tishkin. Before referring her to

Olivia, I had looked up her farm and learned about her yarns, but I hadn't proceeded further. Now I saw how little of her personal information was available online: no Facebook page, no LinkedIn profile, no other social media entries. Evidently a retiring sort of person outside of her business.

I smelled . . . something.

A couple of emails later I was trying to keep my eyeballs from popping out of my head. So this Barbara was Dash Fordhyme's sister? Natalie got this from Sonya after receiving my email. As it turned out, Natalie explained, Sonya did not normally divulge this information. Barbara, Sonya had written, had distanced herself from her brother and did not want to deal with either his detractors or admirers. She disapproved of him and had been estranged for several years. Sonya knew nothing about Barbara's connection to Reve Tierney; she speculated that they may have met as a result of Dash's death.

Sonya said Barbara went to considerable lengths to protect her privacy and Sonya would not lightly violate it. She expected both Natalie and I to be discreet.

A few minutes later Natalie called me.

"Sonya never told me!"

"Well, based on her email I can understand why, can't you?"

"I suppose so. She's always spoken highly of Barbara, but our paths just never crossed and I never met her. I do know Barbara's a widow and also that she votes Democrat."

"Good for her! Poor thing. Imagine having Dash Fordhyme as a brother."

"So Olivia met Reve Tierney and didn't know who he was?" Natalie chuckled.

"That's what she said. She said he was nice and polite."

"Is he now?"

"She really liked Barbara too," I said.

"I heard there wasn't any kind of public funeral or calling hours or anything. It surprised me at the time. Makes more sense now."

"Olivia said Barbara had mentioned going to the funeral home; she thought Barbara and Tierney were going together."

"Fordhyme was divorced; no kids, parents dead, and I'll bet he had more fans than friends."

"Evidently Tierney was a friend. Of one of them, anyway."

Dash did not reappear that night; Reve and Barbara trooped dutifully into the bedroom three times to check.

Reve and Barbara spent a lot of time fussing over the night's sleeping arrangements. Having pulled out the couch bed and tested the mattress they agreed it was probably adequate at best, but it didn't concern either of them. The process of selecting sheets, blankets and pillows took longer than (strictly speaking) was necessary, prolonged by joking, debating and numerous amorous interludes.

They retired rather earlier than usual; both pleading exhaustion. They did not make love, as agreed. Instead they luxuriated in their physical proximity; held hands, and talked about their early lives.

As they grew drowsy, Reve pulled Barbara close and, so situated, they fell asleep.

Chapter Eleven

Between Earth and the Spirit World:

Dash Fordhyme carefully collected his energy, preparing himself for another attempt at communication with Reve. He was now convinced direct vocalization was beyond his powers, but was encouraged by his successful reception of Barbara's communication. He believed Barbara and Reve had likewise received his reply although he'd been almost immediately distracted by his own energy depletion.

Still, while he worked to draw more energy to himself, he considered and rejected several possible approaches to his next effort. And then he got an idea. He examined it closely and it seemed to withstand scrutiny. It was simple, to the point, fast, and doable. What could go wrong?

On Earth:

Barbara awoke. She stretched luxuriously and lay for awhile reflecting on the topsy turvy nature of the last several days and it's startling aftermath. She pondered the nature of the relationship that had so unexpectedly blossomed. As a girl and young woman she'd undergone her share of infatuations; sudden, intense attractions based almost entirely on superficialities. The attractions, at first so compelling, always faded over time. She didn't *think* her feelings for Reve were infatuation.

What *were* her feelings?

She wasn't prepared to use the word "love". It was far too soon. But there was an undeniable affinity. This puzzled her as she couldn't account for it rationally. Or even irrationally. There just wasn't any basis for their coming together.

And could they possibly *be* together? She cherished no illusions about changing other people — she couldn't change Reve. Nor could she see herself being with someone whose labors were dedicated to outcomes she utterly opposed.

Perhaps they'd become occasional lovers, choosing to overlook their differences in exchange for companionship, a friendship of sorts, and sex. Not a thrilling idea, she thought, but it was tolerable.

Was tolerable *tolerable?*

She decided to stop analyzing and instead focus on experiencing. After all, how could she accurately predict the future of a relationship that had sprung from such a notably unusual string of events?

Reve, still asleep, looked . . . peaceful. Barbara found this quite touching. He was lying on his side, facing her, one hand pressed lightly against her. She moved carefully, trying not to wake him, and eased herself out of the couch-bed. She would make coffee.

Reve stirred when she returned. He rubbed his eyes then pushed himself up to a sitting position, reaching to receive the coffee mug she offered. He smiled, pushing his hair off his forehead, and after she settled in next to him, he reached for her hand and pressed it gently.

"Good morning," he said.

"Good morning!"

They sipped contentedly for a few minutes, feeling no need to speak.

It struck Barbara that their ability to enjoy silences together was a significant positive.

For Reve, the morning came as a benediction. He pinched himself twice knowing he wasn't dreaming, but double-checking anyway. If this wasn't a dream, it ought to be he thought. Could it possibly last?

He watched for a minute as she, all unaware, unfolded the newspaper she'd brought in with the coffee and started to read. How was it that she could be almost brutally critical of him while making him feel, simultaneously, completely accepted? He was routinely surrounded by people whose opinions he shared; whose outlooks he mirrored. Yet, as he had only recently recognized, his primary feeling had been one of vigilance. He had been a careful man, circumspect and prudent which presupposed some need for care. Against what had he been so guarded all the time?

Barbara offered him the Editorial page and, to his surprise, he declined. He didn't want to read about the state of the world right now — it would bring reality into their enchantment. He had never been enchanted before. Barbara, innocently sipping coffee in a pair of his cotton pajamas, did not look the part of a spell caster. But in his mind's eye, she *lured* him, and light danced at her finger tips.

Then, Barbara's head turned towards his bedroom, an alert look on her face.

Reve asked: "Is he here?"

"I think so."

This, he thought, is the other side of the spell. Although, I should be grateful — I am grateful — to Dash. Had he not haunted me, none of this would be happening.

So thinking, he adopted a brisk tone of voice, saying: "Let's get to it!" while arising and offering Barbara his hand.

Pajama-clad, they made their way once again to Reve's bedroom.

As they entered the bedroom and beheld Dash, Barbara was struck by his determined expression.

Dash saw them coming. He waited for them to stop a few feet from him. His gaze moved from Reve's eyes, to Barbara's, then back.

Very deliberately he tapped his chest with his index finger and then, extending his arm, closed his hand into a fist, lifted his thumb — creating a "thumbs-up" — and rotated his hand to a "thumbs-down".

He then pointed at Reve and repeated the thumbs-down gesture.

Finally, he pointed to Barbara and, with a slight suggestion of grudging admission on his face, did a thumbs-up.

Reve made a sound like someone recoiling from a punch in the stomach and Barbara dragged her eyes from Dash to look at Reve. He'd gone pale.

"What are you saying? Are you saying — "

"Reve!" Barbara cried.

"Wait!" he answered. He pointed back at Dash, who was repeating his series of gestures, pointing at himself and forming a thumbs-down; pointing at Reve followed by another thumbs-down, then pointing at Barbara and, raising his eyes, pointing upwards with his thumb.

"Dennis! Wait a minute! You don't mean — "

Dash began to fade.

"Wait Dennis! Come back! I need to ask you — "

Dash looked like he heard but, after a resigned shake of his head, was gone.

Reve, feeling as though his bodily fluids had solidified, turned towards Barbara.

"Reve," she said urgently, "don't panic! It's alright! We don't know what he meant!"

Reve moved his head in a vertical circle, then stiffened. A portion of his consciousness was contemplating the option of a dead faint. There was a growing buzzing in his ears and his vision was receding.

Barbara saw him begin to sway back and forth and, snatching at his left arm, pulled it around her shoulders and leaned into him to provide support.

"Reve," she said loudly, "breathe! You're okay! Hang on to me — walk!"

She started swinging him around so they could move forward out of the bedroom. His feet and legs resisted at first, then stumbled a bit, then complied.

They went down the hall into the living room and fell on the couch.

Reve sat, speechless.

Barbara was getting alarmed. She ran back to the study and grabbed his coffee mug. Returning with it, she took his hand, clasped it around the mug, and, raising it to his lips, commanded "Drink!"

He stared at her then took a sip and swallowed it. He put the mug down next to him and looked at her again, his eyes opened wide, pupils dilated. He covered his mouth with his clenched fists, then dropped them.

"I'm going to hell," he said.

"You are not!"

"You saw him. What else could he have meant?"

"I don't know, but you're not going to hell! There is no hell!"

"Who am I going to believe? You or him? He's actually *in* the afterlife. He must know more than we do!"

That was unanswerable. But after a pause, Barbara tried again.

"Yes well . . . I still say you're leaping to a conclusion!"

Reve ran both hands through his hair, front to back, then looked at Barbara wonderingly, as though confounded by her inability to understand something so obvious.

"Barbara, he was very clear in his gestures. He went slowly, he watched us, he was definitely sending a message."

"Yes but the message is subject to interpretation!"

"How would you interpret it?"

"I — well, couldn't he just have been saying that I was right and he was wrong?"

"Then why point at me?"

"Because you were on his side. Have been. When he was alive."

"Then why haunt me? Why didn't he show up in your bedroom to admit you were right and he was wrong?"

She winced. That was a good question.

"Well, maybe — "

"He's telling me I'm going to hell."

"Well, he's not in hell is he?"

"How do we know? Maybe he is!"

"But that doesn't make sense," she objected.

"How do you know? Who knows what a ghost can and can't do? Maybe a spirit *can* make contact from hell."

Barbara shook her head.

"I thought the whole point of ghosts is that they're between worlds. They don't know they're dead or something. I've never heard of spirits sending messages *from* hell. I maintain there isn't a hell anyway."

Reve got up, feeling shaky. Then he sat back down.

"I don't know what to think," he said. "But I feel . . . boneless."

Barbara sat down next to him and took his hand, which was cold. That shook her. She cast about for an argument that would reach him.

"Listen, do you really think he'd haunt you just so you'd be . . . fearful for the rest of your life?"

"What do you mean?"

"I mean, uh . . . maybe there's more to come."

Reve didn't look convinced, but he shrugged and made a "maybe" face.

"And maybe you could talk to a priest. After all, you're still alive, right?"

"So?"

"So, can't you confess and do penance and stuff like that?"

This was arresting. Reve suddenly looked intent.

"That's true," he said. "but — "

He stopped, looking worried.

"What is it?" Barbara asked. "What's wrong?"

"I just — it hit me that I don't know if I believe in confession or the sacraments. I haven't gone to confession for years. I'm trying to think why. Wouldn't I have to believe from the bottom of my heart?"

"I don't know," Barbara faltered. Privately she thought he was probably correct. But then she wondered where such beliefs needed to begin and end. Were there spiritual placebos? Could you be forgiven if you believed you were?

I know this much, she thought suddenly. God, in whatever form he or she or they exists, is not vindictive, unforgiving or merciless. She said that to Reve.

"It's good — I'm sure it's good — that you feel that way," he said slowly. "But, how can I be sure you're right?"

Chapter Twelve

In the Spirit World, Lersaliaz, Veliastan and Xe confer.

"Your assessment Veliastan?"

"We knew there was a risk."

"Yes."

"Reve is terror-stricken. Yes Xe?"

"He does not know what to believe."

"No. Lersaliaz?"

"Dash must undo the harm. Yet, I would not like to dishearten him — he is beginning to find his strength again and I believe he will soon return home. I would rather not delay him if he is so inclined."

"I agree but he should not abandon Reve to this fear. Coming from beyond the grave the impact is exaggerated."

"His ability to communicate remains limited; he cannot be heard. We must find another way. Yes Xe?"

"What about Wynne?"

"Wynne?"

"She has an open channel to us. Could she not receive Dash's message? I have been following the forks. Wynne is now linked to both Barbara and to Reve through different people."

"Is she capable, Veliastan?"

"She knows herself to be intuitive, but direct conscious channeling would be a departure. It would be a new skill, but it lies within the range of reasonable probabilities. It would also open for her new avenues of endeavor. We can consult with her Life Planners to find a connecting path. Separately, you must confer with Dash regarding the nature of his message. He may be more receptive to suggestion now."

On Earth:

Barbara was becoming increasingly worried. An hour had passed since Reve had last spoken and he'd remained seated on the couch, staring blankly.

She couldn't think of anything more to say. She was firmly convinced Reve was on the wrong track, but she couldn't articulate why.

Eventually she decided to shower and dress and then convinced him to do the same. He appeared to be moving on auto-pilot, but he went into the bathroom in pajamas and came out clothed with combed wet hair and a freshly shaved face. But he looked like someone who'd been told he had a malignant brain tumor and was still coming to grips with the news.

She had checked the bedroom three times, hoping Dennis would make another appearance. Was he gone for good? She devoutly hoped not. Not like this.

Each time she found the room empty she returned to the living room and sat next to Reve. He would look at her expectantly, she would shake her head "no" and he would withdraw again.

Reve was battling dire forebodings. Barbara's attempts at reassurance were as matchsticks to a bonfire. He tried telling himself he was overreacting and was mistaken, but remained unconvinced. He'd never considered himself to be a bad person, certainly not someone who deserved to be abandoned by God. But now, he questioned his self-regard — it didn't seem to be providing any support. He was in a situation of uncertainty and his confidence had not hesitated, it had fled at the first sign of trouble.

Preoccupied as he was, it took awhile for him to notice that Barbara had again withdrawn from the living room and someone was knocking on his door.

Between Earth and the Spirit World:

Dash was satisfied. He was pretty sure he'd gotten his point across.

So now what?

He inspected his energy. It was still mostly torn and tattered, but he discerned a few glints of stable color. That was encouraging.

Then he saw a dot of light coming towards him, growing in breadth and brilliance as it neared.

He allowed the light to reach and wash over him for an instant before pulling back and as he did so, the light resolved into Lersaliaz.

They regarded one another.

Then Lersaliaz thought: "Are you ready to come home?" His energy transferred warmth and understanding.

Dash found he couldn't answer.

"You are undecided?"

Dash nodded.

"If you wish to remain here yet more, it would be well if you communicated further with Fadraya. He believes himself to be condemned to hell. That was not your intent."

Situated as he was, between his identity as Dash, and his soul identity of Ukutmanu, earthly emotions were still familiar, but becoming distant. Had he been fully Dash, he would have felt and expressed a combination of frustration, exasperation and disappointment. Ukutmanu's reaction was a pure desire to release Reve from the distress caused by his misunderstanding.

Dash didn't need to speak; Lersaliaz read his every thought and emotion.

"I have some suggestions."

On Earth:

Barbara made her fourth trek to the bedroom in response to a sudden instinct Dash was present. She said nothing to Reve; if Dash was there she wanted to to talk to him alone.

She sprinted into the room and skidded to a stop a foot away from Dash's form.

She wasted no time.

"Can you hear me?" she demanded.

He appeared to speak; she thought he was saying "yes". Then he seemed to realize she couldn't hear him and nodded his head.

"We're you trying to tell Reve he was going to hell?"

He emphatically shook his head "no".

At that, Barbara deflated, folding at the waist in relief. She had gotten quite tense over the last few hours and the release left her weak.

It took her a moment to gather herself; then she stood straight up.

"What. Do. You. Want?" She paused between each word, enunciating with ballistic precision.

He began to speak, but stopped in response to her frenzied hand-waving.

"I can't hear you!"

He looked abashed, began to fade, but then came back, looking determined. He stared at her intently as though trying to will her to understand.

"Alright! Tell me this: do you have a message for Reve?"

He nodded "yes".

"Okay. We'll just have to figure something out . . . we need a medium I guess."

He nodded "yes" again, emphatically

"You think that would help?" she said, surprised.

Another emphatic nod.

"Okay. But if we get someone here will you appear? Can you . . . be around?"

He nodded again.

Suddenly overcome with curiosity, Barbara leaned forward and pressed her hand against Dash's blinking, spectral chest. She felt coolness and — was she imagining it? — an infinitesimal suggestion of pulsation. Or was she just feeling the circulation of her own blood?

Dash watched impassively then he faded, and Barbara turned around to see Reve, behind Olivia, framed by the doorway.

Olivia's eyes were widened to their fullest extent.

"Was that — did you — who — ?"

"What did he do, Barbara? What did he say?" cut in Reve.

"It's alright, Reve, it's alright."

"It is?"

"Definitely. Honest. I'll tell you everything but let me . . . explain to Olivia."

Abruptly, Reve turned and retreated down the hallway. Barbara, torn between wanting to follow him and needing to see to Olivia, remained.

It was hard to know where to begin.

Olivia was debating whether or not she should believe her eyes. She looked imploringly at Barbara as much as to say "please tell me I didn't see what I thought I saw".

"Um, Olivia," Barbara began.

"He said you were in the bedroom. I'm so used to walking around people's houses when I clean them, you know? I should've waited for you to come out. Did I just see a ghost?" Olivia's voice was husky, as though her vocal cords had withered and cracked.

"Well, yes. At least, that's been our assumption."

"Oh sweet Jesus!"

"Yes."

"He just disappeared! He up and disappeared smack in front of us!"

"Yes."

Olivia swallowed.

"Was that your brother? The one who died last week?"

"Yes."

"Have you been walkin' around scared to death all week?"

Barbara shook her head. "Not scared, no. Shocked at first. Worried and mystified. But I got over being scared."

"Mr. Tierney looked upset."

"Yes, he's been quite bothered."

"My Daddy used to tell us about a ghost, in Alabama. A man been lynched. He haunted the woods where the tree had been. People cut the tree down hoping it would end the haunting, but it didn't, not for years. Daddy said he'd seen the ghost when he was a boy. He had nightmares about it the rest of his life."

"I – I'm sorry," Barbara said.

"Don't be sorry. I'm just telling you. Why is your brother haunting you?"

"We don't know. He wants to tell Reve something, but we can't hear him and we can't make out what he wants."

"Oh, so you need a seer or psychic."

"I guess we do. But we have to be careful, you see. We'd like to keep this private and we don't know anyone psychic. I'm going to ask you not to tell people — though you certainly have every right."

"Don't worry — I'm no tattle-tale."

Barbara thought it would require an inhuman level of self-control for Olivia to not share this story with *someone*. But as long as she didn't talk to the press or post it on Facebook, it might not get too far. The fact that people tended to dismiss stories about ghosts would help.

"Well, I would very much appreciate your discretion."

"If there's anything I can do . . . not that I can think of anything, but, you know what I mean," Olivia said earnestly.

"I will let you know if I think of anything," Barbara replied. "And let me pay you for yesterday. Thank you for coming to my rescue!"

She lead Olivia to the kitchen, wrote her a check and promised to reschedule their information interview as soon as things settled down.

Reve, meanwhile, was in the bathroom. He had locked the door, grabbed a large, fluffy towel, fallen to his knees, buried his face in the towel, and, in an agony of release, wept.

It took Barbara a minute to locate him after Olivia left. She went to the bathroom door after looking everywhere else. Trying the handle, she found it locked, put her ear to the door and heard an indeterminate sound. She stepped back; he wanted privacy.

She went into the kitchen to find something to cook. They'd been too keyed up all morning to eat; now she was ravenous.

It was the smell of frying bacon that coaxed Reve out of a numb stupor. He couldn't remember ever breaking down and crying as an adult. He'd teared up at times (when his father died and at a handful of movies), but he'd never been moved to a genuine bout of tears. He felt mildly sheepish and physically depleted. His body felt completely empty, as though it was a thin shell with air inside. Barbara said it was alright and he believed her. He was waiting for relief, but it seemed he had to expel every other emotion he'd been carrying first.

He remembered the visualization he'd done with Barbara and began imagining that every exhalation was ridding him of stress, doubt and fear. And every inhalation filled him with energy and light. After a few minutes the inhalations included a delectable aroma as well and when he identified the odor, he found himself rising. He went to the sink, splashed cold water on his face, towelled it dry, and combed his hair.

He arrived in the kitchen with slightly reddened eyes, but otherwise composed.

"What are you making?"

Barbara smiled and pointed at a ripe tomato on the counter.

"BLT's. Can you slice the tomato? Do you like BLT's? I was suddenly starving and the tomato is perfectly ripe."

"I do like BLT's," he answered.

He got a cutting board and knife and produced five slices. Then he went to the refrigerator for lettuce and mayonnaise.

"Shall I tell you what happened?" Barbara asked.

"Please."

They made toast and assembled sandwiches while Barbara described her exchanges with Dash.

"So he does have a message for me, but it isn't about hellfire and damnation?" asked Reve tentatively as they settled at the table.

"Right."

"And we need to find a psychic so we can find out the message?"

"That's what it looks like."

He sighed, then took a bite of his sandwich.

"I really, you know, thought I was damned," he said. "I feel kind of silly now. But it was . . . "

"I know."

"I have a lot to think about, don't I?"

She nodded. She nibbled a bit of tomato — it was *tasty.*

"But not just now," she said decisively. "I think the best thing for you now is some, oh, fence mending."

"You do?"

"Seriously," she said. "Let's finish eating, get out of here, spend some time outside, commune with my sheep, fix the fence in my north meadow and clear our heads. We'll feel better and then we can figure out how to find a psychic."

Upon the receipt, via Melvin Thornery, of Wilksie's report about Peter Gilen, Congressman Wayland swore.

"A liberal Baptist church!" he wailed, "Why couldn't he just be gay?"

Thornery made supportive noises.

"We've got to be very careful with this. The last thing I want is for the kid to go liberal on us and leave. Especially if he's public about it. The liberal media will have a field day!"

Thornery agreed.

The Congressman's sigh nearly ruffled Thornery's hair through the phone.

"Maybe you could appeal to him," Thornery suggested.

"How do you mean?"

"Maybe you can get him to come clean with you and urge him to go see Reverend Derbyshire. Derbyshire can probably scare him into line."

It was an attractive idea, but Wayland, reluctantly, rejected it.

"Odds are Derbyshire would be his last straw. Gilen's devout. If he's feeling doubts, scaring him won't work."

"Well, maybe you could get him to go quietly if he's going to leave. You know, for loyalty's sake."

"That's possible. When can I sit down with him?"

"Maybe Tuesday. Tomorrow you'll be lucky to squeeze five minutes out of your schedule to go to the can."

"Figures. Well I'll have to pray he doesn't do anything until I can talk to him."

"Yes, sir. Should I call off Wilksie?"

"Hell yes. We already know the worst."

Peter had gone to Reverend Fenimore's Sunday service. He'd battled a strong feeling of disloyalty as he made the drive.

Driving home afterwards he wasn't sure if he felt better or worse.

Despite his best efforts, he'd started to enjoy himself at the service. It had been a long time since he'd felt euphoric; felt the transcendence that convinced him not only that there was a God, but that God was powerfully, indescribably good. For a few blissful moments that morning he'd felt flutters of the old connection, then realized he'd been deliberately holding back. What was more important, he wondered, the feeling of connection or the pathway *to* the connection?

He meditated on the meaning of loyalty.

Was it more important to be loyal to his upbringing? To the church he'd been raised in? To the people he worked for?

Or was it more important to be loyal to himself? To his evolving views on what was important and true? Did he have a right to views that differed from those he'd been raised to believe? Who was he after all? Just another sinner.

To change churches was, to some degree, simply changing authority figures. Which authority was right? Reverend Fenimore or Reverend Derbyshire? Both seemed to know the Bible backwards and forwards, but they looked at it and saw different things.

Reverend Fenimore emphasized helping people, spiritually and physically. Reverend Derbyshire, Peter admitted to himself reluctantly, appeared to focus on judging people, and having rendered judgement, leaving those who suffered to get on with it since he assumed their suffering was God's judgement.

But the Good Samaritan didn't leave the robbed and beaten man on the side of the road.

Hadn't John said: "But if anyone has the world's goods and sees his brother in need, yet closes his heart against him, how does God's love abide in him? Little children, let us not love in word or talk but in deed and in truth." (1 John 3:17-18 ESV)

Then there was the question of homosexuality.

Connie was gently, but persistently, urging him to consider acceptance of homosexuality. In practice he was already tolerant; he would never treat someone badly in response to their sexual orientation. Had he been so inclined, his relationship with Connie would have been over long since. But while he wouldn't mistreat individuals, he'd been raised to believe homosexuality was wrong and he remained conflicted.

Connie said many animals, in addition to humans, exhibited homosexual behavior which meant it was part of nature and God must have had his (or her - she always added "her" with a smile and a slight hint of steel in her voice) reasons. God also made sex enjoyable and she emphatically rejected the idea that non-procreative sex was sinful. Predatory or coercive sex was sinful. She was divided on prostitution — she didn't think it was sinful so much as sad (when voluntary) and horrifying (when forced upon someone, especially children).

She supported gay marriage for the simple reason that gay people wanted access to the same emotional and legal rewards and protections that straight couples enjoyed. And why shouldn't they? The response that they shouldn't enjoy anything because they were sinners hadn't gone well the only time he'd said it.

Among other things, Connie had reminded him more than once, Jesus hadn't said a word about homosexuality one way or the other. This had lead to a discussion about how people can find something in the Bible to support just about anything and he'd had to admit that was true.

"At some point," she'd said, "you have to decide for yourself what is or isn't right. The Bible is full of contradictions. If you're going to use it as your guide, you *must* pick and choose."

He would pray on it.

Barbara and Reve had spent several hours doing odd jobs around the farm. They were dripping with sweat and famished.

Reve was in good general health and worked out regularly at a gym (the better to maintain his image for television), but his treadmill and rowing machine routines did not prepare him to swing a sledgehammer or wield a shovel. He had activated normally quiescent muscles and would, he knew, pay a price tomorrow but he didn't care. Sometimes, he thought, the best response to an existential crisis is a session of simple physical labor.

Barbara, monitoring him unobtrusively, was satisfied she'd landed on the right remedy for what ailed him.

As they completed each task both felt a sense of accomplishment and Reve's mood improved.

Barbara had advised him to empty his mind and concentrate on his physical sensations.

"You're all tangled up right now," she said, "and you need a break. Let your unconscious sort things out for awhile. Leave it alone. *Feel* the dirt and the hay and your muscles working. Smell the air. Watch Sabrina herd the sheep — she's in the moment. Renew yourself."

Okaaay, he'd thought. Then he had looked into her bright eyes and saw both understanding and a touch of challenge. She knew what he was thinking.

He'd looked down then and thought "why not?"

He didn't want to think about Dash anymore anyway. He didn't want to think about his life or his work or what he thought about the world. He shied away from thinking about *them,* as well. He wasn't in a fit state to imagine a future either with Barbara or without her. There were so many complications.

But being with her, walking around the farm — that was simple. It felt good and it felt right.

He wanted to re-conjure their private bubble; retreat inside with her and seal them in, but they hadn't kissed or held hands since early morning and he felt tentative and unsure. When, late in the afternoon, Barbara unselfconsciously reached for his hand as they walked across the field towards the barn, he felt profoundly relieved.

They had brought a selection of food supplies from his condo and debated what to cook for dinner. They decided on a pasta primavera with garden vegetables — Barbara had a recipe that was speedy and tasty, especially with two people available for chopping duty.

As they worked they discussed the question of finding a psychic. It was a surprisingly daunting undertaking. How could you possibly evaluate a psychic in advance? And how could you know who to trust? Anyone could say anything, after all. Neither of them knew anyone who could make a referral.

"We'll just have to talk to people and trust our guts," Barbara said, "what else can we do?"

That conclusion reached, Reve wanted to shelve the topic and concentrate on normal learning-to-be-a-couple conversations and activities.

Tonight they would sleep in *her* bed. They'd made that choice earlier, a simple decision, but as bedtime approached they both wondered precisely what they would do and where it would lead.

After last night, the notion of separate beds hadn't even been broached; both assumed they'd sleep together. But while Barbara had been content to restrict their interactions last night, tonight she wasn't sure. Part of her felt it was still too soon to have sex *or* make love (since she wasn't sure which it would be), but another part of her was getting increasingly anticipatory. Still, she sensed that Reve was in something of a delicate state. Men had the whole pressure to perform thing going on and confidence (so she understood) was integral to success. She didn't think his overall confidence level was high at the moment. She wondered if he was worried or concerned or alternatively, consumed by desire. It was a dilemma as the last thing she wanted to do was diminish his confidence by questioning it.

It might be safest, she thought, to issue another proclamation of limitation for the night. But she didn't want to.

Reve was similarly torn. Had she but known it, concern about his physical capability hadn't entered his head. But he just didn't feel quite right in himself. He couldn't decide if that mattered.

As their thoughts revolved, they separated to shower and prepare for bed.

Barbara shaved her legs (just in case) and Reve shaved his chin (just in case).

They met in her room, both smelling clean and soapy, and, in Barbara's case, very lightly perfumed. She'd chosen a pair of white cotton pajamas with a lacy, scoop-necked sleeveless top. They were, she thought, subtly romantic without being overly suggestive.

Reve, who had thought her sexy in *his* pajamas, was rendered breathless by hers. She stood across the bed from him and the lit lamp on her nightstand shone through the thin cotton and outlined the curve of her hip.

Acting entirely on instinct, his arms came up and he reached across the bed towards her. His body followed. Meanwhile, she too climbed onto the bed and they met in the middle, kneeling, facing one another, a few inches apart.

For Reve, all was quiet save for the thudding of his heartbeat. He swallowed her with his eyes; breathed her scent, then lowered his head and then his lips to the hollow between her neck and shoulder.

Barbara shuddered.

Then the universe was reduced to tangled limbs, and hair and searching hands, lips and tongues and fire and more fire and then those fleeting but glorious seconds that suspend time.

Sated, they lay entwined while the world began to reassemble into the everyday version of itself in which they could, if they chose to, speak, hear and think. But as they looked at each other, they sensed an exchange taking place that hovered just above or below normal communication, somewhere speech couldn't travel.

Then Barbara moved, reached, and turned off the lamp.

Chapter Thirteen

Monday morning came too soon.

"I'm going to have to go to work," Reve said. He stretched then clasped his hands behind his head and looked at the ceiling. Although he enjoyed more freedom than most employed people, he did have projects pending and his boss was getting anxious. He also had a call from Melvin Thornery to return (he'd done some consulting work on Congressman Wayland's last campaign): Wayland was seeking advice about his primary challenge.

Barbara sighed. Life insists on intruding, she thought glumly.

Reve was no happier. The last thing he felt like doing — the very last thing, he thought — was to go back to work.

He didn't know what to tell Congressman Wayland. The usual prescription for a Republican facing a challenger from the right was to go even further right. But things were getting awfully tight on the right — there was very little room to maneuver. The point of no return seemed imminent.

Meanwhile, his boss would be curious about Barbara and insistent in his inquiries. His co-workers would be who they'd always been: dogmatic ideologues bolstered by generous salaries, good educations and high opinions of themselves. Until last week he'd felt perfectly at home in their company.

Now he felt . . . he didn't know. Different. Unsure.

And that was a problem. His think tank job was, in its essentials, that of an "opinion-shaper". It was work requiring confidence, ego and sturdy belief in his own (or his party's) rightness. Or, failing rightness, a sturdy belief that factual wrongness could be justifiably promoted for a greater good which demanded a sturdy belief that he labored for a greater good. Which, in turn, required some belief that he knew what the greater good was, and why it was good.

Right now he wasn't sure what he believed about anything.

Except for Barbara. Which was the root of the problem really, he thought later, driving to IPR. His job, his political life, most of the people he knew, were antithetical to her on almost every dimension. She should repel him. Instead, she was positively magnetic.

As he worked his way through intricate traffic, he wished he was tramping around her farm.

They'd left open the question of where he'd stay that night. He didn't want to go back to his condo and sleep alone, especially after last night. But it was a long drive to her farm and he might have to work late. On the other hand, he wasn't sure he could face staying at the condo by himself. They really needed to find a medium, get Dash's message, and move on from there.

Peter, going through the motions of his job, hoped he wouldn't need to work many more Mondays in Congressman Wayland's office.

He didn't like pretending. He didn't like saying things he didn't believe, especially to constituents, who, presumably, took him at his word. With staff he felt less guilt as he'd internalized the realization that Wayland, Thornery and the others were first and foremost, *political.* Their highest goal was to retain the position of Congressman for Wayland and to that end morals, standards, principles and facts could be flexed, promoted or dispensed with on an as-needs basis. He'd figured this out some time ago but had been, as he now recognized, making excuses.

He noticed that Melvin Thornery kept looking at him in a penetrating way. He didn't know what to think. Surely they couldn't know what he'd been up to, could they? How? Probably, he thought, he was projecting his feeling of being out-of-place onto Thornery and Thornery was looking penetrating because that was his way. Nevertheless, Peter felt relieved when Thornery, in company with Wayland, announced they'd be gone for the rest of the day.

His relief was short-lived. A few minutes after they departed Peter received a text message from Thornery: Peter was to be available on Tuesday at 9:15 a.m. for a meeting with the Congressman.

Reading the message, Peter knew they knew.

He checked the time: 10:17 a.m. There were people around and no privacy available. He wanted to call Connie for general reassurance and Wynne for strategic advice. He'd have to wait until later.

After Reve left, Barbara commenced her work day: physically occupied with the tasks at hand, mentally focused on reviewing the complications engendered by their unexpected relationship. Principally, she struggled over what to do about Reve's job which intruded into their nascent happiness like a bout of the flu at Thanksgiving dinner.

Had Reve been the sort of Republican her father had been, their political differences would be workable. She thought her father's Republican Party started withering during the Clinton Administration and Dennis and all his acolytes bore a large share of responsibility for its decline. Dennis had been a player in the endless scandal mongering purveyed by cable news and talk radio during those years. She'd grown disgusted by the relentless manufacturing of innuendo and ceaseless leveling of fact-free accusations made by obviously tainted people.

Sadly, what had begun as an ad hoc set of tactics used by conservatives to weaken Bill Clinton and other Democrats became the Republican Party's entire modus operandi. They abandoned debate and good governance and embraced exclusion, accusation, blame and defamation. With the rise of the internet, Hillary Clinton's "vast rightwing conspiracy" was unmasked as the unholy nexus of corporate-owned media outlets, think tanks, New-Deal-hating-billionaires and shadow 501 3C institutions tirelessly trumpeting each others' propaganda.

While the Democratic Party's weak and ineffective response to this onslaught hadn't impressed her, the Republican Party's fervent adoption of destructive politics repulsed her. She'd ended up a Democrat by default, suffering, as many Democrats did (particularly during the Bush/Cheney years) from the feeling that her choices had been between *bad* or *worse*. It wasn't a happy place to be as a voter and it was a very bad place to be as a country, but there it was.

Reasonable people can disagree, she thought, but there's a difference between, say, preferring a smaller government and claiming every person getting government assistance is automatically a lazy, lying parasite. Instead of promoting and defending legitimate (if debatable) points of view, Republicans now spent most of their time slandering people who disagreed with them. Some of them sank lower — they dehumanized their opponents. Reason enough, Barbara thought, to bar them from positions of power indefinitely. Using dehumanization as a tactic was the last step before direct physical assault. It was reprehensible.

Reve, though, doesn't stoop that low, Barbara decided. But he's an active player in this dark game and I can't disregard his involvement indefinitely. But neither can I ignore last night. And I'll miss him tonight if he stays in town...

By lunchtime Barbara came to the conclusion she'd devoted too much mental energy to a question she couldn't answer. It was too soon. And she wasn't alone in this — Reve had his part to play. The two of them were going to bounce off of one-another and would thereby create new conditions which would impact their choices down the line.

With a shake of her head, she decided to redirect her energy to finding a psychic who could transmit Dennis's message to Reve.

Her initial online search supplied a long list of potential psychics. She envisioned them coming to Reve's condo one by one, seeing Dennis's ghost and failing to hear his message. Of course, the first one might not fail, but what if she did? And how much would it cost?

It then occurred to her that she now had a great deal of money — cost needn't be an issue.

Even better, she thought suddenly, maybe she could pay someone to do initial contacts and assessments. Olivia, for instance. Olivia already knew about Dennis.

Olivia could call some psychics, using her own cellphone, and describe the situation in broad terms, naming no names. Hopefully, she could then make preliminary recommendations. In the end, they'd have to trust someone, but at least the first round of screening could be done with minimal risk.

As she tapped in Olivia's phone number, Barbara wondered if Olivia was glad or sorry they'd ever met.

As it turned out, Olivia was delighted to help. She'd been thinking about the haunting and was naturally interested in knowing, indeed participating in, its resolution. Should she come to the farm and make calls so that Barbara could listen on speaker? She could reschedule some cleaning appointments and be available tomorrow afternoon.

"Perfect," said Barbara, "just perfect!"

I got a call from Peter just as I was about to eat. I'd gotten some Thai takeout and it was smelling heavenly, but it seemed it would have to wait. Peter was panicking and I needed to talk him down.

"Okay, okay," I said as soothingly as I could, "lets work through this. Relax! Where are you?"

"I'm home!"

"Great! Can you get yourself something to drink?"

Beer, vodka, rum? I thought a bit wistfully. But Peter, as I assumed, drank alcohol very rarely and had none in the house.

Oh well.

"Tell me everything," I said and as he spoke I was able to sneak a few bites of my dinner.

It boiled down to a meeting Tuesday for an unspecified purpose. Peter was agitated because he'd never had such a meeting scheduled with Wayland before, plus Melvin Thornery had been giving him piercing looks all morning.

It wasn't a lot to go on, but I respected his conviction that the meeting was going to be confrontational. It wouldn't surprise me if they'd noticed all was not well with Peter — he wasn't comfortable with subterfuge and they, I suspected, were. Which, in a weird way, would make Peter's kind of profound sincerity conspicuous in both its presence and absence.

"Alright," I said, "let's look at the best-case scenario: they've noticed you seem unhappy and want to know what's up. You can respond directly or indirectly and we can talk about approaches. "

"Okay."

"Now, how specific could they be about anything else? I mean, what could they know? Could they have found out about Connie?"

"I don't know . . . maybe. We've been very careful, but I suppose someone may have seen us somewhere. Seems unlikely but not impossible."

"So we can strategize how to handle it if they confront you about Connie."

"Okay," he said again. He was calming down.

"Other than Connie, what else could they have? You haven't talked to any Democrats about jobs yet have you? Or anyone else that would raise red flags if they heard about it?"

"No, not at all. The only new person I've spoken to is Reverend Fenimore and how would they know about him?"

It crossed my mind Peter may have been spied on, but I decided not to mention the possibility. It would just make him paranoid. So I put it as a hypothetical.

"Let's pretend they've been tailing you around town — is there anything else you've done or places you've gone that would concern them if they knew? I just want you to be prepared for anything."

"Well, there's you."

"That's true. I would be hard to explain . . . anyone else?"

"I don't think so."

"Okay, so you need to be ready for general dissatisfaction, Connie, Reverend Fenimore, and me . . . "

I pondered and chewed for a minute.

"Do you — "

"Give me another minute," I interrupted and he subsided while I organized my thoughts.

"Peter," I then said, "there's no reasonable way they could know about Connie, the Reverend, or me — which doesn't mean they don't know about any or all of us — but I doubt they'll confront you directly. They'd have to explain how they found out."

"So . . . ?"

"So my guess is they'll try to get you to volunteer the information."

"Ah . . . oh."

"Yes. Now, what they *can* bring up is concern about your work or attitude or however they choose to frame it. Then they can ask a few leading questions and if you spill, then you'll have teed up the confrontation conversation."

He mulled this over while I ate a few more bites.

"So," I went on, "I think there's a couple of ways to play this, depending on what you want."

"What do you mean?"

"Is your objective to retain your job? Or do you just want to get the inevitable confrontation over with in the most constructive way? Or don't you know?"

"I . . . hmm. Good question."

I nodded to myself. The moment is going to come sooner or later, I thought; should he just get it over with?

"I guess I was hoping to have more money saved or a definite job lined up. But I'm also really uncomfortable at work these days so it might be a relief to leave now. I'm torn."

"Exhausting, isn't it?"

I heard him sigh.

"All things being equal," I said, "it would probably be better for you to stay until you're ready to go. You're miserable, but not miserable enough to embrace this as an immediate way out. Personally, I don't think you're quite ready — you haven't finalized your direction yet."

"No."

"On the other hand, it's conceivable you could get fired tomorrow. It won't be the end of the world though I know it's a scary thought. So I think we need to prepare you to try to keep your job. But, if they have other ideas, you'll want to handle yourself effectively."

His "okay" came out low and worried.

"Let's start with the easiest scenario: they ask you if you're unhappy with your job. The safest response would be to say you're quite happy with your job and ask why they're asking. You can act surprised, worried, indignant. They'd have to justify themselves and would probably say general things about how you don't seem as happy as you once did and you can reply that you're sorry, you've been working a lot of hours and have been homesick a bit and promise to do better. Conversation over."

"I'd be lying though."

"Right. You'd be lying. You're lying every day now just by showing up at work."

"True. But it's . . . indirect."

"Does that mean you won't go there?"

"I'd rather . . . I'd rather not. Does that mean I'm sunk?"

"We-ell," I said slowly, "possibly. Unless . . . let's try this out. They ask if you're unhappy with your job and you say you're sorry they've noticed; you hoped to work it out yourself. They'll want to know what's wrong and you can tell them you've been unhappy about — about — "

"About people's struggles. About constituents having problems and feeling like we're not helping them, as a party."

"Yes! Good! What do you think they'd do?"

I could picture him thinking this over.

"I *think* they'd try to make me feel better," he said.

"Then the problem's solved."

"It's not the whole truth, though."

"Its true in that you *are* unhappy about the party's failure to address real problems. You just aren't elaborating on your opinion about *why*."

"But its still deceitful."

"Eeee-yeah," I conceded. Strategy and 100% honesty do not natural companions make, I thought.

"Is it humanly possible for me to be honest and keep my job?"

"I don't think you can tell them you're dating a Democrat and have been seeing a career counselor to help you decide how best to leave your job and not have them fire you." I said. "Unless — " I stopped. Maybe . . .

"Yeah?"

"Alright, how about this," I said slowly, "what if you take the offensive? Tell them you've been getting increasingly unhappy about how the party is approaching several issues and you've been thinking about leaving. Tell them you've been seeing a counselor to help you sort out what you should do. Tell them you've been having a crisis in faith and sought out Reverend Fenimore to get a different perspective. Tell them about the poverty simulation — that you want to participate in it and ask if Congressman Wayland would be willing to join you. Because — here's the good part — if he did he might actually learn something and he might try to do something."

"Whoa!"

I smiled. "I don't think they'd see that coming, do you?"

"Absolutely not!"

"Doesn't mean he won't refuse — he probably will — and it doesn't mean he won't fire you. But my guess is he would prefer not to fire you. He's looking down the barrel of a primary from the far, far right. You could, if you chose to, create problems for him that he doesn't need right now. He won't want people to think working with him disillusioned you. On the other hand, most of these guys wouldn't think twice about destroying you if you became a threat. They are very good at character assassination. On the third hand, they lose much of their ability to hurt you if you're prepared to switch sides. They might still try, but I think Wayland is smart enough to know it could backfire."

"My head is reeling!"

"You could tell Wayland he might be able to use the poverty simulation to his advantage — note to Wynne: stop giving good advice to Republicans — "

Peter laughed, "What do you mean?"

"Wayland is old school Republican, notwithstanding his evangelical roots. He's getting backed into a corner by Tea Party fanatics. If he decided to make poverty his issue, he'd have some credibility, religiously, wouldn't he? I know there's disagreement among Evangelicals about social justice and helping the poor, but who would be more appealing to your parents: Wayland quoting scripture or a Tea Party Libertarian saying we should cut Social Security?"

"Hmm."

"He'd have to craft his message, obviously, but, among other things, it would have the value of being unexpected. I think he could put his challenger on the defensive — he could go *on* the offensive. He can fight on their turf, or make them fight on his. I know what I'd do."

"That's a good idea. I know he's worried about being primaried and isn't sure how to handle it. But . . . "

I knew what was coming.

"Yes?" I said.

"It still wouldn't be truly honest. It would be a delay tactic. Even if he participated in the poverty simulation, even if it changed him, I don't *think* I'd stay. However, I might not leave as soon."

"Peter," I said patiently, "you can't have it both ways. If you insist on telling them everything you'll just have to take the consequences."

He sighed.

"Although," I said, as another angle occurred to me, "there might be a way you can be honest and still keep your job for some period of time, anyway."

"How?"

"You could tell Wayland you've been increasingly unhappy about the party not helping people and you've been thinking about leaving, but haven't decided what to do next. You can say you've been agonizing because you feel loyalty towards him and gratitude for the opportunity you were given and so were trying to find a way to leave without damaging his reputation. Depending on what he does or doesn't say, you can bring up Connie and me, or not. At that point I don't think it would matter. You could tell him about the poverty simulation and ask him to participate in it because you think it would be a good experience for him and, also, you think he could use it against a primary opponent. You could say you understand if he wants to let you go, but if he is willing, you'd rather stay a bit longer and leave in a way that would make everyone look good."

Peter didn't respond for so long I thought we'd been cut off. But after a couple of "can you hear me's?" he came back on the air.

"It's terrifying, but I like it."

"I think the odds are fifty-fifty. You'd have to be prepared to be fired. But your principles will have been respected and if it works, it will buy you some time and you won't have to feel dishonest."

You'll also be doing far more for Wayland than he deserves, I thought to myself. Still, I liked the idea. In the dance of seeking and keeping jobs, honesty is so rarely an option. Or so it seems. Food for thought . . .

"I think it's a great idea," Peter said. "What should I do if they get angry?"

"Bow your head and say you're sorry. Tell them it's been a struggle for you and you didn't want to make them angry. They could go crazy on you, but I don't think they will. Although I could see Wayland huffing and puffing a bit; he's that kind of guy."

"Yeah. I've heard him tell a few people off. He does have a temper. But really he's been pretty decent to me personally."

"I'm glad he's been decent to you personally, but he has voted for a number of indecent things, don't forget," I couldn't help saying.

"I know. Does it count if he really believes he's doing the right thing?"

"I think intentions do matter. But so do intelligence and responsibility. I don't think it's forgivable for a powerful person to accept demonstrably stupid, false or harmful things and then use their power to promote them. He doesn't get a pass from me, but I can understand why you feel differently."

"Thanks. I guess."

I laughed.

"Anyway, do you feel better? Are you going to be okay tomorrow?"

"I think I will be. Thank you for helping me."

"You're quite welcome. Call me tomorrow and tell me how it went. I'll be rooting for you!"

We wrapped up the conversation and I was able to finish my dinner. I couldn't help chuckling at the thought of Peter asking Wayland to participate in a poverty simulation. I was convinced if Wayland agreed his motives would differ dramatically from Peter's. Motives aside, it would be genuinely interesting to observe Wayland's reaction to the exercise. But it seemed far more likely that Peter would be out on his ear and I could only hope Wayland would merely fire him and not *destroy* him.

Or try to. I would see he didn't succeed, I thought, and was surprised to discover how fierce was my feeling.

For Reve the work day couldn't end fast enough.

He'd disposed of Melvin Thornery by promising to call back Wednesday and schedule a meeting.

As he'd anticipated, his boss (Elliot Bauers) wanted to know all about Barbara and whether they could get money from her for their endowment. Reve suspected Elliot had heard about Reve and Barbara's lunch from Gerald Kaboulis.

He felt beleaguered. He had no intention of approaching Barbara for money under any circumstances. He also had no intention of describing his feelings to Elliot. The simple reduction of Barbara to "potential donor" was distasteful, ironically because he knew he'd many times looked at other people in exactly the same way.

He settled for saying they'd only just met and he wasn't comfortable approaching her for money at this point. The "maybe in future" was implied and satisfied Elliot, for now. Reve knew it was only a temporary reprieve.

Then there was the work waiting for him. The Republican Party was committed to providing unyielding support for the NRA and, shortly before Dash's death, Reve had been tasked with preparing a set of talking points and supporting editorials to explain why unlimited gun ownership was prudent, intelligent and concordant with the American Way. Freedom, he was to declare, rested on all citizens' access to unlimited guns of most types and security depended on Americans' God-given rights to openly carry said weapons anywhere, all the time.

"It's a bit of a gamble," Elliot had explained, "but our sponsors want us to provide some push-back to the opposition. Too many shootings being reported; several leftwing websites are making a point of highlighting every Tom, Dick and Harry in America who accidentally shoots himself or his kid or neighbor or whoever. Or worse, when some eight-year-old shoots his baby sister because his idiot parents didn't lock up the weapon."

"Some gun owners really give gun ownership a bad name," Reve had remarked in an expressionless voice.

"Yeah, well, we've been lucky so far — anti-gun legislation has stalled in the Congress, but there's a couple of trials happening now in Stand Your Ground states that could go badly. I think the policy of keeping quiet in the weeks after a school shooting is sound, but we can't go quiet all the time or the other side will start getting traction. See what you can do."

Sitting at his desk, Reve now wondered how many bottoms you had to drill through to reach the bottom-most rock-bottom. He couldn't specify just when his job had crossed the line from strenuous partisan argumentation to clever persuasive pimping, but it had.

He'd told Elliot at the time he wouldn't do any public appearances in support of NRA positions and Elliot had acquiesced on the condition that Reve provide the copy. His editorials could appear under other people's names; his talking points could be fed to legislators and reporters as coming from IPR.

Up until now, Reve realized, he'd never even *considered* refusing. It was part of the job; a job that afforded a number of perks which he thoroughly enjoyed. He thought it was his duty to suck it up and do the work. He had told himself he was operating from duty, loyalty, gratitude even — all worthy qualities. Now he wondered if he peeled away duty, loyalty and gratitude would he see greed, cowardice and expediency?

And even if he *could* absolve himself of the lowliest motivations; if his intentions were as pure as he'd like to think, was he culpable for the results of his output?

He'd taken plenty of credit in the past for his contribution to various conservative successes, so . . . so . . .

A news item came through one of his RSS feeds: "Judge Sentences Mississippi Killers." He remembered something about the case; he did not need to read the news item.

He did not want to read the news item.

He would not read the news item . . .

He knew the background: just before dawn on a Sunday morning in 2011, a group of ten drunken white teenagers drove to Jackson, Mississippi to find someone — anyone — black, to harass. This was not their first such foray. They found a man in a parking lot who they beat up and then *drove over* in their pick-up truck. The victim was black and gay, who, with his partner, was raising an adopted child.

He gave in and read the news item.

The judge who presided over the sentencing of three of the young men had made a moving statement which was being widely distributed online. In it, the Judge described the history of brutal violence against black people in Mississippi and lamented the existence of a new generation of people following in the bloody footsteps of their forebears.

As Reve read accounts of the killing and the judge's remarks, a cold hollow formed in his interior, made of nothing yet heavy enough to pin him to his state-of-the-art ergonomic office chair. For a few minutes he couldn't move and didn't breathe.

Olivia's face appeared before his mind's eye.

Then he thought about Dash and all the Dash imitators distributed around the country spewing their variations of sneering, jeering, contemptuous vilification. How much exposure to such influences was required to turn high-school students into murderers?

He looked up and around at the cubes and offices where his co-workers did their bits to promote the Republican Party and its associated special interests. *We* don't descend into the real muck, he thought. *We* talk about taxes and trade policy, the deficit and entitlements, freedom, the Constitution, job creators, the free market. *We* don't personalize.

Other people do that for us.

We're not them.

We just have drinks with them and go to events with them and appear with them and give awards to them. Sometimes we run them for office and we vote for them.

Bile rose in his throat. He broke into a sweat and for several exceedingly unpleasant seconds he battled nausea.

Mercifully, it passed.

He didn't . . . he couldn't . . . it was too much. He couldn't deal with this right now. He had Dash to contend with — wasn't that enough?

He tried thinking about Barbara, then felt almost unclean. He shouldn't use her as an antidote for . . . for . . . he shouldn't use her as an antidote.

He got up, wobbling slightly, and fetched a bottle of water. They would get Dash's message. Then — well until then he would go on as usual.

He gritted his teeth, forced himself to write, and finished the day in a fiendishly foul mood. His head ached. He wanted to see Barbara, but she'd either confront him about his job or they'd avoid the topic. But it would be there, like a tiny malignant tumor destined to grow.

He decided to spend the night at his condo, not without some apprehension. When he entered his unit everything seemed normal. With leaden steps he approached his bedroom, but it was empty. The indescribable sensation of an otherworldly presence was blessedly absent.

He went into his study where the couch-bed was still pulled out and dressed with sheets and pillows. He rather thought he could detect a suggestion of Barbara's scent and decided he'd sleep there.

That settled, he headed to the kitchen to muster up a sandwich and something to wash a couple of aspirin down.

He found the coffee cups they'd last drank from and cold coffee in the pot. Suddenly, eating seemed like way too much trouble and he sank into a chair by the table and debated whether to go straight to depression, or get a snifter of brandy first. The thought scared him — he didn't want to start depending on brandy to cope with bad moods.

He pulled out his phone.

"Barbara?"

"Reve! How are you? How was your day?"

"I've had better. How was yours?"

"Good. Odd. I ended up calling Olivia again. She's coming over tomorrow to make first contact with some psychics. She'll screen them using her phone so I can avoid giving out my name and number."

"Great idea."

"I think so. It was a big relief. After talking to Olivia I was able to get a lot done — so that was nice. But now I'm missing you."

"I miss you too," Reve said, and his mood registered a microscopic lift. "I have a headache and decided to come home. I need to eat something, but I don't feel like cooking."

"Should I come over?"

"There's nothing I'd like more in the world, but you'd have to make arrangements and it's late. Let's plan to see each other tomorrow or Wednesday night for sure. I'll call you late afternoon."

"Alright. Are you okay there alone?"

"I don't feel Dash's presence at all. Although, I'm going to sleep in the study, just in case. But actually I think it will be fine."

"That's good. Well then, let me talk you through eating. Do exactly what I tell you."

"Yes ma'am!"

"Get up, go to the refrigerator and tell me what you see."

Complying, Reve felt his appetite returning and his headache fading. A little.

Chapter Fourteen

For Peter, Tuesday dawned fair following an extremely heavy night's sleep. After talking to Wynne he'd spent an hour at prayer seeking strength. He was highly principled, but he was equally intelligent and knew his insistence on honesty could cost him his job. After prayer, he'd concluded God's will would be done and stopped fretting. He'd feared a sleepless night, but instead dropped off and resumed consciousness almost eight hours later with no recollections of night wakings.

Inspecting his mood, he found himself strong, with the barest hint of apprehension. He called Connie, who expressed her love and wished him luck and, thus fortified, he dressed, ate and made his way to the office.

His meeting was at 9:15 am.

Thornery, surreptitiously observing him, thought Peter was nervous which meant Peter felt guilty. Which meant Peter was up to something at that church Peter knew Wayland wouldn't like. The tricky thing would be getting a confession without disclosing Wilksie's surveillance. Fortunately, Wayland was a crafty old fox and Peter was young and honest — should be no contest.

At 9:14 Peter went to the corner of the office where the coffee machine and water cooler stood and got a drink of water. Wayland had arrived a few minutes earlier and was going over his schedule with Thornery.

After breathing a short prayer and drying his suddenly sweaty palms on his pants, Peter followed Wayland into his office.

"Sit down Peter," Wayland said in a genial voice. While Peter pulled up a chair, Wayland walked around his desk, sat down, moved some papers aside, settled his elbows on the desk, rested his chin on his clasped hands and cleared his throat.

He looked at Peter steadily for a minute letting the silence build. Peter found himself crossing and uncrossing his legs, then he broke down and said: "Is something wrong, sir?"

"Is something wrong?" Wayland repeated, continuing his steady stare for three beats, then: "you tell me Peter."

Well, thought Peter, here we go.

And that's when the interview, thought Wayland, began to go wrong. Peter spoke, outlining his growing unhappiness with the Republican Party, ticking off points with his fingers and asking a list of rhetorical questions Wayland would have been hard-pressed to answer. As Peter continued, now describing his crisis of faith and his search for a church "focused on helping people instead of judging them," Wayland felt the initiative evaporating and his own position sliding inexorably from the offensive to the defensive.

When Peter began describing the poverty simulation exercise, Wayland relaxed briefly (Poverty simulation: was the boy insane?) only to be horrified when Peter asked him to participate in one scheduled for Thursday evening. While he was still trying to frame a reply, Peter added his idea that Wayland might be able to use the exercise as an offensive measure against his Tea Party challenger effectively short-circuiting Wayland's instinctive refusal. And while Wayland was still grappling with *that* idea, Peter closed by saying his gratitude for the opportunities he'd enjoyed through his job, and his loyalty to Wayland, had caused him to vacillate. He said he knew he was ultimately destined to leave, but wanted to find a way to do so that would preclude him damaging Wayland's prospects given the delicacy of the situation and tendency of the media to manufacture scandals out of the thinnest material.

Then Peter stopped talking, looked at Wayland earnestly, and waited.

"Peter I, I don't know what to say." Wayland was appalled to hear himself utter. He shook his head, cleared his throat again and tried vainly to think of a way to regain the upper hand, but to what end? What was his objective? And then, floating out of the muddle of his confusion came the topic most worthy of pursuit.

"What," he asked carefully, "was it you said about this poverty thing and my primary?"

Barbara's conviction that selecting a psychic would be difficult was amply confirmed. After Olivia arrived, they sat down together at the kitchen table and compiled a list of potential contacts. Barbara had found a phonebook, still shrink wrapped, which yielded an abundance of names. They went online and did a search on each name.

A further review of the psychics' websites and Facebook pages reduced their list dramatically: they weren't interested in fortune-tellers, tarot card readers, mind-readers and entertainers, healers, numerologists, or astrologers. More prospects were cut as they dug deeper and began eliminating channelers who spoke to specific familiars; intuitionists who specialized in advice about life decisions, or witches offering spells and potions.

At that point they realized they'd crossed off every single prospect with an online presence. They had seven remaining names they'd have to call for screening.

"What if they're all astrologers or witches or something?" asked Barbara, discouraged.

"Maybe we're looking under the wrong category," Olivia replied "Maybe we should look up ghost hunters."

"Good idea!" And so another round of research began.

This, too, was discouraging. Area ghost hunters were represented by websites that looked 15 years old and screamed *mad scientist.* Then there were people who arranged tours of reportedly haunted houses, buildings and landmarks, and people who lectured on paranormal topics.

"Some of these guys might be able to refer us to someone reputable," Barbara said, though without conviction.

"Maybe," Olivia agreed. "Why don't I call the people we still have on the list and if we strike out we can check with one of these groups?"

An hour, two "no-longer-in-service" messages and five completed phone calls later they had a single possibility: a professional medium who said she could see spirits. She had sounded intelligent and credible.

Still, Barbara hesitated.

"After all *we* can see him," Barbara said; "It's hearing him that's the problem."

"She said she's gone into trances and spoken for spirits," Olivia said.

Barbara's brows puckered.

"At some point I'm going to have to trust someone, but it's hard."

Olivia nodded. Then she looked at the time on the laptop and, with a squeak, announced she had to run.

"Is it that late already?" asked Barbara. "Wow, it's after five."

"Should I come back tomorrow and see if we can come up with some more names? I could come around 2:00 and stay til 5:00 again."

Barbara agreed and Olivia quickly gathered her purse, phone and a check from Barbara then jogged to her car. She had a cleaning appointment for the evening.

After Olivia left, Barbara put her phone in her pocket, called to Sabrina and headed out to the barn. She was expecting Reve to call and was debating whether she should drive into town to see him. But, as it turned out, he was unavailable, having gotten a last-minute request to do an appearance on CNN that evening.

"But I should be free tomorrow," Reve added quickly. "Should I come out or would you rather come into town?"

"Um, let's decide tomorrow. Olivia's coming back."

Barbara went on to describe the meagre results of their psychic-hunting efforts.

Reve, who was already in a low mood, fought his instinct to sink even lower and made some encouraging remarks.

Barbara replied in kind, and in an effort to cheer them both up, asked what time he'd be on television.

"Oh God, don't watch me," Reve said, with unexpected intensity. "I've got to present the conservative defense of Voter ID initiatives and you won't like it."

He didn't add that he, personally, knew Voter Fraud was virtually nonexistent and the Voter ID initiatives were poorly disguised efforts to make voting difficult for Democrat-leaning citizens. He didn't add everyone at IPR knew it as well. He didn't add that, until recently he hadn't cared. He did say he would much, much rather spend the evening with her.

"You would, huh?"

"More than anything. But — oh hell, I have to go. But let's do tomorrow, no matter what, okay?"

"Okay."

After they disconnected, Barbara squatted down and started stroking Sabrina and staring pensively at nothing.

I watch very little cable news. A few shows on CNN and MSNBC stand out, (FOX News is, of course, revolting and entirely unwatchable). But most of the time, anchors and guests seem to engage in a breathless tizzy of speculation lightly seasoned with reporting.

The same tired faces appear over and over, many whose analytical or predictive abilities have been proven woefully inadequate.

The "both sides do it" mentality prevails on most shows. Some event or issue is presented, then a "liberal" and "conservative" is brought on to "debate". (Or more often, three conservatives and one liberal, with the liberal nearly always occupying the center-left rather than the lefty-left.) Occasionally there's an interesting exchange, but usually you get a round of talking points and very little in the way of insightful comments or questions from the hosts. Factual corrections are also rare; people (almost always Republican) make inaccurate statements and assertions every day that go unchallenged. (A couple of the hosts do a good job on fact checking; most don't.)

Also glaringly absent is full disclosure about guests. People appear on news shows every day to support political positions that also financially benefit them or their connections. The financial benefit part is always suppressed.

Lefty leftists tend to make less money, sometimes almost no money — their focus and interests are simply different. It seems this lack of money-focus renders them ineligible for television (one of the reasons Republicans and conservatives outnumber Democrats and liberals by almost three to one on TV *every* week). Corporate-owned media is not interested in the views of people who think corporations have too much power, or think rich people or institutions shouldn't be able to write legislation, or buy legislators, judges or political offices.

So, I missed Reve Tierney on CNN. I was working on a blog post until one of my RSS feeds alerted me his appearance had not gone well. I started checking out my usual online haunts and Twitter. It took awhile for the video clip to be available online, so for a few hours I had to be satisfied with people's descriptions and commentary.

Apparently the topic of discussion was Voter ID legislation and Tierney was brought on to make the conservative case.

When I was able to watch the actual video I judged the fuss was a tempest in a teacup — almost. It wasn't like he completely crashed and burned, nor did he make some kind of painful gaffe that would forever rocket around the blogosphere. What people were reacting to was his delivery, variously described as "robotic", "detached", "off-key", "programmed". One blogger said Tierney looked like someone reading his own ransom note on camera.

Tierney recited the usual litany of talking points without enthusiasm, and you could see his Democratic counterpart sense weakness and pounce. Usually in these exchanges a certain amount of yelling and talking over one another occurs with the host mediating and deciding to whom to give the last word. In this segment, Tierney made his first statement and sat mum while his opponent took control and delivered a spirited denunciation of Voter ID efforts and their sponsors. Tierney's rebuttal was boilerplate, he deflected no specific charges. He was unemotional in the face of his opponent's zeal and he allowed himself to be quashed in mid-sentence. It was such unusual behavior for Tierney that the host actually asked him if he was feeling well, to which Tierney replied "I'm fine, thank you."

The host, recognizing it was up to him to deliver the formulaic "balance", began making some of Tierney's arguments for him which the Democrat swatted down with zest.

At that point, people had started tweeting positive comments about the Democrat and sarcastic or questioning comments about Tierney. No one on the right defended him.

Someone tweeted: "Hang it up Tierney. Your heart's not in it."

I started wondering if he was trying to get himself fired.

After Reve was through, he announced he had to go and promptly left the studio thus avoiding conversation with his recent opponent, host and other staffers. He frequently appeared on CNN and was well-liked; his performance elicited genuine concern.

His phone vibrated while he was still in the parking deck; it was Elliot and Reve let it go to message. Wondering if he was irrevocably burning his bridges, he got in his Mercedes and aimed it towards Barbara's farm.

Barbara had seen the show — she'd been unable to resist turning it on. In a detached way she'd wondered how she would react. She expected to deplore what he would say. Then what?

To her delight, she watched a performance she felt was just for her. Reve's appearance had been, judged by normal standards, terrible. His spiritless defense of voted ID legislation was acutely gratifying to Barbara.

She wondered if he would call her — he hadn't said he would and he wouldn't know she'd watched the show. She wondered if she should call him.

She turned off her television, called to Sabrina and strolled over to the barn. It was a warm evening, just a bit more light than dark. Nothing was happening or needed doing, she just felt restless and had no one to talk to. She wasn't ready to discuss Reve with anyone anyway.

After a period of aimless meandering she headed back towards the house, ultimately coming to rest on a chair at the south end of her wraparound porch. There seated, she stretched out her legs and, stroking Sabrina, began (although she didn't realize it) to wait.

Some thirty minutes later she saw a car turn into her driveway.

"Hello," she called, as Reve climbed out of his car. He'd had the air conditioner on; the warm, humid air slid over him, wilting his collar. He took off his jacket and tie and threw them into the backseat. Sabrina trotted up to him, sniffed gravely and returned to Barbara.

Reve approached the porch at a deliberate pace and halted in front of her.

"You watched?"

She nodded.

His sigh went on for a long time.

She got up, took his hand, and lead him to the porch stairs where they sat side by side with Sabrina curled up behind them.

For awhile they watched fireflies.

"I couldn't do it," he said.

"I know."

"That is, I did it, but every word — I had to force out each one. Then I got the hell out of there."

"I wondered if you'd come here."

He looked at her. She had her hair pinned up and was wearing a sleeveless white blouse and oatmeal-colored linen pants with a drawstring waist. Her hair was damp around her forehead; her sandaled feet carried bits of hay. She looked, in short, unthreatening. Unassuming. Which was completely deceptive.

"You did this to me," he said.

She smiled slightly but shook her head.

"I blame Dennis."

"No," he said firmly, "Dash knocked me off-balance. I teetered. I could have gone either way. You made me fall here."

At that she laughed and said "You're a free agent. The choice was yours."

"I didn't have any choice," he replied. "Not really."

Her smile became mischievous; she placed her hands on both sides of his face, leaned in, kissed him lightly and said "Was it my deeply principled philosophy of life that captured you? Or," she paused, kissing him again more forcefully, "was it my irresistible physical allure?"

"Both," he whispered. He threaded his hand through her hair, gripped and pulled her head back and began a ring of kisses around her neck. Just as she was starting to melt he stopped and said, "Plus, the sheep. Let's not forget the sheep."

They smiled at each other and, shakily, got to their feet.

"Have you eaten?" Barbara asked.

"Um . . . no. I never seem to eat these days."

"C'mon," she said, taking his hand. "Let's get you fed. Are you going to spend the night?"

"I don't know. I didn't pack anything. I wasn't planning to come tonight. And I'll have to face the music tomorrow."

"Are you . . . what will you do?"

"I don't know."

She wanted to say 'Quit tonight! Start over! Anything's better than what you do now!' but she didn't. She just led him to her kitchen.

I was still reading tweets and comments on blog posts about Reve Tierney's CNN appearance when Peter finally called. I'd been in suspense all day wondering how his meeting with Wayland had gone.

Turned out Wayland had zeroed in on the poverty simulation as a potential kick-off to a possible new strategy to beat his ultra-right primary challenger. He wasn't sold, but was cautiously interested.

"He doesn't want to try to out-conservative his opponent." Peter said. "He doesn't think it will work because he doesn't think he can be convincing. He's actually, if you can believe it, reached his limit."

"No kidding!"

"Nope. He considers himself a conservative Republican, and thinks the Tea Partiers aren't really Republicans."

"Amazing."

"I know. He brought Thornery in and had him shift his schedule around. We spent 3 hours talking about how to position him as — don't barf — a compassionate conservative. For real."

"For real as in he's suddenly discovered compassion? Or, for real as in he's decided pretending to have compassion might be a winning strategy?"

"I don't know. But my thinking is I'd rather have him try to do some good regardless of why. And who knows? Maybe he'll learn to like it."

"He could make a bunch of promises and renege as soon as he's re-elected," I countered. "Happens all the time."

"He absolutely could. He might. I can only hope he won't. And, at least, I can keep my job a little longer without feeling like a fraud. I'm going to treat him like he means it."

"You're trying to save him aren't you?"

"Oh, he's been saved."

"I don't think he's been saved the way you've been saved."

"Well . . . only God knows what's truly in his heart."

"Yeah," I said a bit sourly. It was going to be *truly* ironic if my idea became the starting point of a winning campaign for Wayland. But then, I decided Wayland would probably beat whatever Democrat was mustered to run against him anyway and separately, while Wayland was detestable, his Tea Party opponent was even worse.

And there was probably at least a twenty percent chance Peter could be a positive influence on Wayland.

"So, is he going to do the poverty simulation Thursday?" I asked. "Are you? I am. Should I pretend not to know you if you're there?"

"He hasn't decided. Or hadn't when I left today. Thornery was worried because he wouldn't be in charge of the event. You know how things go — congresspeople hardly ever do anything spontaneous. Everything is figured out in advance. Also, you don't have to pretend not to know me. I told him about you."

"You did?"

"I said I'd been working with a career counselor and if he comes, I'll introduce you. I'd rather not pretend. Although, I didn't tell him about Connie. I really do think that's personal. Plus, it could cause problems for her too. We'll come out, so to speak, after I resign."

"You're right. Both your bosses would have reason to be paranoid about the two of you exchanging information. Although, it can't be fun to have to be so secretive."

"It's getting old," Peter agreed. "Hopefully it won't be for much longer."

"Did Wayland seem to know about anything?"

"Nope. He did just what you suspected he would — he got me to talk by giving me a significant look and a leading question. I could have denied everything. Maybe I should have, just to see what he might have said."

"It would have been nice to know."

Peter agreed, then he chuckled. He was jazzed.

While Barbara puttered around the kitchen warming up dinner leftovers, Reve sat at her kitchen table staring at his phone. Elliot had called twice and sent an email asking what had gone wrong on CNN.

Reve was debating what to do. The last two days had been ordeals. He decided to take a sick day Wednesday. He would send an email telling Elliot he'd been hit with an intestinal complaint and would blame his poor television performance on a painful stomach. Elliot might not believe it, but it would buy time. He'd call Melvin Thornery and schedule something. He'd help Barbara find a psychic; they'd get Dash's message and maybe then he'd know what to do next.

It was a plan.

He sent the email and got an "OK" in reply followed by a "We'll talk Thursday."

He spent the night. They'd retired soon after he'd eaten; partly because he was exhausted and partly because, despite his exhaustion, all he wanted to do was make love. The result had been brief and shatteringly intense.

For Reve, the physical build up and release mirrored the emotional turmoil he'd been experiencing — the collision of his previous life with his desire for her. At first, he was primal — *this*, his body said, is what's at stake — everything about my life will be sacrificed for *you*.

And her body said: claim your reward.

Then there was just deep satisfaction.

Reve was soon asleep; spent, empty and temporarily at peace. Barbara had lain awake for awhile, trying to get at the underlying meaning of the encounter, certain there had been a meaning but one she couldn't form into words. Nothing definite emerged so she abandoned the effort and drifted off.

Chapter Fifteen

Wednesday dawned hot and sunny. Barbara awoke at 7:30 and padded down to the kitchen to make coffee.

She moved quietly. Reve was still asleep and she thought he needed as much sleep as he could get. Big decisions were pending and, she suspected, he was likely to feel worse before he felt better.

Barbara wanted Reve to leave his job, *but not for her.* He needed to leave because what he was doing hurt people and made the world worse instead of better. She thought he was working his way to that realization but he hadn't arrived.

Would Dennis's message get him there? Something had happened to Dennis when he'd died, something so devastating he'd literally refused to finish dying. She had been so angry at Dennis for so long; so disgusted at the misuse of his gifts that she'd felt, she suddenly recognized, little sympathy for him.

Mostly, she thought, whatever he was suffering he had it coming. The scales had to be balanced somehow. If there was any sort of afterlife, it must involve some kind of accounting for the life just lived. She didn't believe in hell (that was firm), but everything else was fuzzy. She was attracted to the concept of *Karma* but had, she knew, a fairly superficial grasp of its purported workings. She'd read enough to know Buddhism and Hinduism held disparate views about Karma and how it manifested. She preferred the Buddhist approach, at least insofar as she did not accept the Hindu concept of caste. But she knew there were intricacies she'd never explored. Both Hindus and Buddhists believed in reincarnation, an idea that attracted her. However, she wasn't sure reincarnation was real and didn't know how to be sure.

Beyond Karma, she also retained a vague belief in purgatory. Really, it boiled down to the idea that there must be some kind of accounting after death. God might love the worst sinner, but did he/she simply welcome a mass murderer into heaven without any sort of reparation required?

The point is, she told herself, she didn't want Reve to undergo whatever it was Dash was experiencing. She didn't want Reve to *deserve* it.

She reflected while the coffee dripped, staring out her kitchen window.

When the pot was filled, she poured a cup, added some cream and sipped thoughtfully.

She recalled the previous night with a shiver of desire. Their views might diverge, but their bodies aligned in complete agreement. Why hadn't they met years ago?

Sabrina, who conducted series of rounds about the farm every day and night, trotted into the kitchen through her dog door. She looked at Barbara, as much as to say "all present and correct ma'am!" and sat. Barbara crooned a greeting and patted Sabrina's smooth head approvingly. They both turned at the sound of Reve entering from the hallway.

Before retiring he'd remembered he had a set of workout clothes in his car and thus was able to don a red t-shirt and a pair of grey athletic shorts. His feet were bare, his hair rumpled and his face in need of a shave.

"I was trying not to wake you," Barbara said.

He dropped a kiss on the top of her head.

"Good morning!" he replied, smiling, then he stroked Sabrina's head.

"I usually get up around now," he added.

He strolled to the sink and looked out the window; Barbara joined him there.

"It's going to be another scorcher today," he said.

She nodded and went to pour him a cup of coffee. He took it, thanked her, and went to the refrigerator for cream while Barbara fetched a spoon.

Enjoying the simple domesticity of the morning coffee ritual, they meandered to the kitchen table to sit and contemplate their drinks and one-another.

"Is it too soon to ask if we can do this for the rest of our lives?" Reve said. Then they both processed what he'd said and a kind of electricity passed between them.

Barbara looked at him searchingly, then smiled and said "Probably . . . yes, it's too soon. But provisionally, no, it's not too soon since I was thinking the same thing. Although . . . "

"I know. There's things to resolve first and Dash to get settled. It was premature. It's just that right now I'm so happy and yesterday I was so unhappy."

Barbara got up, stepped behind his chair, snaked her arms around his neck and rested her chin lightly on the top of his head.

"I'm glad you're happy today," she said.

Reve covered her hands with his own for a moment, then lifted her right hand to his lips.

"I am," he said firmly. To hell with everything, he thought for good measure. Except this.

He rose and pulled Barbara into his arms, pressing her head against his chest. Then Barbara began to chuckle.

"What?" Reve asked, stepping back.

"Honey — "

"Yes?"

"Your shirt is a bit . . . ripe."

"Oh god, I'm sorry! It's been in the car since my last work out — "

"Not a problem! I have a washer and everything!"

Olivia was enjoying her second information interview. She was meeting with Steven Wrayner who, in partnership with his wife, ran a small but growing permaculture practice (Wrayner-Kirk Permaculture, Inc.). Steve was a close friend of Natalie's brother and his older sister had been a client of Wynne's.

Olivia met him at his home office in Tacoma Park and was introduced to his wife (who was on her way out), and two other young men who were likewise passing through.

Steven was a medium-sized man in his late thirties with an athletic build and a closely-cropped, wavy, dark red hair. He was wearing a blue polo shirt and tan chinos, which was "dressed up" for him, he explained. His normal garb was beat up shorts or pants with lots of pockets, t-shirts, and canvas hats to keep the sun off — utilitarian clothes he didn't have to worry about since he spent most of his days outdoors either physically laboring or observing a habitat.

They'd settled in his crowded office at a large table that looked like it functioned as both a work surface and meeting space. His computer was on a corner desk surrounded by stacks of books, catalogs and drawing tablets.

"The basic idea," Steve explained, "is to deliberately mimic the way nature optimizes every element in a particular landscape or ecosystem."

Olivia blinked.

"Okaaay," she said. "And that means?"

Steve laughed.

"In nature, nothing is wasted, especially effort, because everything serves more than one purpose. Different parts of plants feed or water different creatures whose activities support other plants, animals, insects, worms, birds, etc. One animal's poop is another creature's dinner. Plants are mixed and scattered instead of clumped altogether in one place which keeps them from being eaten wholesale. You know how your backyard garden attracts various pests?"

"You mean like slugs or rabbits or deer?"

"Right. Most people's gardens are stuck in the middle of a cleared space with all their crops planted in groups. Easy access and bountiful offerings — can you blame the rabbit for raiding your garden when you're providing row upon row of his favorite food?"

"I see what you mean."

"In a healthy microenvironment or ecosystem, the mixture of plants, animals, birds, bugs, worms, fungi and so on control pests, diseases and predators. The rabbit has to forage for his food; he'll never find it all or eat it all. Furthermore, the rabbit doesn't have to plant his food year after year, it just grows. It grows as the byproduct of the activities of other creatures. Likewise, in nature you don't have to do all kinds of things to replenish the soil because nature takes care of it. Healthy soil has a lot of living things in it and they, just by living, replenish the soil. They aerate it. They fertilize it by breaking down nature's wastes and becoming nature's wastes to be broken down by other creatures."

"So, the way I do my gardening is all wrong?" Olivia asked, dismayed.

"No, no, not *wrong*. It's a perfectly valid approach and yields foods and flowers, right?"

"Right," she said, looking happier.

"It takes a lot of work, though, doesn't it? Hoeing, planting, weeding and dealing with pests?"

"Isn't that what gardening *is*?"

"It's a kind of gardening, yes. But using permaculture techniques would allow you, over time, to reduce your labor requirements dramatically while improving your soil and your harvest."

He briefly listed and described the techniques involved while Olivia began taking notes. Then he went on.

"But permaculture isn't only about gardening or agriculture, although that's where it started. Permaculture is about getting the greatest use out of any environment or endeavor. Landscaping, for instance. A permaculturalist will look at every element in a space — the buildings, the water sources, roads, sidewalks, trees down the street — and create a landscape that use those elements to support edible and ornamental plants, trees, fruits, berries, and mushrooms for humans. But also for other critters who, in exchange, provide services to the space. They may sow seeds, improve soil, eat or repel predator insects, protect fruit trees and on and on. They also help support spaces humans like to inhabit."

"That sounds really interesting!"

"It is! And we're not done yet. You can use permaculture principles to plan or improve neighborhoods, clean up polluted ground or water, retrofit cityscapes and reclaim lands that have been abused. Places where the soil is depleted or is getting washed away can be regenerated. You can create oases in deserts and combat draughts."

Olivia's eyes gleamed. Noting this, Steve gave her a list of books to read and websites to visit. He described some of his company's current and recent projects including a brownfield site with contaminated soil.

"They're all over the place," Steve explained. "Manufacturers have contaminated air, water and soil, but so have others. For years people didn't know any better and they dumped or disposed of chemicals in their yards. Houses and buildings shed lead paint into the ground. Military bases are very toxic to their environment. Old gas stations have buried tanks that leak; dry cleaners use solvents that contaminate soil. And on and on. We're doing some experimentation on a contaminated site to see what works. We believe the knowledge we gain is going to be incredibly important as time goes on and the scale of environmental contamination becomes clear."

That topic sparked a particularly potent surge of interest in Olivia. She liked cleaning things — the concept of cleaning soil itself was intriguing. She liked the idea of taking dirt — something she worked to banish — and converting it to soil, something that had value. She said as much to Steve and he was delighted. He offered to take her to the brownfield site and show her what they were doing and why.

"I'm going there this afternoon if you're free," he added.

Olivia said she'd love to go but she'd have to get back to him with a date as she had another appointment that afternoon.

When they were winding up the meeting they chatted about the contacts they had in common: Natalie and Wynne.

"So Wynne did her psychic thing with you, eh?" he said.

"What?"

"Her psychic thing," he repeated. To her surprised look her, he said: "didn't you know?"

"I knew she was *intuitive* but we never really talked about it. I don't think of her as a psychic."

"Well, I guess it's all a matter of degree. She helped my sister you know. Wynne read her and knew exactly what she needed to do and my sister has never been happier."

"So she read me?"

"Don't take my word for it. Ask her."

"Oh I will," Olivia said, smiling sunnily, "I will."

As she walked to her car, Olivia wondered if Wynne could be the person they'd been looking for. Olivia knew psychics had different specialties and Wynne's ability in one area might not translate to ability in a different area. Was it worth finding out?

Barbara's biggest concern was confidentiality. Olivia thought Wynne was trustworthy. Even if Wynne couldn't hear Barbara's brother speak, maybe she'd find a different way to help. Maybe she could read the ghost like she read people.

Should she talk to Wynne and get a reaction before approaching Barbara? It might save her from having to spend another afternoon looking for psychics — not that she minded! The money was good. But it was a long drive to the farm and there was no guarantee they'd get results. And if she didn't need to go to the farm, she could go with Steve to check out the brownfield instead.

She looked at her watch. She had a little over an hour before she needed to start the drive if she was going to Barbara's. She drummed her fingers on the steering wheel. She called Barbara and explained her thinking about Wynne.

"Your career counselor? She's the woman who knows Sonya, right?" asked Barbara.

"Right. I just thought of her because this man I interviewed with this morning was talking about her being psychic. She'd worked with his sister. She doesn't make a big deal out of it and it just didn't occur to me before. I don't know if she's the right kind of psychic, but she reads people — maybe she could read your brother?"

Barbara hesitated.

"The thing is I trust her," Olivia said after a moment.

There was more silence, then Barbara said she wanted to talk to Reve and would call right back. Could she wait?

"Sure thing."

Olivia remembered a sandwich shop a few blocks away from Steve's house and decided to head over and get some lunch. Then, she'd either drive over to Barbara's or she could call Steve and ask to go with him after all.

She was in mid-chew when her phone played Barbara's ringtone.

Barbara had decided to give Wynne a try.

"When can you talk to her?" Barbara asked.

"I can call her now and see when she might be free; I want to talk to her in person. I'll let you know when we've talked. That may not be until this evening, okay?

"Certainly. And thanks!"

Olivia's next call was to Steve.

"Steve? This is Olivia. We just interviewed — "

"I haven't forgotten!"

They both laughed.

"Well, my schedule has changed and I'd like to go see the brownfield with you if the offer's still open."

"Terrific! When can you get back here?"

"I'm eating lunch a few blocks away. When did you plan to leave?"

"When I finished eating. So, swing on by when you're done and that should be about right. See you soon!"

Good! she thought. She munched the remains of her ham and turkey sub, finished the last of her chips, wiped her hands, and then called Wynne.

Wynne could see her after 3:00 p.m. Enjoying a sense of accomplishment, she cleared up her booth and departed.

Olivia asked if she could stop over briefly to talk about something delicate. I was wrestling with a blog post that was fighting back and I welcomed the interruption. I poured us both some iced tea and we settled down in my living room. She embarked on her story.

"You're kidding, right?" was my first response.

"I swear to God."

"A ghost. You saw a ghost, Barbara Tishkin's brother, at Reve Tierney's condo?"

She told me the story again, ending with her startling notion that I could do something about it.

"Me? Why me? I don't know anything about spirits or exorcisms!"

"But you're psychic and they need someone who can find out what the ghost wants to tell Mr. Tierney."

"But — "

"Barbara has been really nice to me and I know you'll like her. And Mr. Tierney is stressed."

"Stressed, is he? Do you know who Barbara's brother is? Was?"

"No."

"Dash Fordhyme."

"Dash Fordhyme, Dash Fordhyme," Olivia murmured, trying to place him.

"Radio guy. Total creep. Sexist, racist, misogynistic jerk."

"Oh, *him.* I've heard about him. Euw."

"Exactly. To be fair to Barbara, I'm told she totally rejected his schtick so we shouldn't hold him against her."

Olivia mused for awhile.

"It had to be hard for Barbara," she said. "And now she has to deal with his ghost and that's hard too. Although," she added, with a sudden glint in her eye, "now I know who he is, I'm curious what he's got to say. Aren't you?"

It was my turn to muse. Yes, I was curious. Assuming this was on the level and not some bizarre mistake.

I admitted to curiosity.

"Okay then. If Barbara says she'd like your help you'll do it?"

"I'll *try* to do it. I have no idea whether I'll be able to — what will I be trying to do?"

"To *hear* him. He talks but they can't hear him."

"I see . . . what did you tell Barbara about me?"

"I said you read people and you figure out things."

"Hmm."

After another minute, I said: "I take it you believe in ghosts."

"I do now!"

She told me about her father and his story about the man who'd been lynched. Very disturbing.

"But this isn't like that," she said. "Barbara isn't scared."

"Hmm," I said again.

In principle, I have no problem with the idea of ghosts. I believe in reincarnation. And if reincarnation is real, then there must be a whole lot of other stuff going on. I also believe in free will and if *that's* real, then a slew of implications must follow such as souls going AWOL or getting angry (at things like being lynched). And the idea of dealing directly with a ghost — the idea of simply *seeing* a ghost — was eerie but exciting.

Although, it would have been nice if the ghost was someone I liked, or, at least, didn't dislike. Still, it would be interesting to find out what Dash Fordhyme had to say about being dead.

Chapter Sixteen

Peter spent Wednesday morning conferring with Reverend Fenimore about the poverty simulation scheduled for Thursday evening. Congressman Wayland had provisionally agreed to participate although Peter harbored some doubts: he thought it quite possible Wayland would change his mind at the last minute.

He, Wayland and Thornery had considered and debated a new approach — based around the central idea of "less judging, more caring" — to Congressman Wayland's campaign. Peter argued strenuously in favor of the new approach, asserting that if they went for it, no holds barred, they could generate a massive buzz and, more importantly, get their opponent on the defensive.

Thornery worried it would backfire, alienating many of their longtime supporters while failing to convince a very cynical press corps that Wayland was sincere.

That, Peter said, was why the poverty simulation was useful.

"If it's persuasive, it can be the impetus. The Congressman can start to talk about it in his appearances and everything can unfold organically from there."

"What if it isn't persuasive?" Thornery asked, "What if it's a waste of time?"

"Then we wasted a few hours. Who cares? We don't have to go public with it and if the press finds out he participated, we can say he learned some things and move on."

Everyone looked at Wayland who had been uncharacteristically quiet throughout their meetings. It was obvious he was undecided, but the sheer fact that he was entertaining the idea was significant.

Eventually, the pressure of expectant stares goaded him into speech.

"I haven't made up my mind, but I'm seriously considering it," he said. "Melvin makes good points, but so does Peter. One thing is definite: I have to do *something* or hang it up. I have a legacy to think about, too. Maybe I'm just gonna lose this time, but I won't go down whimpering."

Voices blended together in a chorus of encouragement.

"On the other hand, a major shift in emphasis is going to scare some supporters and donors . . . " he trailed off.

"If we lose some extremists, can we gain some moderates?" Peter asked.

"Which people are those?" Thornery asked. "Where you come from those people are called Democrats and they don't vote for us."

"Yeah, but you know people didn't used to be so hardcore," Peter said. "And something has to change. We know demographics are against us if we keep narrowing our message."

"That's way more important for senators, governors and presidents. Congressional districts are much smaller slices of the pie and our district is very red," Thornery replied.

"But you know there's Christian Red and Libertarian Red and they're not the same things. Tea Partiers have a Libertarian focus — they're about lowering taxes and cutting the social safety net. My people are dead set against cutting social security. Basically it's a battle between a Libertarian and a Christian."

"Our opponent is a Christian."

"Well, what kind of Christian? That's what it comes down to."

"Peter, that's not something we want to debate. It's better if we leave that alone and don't make voters have to take a position on their flavor of Christianity."

"Yeah, but it's a primary challenge. We have to create some kind of contrast don't we?"

"Contrast, yes, but not that way. Anyway, if you challenge people on a religious front they'll just get defensive and close down. We will not win by telling voters they're the wrong kind of Christian."

After a pause, Peter agreed it would be poor strategy.

Thornery was generous in victory.

"We do have to create contrast, though, you're right," he said.

And so it went on. In the end, Wayland decided to participate in the poverty simulation if only to settle the question of whether it could provide an angle they could use.

"We haven't come up with anything else — Peter's is the only idea on the table. So lets see if it has legs."

On that basis, Peter had set about making arrangements to get Wayland to the event and enable him to participate without disrupting it for other participants (or generating undue attention).

"I can't make people sign non-disclosure forms," Reverend Fenimore said when Peter called him. "If the Congressman participates, people are going to talk about it. They'll have it on Facebook before we even start. Which, I am fine with, by the way. I'm thrilled he's coming and his involvement will draw attention to the issue which is just what I want."

"The problem is we don't want people demanding his reaction before he has a chance to think about it."

"Did you know Congresswoman Tesarik is participating too? And Connie?"

"I knew Connie was broaching the idea, but didn't know if Tesarik had agreed. So she has, huh? That might just scare Wayland off." He'd have to tell Thornery and Wayland and it wouldn't surprise him if they summarily pulled out.

"I can't tell you how to do your job, Peter, and I'm no political strategist. But I think it would be a terrible shame of the Congressman avoided this chance to learn something important because he feared — what, exactly?"

"Being labeled bipartisan. Doesn't fly too well where I come from."

"My, my. Is that inevitable?"

"Depends. The media is incredibly predictable unless we push the right frame. And we haven't figured out what the frame is yet."

"I see. Hmm. Well Peter, if he changes his mind we'll just have to live with it. You'll still come won't you?"

"Absolutely. If nothing else I'd be able to tell him what it was like and maybe get him to another one."

"I'd like every single member of Congress to go through one of these."

"I know. Seems pretty unlikely though doesn't it?"

"You never know. Anyway, do your best and call me if you need anything else."

After disconnecting, Peter put his chin in his hand and started thinking. He wished he could consult Wynne. Failing that, could he think like her? What would she advise if he *did* consult her?

After the meeting broke up, Congressman Wayland pulled Thornery aside.

"Have you spoken to Tierney yet?"

"He's supposed to call me this afternoon."

"See if you can convince him to meet me at this thing. I'd really like to get his take on it and on Peter's idea."

"I'll see what he says."

Good! Thornery thought to himself. Tierney will tell him not to take the risk. I hope.

I had a very pleasantly surreal conversation with Barbara Tishkin. She'd gotten my number from Olivia and called me just before dinner.

She sounded a bit shy, but very nice and pretty much the opposite of Dash Fordhyme. After some hesitation, she took the plunge and told me the story, winding up with Olivia's suggestion that I might be able to act as a medium and help them learn whatever it was Dash Fordhyme was trying to tell them.

I had already decided I'd give it crack, but I felt compelled to offer full disclosure about my opinion of Dash Fordhyme and Reve Tierney first.

"I think you have a right to know I was not a Dash Fordhyme fan, nor, for that matter, a fan of Reve Tierney's," I said. "I would be doing it for you, not them."

There was a pause.

"I wasn't a fan of Dash's either," she replied. "But at one time I was close to my brother Dennis, and that is really who I'm concerned about."

She spoke slowly, seeming to choose her words carefully.

"Like you," she went on, "I also don't like Reve Tierney's . . . politics. I had never met him until Dennis died and all this started. But since we met we've gotten rather . . . close. I'd appreciate it if you could meet him with an open mind."

"Fair enough," I said.

"I can't make any promises," I added. "I'm *sensitive,* but I've never attempted anything like this before. I'd like to try, though. I understand why you'd want to keep all this quiet and I promise you I won't betray you, even if you change your mind about me. But I feel constrained to say that you might do better with someone more experienced."

"I appreciate your honesty and you're probably right. But you can see my difficulty."

According to Barbara, Dash had indicated he could appear at will and would be waiting for us so it was down to my availability. Barbara wanted to proceed as soon as possible. Their lives (hers and presumably Reve Tierney's) were in a kind of limbo, she said, but didn't elaborate.

Reve was apparently spoken for on Thursday, as was I, and Friday was questionable for him. We decided to meet at Reve Tierney's on Saturday morning.

In the Spirit World, Xe and Veliastan confer:

"Wynne has agreed to help Barbara and Reve. She is intrigued."

"Excellent, Xe! You have merged with Neriante many times now; are you enjoying it?

"Very much. Will she be able to hear Dash?"

"Not physically, but I will ensure she receives his words telepathically. It will *seem* to her that she is hearing them — that will be less unsettling for her."

"And Dash?"

"If this works, Lersaliaz believes he'll be ready to come home."

"He will have a happier homecoming."

"Yes. He has difficult times ahead. He will have to prove himself and overcome many trials."

"Will that happen to me?"

"It is not inevitable. It is expected souls will make mistakes and do wrongs, especially in their early incarnations. I did, Lersaliaz did and you will. You cannot learn otherwise. But some do more wrong than others and consequently have larger karmic debts. A very few will fail so disastrously they will never be allowed back. I do not anticipate any such outcome for you."

Chapter Seventeen

This, I thought, is one for the memoirs. I would be participating in an exercise designed to enlighten people about daily life for modern Americans living in poverty, in the company of Reve Tierney (a man I had hitherto despised but now felt a bit sorry for) and Congressman Wayland (a man I still despised). Also participating were Connie Milleray, Peter Gilen and Congresswoman Tesarik.

There were forty-five of us in groups of three to six persons. Each group represented a household with a cast of characters and a storyline based on real life situations. An additional sixteen people portrayed service providers with whom people in poverty typically interact. They manned tables around the room with signs: School, Department of Health & Human Services, Mortgage Company, PayDay Lender, Pawn Shop, Police Department, Grocery/Drug Store, Bank, General Employer, Homeless Shelter, Local Charity Service, Food Bank, and Daycare Center.

Facilitating was the Reverend Fenimore, a dynamic, charismatic individual who was visibly delighted at having netted two Congresspeople for the event.

So there we were, knee to knee in groups of chairs that filled the basement of Fenimore's church. Most of the participants were church members; a smattering were friends of members. Based on wardrobes, grooming, and cars in the parking lot, this group was reasonably well off. Which was the point, of course. People already struggling financially don't need a simulation to illuminate what it feels like.

The six of us were divided as follows: Congresswoman Tesarik was in a group that included Connie and a young man; Peter was in a group with a teenaged girl, an older man and and a middle-aged woman, and I was in a group with Wayland, Tierney and a young woman named Lily. We were surrounded by similar mixtures of age, sex and race though most of the people were white. While awaiting direction, group members exchanged names.

"Nice to meet you Congressman Wayland," I lied, "my name is Wynne Frost."

Wayland smiled heartily and shook hands. I think hearty is his game face. He assumes a hearty persona in public and he'd been beaming heartiness at people since his arrival. But then recognition dawned and he said "Wynne Frost, eh?" with less enthusiasm.

So, I thought, Peter had told him who I was. Although, in what terms I didn't know. I waited to see if he had anything further to say, but he didn't so I turned to shake hands with Reve Tierney.

He cleared his throat and said: "How do you do, Wynne. I'm Reve Tierney."

"Nice to meet you," I replied. I gathered he was with Wayland, presumably in an advisory capacity. I knew he occasionally consulted on Wayland's campaigns.

Separately, I was to meet him Saturday to deal with his haunting and could tell he was concerned lest I let the cat out of the bag. So, I generated an expression of utter blankness, hoping to telegraph my intention to be discreet, and decided, as his expression relaxed, the message had been received.

We sat and an awkward silence began to build between the three of us. (Lily was unaffected.) Then, Wayland tapped Congresswoman Tesarik on the shoulder and they had a low-voiced exchange. Connie and I spoke and Reve Tierney stared at his knees.

Turning from Connie (who's chair was backed up against the back of mine), I tried to get a read on Tierney but couldn't glean much. The result, I think, of the press of people, my awareness of all the secrets I was juggling, and Tierney's self-protective psychic shield. This guy, I thought, is feeling fragile and needs to guard his "himness" from the world. Was this normal or the result of his being haunted?

Must be weird to be haunted, I thought, it would freak anybody out. Then I reflected bitterly on the fact that I was rubbing elbows with two people I'd have paid money to be able to throw pies at, and conditions were exactly wrong for me to voice my distaste to either one. Wayland was doing a good thing, probably for the wrong reasons, but nevertheless. And, Tierney was radiating a high degree of vulnerability. With a sigh, I decided to repress my hostility and focus on the exercise.

Reverend Fenimore mounted a small dais at the front of the room and asked for our attention. With some shifting of chairs by those facing the other way, we quieted and he began.

"I want to welcome you all and give a special shout out to Congresswoman Tesarik and Congressman Wayland!"

He waved in their direction; they waved in acknowledgement and people clapped.

"The purpose of this simulation is to give all of you a visceral sense of how it feels to be poor in America today. Americans hold a lot of views about folks who live in poverty, but as the saying goes, 'never judge a man until you've walked a mile in his moccasins.' That's what this evening is about."

"I can recite statistics (he did) and, now that you've heard them, what do you think we should do? I won't put our Congresspeople on the spot and we don't have time for a discussion but, with a show of hands, how many of you have something to suggest?"

Four tentative hands went up and the rest of us looked a bit sheepish. Fenimore nodded, point made.

"We'll see what we think after the simulation. Here's what I ask of you: make a mental list of your beliefs about poor people in this country. What are your attitudes towards them? How do you think they got where they are? Why don't they simply make more money? Why don't they just pull themselves up by their bootstraps? Some of them have big screen televisions and most of them have some kind of cell phone. What do you think about that? Don't tell me" he said, as some hands went up, "just make that mental list. We'll revisit it later."

After a pause, while we did as directed, he resumed.

"Let's get started. Our volunteers are going to distribute information packets and I'm going to give you a few minutes to read your family description which will describe your group's circumstances. Then I'll explain the rules of the exercise."

I was handed a name-tag and a clear vinyl packet. The name tag had a paragraph on the back which I read out loud: "I am Gemma Gordon, age 30. I am a high-school graduate who works in retail. I would like full-time hours, but never get more than thirty hours a week and my schedule constantly changes. I earn $8.00 an hour, 75 cents more than minimum wage in my state."

The name tag was on a cord so it could be hung around my neck. I put it on and looked at Tierney and Wayland.

As the swell of everyone reading their name tags surrounded us, Tierney read the description on his: "I am George Gordon, age 32, employed full-time earning $9.25/hour, two dollars an hour above minimum wage in my state. I have a high-school education and a year of community college, general coursework."

Tierney hung his name tag around his neck and we looked at Wayland.

"I am Gerald Gordon," Wayland read, "age 60, widower, George's father and Gemma's father-in-law. My wife died a few years ago and I am still paying off medical bills. When she became ill our insurance costs skyrocketed and then my employer went out of business and I lost my job and insurance. After my unemployment benefits lapsed, I was unable to get a full time job and worked part-time and under-the-table jobs. I began drinking after my wife's death and was convicted of a DUI. My driver's license is suspended for a year. I had been living off my dwindling 401K, which I funded with a lump sum pension buyout when my employer closed. It lost 40% of it's value in the 2008 crash and is now gone. My kids moved in with me to help with expenses until I can collect Social Security."

Lily was next: "I am Gina Gordon, age 8. I am a good student, but I have asthma and sometimes miss school due to flare ups."

"Okaay" I said, while Wayland placed his name tag around his neck. Then he and Tierney looked back at me. I pulled the sheet out of the vinyl packet headlined "Family Situation" and read it out loud.

"Gerald's house is paid off so there are no mortgage payments, but there are monthly house insurance and property tax payments. Gerald owns an older model car; George has a newer model car with four more years of payments.

Due to his license suspension, Gerald cannot drive. Gemma's been using Gerald's car to get to work.

The Gordons live in a suburb with no bus line within two miles. Gina rides a bus to school.

When the Gordons moved in with Gerald they shared expenses, but Gerald's 401k ran out three months ago and each month since the family has fallen further behind. Gemma occasionally gets more work hours, but not enough to cover their shortfalls.

After taxes George brings home $1100 a month and Gemma brings home $700/month, so income is $1800 a month for four.

Expenses

$200/mo George's car payment: due Week-2

$120/month house insurance/property tax payment: due Week-2

$90/mo to insure both cars: due Week-2

$250/month gas, electric, water, trash: due Week-2

$120/month phones: due Week-3

$150/month payment plan for Gerald's wife's medical bills: due Week-3

$300/month gas for both cars

$90/mo cable/internet access: due Week-3

$70/mo health insurance for Gerald: due Week-3

> $80 past due for utilities: paid $20 less then full amount due for gas, electric, water and trash.
>
> $90 for car insurance: you are not cancelled, but you are in the grace period before cancellation.
>
> Must pay car insurance in Week-1 to avoid cancellation.
>
> Must make a second payment of $90 for car insurance in Week-4 to meet this month's obligation.
>
> $2040 - $1800 = $240 deficit + $80 past due utilities + $90 last month's car insurance = $410 deficit.
>
> You will begin the month $410 short of what you need for your month's payments due, your past due utilities balances, and ongoing expenses such as food, gas, toiletries. Plus, unexpected costs. You have no savings.
>
> You must make sure Gina goes to school every school-day.
>
> You must get food in Week-1; your cupboards are bare.
>
> You must pay the utilities by the end of Week-2 or expect a shut-off notice and an additional fee to reinstate service.
>
> Gerald must be able to go to an AA meeting twice a week and keep a telephone to ensure access to his sponsor or he will begin to drink again."

I stopped. We all took a minute to absorb what I'd read.

I went on: "Okay, so we need an additional $410 to catch up for last month."

"$410?" said Wayland, "That seems manageable."

Tierney looked skeptical while Lily looked rarin' to go. Then, Reverend Fenimore called us to attention.

"By now you should know your family's situation. Now check your packet for your easily sellable assets and available cash."

I pulled out a stack of cards.

"It looks like we have a ring, worth $100; a television, worth $100; a digital camera, worth $100; furniture, worth $250; a microwave, worth $50; a refrigerator, worth $100; and a stove, worth $100."

There were two bus passes with a face value of one dollar each.

A sheet said:

> Gas for George's drives to work each day is $50/week or $10/day. Gas for Gemma's commute is $20/week or $5/day. Gemma works 4 days/

week. There is no bus route available for George, but Gemma *could* ride the bus. She would have to travel two miles to the bus stop and must have a bus pass for each trip to work and home. Plus, a pass for any other place she visits by bus. Gerald can also use the bus and must have a pass for every place he visits by bus as well as a pass to return home. You must purchase more bus passes if you run out.

Alternatively, Gemma can drive George to work, then drive on to her job. Her shift ends an hour later than George's. He would have to wait for her to pick him up. The utility office, bank, government office and community services office will all be closed by that time. The grocery store, food pantry, homeless shelter, Payday lender and pawn shop would be open.

If George leaves work for an emergency he will lose a day's pay. If Gemma leaves work for an emergency, she will lose a day's pay. Any work days missed mean a loss of the day's pay.

There were two cards with boxes for the twenty work days in the month: one for George and one for Gemma. We were to check off each completed work day. At the end of Week-1 and Week-3 we would get paychecks.

There were Social Security cards for each of us and $30 in Monopoly money.

Lastly, there were four little notepads and several sharp pencils.

After reading the instructions, numbers started to blur in my head. Mutely, I offered the sheet to Tierney, who scanned it quickly, grunted, and handed it to an impatiently waiting Congressman Wayland.

Poor Lily, we kept saving her for last. She had just started reading the instructions when Reverend Fenimore began again.

"OK, here are the rules. Our month is composed of four 15-minute segments. I will blow a whistle to start and end each one. People employed full-time must report to General Employer over here," he pointed to the table at his right, "and must stay there for the first seven minutes of each 15 minute period. Part-timers report there," he pointed to a table at his left with a sign: Part-Time Employer, "and stay there for the first 5 minutes of each 15-minute period. Anyone without a car must give up a transportation pass at every place you visit and you need a pass to get home. These passes represent costs and time used in getting places. Kids must report here," he pointed to a group of chairs, "for school and stay for the first 7 minutes of the 15 minute period. Kids do not need transportation passes to go to and from school, but they do need them to go anywhere else."

There was a brief buzz as people oriented themselves, then the Reverend resumed: "Your goal is to meet your financial obligations and come out in the same place or ahead by the end of the month. Remember, you need food; kids need attention; younger children should not be left unsupervised. Try to envision creating a healthy, positive life experience within the parameters of the education and income level of the people you're portraying. Now, take the next 10 minutes to develop a plan for dealing with your situation. Then I'll blow the whistle and the week starts. Everyone understand?"

We all nodded or murmured affirmatives whether (I suspected) we understood or not.

"Okay, ten minutes to plan starting now!"

Automatically, we pulled our chairs closer and leaned in, then waited to see who would take charge. Oddly enough it was Lily who kicked things off.

"How are we going to get $410?" she asked. "Should we get a loan?"

"No!" the rest of us cried in unison so loudly she reared back in surprise.

"Last resort," I said.

"Interest rates will be punitive," Tierney said, and I nodded.

"What can we cut from the budget?" Wayland asked.

There was quite the pregnant silence while Tierney and I exchanged glances. Tierney got the joke, which made me like him a bit; Lily looked puzzled and Wayland, oblivious.

"Yes, I said, "what can we cut from the budget? Let's look."

I held up the sheet with our budget figures.

"Looks to me like the only truly expendable items would be the cable/internet access for $90; the clothing allotment of $50 and probably the toiletries for another $50. That's $190. $410 minus $190 leaves . . . "

"$220," said Tierney promptly.

"$220," I echoed.

"I bet Grandpa watches cable," said Lily, "he'll miss it. He's unemployed and can't drive. What's he doing all day?" She said it with a slight chuckle and I looked at her closely. Yep, I thought, she's got a sense of humor and is finding her bearings.

"I'll live," said Wayland. "I agree it'll have to go. We don't have much choice. But we still have a shortfall."

"George is already working full-time; I'm only working part-time. I should apply for full time, where . . . ?" I looked around. "At General Employer I guess. So I'll do that. Not that there's any guarantee."

"True," said Tierney, "I think we'll have to sell some of our stuff."

"I'll apply for jobs," said Wayland.

"I suppose you can," I said, "but then you won't be here when Gina gets home from school. Someone has to be."

"There's a childcare facility," Tierney said, pointing at another table. "We need to find out what it costs. Can we net more money with Gemma or Gerald or both working full-time while paying childcare?"

"Yeah, we need the cost," I agreed. I dug into the zipper bag and handed out pencils and notepads. "What's due when? Some bills get paid in the second week so we need money for those first. Even if we get jobs we probably won't get paid in time for them."

"How much will there be after you two get paid the first time? When do you get paid again?" asked Wayland.

I consulted the situation sheet.

"Paychecks at the end of week one and three. So we don't see any of that in our first week. We'll get $900, right? Half of the total take-home of $1800?"

"Will they take out gas money?" Tierney asked.

"Oh right," I said. "We have to check off our work days. So they probably will. It won't be $900, it will be $800 or whatever, depending on whether I drive or take the bus."

"That's right," said Wayland. "We can save money if you take the bus."

"How much do we save?"

Lily had been poring over the situation sheet.

"$80 a month or $5 a day. Which becomes $3 a day because you need $2 a day to ride the bus. You work 16 days. The bus costs $32 a month so we gain $48"

"That doesn't seem like much, does it?" I said. "Still, if Gerald loses cable I guess I can take the bus. Though its 2 miles away. Is that realistic? Do I drive to the bus stop and park the car somewhere so I can drive home then? Or do I walk two miles there and back? It's not *that* far . . . "

"Couldn't I drop you off?" said Wayland.

"You can't drive Grandpa!" said Lily, "your license is suspended."

"Oh that's right," he said, shaking his head at himself.

"George can drop you off at the bus stop on his way to work," Tierney said, "then you'd only need to walk home."

"Okay," I said, "we can add $48 to our total — what do we have now?"

"$220 is the gap so far. $220 minus $48 leaves $172." Tierney replied.

"So we sell stuff now and buy it back after payday," said Wayland.

"I don't think we'll be able to buy it back unless one or both of us gets work," I said. "Unless something changes, we'll have a shortfall every month. If we catch up now the shortfall will only be . . . what was it . . . ?"

"$240, less the cable/internet bill of $90, so $150. We'd be short $150 for next month," Tierney answered.

"Oh Lord, we can't worry about that now," said Wayland, "one thing at a time!"

Once again Tierney and I exchanged glances, then Tierney said: "We can sell stuff to make up the remaining $172, although we're supposed to buy food, right?"

"Let me see that," Wayland said, holding out his hand for the situation sheet. He reviewed it.

"Yes, we need food. Cupboards are bare. We're supposed to spend $560 a month for food, so $115 a week. What do we have for cash?"

I held up the $30 in monopoly money.

"Thirty bucks," I said. "And we need transportation passes. We only have two representing one bus trip somewhere and back."

"So, by not spending on cable etc., we save — " I started scribbling on my notepad, "$410 minus $172 is $238. We save $238. We can sell stuff to get the $172 *or* we can sell stuff to get $115 for food now and see where we are by the end of the week on jobs. We don't have much to sell and it's one thing to sell a ring and quite another to sell the stove."

"What can we sell again?" Tierney asked.

Wayland checked the sheet.

"A ring, worth $100; a television, worth $100; a digital camera, worth $100; furniture, worth $250; a microwave, worth $50; a refrigerator, worth $100; and a stove, worth $100." he read.

We all agreed the ring and digital camera could go.

"So, to summarize, we've cancelled our cable and will forgo toiletries or clothing purchases for the month. I'll take the bus to work, and will apply for a full time job at General Employer. We will sell — where will we sell our stuff? Are we pawning it?"

"I think for purposes of the simulation we probably have to," said Tierney. "I suppose in real life we might sell things through Craigslist or something. Or maybe we could wander around and ask people if they want to buy our stuff?"

"I'll try that," said Wayland. "You two have to go to work. I'll try to sell stuff to people and if I get no takers, I'll pawn them."

The whistle blew and the week commenced.

Chapter Eighteen

There was a burst of activity as people headed for the Employer and School areas. We part-timers were seated and given handouts listing statistics about poverty in the U.S.

They were depressing.

After reading them I looked around. I could see Tierney seated and holding, presumably, the same handout; Lily, ditto with the other students. Wayland was walking around with the cards representing the ring and digital camera. He stopped people and pitched the items. He didn't seem to be making any sales. After a few minutes he went to the Pawn Shop and got in line.

Meanwhile, other people were scurrying around doing whatever they were doing at the Store, Bank, PayDay Loan table and other stations. I was anxious to leave "work", but when we were released, I realized I'd need to go "home" first and get Gerald's car to drive to General Employer and apply for full-time work. I zipped to our clump of chairs. Wayland was waiting.

"I could only get $100 total for the ring and the camera. Pawn shops don't give you what items are actually worth or they couldn't make a profit. They gave me $50 for each."

"Okay, well, I still have the $30, but we're going to have to get more transportation passes."

"Oh, right. I used up the two we had."

Lily arrived with a square sheet of red paper that said *Needed: $15 for school supplies.*

"What? Crap!" I said.

"I'm sorry Mom," said Lily gamely, "but they cut the budget at our school so we have to pay for supplies."

"Alright. We need change so I can give you $15, all I have are tens. Do we wait until George gets home with the car? If I drive won't that cost us?"

Before anyone answered, Tierney arrived.

"What's happening?" he asked.

"Gerald got us $100 for the ring and digital camera — " I began.

"That's all?" said Lily.

"Pawnshops never give you the full value of the item or they couldn't make a profit if they sell it," I explained.

"Oh."

"Anyway, we have $100 and Gina needs $15 of it for school supplies. We also need to get to the PayDay Loan store to get transportation passes for Gerald or he won't be able to go anywhere. So, you drive us."

We all walked together to the PayDay loan store and got in line. I bought five passes for $5 and gave them to Wayland; gave Lily $15 and kept the last $10.

"Okay, where to next?" I said.

"How much time do we have?" asked Tierney.

"Can't be much" I said.

"Let's get groceries," said Lily.

We looked at each other, nodded, and trooped over to the General Store.

The fellow at the table checked our name-tags and asked how much we wanted to spend on food and how much on toiletries or clothes.

"Just food," I said. "We have $110," I added, looking at the others, "do we spend it all on food or save some just in case?"

"Make a note that you're spending less than your allotted $115 budget for the week," said the grocery man.

"Yeah, okay," I muttered and hurriedly recorded the amount.

"Spend $90," said Tierney, "keep $20 for emergencies."

I gave the man $90 and he made a note next to "Gordon" on his clipboard.

As we were walking back to our "house" a man walked up, waved a toy gun at us and said "I'll take that" snatching the $20 I had clutched in my hand.

A cacophony of protests erupted from us, but he winked and fled.

The whistle blew and Reverend Fenimore spoke: "Everyone return to your homes. Unless you've been evicted, in which case, stay at the Homeless Shelter. We'll take a few minutes to distribute the end of Week One paychecks and you can start strategizing for Week Two."

We all started talking at once.

"Settle down everyone!" I said, rather loudly. "Oh heck, I never did apply for full-time work, did I?"

"Neither did I," rumbled Wayland.

"Did anyone find out how much daycare would cost?" Tierney asked.

We looked at him blankly, then I said: "No. We forgot about it."

"Geez, we suck at this!" Lily said.

"Alright, we'll do better next week," Tierney said. He said it soothingly and we all basked for a few seconds, as though we really would do better next week.

A woman stopped at our group.

"Gordon?"

We nodded.

"George Gordon: did you miss any work?"

"No," said Tierney.

"You drove?"

"Yes."

She consulted a spreadsheet and said: "you get $450 — that's your pay minus gas."

She counted out monopoly money and handed him a wad of it.

"Gemma Gordon: did you miss any work?"

"No."

"Did you drive?"

"No, I took the bus."

"OK, you get . . . $167 for this week and $155 for the previous week, when you drove. So total of $322."

She gave me the bills and left.

"So now we have?" I asked.

"$772," said Tierney.

"And what do we need to spend it on?" Back to the situation sheet. "Someone write down $772 and start a list," I said.

"I will," Lily said, pulling out her notepad and pencil.

"Alright, here's the list again. $200 for car; $120 for house and taxes; $90 for car insurance; $250 for utilities are all due in this next week — what's that add up to?" I said.

"$660," said Lily.

"$772 minus $660 is wha — "

"$112," said Tierney. Man he was fast.

"So we have $112 for food," I said.

"No we don't. We have $112 left, but we have bills due in Week Three and we don't get paid again until Week Four," said Tierney.

"So we're not going to have money in time for Week Three bills?" I asked.

"Let me see," said Wayland, taking the sheet. "Forget Gerald's medical bills until Week Four. Then we'll catch up."

"Aren't there other past due bills? What were they? We came into the month behind on stuff, right?"

"It was $172," said Tierney. "Let's write this down. We started out $410 down and saved by stopping our cable and not buying any clothes or toiletries. Plus, we have to pay for phones in Week Three. That's another $120."

"I don't think we can be late on the phones," I said. "If the phones go off Gerald can't talk to his AA sponsor, plus all the other inconveniences."

"Wasn't there something about the car insurance?" Lily asked.

Wayland, who was looking grim, said: "We're in the grace period on the car insurance — we didn't pay last month. We need to pay $90 this week and another $90 in Week Four. If we don't pay $90 this week we'll be cancelled."

"Oh yeah. That was part of the $172. The rest was past due utility payments." I said.

"$660 plus $172 is $832," said Lily. "$832 minus the $772 we have is $60. Can we come up with sixty more dollars?"

"We can sell something else I guess," I said doubtfully. We were forgetting something . . .

"What about food for the two weeks?" Tierney asked.

That was it!

"Oh nuts!" I said. (If we hadn't been in a church I would have used a different word.)

As we helplessly looked at each other, I tuned in to the surrounding noise which was tinged with hysteria. People were all talking rapidly, looking worried and harried. Evidently they were wrestling with similar shortfalls. It was funny, none of this was real but we were still feeling, well, a bit of panic.

I looked at the stations around the room.

"Is this when we decide to visit the Food Bank?" I asked.

"Are any of us eligible for food stamps?" Wayland asked.

"Maybe you would be since you're unemployed," I said. I looked at Tierney to see what he thought. He shrugged. He didn't know.

"Lily?" I said.

"You might be," she said, "since you're employed part-time. Isn't that how Walmart works? Most of their employees get food stamps or whatever it's called now. I don't think they call them food stamps anymore."

"Alright," I said, "I need to apply for food stamps or whatever they're called and so does Gerald. And we both need to apply for full-time jobs. And one of us needs to go to the Food Bank. George, you check out the Food Bank after you leave work and find out about child care costs."

"Gerald will need to pay some of the bills — I think we probably have to go to the Utilities Table and the Bank and so on to make payments," said Tierney.

"Give me all the money then," Wayland said, "and I'll make the rounds."

The whistle blew and Reverend Callahan said: "Commence Week Two!"

"Don't get robbed!" I said to Wayland.

Back to the Part-Time Employer table where we were given handouts about budget cuts affecting food banks and homeless shelters around the country.

But I couldn't concentrate on them, I was thinking about our bills and wondering if we should sell Gerald's car. That's when I gave myself a metaphorical slap and reminded myself none of this was real. So I ceased that train of thought and looked around to see what anyone I knew was doing.

Congresswoman Tesarik was in the line applying for Food Stamps. Connie was sitting in the group at General Employer, and Peter appeared to be . . . in jail? Yep, he was in jail. I wondered how that happened.

Meanwhile, Tierney was seated in the row behind Connie. Wayland was standing in front of the General Employer table filling out a job application and as I was trying to locate Lily, a woman tapped me on the shoulder and handed me a square red sheet of paper that said: "Your daughter is having an asthma attack and needs to go home. After work you must stop by the school to take her home. If you leave now you will lose a day's pay."

"Oh no," I said, "really?"

The woman nodded an emphatic "yes" and left me.

I wondered what I'd have done for real. For fake, I wasn't going. If Gina was at the school office she'd be fine until I could get there. Of course, I would have to go home by bus and then pick her up in the car, but that would be a much smaller income loss.

A minute later we were released and I headed "home" then left again and walked over the the School Table. Lily was in a chair next to the school person who gave me a stern look and said Gina had been miserable and I should have come two hours ago.

Feeling defensive, I just managed to repress a snarl of indignation before, once again, remembering this wasn't real. I collected Lily and we went back to our chairs.

"I know I was supposed to do something else now — what was it?" I said.

Mutely, Lily handed me a square-cut pink sheet of paper that said: "Gina is 8-years-old and ill. She should not be left alone. One of the household's adults must stay with her for three minutes, representing one sick day."

"This means I lose a day of work?"

Lily said: "Sorry Mom!"

"Unless Gerald gets home. He can do three minutes."

"Where is he?"

We peered through the milling people and saw him at the Bank table. Then we looked for Tierney, who was at the Food Pantry.

"We're going to count this time as you staying home from school," I said.

"Then you lose a day's pay," she reminded me.

"Well, but, I can't leave you to go do anything. I need to apply for a full time job and for food stamps."

"Let's try to get Gerald's attention," Lily said.

We waved madly and yelled, but it didn't penetrate. Foolishly, we were yelling "Gerald!" instead of "Congressman Wayland!" so he remained unaware for a good thirty seconds. Then someone nudged him and he turned around.

"Get back here as soon as you're done," I shouted at him.

"I need to pay the utility bills!"

He pointed at the Utilities Company table."

"I'll go!" I yelled.

He nodded and joined us a minute later.

"What's up?"

"Gina is sick and someone has to stay with her for 3 minutes — if I do, I'll lose a day of work."

"Okay, go!"

I ran over to the Utility line, then ran back to get cash from Wayland, then ran to the line again.

Tierney had joined Wayland and Lily; I wanted to know what he'd found out, but I was stuck in line. It was a long line.

I waved at him to come over.

"I know we're cheating, kind of, but I'm stuck in this line and wanted to know what you'd found out."

"I was able to get this week's food from the Food Pantry."

"Oh good! That's great! $115 we don't need to come up with."

"Right."

"What did Gerald get done?"

"He applied for a job and was told he'd hear something next week. He paid the car payment, car insurance — the $90 that was past due — and the house insurance and taxes."

"Ok, so what do we have left?" I said, and started counting the monopoly money in my hand. "I've got $362."

Consulting my little notepad I saw that we had to pay $250 for utilities plus another $80 for past-due utility charges.

"Need to pay $330," I said. "We'll have $32 left heading into next week."

"Someone at General Employer said the Food Stamps table is for the TANF program: Temporary Assistance for Needy Families. They give money, not food stamps."

"Really? Okay, that's gotta be my next stop. I'll apply."

I turned around. I was two people away from the front of the line when the whistle blew.

"Sorry folks, the bank is closed!" announced the man at the bank table.

"Everyone back to your homes!" shouted Reverend Fenimore.

"What?" I said. "C'mon, I need to pay my utility bills! I have the money!"

"Sorry Ma'am. Bank is closed," replied Bank Man, "come back Monday."

"Come back Monday," I muttered as Tierney and I went back to our chairs.

"We have to tally up some things. Please take this time to make your plans for Week Three," said the Reverend.

"I couldn't pay the utility bills because the bank closed," I said. "So I have $362 in hand, but $330 is spoken for; we have $32."

"George got a week's worth of food from the Food Bank and Gerald applied for a job," Lily said. Wayland nodded.

"Okay," I began, when a head appeared over Wayland's shoulder.

"Utility man!" said this person. "Gordon family owes $330 in utilities including past due balances. Payment wasn't made on time; this is your shut-off notice unless you can pay me now."

"We can!" I said.

"$330 plus late penalty of $15 — "

"We've got $362," I said.

"Per utility. $15 for Gas, $15 for Electric, $15 for water and trash."

"We've got $362," I repeated.

"You need $375," he replied.

We made incoherent protests.

"You have enough to pay two out of three. Which utility would you like to shut off?"

We looked at each other.

"It's summer," said Tierney. "Shut off the gas. We'll heat water with electricity and get the gas turned back on later."

"Good choice," said Utility Man, "$250 please."

I handed it over and he gave me a square-cut orange sheet of paper that said: "$50 fee to turn gas back on."

"Oh great," I said and showed everyone.

"Oh this is ridiculous!" Wayland burst out. "People can't live like this!"

We looked at him, I wish I could have seen our faces. From the inside of mine, I was expressing "people *do* live like this — that's the point". I didn't get a chance to look at Tierney or Lily.

Wayland reddened and drew his lips into thin lines. He started to speak, then closed his mouth.

Tierney cleared his throat and looked at me.

I took a breath, then said: "Be that as it may, if we were really in this fix, what's our next move?"

Tierney looked at his notepad.

"We need $120 for phones," he intoned, "$70 for Gerald's health insurance and $150 for Gerald's wife's medical bills. That's $340. Plus $50 now to turn the gas back on. $340 or $390."

"And we have $112" I said. "We'll probably have to skip the gas for next month unless something comes up. I'll apply for the TANF benefits. Or, should Gerald? Or both of us?"

"We'll both apply," Wayland said.

"I still haven't applied for a full-time job," I added.

"I didn't find out about child care costs either," said Tierney.

Another head popped over Wayland's shoulder: a young woman.

"Need money?" she said.

We looked at her inquiringly.

"I have a little job that needs doing," she said. "All you have to do is take this bag and hand it to a man who will be waiting next to the school on Monday. Deliver the bag and I'll give you $500."

I'm quite sure that each one of us considered the proposition. I saw it on their faces and they saw it on mine.

But we said no.

"We're not that desperate," I said. Mentally I added "yet."

Chapter Nineteen

Weeks Three and Four degenerated into a downward spiral of cascading difficulties. Neither Gerald nor Gemma were eligible for TANF benefits as Gerald owned his home and wasn't disabled and Gemma wasn't paying for child care. We could reapply should those conditions change. We also requested help with our gas bill and learned heating assistance wasn't available in the summer, but would be in October.

I applied for full-time work at General Employer although the month ended before I received a decision. Gerald was turned down by General Employer so he wanted to apply at the Part-Time Employer. We were out of transportation passes so I drove to work in Week Three (instead of taking the bus) and took Gerald with me. When Gina's school was unexpectedly closed due to a burst water main, Gerald decided to drive and collect her, leaving me at work and saving my hours. Thus, the Congressman became a lawbreaker (had he been caught driving on his suspended license the car would have been impounded, among other things).

We discovered the Community Charity Organization which gave us clothing and toiletry stipends and $50 in cash and we got more food at the Food Bank.

We received another square-cut paper notice informing us that George had a painful cavity and our medical insurance did not include (naturally) dental. Poor George was destined to suffer.

We got a notice Gerald's sister in South Carolina had died. There was no way we could drive or fly there for the funeral.

At one point, Gina spotted a $20 monopoly bill on the floor and we pounced on it frantically and cheered like it was $200 or $2000.

We were desperate to pay for phones and ended up at the PayDay Lender getting an advance on George's next paycheck. We figured we'd make up the difference by getting food at the Food Bank for a few more weeks. With the gas turned off, we'd save on the next utility bill and we could all hope Gemma would get a full-time job. Or, Gerald would get a part-time job, or both.

By Week Four everyone was shuffling around. The manic energy fueling the beginning of the exercise had dissipated. I was physically tired and emotionally drained.

When I was handed yet another square-cut paper telling me Gina wasn't getting appropriate nourishment and it was affecting her performance at school, I just hissed and handed it to Tierney. He grunted and handed it to Wayland, who snorted. Lily said "poor Gina" and we all nodded.

I looked around. It was amazing how wrapped up I'd become in our situation — I'd paid virtually no attention to anyone else during our last two weeks. I now saw that Connie was at the Homeless Shelter, Peter was across the room arguing with the Utility Man, and Congresswoman Tesarik was in jail.

A lot of people seemed to be in jail.

I looked at Tierney. His hair was ruffled and his tie was off-center. He'd had a vibe the entire time of someone wanting to be elsewhere and was running on sheer will power. He'd been pleasant, polite and done his part, but his limit was fast approaching.

I looked at Wayland. He reminded me of a cat settling down after a back-arching, tail-puffing episode with a barking dog. He was smoothing his hair, adjusting his sleeves and jacket, trying to get himself under control. He wasn't used to surprising emotions, I suspected. Still less was he used to exhibiting them publicly. To give him credit, he'd thrown himself into the simulation and had reacted authentically, as we all had. The question was, what would he take away? Had any consciousness-raising occurred?

Mercifully, the last whistle blow sounded and we could stop.

There was a delay as people wound up whatever they'd been doing and returned to their seats.

"So," said the Reverend,"what did you learn?"

There was an explosion of discussion which he waved into silence.

"A thing or two, evidently," he said, smiling. "Let's go around the room and have each family present their situation and tell us whether they came out ahead, behind or in the same place they were when the month started."

And so, people presented their scenarios: single moms with kids and no jobs; ex-offenders trying to survive when no one would hire them and they were ineligible for many types of assistance; elderly women dependent on small Social Security checks; families struggling to get by on full-time, low-paying jobs; troubled kids and teenagers who were dropping out of school. In all sorts of combinations of age, situation and sex we all faced the same problem: we didn't have enough money to meet basic expenses. The one group that paid all their bills with a few hundred dollars to spare succeeded only because they sold drugs.

One enterprising man had purchased two of the guns for sale at the pawn shop which he'd sold at a small profit to two different people who'd been robbed.

Several people landed in jail because they'd gotten speeding tickets (on bright yellow square-cut sheets of paper) and couldn't afford the fines.

And everyone had gotten a taste of what Reverend Fenimore referred to as "the tyranny of the moment".

"One of the conditions that characterizes poverty is this tyranny of the moment," he said. "When you must continually put out fires and decide between nothing but bad choices — do I pay my car insurance or keep the electricity on? — you, wait, let me ask you all — what happens?"

Hands went up.

"You get really tired," said one woman.

"You get really angry," said a young man.

"You get depressed and fatalistic," said an older man.

"You make short-term choices, sometimes bad choices, like getting high-interest loans you probably won't be able to pay off," said Lily.

"Did any of you turn to crime or knowingly break the law?" the Reverend asked.

Several heads nodded. I noticed Wayland's remained still.

"Did any of you consider committing crimes?"

Many more heads nodded and several people said they were surprised to find themselves exploring the possibility.

"What about planning?" the Reverend asked. "Did you all figure out how you would manage to go to college and get the education that is supposed to lift you out of poverty? Or how about meal-planning? I've read articles about how low income people can carefully plan out menus so they can stretch their $115 a week for food into healthy meals for four people seven days a week. Did you feel like doing that?"

Some people took exception to his question and one man raised his hand.

"I don't know if that's fair," he said, "we didn't have time for that. In real life people have way more hours in the day for planning."

"Fair enough," said the Reverend. "Anyone else?"

Connie raised her hand.

"There are more hours in the day, but that just means there's more time to be stressed and exhausted. Retail and restaurant jobs are physically demanding — you spend hours on your feet. And many people work more than one of those jobs and still can't earn enough money. It's amazing *any* of them manage to go to college and now I understand why a lot of people don't graduate. And don't get me started about the burden of student loans!"

Several voices rose in agreement.

"The thing that strikes me," I said, "is $115 a week for food. How many of us have spent $115 in one evening at a good restaurant?"

Lots of "yesses".

I continued: "I've read articles and online discussions about how to eat on the money provided by SNAP or food stamps or whatever the program is now — and you always see people recommending eating beans and rice and store brands instead of name brands, etc. I'm sure they're right. But imagine having to do it month after month after month! It's one thing to do that to get through an unusually lean time, but what if it's lean all the time? What happens to your head when you go into a grocery store and you can never get treats? Or even just a good cut of meat?"

"What happens to your head when people feel they have the right to judge what food you buy for your family?" said a voice behind me.

"I read an article in USA Today," said a man in front of me, "about how to eat healthily on low incomes. The thing I remember was about how people spend too much on drinks — referring to soft drinks. The expert said you should plan to drink, and I quote, 'tap water and skim or two-percent milk.' It really bothered me. I mean, I can see the point. Milk and water are healthier than soda-pop, but still . . . that's pretty grim. It made me think of gruel and Oliver Twist, y'know?"

"Yeah," said a young female voice, "I think there's a big difference between eating a certain way because you *want* to, and having no choice."

Several small conversations broke out, and Reverend Fenimore let them go on for a bit before calling everyone to order.

"Regarding meal planning," he said, after everyone had subsided, "setting aside how doable, enjoyable or possible it is to feed four people on $115 a week, what strikes *me* is how it is yet another burden laid upon people who are already undergoing stress. I know many of us here try to keep to spending budgets, but I suspect most of us have wiggle room and most of us include a few luxuries as a matter of course, don't we? Can you share the food luxuries you buy every month?"

I thought about my Starbucks coffees, organic dark chocolates, wine, cut flowers, organic fruits — especially blueberries and strawberries all summer.

People mentioned all those and others: pricey free-range organic meats, artisan sausages, bakery breads, seafood, vitamin-infused flavored waters, exotic spices, baking extracts, imported extra-virgin olive oil, high-end salad dressings . . .

"However much they would like to enjoy such things, many Americans literally cannot. They must go into a grocery store, week after week, and get the cheapest, most basic foodstuffs. If they indulge, it will be on low-cost, highly processed, high-fructose-corn-syrup laden junk because the good stuff always costs more. And what about other pleasures?" Fenimore looked around the room. "Going to the movies, out to dinner, to the store for some new item just because they feel like it? New tools from Sears? A vacation?"

Another wave of conversations broke out. I took a furtive look at Tierney, who's eyes were downcast, and Wayland, who's impassive countenance revealed nothing (which told me both were bothered but unwilling to show their concern). In contrast, Congresswoman Tesarik was speaking intently to Connie, her expression open, unguarded, animated.

"What can poor parents provide for their children? Piano lessons? Braces for their teeth? Networking and career building opportunities? Home computers? Many of you portrayed parents. How did you feel about not being able to provide food, let alone luxuries?"

"Rotten!"

"Pissed!"

"It was numbing."

Lily raised her hand: "Speaking from the child's point of view, I felt helpless. I felt like a burden, plus I couldn't do anything to help. Except not eat."

"Yes," said the Reverend, "and its not uncommon for people to judge poor people's parenting, isn't it? If their kids go bad, it's always the parent's fault, right? Parents are unloving, lazy, stupid. They let the kids get into bad company. You don't have to answer this, but how many people here have had those kinds of thoughts?"

Tierney and Wayland looked even more rigid.

"Recent events in the news have publicized aspects of poverty about which most Americans are blissfully unaware. I'm speaking about how low-income people are preyed upon by law enforcement. Budgets get cut at the federal level, unemployment is high and most new jobs pay badly. So state, county and city governments all over the country are strapped for cash. What do some of them do? They enforce all sorts of technical laws on poor people in order to generate fines. Things like loitering, jaywalking, driving while black. In certain parts of the country people can be jailed because they don't have the money to pay a fine. Talk about the criminalization of poverty! And why pick on poor people? Because they can't afford lawyers. How many of you would accept being jailed for jaywalking?"

I lowered my head and chanced another unobtrusive glance at Tierney and Wayland. Tierney's hands were clenched and his fingers were white; Wayland's ears were bright red.

Peter raised his hand: "One thing I became much more aware of is penalties. I'm able to pay all my bills on time so I don't usually get late fees. But now

I see the lower your budget the more you pay for things. You pay extra to get your checks cashed. You pay insane interest rates on loans. And the world runs on 30-day schedules, so if you're a day late because you didn't have the money, your bill gets bigger. All these institutions we pay: utilities, insurance companies, banks, internet providers — they each have twelve chances a year to add penalites to your bill."

"Legions of psychological studies have concluded that feeling powerless is the highest stressor people can experience," said the Reverend, "and powerlessness is a defining characteristic of poverty. Everywhere you are faced with people and institutions that can control you, penalize you and prey on you."

I think the Reverend had more to say, but he stopped because someone was crossing the room. I recognized Melvin Thornery (Wayland's Chief of Staff). He bent down and spoke in Wayland's ear, then Wayland stood up.

"Congressman?" said Reverend Fenimore.

"I want to thank you Reverend, and all you fine citizens who participated in this very educational experience. Unfortunately, something has come up and I have to leave, but I won't forget this day."

There was a reasonable level of applause as he did one of those politician waves and strode towards the back stairs. Something about it . . . I turned and caught Peter's eye. He winked.

Ah hah! I thought. Peter had set this up in advance so Wayland could escape having to comment or take questions. Smart move.

I wondered what Tierney was thinking.

The Reverend resumed: "Recently I saw statistics that fifty percent of Americans do not have *any* money available for an emergency. How many Americans live to work and work just to live? And when you have no extra income to save, let alone invest, what happens? You rob Peter to pay Paul. You buy cheap, used and old. Your beat up car needs constant repairs. You can't buy the expensive appliance that uses less electricity because you'll never have an extra $2000 to spend. And you learn that loans are traps — late payments or missed payments mean late fees and skyrocketing interest rates. If *our* car has a problem we get it fixed. But for a lot of people, a car breakdown can literally cost them their job."

I thought about Olivia driving all over to clean houses. She *had* to have a car.

"For the last forty years incomes for roughly eighty percent of Americans have remained stagnant or dropped. But costs have risen steadily. Is anything less expensive? Are utilities cheaper? Costs for cars? Appliances? Homes? Rents? Utilities? Food? Gas? Education? Medical care? Dental care? Sales tax, in particular, disproportionately affects low-income people."

Nods and murmurs of acknowledgement.

"A few final thoughts for the evening," he said. "First, there's a lot of debate about raising minimum wage and people often point out a relatively small number of Americans actually earn minimum wage. But as we've learned, you can earn more than minimum wage and still be in poverty. Personally, I think raising the minimum wage is important not only because it will greatly help those who earn it, but also because the next couple of wage tiers should go up as well."

There was a ripple of reaction in the room.

"In much of America being homeless is a crime. We have enacted laws that have completely eliminated avenues for people who don't have money. You can't just pitch a tent somewhere, as the Occupy protesters found out. You can't camp in parks. You can't legally squat in empty houses of which our neighborhoods are full. And, it's very hard to find and maintain employment when you don't have a phone, access to computers, clean clothes, clean hair, etc. Our social safety net has lots of holes."

Many nods.

"America's working poor do a lot of unexciting, unrewarding, non-prestigious jobs. And yet, think how much we all rely on them. Their labors provide us with many conveniences. Big money is made for small numbers of people on the backs of America's working poor. People scorn or dismiss the fast-food worker, but they don't scorn the money made by McDonalds as a corporation, do they?"

More nods.

"I think there is something fundamentally, profoundly wrong with expecting people to work full-time and still be unable to meet basic expenses, let alone enjoy anything or be able to save. But until I did a poverty simulation, I didn't realize part of me thought the poor should *just stop being poor.* As though it hadn't occurred to them. As though they just weren't trying enough. Now I realize the pernicious nature of the trap they live in, which is worsened by lack of respect, judgmentalness and indifference. So, here's what I'll ask you all to do."

There was a palpable frisson of people-sitting-up-straighter and ears pricking up.

"Going forth, I ask you to treat your working brothers and sisters with respect. And on days when you're tired and irritable and you don't get perfect service, give them the benefit of the doubt. Chances are their lives are far more difficult than yours."

Someone shouted "Amen!" and I felt both uncomfortable and oddly pleased.

"Going forth, I ask you to support your local food bank and homeless shelter."

"Yay Father!"

"Going forth, I ask you to learn about and support efforts by your political representatives to address poverty. Visit your congress people and let them know it's important to you. Support them when they do good; call their offices — respectfully — and ask them to justify their neglect or abuse when they do ill."

I gave a loud "Amen!" to that one.

"Going forth, look for the problem-solvers. As Matthew says: 'You will recognize them by their fruits.' Seek people who look for ways to make things better; *be* people who make things better!"

We applauded, even Tierney, then the Reverend bowed his head, said a short prayer, and the event was over.

I turned and saw Tierney walking towards Peter. Meanwhile, several people were moving towards Congresswoman Tesarik. Connie had pulled out a small video camera and was filming what appeared to be an impromptu town hall meeting. If it went well, Connie would post it on the Congresswoman's website and YouTube.

Looking back at Tierney, I saw him hold a brief conversation with Peter. Then Tierney came back to me.

"I'll see you Saturday?" he asked.

I nodded an affirmative.

"Good," he said, then added: "bye Gemma."

"Goodbye George," I replied. As he snaked his way swiftly to the back stairs, I sighed.

Had the poverty simulation penetrated the hides of either Tierney or Wayland?

I looked at Peter. He was now talking to the man who'd worked the Homeless Shelter table. I went over to Connie.

"What did you think? What did she think?" I whispered, pointing to the Congresswoman.

"She thinks everyone on the Hill should do one of these," Connie whispered back, still filming. "I think it was great. How'd Wayland react?"

I didn't want any of my speculations captured on tape so I motioned to her to phone me later. Then I found a chair, sat, and listened to Congresswoman Tesarik take questions. People were liking her; questions were friendly and her answers were genuine, not political-speak. Virginia isn't her state and these folks can't vote for her, but (as Connie told me later) these same folks could contact their own representative and encourage them to work with her on poverty issues going forward.

Eventually, Peter found me.

"How'd Wayland do?" he asked.

"He threw himself into the simulation and got emotional and frustrated like the rest of us, but then he shut down. I expect he's feeling a lot of conflict right now. It would take a colossal amount of courage for him to embrace poverty relief as an issue. It's what I call a 'risk big, you win big or you lose big' move. It would make for a more interesting primary campaign, though, wouldn't it?"

"Amen to that. We'll know tomorrow I *think*. How'd Tierney do?"

"Tierney was . . . remote. He did everything he needed to do, but I felt like he was only partly here. I think he's even more conflicted than Wayland."

"Hmm. That's interesting. I wonder what his advice will be?"

"Me too. What did you think? Glad you did it?"

"Oh completely. I'm going to volunteer to work one of the stations the next time the Reverend has one of these. I'm thinking I might have my folks participate in one. It would help them understand why I'm changing direction spiritually and vocationally."

"That seems like a good idea — if they'd be open to it. Would they?"

"We'll see. It's worth a try."

Chapter Twenty

As he made the drive back towards the Capitol, Reve Tierney considered what advice he'd deliver to Congressman Wayland. He was never fully comfortable with hard-core biblical literalists, but he'd always respected Wayland's ability to win elections and had been flattered to be consulted on the occasional issue. In this case, he couldn't work out whether he'd been asked to help Wayland determine how to make poverty an issue he could run on, or come up with persuasive excuses for why he couldn't.

As to his own reaction to the exercise, he was alternating between feeling ashamed and defensive. He couldn't deny he'd previously been oblivious to the practical and emotional difficulties faced by low-income people in America, but he felt he was hardly alone in his ignorance. Indeed, that was precisely why such simulations were held. Congresswoman Tesarik had been there to be enlightened and she was a liberal who was supposed to know those kinds of things, wasn't she?

Of course he'd been aware, in an abstract way, of the predations visited upon the poor by the police, payday lenders, banks and others, but he'd categorized such things as part of life's general unfairness. It sucks to be poor was his attitude; it always had and always would. He'd never — and when he realized this he felt deeper shame and simultaneously greater defensiveness — connected the dots between the sorts of policies he supported and the way they played out in the lives of struggling people.

After having that thought he got angry, then he realized his anger helped push away the guilt hovering on the outskirts of his consciousness. If he let the guilt overtake him, where would it end?

He thought about Barbara. She was . . . fundamentally . . . good. A good person. Was he a good person? Or was he, as he was starting to believe, a completely hollow piece of shit?

Reve realized he was gripping his steering wheel so hard his hands hurt. He forced himself to relax, shocked. He had never, throughout his charmed life, used a profanity to describe himself.

That was probably what Dash was trying to tell him, he thought, and laughed humorlessly. Dash was going to tell him to stop being such a hollow piece of shit. Stop, or die and awaken in some empty dimension between life and afterlife where all you could think about was how you'd been a hollow piece of shit.

Distracted by a vision of himself as a Dash-like ghost, Reve almost missed his exit. Instinctively swerving into the lane to his right, he incited a furious horn-blowing from an SUV emerging from his blind spot. The SUV hit the brakes just enough to avoid hitting Reve or being hit in turn by a Lexus sedan.

Heart thumping, Reve thought: Please God, let me make it home alive. Don't, don't let me die now. Give me a chance to fix things.

At the bottom of the exit ramp he turned right, then pulled off into the parking lot of a shopping center. Shaking, he pulled into a relatively empty area of the large lot. He turned off his car, made sure his doors were locked, and, for the first time in his adult life, began seriously to pray.

In the Spirit World, Xe and Lersaliaz confer:

"Fadraya is in deep distress. He calls for help. What is your response?"

"I have sent him energy. Some anguish now will prevent much anguish later."

On Earth:

After several minutes of impassioned pleading for spiritual aid, Reve began to settle down. He could not, he decided, face Wayland tonight. He would call Wayland and tell him the simple truth: he needed time for reflection before he could possibly provide useful counsel.

He said as much to Wayland and their phone conversation was mercifully brief. Wayland was himself tired and needed time to digest the experience. They could meet at Wayland's office on Friday — he'd have Thornery call with a time.

Gratefully released, Reve re-embarked, heading for Barbara's farm.

Turning into Barbara's driveway, Reve released a lungful of pent-up breath. Travel to the ends of the universe, he thought, and take all my darkness with you.

Opening his window, he focused on the scent of growing things floating in the eddies of the warm, humid night air. Green things, he thought vaguely: grass and hay and wildflowers and trees. Ahead stood the house with the big porch, golden light in the windows and, exiting the car he saw — yes! — Sabrina trotting towards him. She didn't bark at him, he was no longer a stranger. She was there to greet him and conduct him to the house. He found that overwhelmingly touching and for an instant couldn't move. Then Sabrina nudged him lightly with her head; was he coming or not?

Passing over the front threshold he heard Barbara call out: "Reve? I'm in the kitchen."

Walking down the central hallway towards the back of the house, he wondered what he would say to her and realized he didn't know. His mouth would open and presumably something was going to come out and he had no idea what it would be.

It was a strange feeling.

Barbara was at the kitchen table engaged in some sort of activity involving tape measures, skeins of yarns, several knitting needles, a stack of paper, colored pencils and her laptop. She looked up and smiled at him as he entered.

"Working out the gauge of one of my yarns," she said.

His expression accurately conveyed his complete lack of comprehension. She laughed and said she'd explain later. Waving her hand toward the kitchen chair opposite her she said: "Sit down! Tell me how it went!"

Reve took off his sport coat and sat. He loosened his tie, unbuttoned his top shirt button, leaned back and stretched out his legs. Then he sat up straight, looked at her, opened his mouth and closed it.

She looked inquiring.

"How it went," he said. "How it went . . . "

Her eyebrows went up.

"That . . . bad?" she hazarded.

"No, not *bad*. Unsettling. It made me feel rancid, but on the upside I met your Wynne Frost. The reverend running the show seemed like a good guy. I have no idea what I'm going to say to Congressman Wayland."

"O-kay," she said. She put down her pencil and gave him her full attention.

"I'm . . . hmm, I feel," he paused, "if I wasn't . . . questioning myself, would you hate me?"

"Reve — "

"Seriously. Would you?"

"I don't see how you could go through all this without questioning yourself."

"You're not."

"Dennis didn't point at me and give me a thumbs down."

"No, he didn't. But you didn't answer my question."

"Reve — how can I say this?"

Barbara reached across the table and grasped his hand for an instant, then let it go.

"I think what you do for a living is unworthy of you and the views you promote are not only wrong, they're *malignant*."

He flinched; she continued: "The political machine you're a part of makes me angry. You know this. But . . . "

"Go on," he said.

"What I *think* about what you do for a living angers and saddens me. What I *feel* when I'm with you, on the other hand, is happy. So, then what?"

"So then what," he echoed.

"And it's all inextricably connected to this whole crazy experience we're having and I can't tell you how I would feel if we weren't having it."

"You don't do hypotheticals?" he asked with a wry smile.

"Nuh-uh. Not in this case anyway. I decided early on to go with the flow, as they say. You're being haunted. That is uncharted territory. Everything happening has been unpredictable so trying to analyze our . . . attraction seems pointless to me. Analysis is a thinking tool. This is about feeling."

"But why is my work so very bad?" he asked with sudden vehemence. "I'm not like Dash! I'm not racist or sexist or homophobic!"

"But you give ammunition to people who *are* racist, sexist and homophobic. *Powerful* people who create and change laws, impacting the country and the world. And focusing on the "isms" — the sexism, racism, is too narrow — your work supports corporate power over human rights. You've supported the criminally botched Iraq War; you've supported the dismantling of the New Deal and the Voting Rights Act; you've helped turn the judiciary into a partisan wing of the Republican Party — I could go on and on. And it's all based on lies. The heart of conservatism is rotten; it's built on propaganda and fear. A lot of things have been going wrong in this country and they all start with the lies."

Reve's face darkened and he spoke grittily: "Look, Democrats have held power too. You can't lay everything that's going wrong with this country on Republicans."

"I don't. Democrats have failed us many times, but mostly through *appeasement.* They should have condemned Dennis twenty years ago. They didn't. They made no effort to prevent the corporate takeover of our media outlets and the creation of media monopolies so that now our news outlets are corporate proxies focused on ratings instead of news gathering. Democrats let the Bush administration lie us into a horrifying war and then let everyone get away with it — even when they learned about the torture. And sometimes they've just been stupid and shortsighted like when they repealed Glass-Steagall. Oh, the Democrats have much to answer for — but that doesn't excuse you, Reve. It doesn't excuse your party."

"Look, our job is to oppose. We are the loyal opposition when we're out of power."

"No. The loyal opposition is supposed to dissent when there is a genuine disagreement, but they're supposed to be loyal to the government in principle, and are supposed to serve the country. Losing elections isn't a license to burn the country down out of spite."

Reve got up and walked across the kitchen to the window where he gazed, unseeingly, at the summer night. After a pause, he said: "What do you want from me?"

"I want you to be honest," she answered. "And I don't want you to end up like Dennis."

He turned around.

"You think if I'm honest I won't end up like Dash?"

"I think if you're honest, a number of things will follow. One is that you won't end up like Dennis. Another is I could both sleep with you *and* respect you in the morning."

Their eyes met and they both smiled. Then Reve became serious again.

"So you think I'm dishonest," he said.

"In terms of your work, yes, I think you are dishonest. With yourself. You know how I can tell?"

"How?"

"You can't complete an argument. You always veer off. You change the subject. All conservatives do this. They change the subject. They're told the actual cases of voter fraud amount to less than 10 or 20 in a voter pool of several million and they reply it's not that hard to get a photo ID. They don't address the non-existence of voter fraud — they change the subject. Because they're fully aware the fraud they peddle doesn't exist. Happens on issue after issue. The stupider people make things up. Literally invent things. Pull numbers out of the air. I don't think you make up numbers, but I think you evade numbers. And facts. And connections. You do it in public — that's your job. And to live with yourself you do it in private, too. You evade. You stop thinking about it. You change the subject."

Reve took this in.

"You are . . . *implacable,*" he said. "And yet, oddly sympathetic. How do you manage that?"

"Notice how you changed the subject?"

He winced.

"I just did, didn't I?"

"Might not be a fair example. You made an observation, really. We weren't debating. I don't think. Still — "

"No, you're right. It's almost, well, automatic."

"Pretty much. I think you got in the habit, probably a long time ago, and it works so you do it. No one calls you on it because everyone you know does it too. And the whole point of habits is their invisibility. They become things we do unconsciously."

He sighed heavily and, crossing back to the table, dropped into a kitchen chair.

"God, I am basically a sniveling, rationalizing, dishonest bastard, aren't I?"

"Fraid so."

"You could have waited at least a second before agreeing!"

"Well, I don't think you're a bastard. I do think Dennis was, though. And you don't snivel."

"That's better."

"But what you are," she said, "or maybe more accurately, what you were, is complacent. A not uncommon condition inside the beltway."

"Complacent?"

"There's so much money in Washington, and so many well-off, well-educated people interacting with each other. You're all so removed from dreary, exhausting problems. Your problems are so much more exciting! I think it all becomes a kind of game. This poverty exercise you did — what did you learn?"

Reve frowned for a minute, thinking.

"The short answer," he said slowly, "is poverty is a condition of practical difficulties over which people have little or no control, and their problems are intensified by institutions that profit from them. Our social safety net may help people literally survive, but not much more. Too many people don't make enough money even working full-time and lots of people who want work can't get it."

"Okay, now, didn't you already know that?"

"Well, that's the point of the exercise. Knowing those things in the abstract isn't the same as experiencing them. So yes, with respect to poverty I would agree that I was complacent. And so is everyone I know. I'm not excusing myself, I'm just saying complacency is probably the rule not the exception."

"Yes, I'm sure its the rule. To be fair, not just inside the beltway, but anywhere people are comfortable. And removed from people who aren't. But its the job of our elected officials to represent *everyone.* So I consider them more accountable than me. When they allow themselves to become complacent and comfortable and ignore or even worsen living conditions for a large chunk of the citizenry, then they're derelict in their duty."

"Could be."

"They should know better. They shouldn't be so easy to fool. They shouldn't have let Dennis succeed. Or you succeed, for that matter. They should have seen through it."

"What do you mean?"

"When Dennis talked about poverty, for instance, he had a purpose."

"Which was?"

"He maintained that low-income people are lazy, shiftless, dishonest and criminal and any efforts to aide them encourages bad behavior. Folks like you take the same ideas and pretty them up. Other media outlets provide platforms for people to debate or report on those points, giving them legitimacy. So your average person hears all kinds of celebrated people discussing these ideas and so they enter the mainstream and are taken seriously, even when they're factually wrong — which is often. Then groups conduct polls and surveys and produce results showing many Americans think welfare benefits are too generous and government money should be allocated elsewhere. Politicians see these survey results and start considering really stupid things like further weakening the social safety net because they think that's what the public supports. And isn't that great, since many of their rich funders agree! It's a perfect circle where everybody wins except the American public."

Reve grimaced. In actuality, one of IPR's standing gigs had been the delivery of talking points *to* Dash to use on his show. So Barbara was backwards there. But he decided not to correct her on that point.

"All of which is bad enough," Barbara went on, "but Dennis went further. He encouraged the next rung or two above poverty, people themselves struggling, but not desperate, he encouraged them to blame their struggles on the people at the bottom. Those with the fewest resources and the least amount of power are, according to him, responsible for everything going wrong in America. Folks like you recast the same ideas in more palatable forms. And the result? Everyone focuses *downward.*"

Reve was silent. Barbara got up and began pacing the kitchen.

"The hate-radio jocks like Dennis; the fanatical clergy and far-right politicians; the entire FOX News cast; the right-wing think tanks like yours — you're all like money launderers for drug cartels: you take lies and transmute them into conventional wisdom. You do it because it deflects attention from the powerful interests that both cause and benefit from poverty, as well as other things you all promote, like wars and too-big-to-fail banks and trade agreements that benefit a few large corporations and hurt everyone else, including the environment."

Barbara came back to the table, sat, and looked at him challengingly.

"Am I wrong?"

Reve, who had been staring at the table, met her eyes.

"So that's how you think it works?"

"That's how I think it works."

"I agree that a good deal of politicking involves sleight of hand and other forms of manipulation in order to convince people to vote certain ways. I'm not prepared to concede that my motivations are as sociopathic, irresponsible or just plain hateful as you imply."

Barbara's fierce expression softened.

"I will grant you that," she said. "If you were a sociopath or just plain hateful I really couldn't have any sort of relationship with you."

"You left out irresponsible."

"Well, that I can't give you."

"Why not?"

"Because what you do is a matter of degree and not kind. You're on one end and Dennis was at the other end, but it's the same stick. Dennis nourished hate, which leads directly to things like violent, right wing militia groups and hate crimes. Right wing politicians have made threats against President Obama, against judges they disagree with, against ATF agents and others. Many Americans are under relentless financial pressure and pressure messes people up. You guys poke sticks into wasp nests and stir, then step back and pretend you aren't responsible when bystanders get stung."

Reve thought about the teenagers in Mississippi who'd killed the black man and found he couldn't speak.

Something outdoors attracted Sabrina's attention and she shot through her dog door; they listened to her barks diminishing into the distance.

"Enough," said Reve.

"Enough what?"

"Stop. I can't listen any more. Can we stop for tonight?"

Barbara put her elbow on the table and rested her chin on her fist, suppressing the queue of arguments that were trying to push their way out of her throat. "Okay," she said levelly.

Having acquiesced, there followed an uneasy period as neither knew what to say or do next.

Then Barbara went back to her yarn, pencils and papers, while Reve fetched a glass of water. He drank it slowly.

"I bought a bottle of brandy today," Barbara said, tentatively. "I left it in the car. Do you want to go get it? I don't have snifters though."

"That was thoughtful — thanks. I'll get it."

Exiting the kitchen he followed a bricked pathway to the side of the house. Sabrina accompanied him, waiting politely while he opened the door of the car and hunted for the bottle. He found it in the back seat, next to the cardboard box he recalled (with a start) contained Dash's ashes. He stood for awhile looking at the box. He stroked Sabrina's head and took several deep breaths.

He really couldn't think anymore tonight. Not about anything serious anyway. And he might as well let Dash have his say, he thought, then he would . . . he would *figure things out.*

Walking slowly back to the kitchen, he gave his attention to the problem of Dash's ashes. He'd pour them both some brandy, he decided, and while Barbara did her thing he would go online and research what to do with cremated ashes. He remembered Barbara doing a similar search in vain. But she hadn't spent much time at it. Maybe he'd get lucky.

Re-entering the kitchen he found two red wine glasses and two highball glasses on the counter.

"Which do you think would work better?" Barbara asked. She was back at the table engaged in her mysterious activity.

"Oh, either will be fine. Which would you like?"

"Hmm . . . the wine glass I guess."

"Coming up."

After pouring a few ounces in each wine glass he delivered one to Barbara. They both took a sip.

Then he took out his smartphone and, pulling up the browser, began his search. Looking up he saw that Barbara was curious but hesitant to intrude.

"I'm looking something up," he said. "I'll tell you about it later if I find what I'm looking for, okay?"

"Sure. Of course. I'll just get back to what I was doing."

As each became engrossed in their respective activity the emotional temperature of the room lowered.

The brandy helped.

Barbara felt she'd had her say; it was up to Reve now. In any case, he needed time and she needed to regain her composure. To that end she cleared the decks mentally and went back to work on her yarn gauge.

Reve got absorbed in the search for the Dash ash solution and after some twenty minutes found what he was looking for.

He pulled out a credit card, asked Barbara for her address and ordered overnight shipping.

"I'll show you tomorrow," he said, when she couldn't help looking questioning. His face reflected a subdued satisfaction; he smiled to himself and that made her smile.

Her smile caused him to look at his watch and say: "Wow, look at the time! I've had a long day. Time to turn in?"

"Yes, it's late, isn't it? Perhaps we'd better."

He reached for her hand. As they touched, he felt the portal through the looking glass open up, and feeling a rush of anticipation and gratitude, pulled her through.

Chapter Twenty-One

Reve woke early. He wanted to organize his thoughts in preparation for his meeting with Congressman Wayland, but he couldn't concentrate properly. His on-its-merits response to the poverty simulation was: *something has to be done* but after that things were murky. He didn't know what could be done or who would do it. He didn't think his Party had any interest in improving the lives of low-income people; Republican economic policies centered around tax-cutting, rule-overturning, oversight-limiting, corporate-empowering initiatives. Theoretically they were trying to improve overall economic performance which should result in reduced poverty — and if conditions never quite aligned such to produce noticeable trickle-down, well, a few more tax cuts should do it. That millions of people suffered in the meantime was, some Republicans thought, regrettable (but not so regrettable as to require action), while other Republicans actually appreciated the existence of poor people, for reasons ranging from the pragmatic to the exploitative to the sadistic.

It was, he thought with a sigh, stony soil on his side of the aisle.

Not that the Democrats were doing any better he thought automatically. But at least they tried, he amended. Some of them, anyway. Others were resigned or perplexed about appropriate remedies, or fatalistic.

Another sigh.

What should he advise Wayland to do?

Moving carefully, he managed to slide out of bed without waking Barbara. Sabrina instantly appeared at his side and accompanied him as he collected his phone and trod softly down the stairs.

He went into the kitchen, started a pot of coffee and wandered over to the kitchen table with his phone to check the weather and his news-feeds.

Looked like a good-sized thunderstorm was coming after which there would be a blessed cooling and drop in humidity. Nice.

Turning to the news, he saw a reference to a state representative somewhere trying to ban SNAP recipients from buying fish and steak.

Idiot, he thought. Even before the poverty simulation I'd have disapproved. What is it with these guys?

Shaking his head in disgust, he put his phone down and, drawn by its enticing aroma, went to get his coffee. As he stirred in his thick, organic cream he thought about not being able to afford anything beyond necessities. The cream was just a little luxury, but — correction, he thought — it was one of *many* little luxuries he enjoyed (and took for granted).

On the day after the poverty simulation, as I was drinking coffee and running through my morning-online-news-gathering regimen, I came across a story about a Republican state representative in Missouri who'd introduced a bill prohibiting people receiving food stamps from buying seafood, energy drinks, sodas, cookies, chips or steak. The rep had, thus far, not explained his rationale for the bill, but according to local reporters, Republican lawmakers in Missouri are convinced benefit recipients choose unemployment (because they are lazy) and gratuitously lounge around eating steak dinners and potato chips. (When in fact, most benefit-recipients are employed but are paid so poorly they qualify for assistance.)

The representative responsible for the bill has quite the legislative history: when he isn't trying to prohibit abortion (unless the woman is "legitimately raped" and has permission from her father), he's demanding creationism be taught in Missouri schools. And, trying to spice up the death penalty by adding execution by firing squad as an option.

I looked up Missouri's minimum wage: $7.65/hour. Meanwhile, Missouri state reps get a salary of $35,915 for working an average of seventy days a year. On days they show up at the state house, they receive a $103 per diem for food and lodging expenses. The reps get a mileage allowance (37 cents a mile) and $700 a month expense allowance for "reasonable and necessary business expenses". Oh, and medical benefits, to which they make small contributions while taxpayers pick up the lions's share of the cost. Plus dental, vision and, after six years, a small pension.

Not a bad part-time job. I'm quite sure many of the reps work more than seventy days a year (just like teachers take a lot of work home), but still.

Meanwhile, Missouri has one of the stingier social safety nets with the usual assortment of catch-22s and Orwellian requirements.

Ultimately, there was just something mean-spirited and sanctimonious as well as indefensibly ignorant about this particular legislative gem.

This rep ran unopposed in his last election. Seems like a district crying out for a (I wish) charismatic Democrat who could turn a red district blue. Or a primary challenge.

At lunchtime I texted Peter.

At 9:30 Reve got a call from Melvin Thornery requesting he come to the Congressman's office at 2:00. Free for the morning, Reve went with Barbara to the farthest corner of her property in search of a missing sheep. Sabrina lead the way — she'd evidently located the animal already and needed help to retrieve it. It was warm and muggy, but the sky was a deep pewter and the wind was picking up.

The sheep had an injured foot and between them, Barbara and Reve carried it to the barn for first aid. While Barbara ministered to the sheep, Reve wiped the sweat off his forehead and watched a UPS truck arrive and depart.

Returning to the house, Reve went around front. On the porch was a brown cardboard shipping box, about 24 inches high and a foot wide. He took it to the kitchen and placed it on the kitchen table.

"For you," he said, waving grandly at the box, "I hope you like it."

He smiled as she approached the table, her forehead wrinkled.

"What is it?"

"Open it and see!"

Barbara fetched a pair of scissors and used one of the blades to cut through strips of packing tape. She pulled out what appeared to be a large styrofoam-like container with an image of a green leaf on it. Below it was a brochure. She read it, then looked at Reve.

"It's a biodegradable urn with space for a tree sapling to be mixed with cremated ashes?"

"We get a sapling, add Dash's ashes to it and plant it, and the ashes will become nutrients for a new tree."

Suddenly, Barbara's hands went up to cover her eyes and Reve was dismayed to see her start to cry. He reached towards her.

"Barbara — I thought — I didn't mean — "

He dropped his arms helplessly.

"No, it's wonderful," she said, scrabbling at her eyes and reaching for a napkin. After wiping her eyes and nose she said: "I love it. I don't know why I cried. Thank you."

"My God, you gave me a scare!"

She chuckled; then, one hand holding the brochure and the other taking his hand, she pulled him back down the hall and out the front door. She led him to the padded outdoor chairs at the end of the porch.

The humidity was yielding to cooler air being blown briskly over the landscape. Dark clouds were multiplying and flashes of lightening were distantly visible. A thunder clap sounded.

"We'll probably have to go inside soon, if the rain gets blown under the porch roof." Barbara said. "But, depending on the direction and strength of the wind, you can sometimes stay perfectly dry while it pours. We'll see."

As the rain began in earnest, they looked over the instructions for planting the urn.

"Where should we plant it?"

"Somewhere here on the farm?" Reve answered.

"We could. But who knows if I'll keep the farm? And when I die and someone else gets it, there's no guarantee the tree wouldn't be cut down."

"That'll be true no matter where you plant it, unless you plant it in a protected area of some kind. A nature conservancy or something."

"Ooh, that's a good idea! We'll look into it."

A gust of wind blew her hair; lightening forked the sky and a very loud crack of thunder made them jump.

"I love a good storm," said Barbara exultantly. "If it gets too violent I'll be scared, but if it stays like this I'll enjoy it. Are you okay?"

"I'm fine."

Reve was less enthralled by the storm than by Barbara watching the storm. She had the look roller-coaster enthusiasts wear when they're screaming in joyous terror: ultra-alive.

Elated with the success of his gift he felt a surge of utter contentment. Then he remembered his upcoming meeting with Congressman Wayland and realized he was still unsure what to advise.

He decided to present his problem to Barbara.

"When you can't decide something," she said, "you either lack information or want to do something, but fear the consequences. In your case, you want to tell him to run on doing something about poverty, but think he'd lose if he makes an issue of it."

"Right. I can't tell him to do something he'll fail at, can I?"

"Well, the only way he could possibly succeed is if he tries. You could try to brainstorm a bunch of tactics that might help him win. But if you think it's utterly hopeless and useless, you'd better be honest and tell him so. Do you?"

"Maybe not utterly hopeless. The problems are real and they need to be addressed. There might be a window of opportunity — a lot depends on his opponent. And the party apparatus isn't as monolithic or united as it used to be. A few high-level republicans have started to talk about the struggling middle-class. But it's one of those situations where he could lead the way or be crushed."

"It sounds to me like a "feeling" kind of decision," she said.

"What do you mean?"

"Some things are worth a try, even if you fail. What will he regret more?

Trying and failing or not trying? Sometimes you succeed because you want to *so badly,* even against great odds. Sometimes you fail because you just go through the motions; you're not committed. Those are all emotionally driven behaviors. Tell him he has the power to solve, or start to solve, a serious problem and you'd like him to try. That's what you want to do, isn't it?"

"I guess. I guess I do. But my job is to tell him what I think will help him, not satisfy me."

"You have the logical answer then. But you don't want to deliver it. The logic isn't satisfying you emotionally. You're going to have to feel your way to your decision. And so will he."

Peter didn't know what to think.

Wayland had arrived that morning, greeted him, gone into his office (with Thornery) and stayed there.

The morning hours ticked by. Take-out for two was delivered to the congressman's office at lunchtime. Trying to work, Peter stopped often to stare out his window, eventually noticing a robust thunderstorm in progress.

He was certain they were conferring about his suggested new campaign approach, but he had no idea which way they were leaning.

Clearly they didn't want his input, which probably meant they were leaning "no".

On the other hand, the fact they were still debating (presumably) implied they were struggling with their decision, which might mean there was hope.

Twice he went to the office door, put his hand up to knock, then changed his mind and retreated to his desk.

He didn't know whether Reve Tierney had offered any counsel the previous night.

He wondered if suspense *could* kill?

A text arrived from Wynne with a link to a story and the words "primary challenge?"

He clicked the link. Oh yeah, that guy. He's always doing something stupid and now *this.*

Primary challenge? Definite food for thought.

Then Reve Tierney walked into the office suite. He was dressed in tan chinos and a green sport shirt and his hair was wet.

Seeing Peter, Reve asked: "Is the Congressman in his office?"

On the affirmative, Reve nodded, knocked on the door and entered.

Peter, a healthy physical specimen, was sure he could feel his blood pressure soaring. Mercifully, the office door opened again and Reve, poking his head around the doorjamb, invited Peter to join them.

The Congressman, Melvin Thornery and Reve were seated around an oblong wooden table used for working meetings. Peter sat on one of the remaining empty chairs.

The Congressman cleared his throat.

"Well Peter, as you probably guessed, we've been discussing campaign strategy and last night's poverty exercise. I want to hear what Reve thinks before coming to a final decision."

Peter nodded. He looked at Melvin, whose face gave nothing away, then he looked at Reve, whose expression was equally unreadable.

There was a weighty silence.

Then Reve cleared his throat and heard himself say: "The poverty simulation helped solidify a feeling I've been wrestling with for some time now."

He replayed the words in his head, swallowed and began again: "I haven't been . . . comfortable . . . with where we've gotten to as a party. I haven't been comfortable with my own work. I trust you will treat this as confidential for now."

Wayland thought "Damn! I need advice, not a confession!"

Thornery thought "I knew this was coming. That appearance on CNN . . . "

Peter thought "Yes! An ally!"

Three heads bobbed. No one commented.

"So, Congressman, what Peter has been suggesting represents a definite departure from the party's platform."

"I know that," said Wayland, with a touch of impatience.

"My advice is to go for it," Reve said simply.

"Really?" said Thornery, anticipating Wayland.

"Yes," said Reve. He looked at Peter, who's face was alight with relief and hope, then at Wayland, who's face was twitching, then at Thornery, who looked skeptical.

"Are you surprised?" he asked Thornery.

"Yes and no," Thornery replied.

"You disagree?"

"Yes and no," Thornery repeated.

Wayland emitted a dismissive sound; they had argued both sides all morning long. They'd tried lists of pros and cons; they'd tried ranking the "pain points" on scales of one to ten; they'd sketched little decision-making boxes, and every approach ended in a draw.

Wayland related as much in a few terse sentences and Reve nodded understandingly.

"You're trying to logic your way to this decision," he said, "and, as you have found, it won't work.."

"Well, what else are we supposed to do?" Thornery asked defensively.

"You have to feel your way," Reve heard himself say, then wondered if he could take it back. Wayland and Thornery wore matching expressions of incredulity. But Peter was smiling seraphically.

"He's saying you need to look in your heart," Peter said.

"Something like that," Reve assented. Well, he'd said it; he might as well go the distance. "We all know the choice is risky with respect to its impact on your electability. It could pay off or be disastrous. Obviously much depends on how you present yourself and your ideas, and how you counter your opponents responses. And all of that is dependent on how you feel about it. This is a gut-based choice. You should try to address poverty in this country because you believe it's the right thing to do, not because focusing on it *might* win you a primary. It might as easily lose you the primary. But!"

Reve held up his hand, forestalling comment by Thornery, "But! Handled right, it could be a game changer."

"How?" Wayland asked flatly.

"Politically we treat poverty as a condition of a specific subset of the population. But in reality, a large percentage of the middle class is sliding nearer to poverty every day. Our tactic has been to deflect their attention from the powerful towards the powerless. We've made no actual effort to change the underlying conditions. What if we did?"

"Amen," said Peter.

"What are you talking about?" Wayland demanded. "We've cut taxes, cut spending and cut government interference — "

"And what have been the results?"

Wayland began to splutter but nothing coherent emerged; Thornery cut in: "The results have been we've taken over a majority of governorships, state legislatures, the courts and now the Congress and Senate."

"All of which helps the party as an institution and certainly helps the so-called one percent, but how has it helped the dwindling middle class, let alone the poor?"

"A majority of white working-class men vote for us," Thornery said.

"They do. But not because we've helped them. They vote for us because we've done an excellent job of scapegoating the poor and minorities. We've done nothing to combat forty years of wage stagnation. Neither have the Democrats. But *someone* is going to have to deal with how the economy is failing working people or things are going to get ugly in America. Uglier than it already is. We've been the party of division and invective and obstruction.

We win by rigging the game. Frankly, I don't see that succeeding for much longer."

There was a pause while all thought.

Reve was astonished at the stuff that was coming out of his mouth.

Wayland was wondering where it would all end. He'd spent years extolling the free market, the unshackling of business from inept government entities, and the ability of everyone to make it in America if they just tried hard enough. The ideas all worked together; start tinkering with one and it would invariably impact the next, which would impact the next . . .

Thornery was wishing they'd just fired Peter instead of indulging his misplaced idealism. He was convinced — well *pretty sure* — Wayland could beat his primary challenger via the tried and true tactic of out-conservativing him. The playbook was written; it usually worked, and it didn't require risky strategizing.

Peter was wondering what had happened to Reve.

Reve's phone vibrated. Pulling it out of his pocket, he saw it was Barbara calling. While he let it go to message, he was aware of an uptick to his mood.

Observing the agonized indecision that ebbed and flowed over Wayland's face like the tide washing in and out, he felt a gentle pity. Poor guy, he thought. I'd bet money he won't run on the poverty issue, but he's considering it. Kudos.

He looked at Peter. Nice kid, he thought. Wonder what will happen to him?

He looked at Thornery and knew exactly what Thornery was thinking. He sympathized. A few weeks ago he'd have felt precisely the same way.

"Look," said Reve, briskly, "there's no magic answer here. You all know what the risks are. You have to *want* to do this. You need to feel like Peter does," he glanced at Peter, who nodded. "But if you don't, you don't. Melvin doesn't, do you?" he asked, turning towards Thornery.

"No. I think we've given the idea fair consideration, but the obstacles and risks are too overwhelming. I think we'd lose. The brutal fact is poverty isn't a Republican issue."

"Yes it is," Peter said. "We talk about it all the time, and what we say is that it's poor people's fault they're poor. We don't talk about any of the structural realities that cause poverty and make it really hard to escape from. And we present legislation that makes it worse."

"We don't support legislation with the intent of making poverty worse, we support legislation with the intent of making businesses more profitable. When businesses thrive workers thrive," Thornery retorted.

"In theory, maybe. But I see little evidence of that in our district. Our district has been losing decent-paying jobs, private sector and public sector, and replacing them with low-paying, no-benefit jobs. We have houses sitting empty and busy homeless shelters. Wages are up for the very top and flat for most everyone else. College is increasingly unaffordable. People are not feeling optimistic and they hate Congress." Peter said.

"They hate Congress as an institution, but they like their own Congressmen," Wayland interjected. "That makes a difference."

"Right!" said Thornery. "Congressman Wayland has always done well with Republican voters in his district. We should be banking on that, not contemplating some leftist shift that will only piss off supporters."

"He's being primaried! That tells me his popularity isn't a shoo-in anymore!" Peter retorted, his voice getting louder.

"He's being primaried from the *right!*" Thornery shouted, "In what universe does it make sense to move left when his challenge is from the right?"

"It's not a matter of right or left," Peter shouted back, "it's a matter of right or wrong!"

"Boys! Boys!" Wayland shouted in his turn, "Quiet down! This isn't helping!"

Right or wrong, Thornery was thinking, *Oh please.* Exactly what planet did Peter live on? But he pulled back in his chair and subsided.

"Melvin presents the pragmatic perspective," Reve said. "Peter is the idealist. Pragmatism is predictable and manageable; idealism is inspirational, aspirational and unpredictable. Melvin wants to do what he thinks best increases the odds of a win. Peter wants to do what he thinks is right, win or lose."

"The Congressman can't do anything, right or wrong, if he loses," said Thornery.

"That is true," Reve conceded, "but what he *can* do will be constricted by the promises he makes while he campaigns."

"Not if this is his last term."

"Oh I see. Is that your plan Congressman?"

"I'm leaning that way."

"So you're saying he should lie to get elected and then break his promises?" Peter asked.

Melvin just managed to refrain from rolling his eyes, but the eye-rolling feeling was palpable.

"Look," said Peter, "I know you think I'm being naive, but I'm a believer. *Lying lips are an abomination to the Lord, but those who act faithfully are his delight.* Proverbs 12:22. Don't we claim to be Christian? Does that claim have any meaning at all?"

Melvin pursed his lips, but said nothing. Some people are so literal, he thought.

Wayland bowed his head. Thornery and Tierney understood the realities of the world, he thought; understood why a believer could justify lying for the greater good. But, looking at Peter's painfully seeking expression, he found himself unable to make the case.

Reve was gazing in some fascination at Peter. What was it like, he wondered? To believe something through and through? Not with qualifications or exceptions or rationalizations. There was a qualitative difference between how Peter seemed to experience his Christianity as compared to, well, Wayland, for instance. Peter had melded his inner and outer life; he, Wayland, Thornery and so many others in Reve's experience, maintained a strict separation.

How did Barbara compare? He didn't think she *believed* in quite the same way as Peter, probably because she took her cues from multiple sources and disciplines while Peter's touchstone was the Bible. What they had in common was the simple but, as he was learning, profound need or desire to *follow through.* If they declared a belief they tried to live it.

Could he be like that?

It would be different he thought, and suddenly felt both inspired and impatient. He wished he could reach across the spiritual gulf that separated Peter from Wayland and Thornery and pull them together, but knew himself to be unequal to the task. All this was new terrain to him; he couldn't guide anyone else to a place he'd only just discovered. So there was little point in discussing anything further. Wayland's indecision told it's own tale.

Wayland needed additional stimulus. Having reached this conclusion, Reve looked around. Thornery looked fed-up; Wayland was bleak and Peter was distressed.

"I'm wondering, Congressman, if you should consider soliciting input from Reverend Fenimore?" Reve said.

Peter's expression lightened at this suggestion; Thornery grimaced and Wayland sighed.

"I don't know," Wayland said, "what will he say that we haven't already considered?"

"It may not be what he'll say, it may be how he says it," Reve replied.

"Or maybe Melvin should go through a poverty simulation," Peter said challengingly.

For a few seconds Reve thought Thornery was about to royally lose his temper, but he didn't. He confined himself to a decisive head-shake to the negative. "I'm not disputing any of the facts you learned, or the conclusions you drew," he said, "I'm just saying I don't see a viable way to act on them unless we're prepared for the Congressman to lose. It's just too removed from the party platform as it stands right now. We'd be working in opposition to years of messaging. The party might well cut us loose."

"So you're saying we're locked into this *un-compassionate* conservatism indefinitely," Peter said flatly.

"For the time being at any rate, yes. For this election cycle, definitely yes."

Reve watched Peter absorb this. Then Peter looked at Wayland. "Congressman?" he said.

Wayland cleared his throat, then said: "I think Melvin's probably right." He opened his mouth to add something but closed it again.

"Okay then," Peter said. He looked down for a few seconds, then raised his eyes, then stood. "Do you need me for anything further today?" he asked quietly.

Wayland shook his head.

"I'll just be going then," said Peter, and he began walking towards the door.

"Peter," Reve said, "can you wait a moment? I'll be right out."

"Okay. Goodnight Congressman, Melvin." Then Peter left the office, closing the door carefully behind him.

Reve looked at Wayland who waved his hands in a gesture of pure helplessness. Reve smiled faintly.

"I know," Reve said. "I understand. I wish I could help. But I don't have an office to lose. If it's any consolation, I really don't think there's an easy answer for you. As we learned from the poverty simulation, sometimes all the available choices are bad."

Then he looked back at Thornery. "Good luck, Melvin. Hope things work out."

He started moving toward the door, stopping when Wayland said "Reve!"

"Yes?"

"What are you going to do?"

"I haven't decided. But when I do, I'm sure you'll hear about it. It probably won't be pretty."

"Don't you care?" asked Thornery.

"Oh, I don't know. That's another thing I got from that simulation: perspective. I have plenty of money — I will never be hungry or cold or homeless. Compared to most people I have it really, really good. At the worst, people will rip me up on social media, which I've been through a thousand times already."

"It'll be worse than that. I mean, depending on what you do," said Thornery. "You could be cut off. No more TV, no more access to movers and shakers in the party."

"I'll bear that in mind, Melvin."

"Reve!"

"Yes, Congressman?"

"You're Catholic, aren't you?

"Nominally. I may have to give this new Pope a closer look. Why?"

"Just wondered. Wondered if you'd been saved."

"Oh, I've been saved all right."

After Reve closed the door behind him, Thornery looked at Wayland and said: "He's toast."

Wayland stared at him expressionlessly for a minute, then said: "Melvin, go home."

"Congressman, I — "

"I'll talk to you tomorrow."

Stiffly, Melvin rose, gathered his dignity around him like a cloak, and removed himself. As he exited the office, he saw Reve standing next to Peter.

"Don't mind me," he said morosely, "I've been dismissed for the day and am going home." Turning his back on them, he went to his desk, collected his laptop and bag, and exited without another word.

Reve and Peter exchanged glances and then both grinned.

"But he's not wrong, you know," Reve said, "if the objective is to retain office at all costs."

"I know," said Peter, suddenly deflated, "it's just . . . just — "

"I know."

"Is that what it all boils down to? People attain office and then it becomes all about them?"

"Not necessarily, but more often than not. I don't think they mean it — most of them. They convince themselves their motives are pure, even if their actions aren't. And they tell themselves whoever would replace them would be worse. Of course, some of them don't have a conscience in the first place. But most of them just slowly lose touch."

"I guess." Peter paused, then: "What did you want to see me about?"

"Do you have Reverend Fenimore's phone number?"

Surprised, Peter pulled out his phone and read out the number for Reve to copy into his own phone list.

"Thanks," Reve said. "I wanted to ask him to officiate at a . . . funeral, of sorts," he explained.

"Oh, well. I'm meeting him shortly. He's at a meeting here in town. Do you want to tag along?"

"Tell you what, why don't you see if he can meet us at the Cosmos Club for dinner on me?"

"Really?"

"Sure. And I'll let the Congressman know we'll be there in case he wants to stop by."

"Really?"

"It's worth a try isn't it?"

"I suppose. Let me text the Reverend."

While Peter was engaged, Reve turned away and called Barbara.

"I'll be having dinner in town," he said, "but will come back to your house afterwards, Okay?"

"Of course. Where are you going to eat?"

"The Cosmos Club."

"Oh, nice. And Reve, I found a nursery where we can get a sapling to be the Dash tree."

"Funny you should mention that."

"Why?"

"I'll tell you later."

When he turned back to Peter he got an affirmative gesture.

"Okay, be right back," he said, and walked back to Wayland's office, where he tapped lightly. "Congressman?" he asked.

"Come in."

Wayland was still seated at the table. He looked at Reve tiredly.

"Just wanted to tell you Peter and I will be having dinner at the Cosmos Club with Reverend Fenimore. If you want to join us or stop for coffee or a drink you'll be most welcome."

"I'll think about it," Wayland said. "Thanks."

"You bet."

"Oh Reve? I may want to talk to you about this further. Without Melvin or Peter pulling at me."

"Of course, Congressman. Of course."

Chapter Twenty-Two

Shortly thereafter, Reve was recalling his last visit to the Cosmos Club Dining Room on the night he'd first met Barbara. It was a mere matter of days ago, and a lifetime ago. Then he looked at Peter's woebegone face.

"How did all this come about, Peter?" he asked.

Peter explained how his growing unhappiness had ultimately led him to meet with Wynne Frost and Reverend Fenimore.

"How did you meet Wynne Frost? Doesn't she work with Democrats?"

Visibly hesitant, Peter debated whether he could safely divulge Connie's existence.

"It's okay Peter, you don't have to tell me. I was just curious. When in doubt don't tell — at least, that's my opinion."

"That's the kind of thing Wynne says," Peter replied. "She's been very helpful. And so has the Reverend. I just have to decide what to do now."

"Had you formed any plans on that? I mean, you knew going in the odds were low, right?"

"Oh absolutely. But trying felt like the right thing to do. It made my job worth doing for a little longer. But I think that's over. I've been talking to Wynne and the Reverend and . . . others . . . about going to work as a consultant, with the goal of building bridges between more progressive evangelicals and politicians. I'm still exploring the progressive evangelical side of things myself. Reverend Fenimore is mentoring me. It's a big change."

"Are you thinking of trying to work with Republicans? Or Democrats?"

Once again Peter hesitated.

"You don't have to answer that, but let me assure you anything we discuss tonight will remain confidential."

"Okay . . . I don't know. I was raised Republican and the idea of switching parties is hard to swallow. But I'll have to discover who's receptive. If there aren't any Republicans . . . "

"You'll go across the aisle?"

"I'll have to, won't I?"

"Probably."

"You know, I think Melvin Thornery was expecting you to back him and he wasn't too happy when you told the Congressman to go for it. I didn't know what to expect so I was thrilled. Have *you* had a change of heart?"

"You could say that. About poverty anyway. And maybe some other things."

They both stared off into the distance, contemplating change. Then Reve thought of Barbara and couldn't help smiling.

"What?" said Peter, seeing the smile.

"Well, lets just say on a personal level there can be compensations."

"I know what you mean," Peter replied without thinking, then looked stricken.

Reve eyed him with dawning comprehension.

"Oh, so that's how it is. You've met someone?"

Peter considered his answer carefully, then with a slightly mischievous look, said: "You could say that. You?"

"You could say that."

Arthur, their waiter, arrived with a soft drink for Peter and a glass of Merlot for Reve. As he delivered their drinks, Reve found himself taking a good look at Arthur. Arthur had waited on him many times and looked to be in his forties. Was he married? Did he have children? Was he able to meet his obligations without undue stress? Did he have any money saved? Did he have a pension in his future? Did he own a home? How much money did he make?

Who did Arthur vote for, if he voted at all? Why? If he knew what Reve did for a living would he approve, disapprove or be indifferent?

Reve's gaze moved from Arthur's professionally friendly face to the far reaches of the dining room. He took in the scurrying of the efficient, swiftly-moving staff, bringing drinks poured by the bartender into glasses washed by someone in the kitchen who labored along side the cooks who prepared the food. How much did they make? What were their lives like?

Their work was, generally speaking, taken for granted. Not for them the prestige he enjoyed; the very generous salary, the opportunities to mingle with accomplished and celebrated people as equals. They didn't mingle, they served. But their service, in a minor but nevertheless real way, enriched his life.

One could argue, he thought, the individuals he was watching were interchangeable and replaceable. If Arthur wasn't there, some other man would be. Did that lessen the value of his work? Did it mean Arthur's needs or hopes could be, should be, ignored or exploited?

The Arthurs of the world were *unimportant.*

Unlike him. People had listened to him over the years.

Important people. Powerful people. One important person affecting other important persons.

Had anything he'd done during those years enriched Arthur's life?

His instinct to abandon an uncomfortable train of thought kicked in, but Reve resisted. He would not evade.

No, he decided, on balance his impact on the lives of the people presently serving him had probably been more negative than positive.

Although he was a good tipper, which should count for something.

Still — it was a funny thing, he thought. His work had given him an entree into the halls of power; you could say he wielded power himself in that he shaped the opinions of literally millions of people, including many in very high places. But his work, ultimately, had been aimed at supporting the goals and ambitions of others who sought and wielded more and different kinds of power, in some cases world-changing power.

All that power being sought, fought for and exercised, by so many brilliant, talented, competitive, ambitious people.

And to what end? For whom?

He was still considering that question when he realized he'd withdrawn into a reverie, leaving Peter to occupy himself by monitoring the entranceway for Reverend Fenimore's arrival.

"Peter," he said abruptly, "how did Wynne Frost help you exactly?"

Peter looked slightly uncomfortable.

"She's — she's a bit of a psychic," he said, then waited, to gauge Reve's reaction.

"So I understand," Reve replied lightly.

"Oh, you've heard about that?"

"Somewhere or other. How does it work?"

"I don't know really. It's not like she looks at crystal ball or anything. She just seems to be able to find the essence of a person and point them in the right direction. Or *a* right direction — maybe we all have more than one, I don't know. Anyway, for me she got me to realize I couldn't keep doing work that betrayed my beliefs. I knew that, but I didn't want to acknowledge it because once I admitted my dissatisfaction, I would have to act."

"I see."

"Then she came up with the consulting idea."

"Ah."

"And some other things."

"The poverty simulation?"

"No, that happened through the Reverend and he happened because my — my girlfriend — suggested I talk to a progressive evangelical minister. But Wynne helped me figure out how to approach Wayland while being honest."

"Oh. Interesting."

"And it worked. Got him there anyway," Peter said glumly.

"That's not insignificant, you know," Reve said consolingly. "If nothing else, you've planted some seeds. It was definitely worth a try. He may just need time to let things germinate."

"That's true. I held out for a long time myself, after all. It's probably not fair to expect him to make such a big change this quickly. And here's the Reverend!"

Reverend Fenimore swept in. "Hello Peter! Reve, how are you?"

After appropriate exchanges, the Reverend seated himself and looked interestedly around. Arthur arrived, supplying menus and reciting the evening's specials.

"Well Peter?" the Reverend asked after Arthur withdrew with their dinner orders.

"For now at least the Congressman will stick with the status quo," Peter said, and sighed.

Fenimore took this composedly, remarking it had been a long shot. "And don't take it to heart," he added. "Remember, for those who love God, all things work together for good."

"Amen," said Peter, brightening.

"And I don't doubt it made an impression," he went on. "It's a start." He looked at Reve. "And you wanted to ask me about a funeral?"

"Sort of. Would you be willing to do a blessing over the burial of some cremated ashes?" He went on to explain the biodegradable urn with the tree sapling.

"Where will you plant this tree?"

"Not sure yet. Possibly in a nature preserve somewhere."

"Is this a relative of yours?"

"Not of mine, but brother of a friend."

The reverend looked curiously at Reve. "In principle, I would be happy to provide a blessing. Why don't you contact me with the details when they're finalized," he said.

"I'll do that. Thank you."

"And, don't hesitate to tell me it's none of my business," the Reverend continued, a slightly impish look in his eye, "but, your presence here, with Peter, makes me wonder if you are, um, venturing into more progressive political waters?"

There was a long pause.

"I don't know . . . let's say I'm exploring the terrain," Reve replied.

Fenimore's smile held a wealth of understanding. "Well, well. Perhaps we can all help one another."

"What do you mean?" Peter asked.

"I can provide some amount of spiritual guidance and you two can teach me how to be more politically active.

"Sounds good to me," said Peter.

"Er, just so you know, Reverend, I'm a Catholic. More or less," said Reve.

"Don't worry Reve, I'm not trying to convert you. Although it makes me wonder why you approached me and not a priest for your burial ceremony."

"I haven't been to church for quite awhile and my friend wasn't Catholic . . . "

"I see. So in a pinch any clergyman will do?"

"Well — "

"I'm kidding!"

Relieved, Reve explained that he'd been very impressed by the Reverend's conviction at the poverty simulation. The Reverend thanked him.

Peter wondered whether Congressman Wayland would show up.

Congressman Wayland's car was, in fact, approaching the main entranceway at that moment. Wayland was about to turn into the entrance when he noticed a man walking, seemingly casually, along the sidewalk that fronted the set-back building. There was something familiar about him.

Concentrated inspection revealed the man to be Lloyd Wilksie.

Perplexed, Wayland surveyed him. Thornery should have ended the Peter engagement. Wilksie must be tailing someone else. Who? He thought about accosting him, but realized the effort would be both futile and foolish. Wilksie never told — that was his value.

A sudden urge to be invisible assailed him. He drove on, around the corner, entering the back parking lot. Then he pulled out his emergency cell phone; the disposable phone with the prepaid minutes.

Arthur had just delivered their salads when Reve's phone vibrated. Reve saw an unfamiliar number, name withheld. He let it go to message. A minute later his phone vibrated again with the same number. Something made him answer.

"Reve? Don't identify me! This is Wayland."

"Oh. Hello," he said, surprised.

"Just wanted to give you a head's up. There's an ex-FBI agent we use once in awhile to do . . . background checks who's outside the Cosmos right now. I suspect he's tailing someone. I'm wondering if that someone is you."

"Me?" said Reve blankly.

"Think about it. Could be someone else, of course. Could be anyone. I'm letting you know just in case. Check your email — I'm sending a photo then I'm going home."

The call ended and Reve stared at his phone for a minute, bemused. Looking up, he saw Peter and Fenimore regarding him curiously.

"That was odd," he said. Very quietly he relayed the conversation.

All three of them began surreptitiously studying the other diners but none were at all familiar to Peter or the Reverend and those who Reve knew or knew of seemed unlikely candidates for surveillance.

"Is this a normal thing?" the Reverend asked, quizzically. Peter shrugged helplessly and they looked at Reve.

"Normal? In some circles I suppose. It's a first time for me — if it is me he's watching, which he probably isn't. The Congressman may just be feeling paranoid given that he's been considering a deviation from party orthodoxy."

"But what if he *is* watching you?" Peter asked.

"Well, hmm," Reve replied, "I really don't know. It's not like I can do anything, right? I mean, what could I do? Wait, here's a photo of the guy."

Reve put his phone on the table and they all squinted at it. Taken from a distance, the photo showed a trim man wearing dark colored pants, a plaid short-sleeved cotton shirt and a baseball cap. He was standing on the sidewalk several feet east of the main entrance to the Cosmos club, apparently on his cellphone. His face was shadowed.

"You know what this means?" asked Reverend Fenimore.

"What?" Reve and Peter said simultaneously.

"If the Congressman knows this man, it probably means he's used him before, don't you think?"

Suddenly Peter was indignant.

"You know, I had a feeling they'd found out about me and my girlfriend; did Wayland sic him on me?"

"It's possible I guess," said Reve. "Wayland did say he's used the guy for background checks."

"I'm going out there to ask him!" said Peter, rising, a martial light in his eyes.

"Wait!," said the Reverend, putting his hand on Peter's arm and pulling him back down. "If he denies knowing you or the Congressman, then what?"

"Oh yeah. True. But still — "

They looked at one another in consternation.

"I'm calling Wynne," said Peter.

"Why?" said Reve, while the Reverend asked "Who?"

"Because she's a strategist. She'll have an idea." He started his call while Reve leaned towards Reverend Fenimore and said "I'll tell you later."

They listened while Peter explained the situation. There was a long interval while Wynne either thought or spoke.

"We can't use the photo for identification, can we?" Peter asked, apparently at Wynne's behest.

"If you mean does the photo clearly show his face the answer is no," Reve said.

Peter listened a little longer, ended the call, then smiled grimly.

"Here's the plan," he said.

Chapter Twenty-Three

For Wilksie, the evening was going reasonably well. The rain had stopped, the humidity was low and the temperature a comfortable 79 degrees. After days in the nineties with high humidity, it felt wonderful.

He'd trailed his quarry to the Cosmos Club. Now he needed a plan for getting in and getting a look at who his man was with, and, even better, a photo. But the Cosmos was a private club. To get inside, he would need an invitation from a member. He thought about trying to bluff his way in, but rejected the idea as likely to produce unwanted attention (the last thing he wanted). His goal was to move unnoticed through the world.

Furthermore, the club was a large place, and while he'd be willing to bet his man was in the bar or dining room, he might be attending an event, using the library, visiting another member's room, or even booking a room for himself.

The next-best plan was to wait for his quarry to leave. People often arrived separately but left as a group. But the situation was complicated by the club's multiple entrances, parking lots and the valet parking service. His man had parked in the West Garden lot and strolled around the building to the front entrance. Couldn't use the valet parking, Wilksie thought, and spent a minute swearing to himself. His man might leave through the front door or might use the side exit or might be spending the night.

The best plan, he decided, was to inconspicuously stroll the sidewalk from the West Garden lot to the front entrance and back and hope he got lucky. Fortunately, he could blend in to the steady stream of people entering and exiting the building as well as walking past it.

The club was surrounded by a tall ornate fence and had a course of steps and inclines leading to the front entrance. He might just be able to sit, periodically, on the lowest set of stairs for a few minutes playing the role of sightseer-killing-time.

He had completed two leisurely laps of his route and was several yards west of the main entrance when he noticed Reve Tierney coming out the front entrance accompanied by a man in clerical garb. Delighted, he slowed his pace, looking for a natural slow spot among the ever moving hoard of passersby where he could stop and snap a photo when he felt a tap on his back.

"Excuse me," said a voice and, turning around, Wilksie saw the familiar face of Peter Gilen.

"Can you tell me where the Cosmos Club is?" Peter asked. His usually open, friendly features were oddly rigid and his voice vibrated with suppressed adrenaline, putting Wilksie instantly on the alert.

Wilksie's training kicked in: he made himself look calm and unaffected.

"You're almost there," Wilksie said, turning and pointing toward the main stairs. Two things then occurred in rapid succession: first, he saw Reve and his companion reach the sidewalk and begin walking towards him; second, he turned back to see Peter, cell phone elevated, snap his picture.

"What the — " he uttered, surprised. Then disgusted at his surprise, his face darkened and he took a menacing step towards Peter, who had prudently moved several paces backwards.

"What do you think you're doing," Wilksie said, in a low but surprisingly intimidating tone.

"I am," Peter began hesitantly, registering the intensity of Wilksie's gaze and holding his phone behind his back, "catching you," his voice became more sure, "in the act."

"Now you listen to me, Gilen," Wilksie began when, noticing a look of relief on Peter's face, he turned again to find himself flanked by Reve Tierney and his friend. Both men had phones in their hands and each snapped a photo.

"Who's this, Peter?" Reve asked.

"I don't know his name," Peter replied steadily, "but he knows mine."

"Really?"

Wilksie didn't move while Reve's companion filled the space in front of him. He now stood with Peter to his right, the stranger in front of him and Reve to his left. His back was blocked by the iron fence that ran along the perimeter of the club's property.

Through the operation of a sort of osmosis, people flowed around them resolutely not paying attention.

Wilksie's eyes darted left and right.

"Don't run away," said Reve. "We have photos of you."

Wilksie's hands twitched.

"You'd have to get all our phones," said Reve evenly.

Wilksie closed his eyes, took a deep breath, and relaxed. He opened his eyes again, fixed an expression of friendly inquiry on his face and said: "Okay, fellas, whatever you say. What now?"

"We want to know who you're tailing," said Reve.

Wilksie made a sorrowful face. "Now, you know I can't tell you that," he said. "I'm just doing a job and in my business client confidentiality is *all*."

"Yes, well, I expect anonymity helps, doesn't it?" Reve replied.

Wilksie looked uneasy, licked his lips and remained mute.

"If you don't tell us who you're tailing, we will do two things. First, we'll go back into the club, visit every table, show every person your photo and warn them that you have someone under surveillance," said Reve.

Wilksie's mouth turned down, his eyes narrowed but he still said nothing.

"That doesn't seem to be worrying him," Reverend Fenimore remarked.

"Which probably means he's tailing one of us, doesn't it?" said Peter. "Are you following me?"

"Or me?" asked Reve.

"Or me?" asked Reverend Fenimore.

"Look, I can't tell you," Wilksie said again.

"The second thing we're going to do is post your photo on Instagram and Facebook, and email it to every contact we have," said Reve.

"Now listen guys!" Wilksie protested.

"Why?" Reve asked.

"Look, I'm just doing a job."

"Does that argument work for you Peter?" Reve asked.

"No! You, Reverend?"

"I'm afraid not. Although I hesitate to do this man an injury. And I would counsel you against it. But I might not prevail."

Wilksie began shaking his head energetically.

"Look, look," he said, "don't you understand? I never tell anything about anyone except what I learn about a case to a client."

"Well, we seem to be at a standstill then," Reve said. "Let me give a few tips on how to survive a social media storm. First — "

"Wait!

"Peter, why don't you email your photo to someone you know for safekeeping," Reve said.

"Good idea!"

"Hold on! Stop!"

"Peter — "

"Alrightalrightalright!" Wilksie looked at each of them in turn. Peter looked excited; the stranger, amused. And Reve, immovable. About them all pulsed a barely-repressed excitement — they had the air of men prepared to be drastic.

"Now look," Wilksie began, "if I tell you can I trust you'll destroy those photos?"

"How will we know he's telling the truth?" Peter asked.

"He's going to tell us who hired him and why," said Reve.

"I can't tell you why — I don't know why!" Wilksie protested.

"I expect you do. Or at least have a pretty good idea."

Wilksie grimaced.

"So start with Peter. Who hired you to follow Peter?"

"If I tell you, will you destroy the photos? I need to trust you too."

"I am a man of the cloth," Reverend Fenimore said. He pulled out a business card and handed it to Wilksie. "Here. This is me. I will ensure these men will keep their commitments to you assuming you are honest with them."

Wilksie looked dubious, but he put Fenimore's card into his back pants pocket.

"All right," he said. "Melvin Thornery hired me to tail Peter."

"Why?" Peter asked.

"He thought you were acting peculiar; wanted to make sure you weren't doing anything that could embarrass the Congressman."

"And me? You're following me, aren't you?" said Reve.

"Same kind of deal. Your boss thinks you've been acting peculiar."

"Has he hired you to follow other people?"

"No, this was his first time."

"How did he find you?"

Wilksie began shaking his head.

"Peter?"

Peter pulled his phone up and started tapping.

"Now wait! I've already told you what you need to know."

"Just tell me how my boss got your name. Was it a referral?"

"Reve, Reve," said Fenimore. "Let's not torment this man further. After all, you can ask your boss can't you?"

"I could do that," said Reve, brightening.

He looked at Wilksie and waited.

After a moment's internal debate, Wilksie decided the damage would be more containable if he cooperated.

"Fine. It was Gerald Kaboulis. I've done work for Kaboulis and he's friends with your boss, isn't he?"

"That he is," said Reve, scowling. Kaboulis, he thought. Never, ever liked him. He saw me with Barbara and put two and two together. Swine.

"Now look, I've given you names — you don't know what it's cost me. I'm just trying to make a living; it's nothing personal. If — "

"Are you still working on me?" Peter interrupted.

"No. I closed you out after the trip to the church in Virginia. Are you going to confront Thornery?" He looked at Reve and added, "Or Kaboulis? Or your boss?"

Reve had been thinking.

"Maybe. Do they know about Barbara?"

"Just that you've spent some time with her."

"What else have you told them?"

"Nothing. I'd only started yesterday."

"Would you have reported anything tomorrow about tonight?"

"Depended on what you did tonight."

"I had dinner at the Cosmos Club and then I left and you lost me. Got that?"

"What about him?"

"Peter, do you want to confront Thornery?"

"Yes."

"Aw crap, kid, c'mon," said Wilksie.

"He shouldn't do things like that. It's probably against the law. I have a right to a personal life and to my privacy."

Reve looked at Peter and saw the same stubborn honesty he'd demonstrated in their meeting with Wayland. He doubted he could sway Peter, but he was grateful to Wayland for alerting him to Wilksie's presence and didn't want to repay the favor by having Peter create problems.

On the other hand, since Wayland had warned them, he would know Wilksie was compromised so the damage was done. Fortunately Wilksie hadn't asked how they'd spotted him; best he didn't know the Congressman had given him away.

"We'll discuss it," Reve said.

Peter looked mutinous and Wilksie dissatisfied, but Reve felt it was time to let Wilksie go.

"I think we're done here," he said. "Gentlemen?"

Peter crossed around Wilksie, then Reverend Fenimore stepped towards Reve, who took a step back. Freed, Wilksie, after one baleful look, turned and began to walk away.

"Well," said the Reverend, "so this is politics!"

Chapter Twenty-Four

Between Earth and the Spirit World:

For Dash, the passage of days between his last encounter with Barbara and his pending encounter with Wynne moved swiftly. He occupied himself by re-weaving small areas of his energy. While doing so, he began to remember the colors of his energy in its pure state. He'd been developing orange overtones. When he went home, his energy would be cleaned and repaired, all the darkness removed. His orange would be muted, though. He would have to work to bring back its shine.

When I go home, I'll . . .

There, he'd thought it.

In the Spirit World Lersaliaz and Veliastan confer:

"Ah."

"Yes Lersaliaz?"

"He has realized. He is ready."

"Now?"

"He will complete his communication first. Is Wynne prepared?"

"She is looking forward to her encounter with Dash. I will ensure her channel is unblocked. Is Dash prepared?"

"I believe he understands what he should say and not say."

On Earth:

I arrived at Reve Tierney's just after 10:00 a.m. Barbara Tishkin was waiting for me by the elevator.

The first thing I noticed about her was her calm — this was a person who was firmly centered in herself. At some point in her life she had figured out who she was and what she believed and now she was a rock. Smacking up against Dash Fordhyme's opinions of the world, I thought, could certainly help a person to figure out their own.

The second thing I noticed was that she was happy. She had a pink-cheeked healthiness that was accentuated by the sort of radiance people emanate when they first fall in love.

Interesting.

Entering the unit I was greeted by the man himself. I could feel Barbara's anxious hovering as Tierney and I shook hands. So I cranked up the friendliness in my smile as I said hello. We had the poverty simulation in common and exchanging a few remarks about it broke the ice.

Now that I could focus on him without distractions, I clarified some specific impressions, the first of which was how un-centered he was as compared with Barbara. Olivia had said he was "stressed" by the haunting — at the poverty simulation I'd been struck by the strength of his psychic shields. Now I received the impression of someone who was wounded — spiritually? psychically? — and was, metaphorically, bleeding. In some indescribable way, Barbara was staunching the flow.

It was also immediately apparent to me that he, too, was in love. Perhaps desperately so, in every sense of the word.

I realized they were talking to me and I hadn't been listening.

I apologized.

"Sorry, I was gathering impressions," I explained. "What were you saying?"

Barbara had wanted to know if I needed anything. I think she was just being polite, or maybe concerned as I'd been still for longer than I'd realized. Maybe it was because I was going to try something new — something that was a stretch — but I felt like I was sensing a good deal more than I normally do and I was trying to adjust.

Tierney had thanked me again for coming and mentioned his appreciation for my discretion. I made appropriate noises.

But none of us really had much to say; we all wanted to get on with it. So we trooped down a hallway to Tierney's bedroom.

It was an elegantly furnished space; I really liked the floor mirror. They had walked over to a corner by a window — apparently Dash's regular spot — but it was empty. They looked concerned, but I wasn't. I felt . . . I knew . . . he'd arrive. He was probably already there, just not visible yet.

I closed my eyes and was assailed by a babble of voices. They sounded close, but I couldn't make out words. This was startling, and a wave of alarm washed over me, but it passed. And then, instead of being afraid, I felt curious.

"I'm hearing voices," I said, and opened my eyes. Barbara and Tierney were staring at me so intently I became self-conscious.

"Did I do something weird?" I asked.

Vigorous head-shakes to the negative. They could tell, Barbara said, I was experiencing *something* and they'd wondered what it was.

"You don't hear anything?"

Two more head-shakes, "No".

"Okay then," I said, "sit tight."

I closed my eyes again and heard a whistling windy sound on top of the voices, a few squeaks and some banging.

"It's like a signal in search of an antennae," I said. "Now there's banging — "

"I hear banging!" Tierney said.

"So do I!" Barbara sounded puzzled. "That is — wait, there he is!"

I opened my eyes. I thought I'd prepared myself, but shock still coursed through me; I felt like every vein and artery in my body, down to the tiniest hairlike filament, had turned into silver and was shooting sparks.

I didn't realize my heart rate had tripled until I noticed it decelerating. That's when the voice in my head (after an outburst of hysterics) re-achieved normal coherence, offering, as it's first complete thought: "Man, I hate that guy."

Then I heard a different voice in my head — not mine — say: "The spirit before you is more than the Dash Fordhyme you know of. Please withhold judgement and attend."

Okaay, I thought, then noticed Barbara and Tierney staring at me again. I gave them both a weak smile and directed their attention towards Fordhyme.

At first he looked like the images of him I'd seen over the years: he was tall, brawny and aggressive-looking. He was also semi-transparent. Then I realized he was pulsating. His clothed form was fading in and out, replaced by what looked like a mammoth pile of dirty laundry — all the items being black or grey, jumbled and shredded. Then he seemed to achieve stability in his human-like form and I zeroed in on his face.

He was looking straight at me.

"Can you hear me?" he said slowly.

It was funny. The effect was like a bad DVD where the audio track is out of sync with the video track. I could see him speaking and heard the words, but there was a slight delay.

"Did you hear that?" I asked Barbara and Tierney.

They hadn't.

"He asked if I could hear him," I said. They looked hopeful.

"Yes," I said to Fordhyme.

He looked pleased — I could see it on his face — which was fine, but also bizarre. It was just odd, odd, odd. Surreal.

He seemed to gather himself; he opened and closed his mouth twice. Then, he began:

"I died, and then I awakened." His voice was muted and somehow distant, but clear.

Here we go, I thought; I repeated: "I died and then I awakened."

Barbara and Tierney nodded very slowly, as though they feared fast movement might sever the connection.

Dash said: "Death releases us from our amnesia."

"Death releases us from our amnesia," I repeated. That's interesting, I thought. Say, this is going well!

"I heard the dissonance . . . in Dash Fordhyme." he went on.

Dissonance? Being out of tune?

"I heard the dissonance in Dash Fordhyme," I said tentatively and he nodded in approval.

"I became remorse," he said. A few seconds later I was swathed in smothering layers of desolate, guilt-infused sorrow.

"He became remorse," I choked out. I felt like I'd just driven over a puppy, or my Grandma, only multiplied tenfold. I saw a bottomless well of thick, sticky oozing living liquid — it wanted to pull me in and drown me.

I wrenched my eyes sideways: "He's emanating sadness; it's pouring over me and pulling me down. Can you feel it?"

They dragged their dilated eyes from Dash to me, wearing twin expressions of fearful dismay.

Refocusing on Dash, I said: "Can you stop making us feel so sad?"

I inhaled, exhaled, and felt the sadness begin to recede until all that remained was a hint of melancholy.

Then Dash pointed at Reve, who recoiled. Barbara clutched at his arm protectively.

From behind us came a guttural sound like a rhinoceros swallowing a roll of carpeting. It shot my concentration to pieces. Barbara and Tierney's heads swiveled to their rear. By the time I likewise turned, they were, respectively, gasping and swearing. And together, the three of us watched Congressman Herbert Wayland stagger a step then drop to his knees.

"Oh my God!" Tierney exploded, breaking the spell of astonishment that had congealed the three of us.

We all rushed to Wayland. Arriving, I glanced back — Dash was gone.

"Who *is* this?" Barbara demanded, reclaiming my attention.

"Its Herbert Wayland," Tierney said. "Congressman Wayland."

"Well, for heaven's sake. What's he doing here?"

"I think he wants to talk to me," said Reve. "He must have just decided to come over. He's been here before."

"That was the banging!" I said.

"He must have knocked," Tierney concurred. He wiped his forehead with a trembling hand. I realized my own legs were shaking.

Barbara squatted down next to Wayland. Are you alright?" she asked. "Do you — can I help you up?"

Wayland didn't seem to hear her.

"He's a big guy," I said, "you don't think he's having a stroke, do you?"

"I hope not!" Tierney answered. "Maybe we should call an ambulance?"

Wayland's eyes were fluttering, then with a sudden expulsion of air, he looked up at us.

"Lord have mercy," he croaked, "I saw Dash Fordhyme." He looked at Barbara accusingly and went on: "Were you conjuring him?"

"Of course not!" she said, stung.

"He's been haunting Reve since he died," I added helpfully. I almost started laughing — reaction was setting in.

"What!"

"It's true," Tierney said.

Wayland's eyes narrowed and he looked searchingly at each one of us in turn.

"He has a message for Reve," I said. "We were getting it when you . . . distracted us."

Now he looked at me accusingly.

"Are you some kind of witch?" he rapped out.

I almost said "yes" just to mess with him, but I didn't. I just shook my head "no".

"It must be a demon," Wayland said. "God doesn't allow souls to go roaming around."

"Um," I said, "With all due respect Congressman, how do you know?"

Wayland started shooting out sentence fragments referencing the Bible, his Reverend, and Satan being tricky — at that point Barbara left, returning in short order with a glass of water. Wayland drank the entire glassful and got to his feet.

"Dabbling in the occult opens the door to possession," said Wayland, which seemed to summarize his position.

"We're not dabbling in the occult, as you put it," said Barbara tartly. (Tartness level: Granny Smith apple.)

"Dash has a message for Reve," I reiterated, "we just want to get it. We're hoping he'll move on then."

"It's a snare, a trap for the unwary. When believers die they go straight to God and unbelievers are kept together until Judgement Day. This demon means harm. You are inviting Satan into your living room — he may be here now!" Wayland's eyes did an apprehensive sweep of the room.

"Look" I said, "we do have a haunting going on — you saw him. He appeared without being summoned. Reve would like him to leave. What do you suggest we do?"

"Accept Jesus Christ as your savior and no harm will come to you," he said promptly.

"Will that make Dash go away?" I asked.

"I don't know," he said. "You need to talk to Reverend Derbyshire — he'll know."

I really didn't know what to say. There was a galaxy-sized distance between my and Wayland's concepts of life, death, the afterlife, God and all the rest and I couldn't see a bridge anywhere. Tierney appeared dumbstruck.

Then Barbara weighed in. "I'm sorry Congressman, but I simply don't agree with you," she said, matter-of-factly. "I don't believe in demons or evil spirits and I don't believe we're in any danger."

"Beware your pride," Wayland replied. "Pride goeth before destruction and a haughty spirit before a fall. Proverbs."

"I'll take my chances," she replied calmly.

Wayland's face reddened, then Tierney found his voice.

"Congressman, I think we've got this," he said.

I don't think Wayland would have dropped it, but Barbara made a sound that drew all our attention — she was pointing and we saw Dash once again flickering in the corner.

"Begone in the name of Jesus!" shouted Wayland, "Begone in the name of Jesus!"

Tierney's "Congressman!" clashed with Barbara's "Please stop that!"

Dash's form stabilized.

We all looked at one-another. Then Dash very slowly pointed at Wayland and held up his hand, palm forward, signaling "halt".

"Please Congressman!" Tierney said.

Glowering, Wayland acquiesced.

"Wynne?" said Tierney.

We moved forward. I took a breath and looked at Dash. He looked at each of us in turn as if to say "be quiet and pay attention." Then he looked straight at me and I felt the universe closing in around me. I swear I could hear three heartbeats drumming beside me and in the foreground I heard my own blood coursing. But Dash's voice, when he spoke, blocked all other sounds.

"We live many lives," he said.

"We live many lives," I repeated.

"We diverge," he said. "It is intended."

"We diverge. It is intended," I said.

He then spoke very slowly and I repeated each phrase: "We choose. We live and die. We assess. Savor. Delight. Regret. Atone. Learn."

When I finished the Congressman grunted and Barbara shushed him.

Dash continued: "We contribute to the whole, in the forever."

"We contribute to the whole, in the forever?" I said, tripping over it a bit. Dash nodded.

Then I asked: "Is there karma?"

Dash seemed to hesitate, then said: "That which we sow, we reap. In time all debts are paid."

I guess I didn't repeat Dash's response because Reve hissed: "what did he say?"

"Uh, we reap what we sow. All debts are paid, in time."

Dash pointed at Wayland, who visibly stiffened.

"There are many paths to resonance, to good," Dash said.

"There are many paths to resonance, to good," I repeated.

Dash looked at Reve.

"Find yours," Dash said.

"Find yours," I repeated.

"Me?" said Reve.

Dash inclined his head.

"Neriante can help you," he said.

"Neriante can help you," I repeated automatically. Then Tierney, Barbara and I exchanged looks and said, in chorus: "Who's Neriante?"

Dash pointed at me.

I could feel my eyebrows climbing in surprise. "Me?" I said.

Dash nodded. "And . . . met-Barbara — Barbara." he added.

While I was still reeling from the Neriante thing (being called some exotic name by a ghost is disorienting) I got the impression Dash was listening to someone else. After a pause he started again but I couldn't make out the words. I heard them but they didn't seem to be in English, then it seemed like he was making sounds that weren't words, they were things — words as waveforms.

"I'm not . . . I can't — okay, here we go. The best I can get is: do no harm. Like the doctors say: first do no harm. Something like that."

I heard static and Dash flickered, faded and came back. I think he was weakening.

I heard: "Do not fear death," pretty clearly.

As from a long distance I heard: "All is well. Great love."

"He said not to fear death, all is well, great love."

"Oh," said Barbara. I could hear the elation in her voice.

And then Dash smiled. There was a suggestion of light around him — he wasn't looking at us — then I got a sense of surrender and tremendous relief.

"I think . . . I think he's relieved," I said.

"Dennis!" said Barbara.

But he was fading away.

And then we all stood there watching dust motes sparkling in the sunlight that illuminated the empty space.

Chapter Twenty-Five

"Well!" I said, breaking an enveloping silence.

"Do you think he's gone?" Barbara asked, "I mean, for good?"

"Not having any previous experience I can't say for sure," I replied, "but he's definitely gone now, isn't he? It feels perfectly normal in here now, doesn't it?"

She and Tierney shook their heads in agreement. Congressman Wayland stood statue-like, frowning.

Of the three of them, I'd say Barbara was the least affected, though she was by no means unaffected — she was uplifted.

Tierney was still assimilating.

Wayland was dazed.

I was staggered. This was going to take a lot of processing.

I set my own thoughts aside and tried to tune in to Wayland to see what I could pick up, and hit a wall. I think his circuits had blown.

"Congressman Wayland?" Tierney said.

Like a robot who's power had been switched on, Wayland came to life. He waggled his shoulders, clenched his hands into fists and unclenched them a few times, then said: "This isn't right."

It was hard to know what to say in response.

"You should have let me banish him," Wayland went on.

I did one of those *what can I say?* shrugs.

"No, Congressman, I'm glad we didn't. I don't think you would have succeeded anyway," said Barbara. "We wanted to hear him and I'm glad we did. As to whether it's right or not, how can we know? It happened, it's over. We'll have to decide for ourselves what we think."

"No! Reverend Derbyshire — "

"Reverend Derbyshire wasn't here. And anyway, he's only human. He's not infallible."

I think Wayland would have argued, but Tierney intervened.

"Congressman, you're saved, right?"

"I am."

"Then you are protected, right?"

"That's right."

"Then, why worry? You take care of yourself and we'll worry about us, alright?"

Wayland wasn't happy, but he recognized the futility of arguing further. I felt kind of bad for him — he was going to have to rethink some things or engage in a lot of repression. Both are tiring.

Tierney looped his arm around Wayland and started leading him out of the room while saying: "Let's us go into the living room and you can tell me why you stopped by." Looking over his shoulder he gave one of those smiles that combined mischief and resignation.

Barbara and I followed them down the hall, but went into the kitchen instead.

"All things considered, that went well don't you think?" I asked.

"Oh yes," said Barbara, "thank you!"

We heard the sound of the front door closing and Tierney appeared.

"He's gone," he said. "He came over to talk some more about the poverty simulation, but he's too rattled to concentrate. I told him I would deny this ever happened if he told anyone in the media about it. I'm sure he'll talk to someone — but as long as its not the media, I don't care. Poor guy. I think it scared the hell out of him."

He and Barbara shared a glance and suddenly I felt intrusive. I was a stranger, but I'd been involved in something deeply personal to them — I think they wanted to talk to me about it and simultaneously wanted me to leave so they could concentrate on each other.

"Barbara," I said, "you two need to digest this and frankly, so do I. Is it alright if I call you tomorrow?"

"Absolutely. I can't thank you enough."

Tierney was equally enthusiastic in his thanks, although I felt a bit of strain from him. He'd been given a pretty pointed message and I think it was starting to sink in.

At any rate they ushered me out. They weren't rude and I didn't even mind, although it left me at loose ends.

I got to my car. Once in it, I couldn't decide where to go. I deliberated for several minutes before concluding I could, in good conscience, call Olivia. She already knew about the haunting and was probably consumed by curiosity. Fortunately, she could meet me at my favorite coffee house an hour hence.

After the door closed behind Wynne, Barbara took Reve's hand and lead him back into the kitchen. She felt bubbly, like dancing, but Reve, she could see, was starting to tighten up. He was beginning to consider the implications of Dash's message.

"Sit!" she said, pointing at a kitchen chair.

He sat. Then he expelled a lungful of air.

"So," he said, then he rubbed his eyes.

Barbara sat down catty-cornered from him.

"Yes?"

"Find my path to good, eh?"

"That's what he said."

His eyes traveled to her face, then he reached across the table for her hand, which he held briefly.

His phone vibrated; he let it go to message.

"There's many paths to good," he said. "Evidently I'm not on one."

"That's how I heard it. He said resonance too. I wonder what that means?"

"Resonance," Reve echoed absently. Then he focused on Barbara: "How are you?"

She smiled. "I'm happy. I'm relieved. Aren't you?"

"Yes. To an extent. I'm sorry I'm being so self-absorbed."

"At the end, it was . . . wonderful, wasn't it?" Barbara, reliving Dash's concluding seconds, glowed.

"I guess it was. I need to think about it — he changed, didn't he?"

"He looked transformed! There was light, from him or behind him; I'm not sure. And he said not to fear death. All is well. Great love."

"That was encouraging," said Reve.

"It was!"

"We choose, live, die, assess, savor, regret. Atone," Reve went on.

"And learn," Barbara added.

"As we say in the pundit game, I need to unpack that."

Barbara laughed and Reve smiled a little, then sighed. "He said he felt remorse. *Was* remorse. That was intense."

"Yeah. Such terrible sadness. It rattled me a bit."

"Do you feel vindicated?" he asked, searching her face.

"We-ell — "

"Admit it."

She just looked at him.

"So you're not a sore winner I see."

"It was never about winning for me," she replied. "And now I feel free."

"Free?"

"I was so angry at him, for such a long time, and now I can let it go."

"Let your anger go?"

"Right. I don't need it anymore."

"Did you ever need it?"

"Probably not. But I felt it and, in some ways, it defined me. Not anymore."

With that, Barbara felt an urge to go outside and move around. She wanted to package all the anger she'd collected and carried over the years into an offering to the four winds. She wanted to feel the weight of it dissipate, leaving her to dance on lighter feet. She jumped up.

"C'mon," she said, grabbing his hand and pulling.

"What? Where?"

"Pack some clothes. Let's go . . . buy a sapling to use with Dennis's ashes."

Reve made no comment. He had no objection, nor did he have a preference. Right now he thought he and his feelings occupied entirely separate spaces and the bridge between them was temporarily closed. He might as well select a sapling to fill time until the conduit reopened. So, he gathered up a selection of casual clothes and a few toiletries while Barbara went back to the kitchen and washed the coffee pot and mugs they'd used earlier.

"You know," he said to Barbara as they locked his front door, "it never occurred to me to film Dash. Can you imagine if we had? How bizarre?"

"You're right! It didn't occur to me either! We could have used our phones. I wonder if he would be visible? And if he was, would we share it with anyone?"

"Would people believe us? Or would they assume it was faked?"

"Hmm," said Barbara, "Probably people would believe or disbelieve according to taste. Strangers would assume the worst, don't you think?"

"Oh most definitely . . . still . . . but its not like we'll forget it."

"No, we won't forget it."

In the parking deck, Barbara demanded the keys to Reve's car. He was becoming too preoccupied to drive, she said. He agreed. As they arranged themselves, Reve pushed the passenger seat as far back as it would go and tilted the seat back a few degrees.

Exiting the parking deck, Reve opened the passenger side window, put his arm out and felt the air. The humidity, courtesy of yesterday's storm front, was still low; the temperature a comfortable 81 degrees. He pulled out his phone and checked his weather app; it would be getting hot and muggy again tomorrow. Oh well, enjoy it while it lasts.

Find his path to good, huh?

He looked at Barbara — she was both relaxed and energized. She had been unburdened and was embracing a new freedom. No hesitation; maybe a few regrets.

He, on the other hand, he just . . . there was . . . it seemed like . . . did he really?

Christ I can barely complete a thought!

He looked at Barbara again; she noticed and glanced at him.

"Having trouble with it, aren't you?" she said.

"Trouble with?"

"The whole thing. Dennis's message. Being told to, well, find a new path."

"We assess and atone," he added.

"Yeah, that's really interesting, don't you think?" said Barbara.

Reve pulled out his phone and looked up "atone" in his dictionary app.

"To atone," he read out loud, "to make amends or reparation as for an offense or a crime; to make up for errors or deficiencies."

"Right. It's part of karma."

"Karma . . . I don't know much about karma."

"I think the relevant idea is that, in some manner, you experience what you've done to others. Good as well as bad. If you love people you experience love. But if you hate people you experience hate. If you lie to people you experience being lied to. If you torture people — ugh — you experience torture or physical suffering or something. And it's all bound up in reincarnation, which, until this haunting, I was never convinced was real. But Dennis said we live many lives."

"Do you think we've known each other in previous lives?"

Barbara looked over at him and smiled.

"Who knows? Probably. It might explain why we . . . seem to know each other so well, so soon."

"Maybe it does."

For a few minutes Reve contemplated the idea of knowing Barbara in previous lives. He found the idea charming, as compared to, for instance, the idea of atonement. Another topic I want to avoid, he thought grimly. I wonder how many that makes?

I can't keep doing this.

"It's a lot to take in," Barbara said, seemingly in answer to his thoughts. Her hand stole over and squeezed his. "Give yourself some time."

"You think that will help?"

"I do. Time will help. I'll help. According to Dennis, Wynne can help too."

"Yeah," he said neutrally. He wasn't sure what sort of help he'd want from Wynne. Further help. Well, maybe time would resolve that too. But —

"It's not easy to give up a deeply held worldview," he said, slowly.

"Who said you have to do that?"

"You have. Repeatedly."

"No I haven't."

"What!" he protested.

"I have never said you had to stop being a Republican or Conservative or however you want to label your identity. I have said I'd be ready to argue with you over various issues because I think Republicans are simply wrong about a lot of things. I enjoy a good debate, if it's about facts and ideas. Maybe you'd win some; we'll see. What I have said is the tactics you guys have been using are dishonest and vile — those are what you have to disavow; those are what you have to stop participating in and supporting. Bad tactics don't lead to good outcomes."

"So you're saying I don't have to change my political party?"

"For all intents and purposes, the party is what it does and what it's doing, collectively, is bad. You might have to leave it. Or, you could focus on trying to salvage it. But you have to stop making excuses and rationalizing what you've been doing."

Reve let his head fall back against the headrest.

Making excuses and rationalizing.

He thought about the murdered man in Mississippi. The pure, inescapable ugliness of it all. Barbara would consider Dash culpable in that event, even if the strand tying him to the incident was thin as a hair. Dash was on one end of a stick and he, Reve, was on the other. Did he hold even an atom's worth of responsibility for that killing?

And that was just one heinous act of violence, among many. We're so good at generating anger, he thought, and angry people do stupid and violent things. Especially when they have nothing else to occupy them, like a job, for instance. Or maybe they start to hold the lives of others cheap because they hear their leaders talk about people as being unworthy of respect, undeserving of help, beneath due process . . .

In that instant, Reve felt a tsunami of guilt hit him with all the force of hard rushing water. He'd been dodging guilt feelings; suppressing, avoiding and minimizing them. Now, he gave in and for a few searing minutes wondered if he might literally suffocate. He wasn't sure how guilty he was of anything; he just knew he'd previously refused to even acknowledge the possibility. As soon as he did acknowledge the guilt, it began to abate.

Shaken, he looked at Barbara, who (contending with busy traffic), was unaware anything was happening to him.

"Don't think anymore," Barbara said. "You can't think your way out of this anyway."

It took some effort, but he managed a natural sounding: "I can't?"

"This is about your soul, not jobs or political parties. My suspicion is your soul has been trying to reach your mind for some time but you've resisted."

I think my soul just fashioned a guilt-bludgeon and clouted me on the head, he thought, but he said: "Aren't they the same thing?"

"I don't think so. Our souls provide our life force and our eternal . . . identity, I guess. I think our minds are more like tools or control panels for our bodies. Our minds include the little voice that jabbers away in our heads all the time. The essence of meditation is learning to still that voice; in the quiet you connect with your soul. Souls, in turn, connect to God, or spirit or heaven or wherever Dennis went. I'm not really sure. But it's where we came from."

"You think my soul has been trying to tell me something?"

"You've been refusing to promote gun proliferation. You wrote that weak editorial. You couldn't make yourself defend voter suppression the other night."

"That's true."

"But you haven't been prepared to dig into *why*. I think you've been acting on unconscious messages, but repressing the implications on a conscious level."

"Hmm." *Repressing,* he thought. *Yes.*

"Or not. Its just what I think, I'm no expert. But I do maintain this: you will find your way more easily by relaxing and opening up and being willing to *receive.* Trying to think your way there will just be an exercise in resistance."

"Why?"

"Because you don't *want* to change. We all resist change. The voice in your head is going to be deliberately discouraging. It's normal. That's what egos do. You have to defang yours, basically, by going over its head. Appeal to your soul for help. Ask for insight, then relax and wait to receive it. When the little voice starts naysaying, just mentally say 'thanks for the input' and deliberately redirect your thoughts to something pleasing or innocuous. Or exhilarating, like a good thunderstorm."

Reve stared out the window, then said: "Okay."

Chapter Twenty-Six

"So what happened?" Olivia asked, agog.

I told her.

"Dang!"

"I know."

We both sipped coffee for a bit, marveling.

"So you're a medium now," Olivia said.

"I don't know about that," I replied. "I suspect this was a one-off. Most people never see a ghost. Your Dad saw one and now we've seen one and I don't expect we'll ever see another. What would the odds be?"

"It probably happens more often than we think," she said.

"It probably does. But still not that often. No, I don't see me becoming a ghost interpreter. I like what I do now anyway."

"Of course. Sure . . . how were Barbara and Mr. Tierney?"

"I think Barbara was fine. They're in love, you know."

"I wondered."

"Oh yes. Anyway, I think Barbara took it all in stride. Tierney was having a little trouble with it."

"Could you read the ghost? Why was it so important to talk to Mr. Tierney?"

I hadn't thought about that.

"I don't know," I said. "Something to do with his karma somehow? He said we live many lives. Did he owe Tierney something from a past life?"

"I don't think my Pastor would approve of this. Christians believe we have one life — that's it."

"I can't help you there . . . other than to say you saw him and I saw him and your Pastor didn't. When you learn things you can't go back. I've always believed in reincarnation anyway."

"Why?"

"Oh, the one-life idea always seemed wasteful to me. People are such complex creatures; eternity is so long and lifetimes so short in comparison. It makes more sense to me that people live many times, learn, evolve, grow in complexity. Plus, it explains, sort of, things like tragedy and babies dying and stuff like that. It's all lessons. Free will makes much more sense in that context."

"I've never really thought about reincarnation. It almost feels sinful to consider it."

"With all due respect," I said, "I disapprove of the concept of heresy — you should be able to explore religious and philosophical ideas without fear or guilt. Having said that, I don't actually think it matters what you believe so long as it leads to good action. If you want to be Christian, be Christian. What matters is how you live your life; how you treat people and animals and the world around you."

She nodded, though I could see she wasn't satisfied. It was one of those things she'd have to come to terms with on her own.

"Do you think you can help Mr. Tierney now?"

I made a face. "I don't know if I can help him, still less whether I want to. I'm a bit torn," I admitted.

"Why?"

"I have despised the guy for a long time. Now I have to help him? It's hard."

"He seems nice though. In person."

"I know. How fair is that? I'll probably end up liking him. I like Barbara and she loves him, so . . . but still . . . it's hard. Of course, he may not want my help. He may not need it. But if he asks, I'll have to try."

"Good karma!"

I sighed. "Yeah."

Olivia went on to tell me about her interview with Steven Wrayner and her trip to the brownfield. She'd enjoyed everything about the day. She loved the idea of harnessing nature to clean up messes humans make. I got the feeling her decision about what to do with her life was already made, though she might not yet know it. She had some additional information interviews lined up, so, perhaps I was being premature.

One thing was definite: she was thoroughly enjoying the process of exploration and, to my mind, it was doing her a world of good. She was looking at herself differently; her confidence was increasing and her horizons had already widened considerably.

She had been so easy to help.

As I drove home from the cafe, I tried envisioning working with Reve Tierney and didn't get very far. I anticipated a conflicted Reve Tierney — how could he not be conflicted? He'd enjoyed significant success in his career, a career that came with a lot of benefits and plenty of ego-stroking. Success, ego-stroking: hard to jettison.

Finding his path to good.

Maybe he'd have ideas of his own. Maybe Barbara would.

Oh well. No doubt something would come to mind. I'd have to talk to Barbara and Tierney again because I couldn't talk to anyone else about seeing Dash Fordhyme's ghost and that was the hardest thing of all.

Chapter Twenty-Seven

Reve was restless. The bedroom was lit by moonlight and the voice in Reve's head was chattering non-stop.

Barbara was asleep. Their interactions preceding her surrender to slumber should have rendered him insensible, but it just wasn't happening. He decided to go sit on the front porch with a brandy to savor while he looked at the moon and tried to get his thoughts in order.

Or shut them down altogether — whichever came first.

He was sitting up when Barbara stirred, opened her eyes and smiled sleepily.

"Go back to sleep," he said.

She closed her eyes and he glided quietly into the hallway and down the stairs. Sabrina joined him, shadowing his steps as he poured his brandy and went out the front door. On the porch she stood sentry by the entrance.

Arranging himself on a cushioned chair, he put his feet up on an ottoman covered in water-proof fabric, leaned back, and sipped his brandy.

He thought about how Sabrina followed him and how endearing that was, and about Kaboulis's guy following him and how not-endearing that was.

He thought about Peter's stubborn honesty; how laudable it was and how inconvenient.

Sinking more deeply into the chair, he listened to the sound of crickets singing and realized the sound was both loud and easy to tune out.

He took another sip of brandy and placed the glass on the porch floor.

He thought about Dash and wondered what was happening to him now. He tried to envision the afterlife, but after rejecting the notion of clouds and harps, he found himself at a loss. If the afterlife wasn't like that, what was it like? What did you do there? How much of you remained? When he died would he stop being Reve? Dash had said we live many lives. How did it work?

Dash said death releases us from our amnesia, which meant we had amnesia while we lived. Was that why people so often seemed detached from their own spiritual beliefs? He'd considered himself a Catholic and, looking squarely at the tenets of the faith, found a lot of mystic stuff that had virtually no impact on his daily life. He'd always considered himself to be a moral man and a person of principle, yet he'd spent years being less than honest for a living. Presumably a truly good Catholic would adhere to a higher standard.

People seemed to associate morality with their personal lives and individual relationships, while collective activities, business activities, many professional activities, were exempt. Why was that?

People cut corners and the results were oil spills, train wrecks, industrial and mining accidents and deaths. People knowingly dumped toxic substances into rivers and lakes, poisoning living creatures, including other people.

People at banks and credit card companies put spurious fees on customer bills for as long as they got away with it. Practically everyone connected with Wall Street, including people charged with monitoring the banks, had, by commission or omission, colluded in illegal behaviors leading to the 2008 financial crisis. Financial professionals sold dodgy investment vehicles to pension fund managers, struggling municipalities, and gullible investors.

And on and on, Reve thought. I'll bet most of those people rationalize what they do, just like I did.

He stretched his legs. No more thinking, Reve decided. Why don't I try Barbara's meditation?

Closing his eyes, he pulled his hands behind his head to support his neck and began trying to envision his thoughts floating up out of his head, into the sky, through the atmosphere and into space.

Shortly thereafter, a slight snore caught Sabrina's attention. She trotted over, essayed a couple of sniffs, then went back to her post by the front door.

Meanwhile, Reve was enjoying the sensation of skimming through stars. He looked at his feet and was pleased to see them outlined in light as was proper when traveling. Up ahead he could see a vivid orb of light growing larger. It seemed to be yellow and green at the center with white outlines. He knew that light.

"Fadraya!"

"Lersaliaz!"

Reve felt himself encircled by a warm light; it energized him and filled him with peace. Then it separated from him and reformed into a shining, human-like figure in a yellow robe with sparkles of green and blue.

"Dash visited me!"

"Yes."

"How is he?"

"He is being restored."

"Where is he?"

"Come."

Lersaliaz began to move and Reve, reaching out, seemed to catch hold of a tail of light, which pulled him up and up through stars and energy streams and radiant sparkles into a glowing blue tunnel and out again, coming to rest on a stretch of sand. Behind him lay grass-covered undulating hills lit by a light source he couldn't see. In front of him was blue water that turned grey and then black as it approached a dark structure that seemed to float on the black waters some distance away. The structure was surrounded by a halo of bright light, like a bubble that was simultaneously lit and transparent.

"He is there."

"What is happening to him?"

"His energy is being repaired and replaced."

"Why is it so dark?"

"It is dark because of the concentration of damaged energy in one place. All the souls there returned home with great stores of dark energy attached to them, tearing holes and deforming the fabric of their essence. Removal and repair must be done carefully and slowly so they may retain and obtain lessons from their experiences. The holes must be patched with new, clean energy. The surrounding light is the source of the new energy."

"Do they suffer?"

"They suffer remorse. We must allow them to first experience remorse then move beyond and recruit their energy for restitution. There is no physical pain, but for a time there is sorrow."

"Dash wasn't so bad, was he? Not like people who commit appalling acts of savagery."

"Souls require repair based on the degree of damage they've sustained. Those who go to the Dark Place do so because they need the utmost in skilled assistance. Dash enjoyed enormous influence in this last life and he infected millions of souls. For each soul he damaged, *he also was damaged* so that when he arrived home his energy was severely deformed. The experts in the Dark Place have specialized skills developed over eons. They can help him."

"What will happen to him when they're finished?"

"That depends on him. He has difficult incarnations ahead — he must decide if he can accept the challenges he will face."

"And if he does?"

"He will return to your group and continue to incarnate. It will be up to him to share details with you, or not, as he chooses."

"If he doesn't?"

"It's possible he will cease incarnating on earth and will be redirected to another world where he can better master his lessons and regain his strength. In rare cases, souls will request oblivion, total dissolution of their energy and thus, their immortal identity. I do not foresee that with him."

"He reached out to me."

"Yes. That was a gift. Make use of it!"

They watched the Dark Place for awhile longer, then Lersaliaz said it was time for them to go.

Together they rose upward and then, the blue tunnel was before them. In a flash, they transversed the tunnel and were shooting through a kaleidoscope of lights and shapes that gradually transitioned into stars and space. There, Lersaliaz waved a goodbye and began to recede. Reve watched until Lersaliaz was gone, then he began to flow downward, feeling energy surrounding and pulling him down until he shot into earth's atmosphere, then into sky. He pulled up as he reached the tops of trees surrounding Barbara's house and floated for awhile, enjoying the sensation. Then he dropped down, and with a pop, was back in his body.

Sabrina greeted him and they got up and began strolling around the farm, enjoying warm sunshine and fragrant breezes. Barbara came out the front door wearing Reve's pajamas and sporting sandals covered with bits of hay. In a blink, she was at his side and, in another blink, he, she and Sabrina were at the Cosmos Club eating a wonderful meal. Only, he wasn't sure what the entrée actually was. He was puzzling over that question when Barbara reached over, clutched his shoulder and started shaking him.

"Reve," she said, "Reve, wake up."

"Wha — ?" he said, opening his eyes with a start. For a few seconds he stared at Barbara, then he remembered where he was.

"I fell asleep, huh?" he said, rubbing his eyes and stretching.

"Sabrina fetched me. I think she wanted to go to her bed, but didn't think she could while you were still on the porch."

He stood up, bent to retrieve the empty glass, and followed Barbara.

"I had the weirdest dream," he said as they went through the front door.

"What was it about?"

"You and I and Sabrina were at the Cosmos Club eating and while I liked my dinner, I couldn't figure out what it was. Before that, we were walking around out here and before that I was . . . I was . . . I can't remember. Something interesting."

"Maybe you'll go back to it when you fall asleep again?"

"That would be nice. I think. I never remember my dreams."

"Most people don't."

For Reve, the next day was a blur. He felt like he was swimming in cloudy waters, moving unceasingly but unclear about his location or destination. He described the sensation to Barbara. She advised him to think as little as possible, especially about the question of his future.

"How can I do that? That's *all* I'm thinking about right now."

"And where is it getting you?"

"Well . . . nowhere."

"Right."

"But!"

"Trust. Relax. You want everything to be resolved now but it can't be. Your life was on one trajectory and that has changed. Your mind, your heart, your soul, all have to catch up and fall into line. They have different timetables."

Reve gave her look which blended skepticism, interest and puzzlement in equal proportions.

"Don't look at me like that," she said, laughing. "Just trust me. Trust yourself. If everything is foggy you will not *think* yourself to anywhere useful. Thinking is foreground activity, but the real work is taking place in the background."

"How will I know when the work is done?"

"You've achieved a reasonable alignment when you *know* what your next move should be and you feel no doubts about it."

"And I'll get there by *not* thinking about it."

"Yes."

"That seems backwards."

"I know, but that's only because you've absorbed the idea that thinking is the only tool to use for decision-making. You're trying to remove a screw with . . . with a computer."

As she spoke, Barbara was clearing their breakfast dishes off the table while Reve wiped surfaces and filled the sink with soapy water.

"I should rephrase that slightly. You may not so much know what you *should* do, but you will know something that you want to do or are ready to do. Sometimes change requires one or two big steps, but often it's really a sequence of small steps, the outcome of which are unknown to you when you take them. I never intended to have my farm — I got here by pursuing an interest, by following up on urges to learn something new or talk to someone or read about something. I knew I wanted to make a change in my life, but I had no idea beyond that. I could have sat for a year *thinking* and I would never have landed on what I'm doing now. I spent months mentally going around in circles until I recognized how pointless it was. When I started meditating and learning about consciousness, I began trusting my urges and my instincts and followed up on little nudges that came to my attention. I started to notice the nudges because I could quiet my mind and focus on being open."

"Open."

"Right. Open, meaning that I was receptive to new ideas and information. I was on the alert for new thoughts; I welcomed them."

"Ah."

So, Reve spent several hours following Barbara around the farm and assisting her while resolutely banishing thoughts about his future as soon as he noticed them. He also, when not conversing or concentrating on a task, threw out the occasional thought to the effect that he was open and interested in new ideas and information.

A few times he found himself thinking about Dash and wondering how he was doing in the Dark Place; he also spent some minutes wondering if anyone else he knew would end up there. There were a couple of particularly vicious media figures and a couple of politicians he rather thought — then he stopped himself. What Dark Place? What was he thinking about? Was that new information? Where had it come from? He gave up thinking about the Dark Place when the thought failed to coalesce into anything firm. The Dark Place remained a vague, elusive wisp.

In the middle of the afternoon Wynne Frost called Barbara. Motioning him to follow, Barbara started towards the house, settling on the front porch for a long conversation. Reve listened for a bit, but tired of trying to reconstruct Wynne's dialogue based on Barbara's remarks (they were talking about Dash the ghost). He looked forward to Barbara filling him in on Wynne's reactions, but in the meantime, decided to wander back to the kitchen to review available foodstuffs with an eye towards dinner.

Some thirty minutes later Barbara appeared; Reve was at the kitchen table, a pile of cookbooks stacked in front of him and one open for active perusal.

"Wynne needed to talk about Dennis," said Barbara.

"I thought so. Can't blame her. Will she tell anyone about him do you think?"

"She talked to Olivia yesterday, but said neither she nor Olivia will tell anyone else."

"That's good of them. What else did she say?"

"Oh, we just went over it all again. She's been thinking about what Dennis said — about amnesia and living many lives. She asked if she could call me again as she mulls it all over. I said of course. I also said you may be calling her."

"You did? What did she say?"

"She said that was fine."

"Hmm, well, we'll see."

Barbara smiled. She went to the refrigerator, peered into it briefly, then selected a pitcher of lemonade.

"Want some?"

"Sure, thanks."

Barbara filled glasses, returned the pitcher and joined him at the table.

"She told me about what Olivia's been doing too."

"Oh, yes?"

"Olivia met with a man who has a permaculture practice, and — "

"What's permaculture?"

Barbara explained the basic concepts that defined permaculture and its applications. She described how permaculture techniques could be applied to brownfields to remove toxins from soil and return the ground to health.

"Sounds interesting," said Reve.

"Yes. And it gave me an idea . . . "

And so the following week Reve, Barbara, Olivia and Reverend Fenimore converged to bless and bury Dash Fordhyme's ashes.

"This plot of land has been added to the nearby nature preserve. Steve's company is experimenting with various approaches to," here, Olivia consulted some notes on her phone, "phy-to-re-med-i-a-tion," she read, pronouncing each syllable, then smiling triumphantly.

"What is that?" Reverend Fenimore asked.

Again Olivia consulted her notes, then read: "It's the direct use of living green plants for in-place, removal, degradation, or containment of contaminants in soils, sludges, sediments, surface water and groundwater. This is from a United Nations Environmental Program report," she added.

"Nifty!" said the Reverend. Then he looked sharply at Barbara and said, "It's an interesting choice for a burial. Methinks there's a bit of a statement being made here?"

Barbara raised her eyebrows and smiled but made no comment.

"I see. Give me a moment."

Reverend Fenimore retreated some 20 feet from where Barbara, Reve and Olivia stood. He turned his back and lowered his head.

"He's praying on it," Olivia said.

Barbara didn't respond. She liked the idea of the Reverend giving a blessing and she thought it was sweet of Reve to have arranged it, but she didn't require it. This was where the Dennis-tree would be planted. He had spent years injecting poison into the body politic; the idea of his remains helping to de-poison contaminated land seemed to Barbara to be both appropriate and uplifting. The instant she'd had the idea she'd felt a sense of closure.

She looked at Reve, who shrugged and said "It didn't occur to me it would be an issue."

They said no more, waiting, motionless, until the Reverend returned.

"Okay," he said. "Whenever you're ready."

"Great!" said Barbara.

"Let me," said Reve, taking hold of the shovel they'd brought with them and starting to dig the hole between markers Olivia had placed. The ground was firm; the temperature was in the high eighties with moderately high humidity. Within two minutes of commencing shoveling, Reve was sweating. After five minutes, he was thirsty and had to refresh himself. Fortunately. Barbara had brought water which she supplied. Then she wiped his brow with a handkerchief and he got back to work.

After the hole was sufficiently deep, Barbara got the box of ashes. Olivia opened the container that was positioned under the tree roots, then held it while Barbara poured in the ashes. Olivia re-sealed the container and together they lifted the sapling with it's attached box of ashes and placed it into the hole.

Olivia then surrounded the urn with soil she'd brought with her, carefully tamping down and watering the soil. She stepped back and the four of them arranged themselves in a square around the small poplar sapling.

Reverend Fenimore looked at Barbara; she nodded and he began.

"Oh Lord, we are here today to mark the passing of Dennis Fordhyme. Let us pray together — your response is 'his love is our strength.'"

He began: "The Lord is our shepherd."

Dutifully Barbara, Reve and Olivia responded, "his love is our strength," Olivia's voice ringing out; Barbara and Reve's voices more subdued.

"He banishes fear," the Reverend continued.

"His love is our strength."

"He offers us hope."

"His love is our strength."

"He fills us with Peace."

"His love is our strength."

"He teaches us faith."

"His love is our strength."

"He welcomes us home."

"His love is our strength."

"From Corinthians: 'It is sown a natural body; it is raised a spiritual body. If there is a natural body, there is also a spiritual body.'"

"Amen!" said Olivia.

"We need not grieve, for our brother Dennis is alive and well, beyond the limitations of earthly life. So let us rejoice that Dennis is in the arms of the Lord."

The Reverend paused to look at each in turn, then continued.

"And now his earthly remains shall feed new life and help cleanse the degraded earth; earth that is the gift of God. And we say to God: 'You yourself are the source that gives us life.' (Psalm 36, 10)."

He paused again, then said: "Would any of you like to share with us?"

Reve shook his head "no", as did Olivia. They both looked at Barbara, who said: "Just goodbye. We're here to say goodbye and to wish him well."

"Then, let us bow our heads and say goodbye."

Barbara closed her eyes, pictured her brother as a teenager and, remembering how she once felt about him, felt a swell of sadness and regret. Tears pricked her eyes, but she took a deep breath and let the sadness pass.

Reve closed his eyes and felt so ambivalent he gave up and simply said "goodbye Dash" to himself and waited.

Olivia prayed for Dash's soul.

After a few minutes the Reverend recited:

"Know that beyond the veil there is the source,
And we rejoice that our suffering is ended,
And we give thanks that our wounds are healed,
And we rest as anger evaporates,
And we forgive as hurts are understood,
And we learn as questions are answered,
And we grow as purpose is revealed,
And we love as we are loved

May the Lord bless Dennis Fordhyme, we pray in the name of the merciful God, the Father, the Son and the Holy Spirit. Amen."

"Amen," chorused Reve and Olivia.

"Amen," said Barbara a second later. With a small sniff she dug out a kleenex and wiped her eyes. Then she smiled.

A sense of relaxation descended on the group. They stepped away from the tree and began collecting their materials and loading up the rear of Barbara's car.

While Barbara and Olivia arranged the tools and supplies, Reve and Reverend Fenimore strolled around the perimeter of the brownfield.

"This has the feeling of a chapter ending," said the Reverend, "Is it your chapter, or Barbara's, or both?"

"Both," Reve said.

"What's next?"

"We're still figuring that out. A lot has happened — more than I can tell you. Although, I must say, I'd love to know what you'd make of some of it." Reve seemed to brood for a minute.

"You've piqued my curiosity," the Reverend said.

"I'm sorry. Maybe someday — "

"Of course. If I can help I'd be glad to. You know where to find me! But now I'll say my goodbyes."

After Reverend Fenimore left, Olivia, Reve and Barbara stood and contemplated the Dash tree.

"You feel satisfied?" Olivia asked Barbara.

"I do. This was perfect. Thank you for everything. And Olivia?"

"Yes?"

"I'll be in touch about an idea I have later this week."

"Sounds good!"

After Olivia left, Barbara and Reve clasped hands.

"You have an idea for Olivia?" Reve asked.

"I'm thinking about starting a scholarship program for students interested in environmental work. I'd like to find a way to offer it to non-traditional students like Olivia, who may not have had the chance to go to college right out of high-school. I'm still roughing out the idea. And I don't want to seem to be offering charity. But I'd like to help her go to school and I have a lot of money to spend."

"Why don't you hire her to clean out Dash's condo, and sell his furniture and stuff, and let her put the proceeds towards her education? You don't want to deal with his stuff or keep it. It will be a big job. And maybe you could do something through this Steven with the permaculture practice — you could fund an internship for him and he could hire Olivia to work there in the summers."

"Those are wonderful ideas! Thank you! And thank you for coming up with the tree-planting idea and for bringing the Reverend here for a blessing."

"Thank *you* for everything," Reve replied. He felt like there was so much more to say and at the same time, no need to say it.

It was as they were driving back to Barbara's that Reve felt his next step was revealed. They had been sharing a restful silence when certainty suddenly, quietly, permeated him. He *could* stop. Just *stop.* And in that instant the future, previously so constricted, widened into a panorama filled with possibilities.

"I will resign tomorrow," he heard himself announce. "I've been thinking about it but I wasn't sure . . . now I'm sure."

"Wonderful!" said Barbara, smiling hugely.

"But then, I'd like to spend some time with you while I figure out what to do next. Is that alright?"

"Absolutely!"

"Well that's step one, anyway." A splendid feeling of release engulfed him. It carried him through the rest of the day and into the meeting with Elliot.

"You're resigning?"

"Yes."

"Isn't this a bit sudden?"

"I suppose it is. I'm sorry."

Elliot looked at him searchingly.

"What are your plans?"

"They are unclear at this juncture."

"You have a twelve-month non-compete you know."

"I'm aware — it's not a problem. I don't want to work for another right-wing think tank."

"God help me, you're not going to work for a left-wing think tank are you?"

"What makes you say that?" asked Reve, his eyes sharpening.

"Well, I don't know. You've just been . . . but you wouldn't, would you?"

"Quite honestly, I don't yet know what I'm going to do next, or for whom or with whom."

"Is there anything I can do to change your mind?"

"You can't change my mind but there is one thing you can do."

"What's that?"

"You can call off your P.I."

There was a charged hush, then, after some throat clearing, Elliot said: "How did you — ?"

"Never mind that. But my future activities are none of his business, or yours, or Gerald's — is that clear?"

Elliot, looking both chagrined and defensive, appeared on the verge of an assertive pronouncement which he repressed, instead giving an affirmative nod.

"I told Gerry it was a bad idea," he said, pettishly. "Are you . . . going to . . . do anything about that?" he added.

"I will if I ever get the slightest hint I'm being monitored that way again. Otherwise, no. Do we understand each other?"

Elliot nodded.

"What are you going to tell the others?" he asked.

"Nothing, really. Just what I've told you."

"Why are you doing this? Is it Fordhyme's sister?"

Reve softened. He had always liked Elliot and, on a personal level, felt bad about leaving on such short notice. On the other hand, Elliot operated in a ruthless and amoral environment and Reve felt certain Elliot would sacrifice him (perhaps reluctantly, but invariably) if the Party deemed it necessary or advantageous.

"We have gotten close, yes," Reve said. "But, well, lets just say after Dash's death I did some soul searching."

"She's got lots of money now, hasn't she?"

Reve sighed. That, he knew, would be the first place so many people would go and there was nothing he could do about it. Except sever relations with Barbara which was not an option.

"Yes," was all he said.

"You know if you turn on us I'll have to do what I can to destroy you, right? Nothing personal." This was said without rancor.

"I know. Keep in mind I can spill about the spying if the need arises, and about a lot of other things. So you may want to tread carefully."

They looked at one another in perfect comprehension.

Then they came to terms about how his resignation would be announced.

It took less than an hour for Reve to box up his personal effects. Co-workers watched him, some curiously, some sympathetically and some with hostility. No one approached him. Reve was prepared for this. At the moment, he was an unknown quantity, but the lack of an official announcement by him or Elliot made clear he was not moving into an acceptably sanctioned position for which congratulations would be in order. Nor was he retiring or a party would have been planned. Probably he was leaving to avoid or minimize some sort of brewing scandal that would reflect badly on the IPR or the movement. Or, it could mean he was about to *start* such a scandal. Either way, he might become toxic to know.

So, there were no "good lucks" or farewells as he picked up his boxes and headed for the exit. He suspected one or two people would contact him confidentially and he would be mildly interested in their reports.

As he made his way to his car, he couldn't help laughing a little. He pictured the outbreak of discussion that would have erupted as soon as he was deemed out of earshot. Elliot would be making an announcement shortly; he would state simply that Reve felt he was becoming ineffective at his job and consequently wanted to take a break, assess his career goals and explore alternatives. Reve would be making a more personal announcement on his Facebook page and co-workers were at liberty to wish him well or not, as they chose. They must not, they'd be told, air any negative opinions through social media channels. Reve would be professional and so must they.

The announced reasons for Reve's departure would not satisfy his co-workers and speculation would be rampant.

Ah well, he thought, philosophically, they'd all enjoy themselves for a few days, but as he had no intention of feeding them anything to work with, they'd move on.

At least until he resurfaced publicly, should he decide to do so. But that was a problem for another day.

That evening Reve and Barbara enjoyed a sumptuous summer feast that included just-picked-corn-on-the-cob, a salad made from fresh-from-the-garden vegetables and grilled bluefish. They sat at a patio table with an umbrella and matching chairs. Lit citronella candles kept mosquitoes out of range. Sabrina was curled up nearby.

"A toast," said Barbara, raising her wineglass, "to endings and beginnings!"

"To endings and beginnings," said Reve.

They clinked glasses.

Reve had already received a message from an IPR co-worker; he'd respond in a day or two. For tonight, he just wanted to bask in each moment as it happened.

Barbara, watching him, was happy.

I was looking forward to meeting with Reve Tierney.

I'd talked to Barbara twice since the Dash episode and was deeply engaged in working through the implications of that event.

More than once I'd mused on how lightly we tend to take the meaning of our existence. It must come with the amnesia; I suppose if we spent all our time concentrating on the afterlife we'd fail to engage adequately with the current life experience.

There's probably some ideal balance between living in the here and now and recognizing our thoughts and actions have consequences both immediately and eternally. I don't know what that balance is but I'll spend some time trying to find out.

Meanwhile, I have work to do.

When Reve arrived, I was instantly struck by the quality of his energy as compared to the impressions I'd received previously. When we'd first met, his shields had been up; he'd seemed closed, confused and fragmented. Now he was tranquil and open with a hopeful receptivity in place of his former self-protection.

We sat, arranged ourselves, and locked eyes.

"So," I said.

"So," he echoed.

I smiled; so did he.

"Well," I said, "lets get started."

In the Spirit World:

"Veliastan?"

"Lersaliaz!"

"Where is Xe?"

"He is meeting with a soul mate. She wants to better understand what he has embarked upon. He is very excited."

"Is he ready to incarnate on earth?"

"No, not yet. I want to expose him to more life episodes first. He is learning fast, but as we know, watching is quite different from physically living. He cannot really grasp the magnitude of the difference as of yet. His council is still considering how best to introduce him to earthly life."

"Have you met with his Guide recently?"

"It has been some time. Xe has frequently consulted his Guide. We are all in agreement."

"Will his soul mate likewise attempt Earth incarnations?"

"Very probably. Eventually. Xe will test it out first. If he is successful, he will encourage her."

"As you encouraged me."

"You would have tried regardless."

"Yes, but the encouragement was welcome."

"I'm glad. Ah, I hear the chimes. Will you go with me?"

"Always."

Author's Note

Raised as a Catholic, I have an attachment to the faith and to Christianity in general — certainly to the fundamental precepts about loving one's neighbor and doing unto others. More broadly, I have found some of the works of Karen Armstrong intriguing as they delve into the more mystical aspects of religion, with an emphasis on its place in various historical contexts. My own personal experience of Catholicism growing up was strong on the more heavy-handed and authoritarian aspects of the Church and thin with respect to the more transcendent elements.

Over time I began questioning various tenets of the faith and began exploring other religions and philosophies. Along the way I ran into quantum physics, an area of enquiry that frequently spans the gap between science and metaphysics.

Quantum physics is hard going for me — I'm a classic "liberal arts" type who struggled with algebra in high school and fell asleep in my chemistry classes. But some of the relevant discoveries (grossly simplified) — quantum events can be affected or changed by the observer; particles can be in two places at the same time until they're measured; related particles can communicate instantaneously even when separated by massive distances — illustrate that at the quantum level the rules of classical physics do not apply and our solid-state predictable world is an illusion. This a conclusion humans have come to in various ways, throughout our history.

Another idea humans have kicked around, going a long way back, is the notion of the existence of other realms or dimensions, of which Earth is one. In classical philosophy we have Plato's Theory of Forms (i.e., a physical realm and a separate, perfect realm of forms or ideas). Indigenous Australians, who can be traced back some 50,000 years, have The Dreaming. And, of course, we have all the mythologies from cultures around the globe, including their creation stories, which form the basis of religions practiced today.

The ongoing debate between atheists and theists soldiers on. Not everyone enters into this debate; humanity's degree of belief follows the usual bell curve with strong believers on both ends (strongly belief versus strong disbelief), to more tepid believers (there probably is a God of sorts to there probably isn't a

God but not sure), to a middle where you have lots of people who don't think much about the topic at all or accept whatever they've been taught without much questioning.

To me the atheist/not-atheist debate is predicated on the first, fundamental question: is there life after death? The dilemma (for those who ponder this question) is that while theists can't *prove* there is life after death, atheists can't prove there *isn't.* Stalemate. (Not that the argument doesn't continue to rage!)

My conclusion is we cannot *know,* with the kind of certainty we attribute to experiential things (like "ice feels cold" and "fire feels hot") the answer to the life after death query. But we can nevertheless take a position: yes or no. Why? Because our minds want answers to the questions that concern us (or interest us, obsess us, or plague us — mileage varies) and beliefs that are important to us (for whatever reason) affect how we live. And if I'm wrong, well, I guess I'll die and that will be that; I won't *know* because my consciousness will be extinguished. But my problem is that I'm conscious *now* and find the notion that life is a random accident and consciousness a mere byproduct thereof unacceptable.

So I choose "yes", but fully acknowledge I can't prove my choice objectively. However, having reached this decision I moved on to the next question: if there is life after death, what's it like?

My concepts of the Spirit World comes from a variety of sources ranging from the *Hindu Book of the Dead* to the *Seth* books by Jane Roberts, the *Abraham* books by Esther and Jerry Hicks and the *Life Between Lives* books by Michael J. Newton.

To me, these sources offer lots of interesting details, intriguing ideas (plenty to chew on) and, for purposes of fiction, dramatic possibilities!

As for their validity, versus, say, the Abrahamic religions' positions on matters of existence? In the end, we all have to make up our own minds. But from a creative and artistic point of view, I find the idea of reincarnation, with its attendant goals and lessons, intellectually and emotionally satisfying. On a practical level, the concept of reincarnation presents an interesting schema for the filling of time. Because eternity, I often think, is a *long* time.

Paula Apynys
June 2016

Acknowledgments

My heartfelt thanks to my second and final draft readers for their encouragement and help with fine-tuning the story: **Ted, Anne, Georgann, Jim, Andrew, Sue, Charlie** and **Alberta!**

Special thanks to the multi-talented **Jim Ballard** of *Skylyne Studio* (http://www.jimballardmusic.net) who conceived, engineered and composed the music for my book trailer and to singer/songwriter **Jim Gill** (http://www.jimgillmusic.com), who did the marvelous voiceover work for the same.